FROM ASHES

BEN MARNEY

Ben Marney Books

SPECIAL OFFER

SPECIAL OFFER

Writing is a lonely job, so meeting and getting to know my readers is a thrill and one of the best perks of being an author. I would like to invite you to join my Private Readers' Group and in return I'll give you a FREE copy of *Lyrics Of My Life*. This is a collection of autobiographical short stories about my crazy life.

I think you'll like this book; it's been quite a ride so far and I really would like to meet you. Please join my readers group here: www.benmarneybooks.com

For my friends in the music industry.
When you hear an outstanding performance, live or recorded, what you're hearing is the tip of the iceberg. The years of practice, dedication, and sacrifice it takes to create a brilliant performance lies deep beneath the surface. It's called paying your dues, and for some, those dues can be very expensive.

For my beautiful wife, Dana,
who has gone through a challenging year. Your ability to always see the positive side of things astounds me, and makes my love for you grow stronger every day. You make me a better man.

AUTHOR'S NOTE

I may be wrong, but I believe that every musician and every singer at some time in their life, has dreamed of being a star.

That dream is what gives them the perseverance to get on stage, night after night, year after year, living like a gypsy, traveling from town to town, state to state, and in some cases, country to country.

To some people, living that kind of lifestyle appears glamorous and exciting, and sometimes it is, but most of the time, it's not.

Even though people continuously surround you, they are strangers, and it can be a lonely and challenging life to live.

I was lucky to have lived it with my wife and best friend, but even *WE* were lonely at times, missing our family and friends.

Unfortunately for most entertainers, they are out there on that difficult road, chasing their dream alone, and the results are too often, drug addiction, alcoholism, and divorce.

The characters in this book are based on a compilation of real people I have known in my music career. The happy, as well as tragic events I describe are part truth and part fiction. I will leave it up to you to figure out which is which.

PART I

MARCH 1989

1

RAINE WATERS

R aine Waters knew when the producers saw it, they would know he was right. It was the perfect location for the shoot.

It was built in 1878 by Heinrich D. Gruene, pronounced Green. It was located in the historic downtown area of Gruene, now considered part of New Braunfels, and it was the oldest dance hall in Texas. In the hundred-plus years it had been standing there, physically it hadn't changed much. The 6,000-square foot dance hall with a high-pitched tin roof still had the original layout, with exposed beams in the ceiling, side flaps for open-air dancing, a 40-foot long bar in the front, a small stage in the back, and a vast outdoor garden. Old advertisement signs from the 1930s and 1940s still hung in the old hall and around the stage.

Through the years, Gruene Hall had become an international destination /tourist attraction and major music venue for up-and-coming and established artists.

Superstars like Garth Brooks, Willie Nelson, Merle Haggard, and George Strait had stood on that stage. It had also helped to jump-start the careers of Jerry Jeff Walker, Lyle Lovett, Nanci Griffith, and many others.

He had always dreamed of performing there, and two months later, after the producers had worked out a deal with the owners, his dream was finally coming true. Tonight would be his turn to grace that famous stage.

But it wasn't going to be a regular performance. On this night, there was a handwritten sign hanging on the front door of Gruene Hall that said, "Closed For A Private Event." That private event was the recording of a new Country Music Television (CMT) special featuring the fastest rising star in country music...Raine Waters.

The front of the structure was blocked from view by two large television production trucks parked sideways. Sitting a few feet further away was a brand new 45-foot custom-built Silver Eagle tour bus, glistening in the sunshine.

The ground was covered with large cables running from the television trucks along the sidewalk through the cracked open front doors of the hall.

Bertha Brooks, the six-foot-six, 350-pound mountain of a man who usually stood just off stage during Raine's performances, making sure his loving fans didn't get too close with their affection, was sitting in a chair just outside the open front doors of the hall controlling the entrance.

When he saw her pull up, he lifted his handheld radio and pushed the button. "Jake, you were right, Virginia just pulled up. What do you want me to do?"

Through his dark sunglasses, Bertha watched Virginia slowly walk up the street toward him. She paused for a moment, staring up at the glistening tour bus, then carefully stepped over the cables, walked up to Bertha, and smiled.

Before he could say anything, his radio crackled. "Tell her to walk around the side to the backstage entrance and knock on the door."

Then they heard Jake sigh deeply on the other end of the radio and say, "I might get fired over this, but I'm going to tell her the truth. She deserves to know what's going on."

Virginia tilted her head and looked up at Bertha. "The truth about what?"

Bertha looked away. "I'd rather not say, Miss Virginia. Just go on around that corner there and walk all the way to the back. Jake will be there waiting for you."

"I didn't come to see Jake!" She shouted, reaching for the door, "I came to talk to Raine!"

Bertha stood up and held his hand against the door. "I'm sorry, Miss Virginia, but I can't let you go in there."

"I need to talk to Raine! Please, Bertha, you know who I am! Let me go in! I have to talk to him!"

"I'm just following orders, ma'am. I'm sorry, but I can't do that."

"Whose orders?" She stared up at him defiantly, with tears rolling down her face.

Bertha shrugged his huge shoulders and looked down at her with sad eyes. "I'm so sorry, Miss Virginia, but it was Raine. He told me not to let you in."

Crying, she ran around the corner to the backstage door and pounded on it hard with her fists. Jake opened the door, stepped out, and closed it behind him.

"Jake, what's going on?" She yelled, "Why won't he talk to me? I've been calling and leaving messages for him for over a week. Why won't he call me back?"

"Virginia, I...I don't know what to say to you. With Raine's new record deal with RCA, and now this television special for CMT, he's...he's under a lot of pressure and..."

"I know, I know, and I'm sorry for all that," she said, interrupting him, "but I have to talk to him. It's very important. Please, Jake, let me go in. I promise I won't make a scene." She stared up at him, "I'm begging you. Please let me see him."

Jake took her hand in his and gently squeezed. "I'm sorry, Ginny, I can't. He...he told me to tell you that he would call you in a few days."

She collapsed to her knees on the grass by the steps. "This can't wait a few days. Raine needs to know now; I have to tell him."

Jake sat down on the grass next to her, wrapped his arm around her shoulders, and whispered, "Ginny, look at me. What does he need to know?"

She slowly lifted her head and looked him in the eyes. "I'm pregnant."

He dropped his head. "Oh, God, no! Are you sure?"

"Yes, I'm sure."

Jake jumped to his feet. "Stay here. I'll be right back."

Virginia sat on the back steps, pulled her knees close to her chest, and rocked. She waited there for over twenty minutes before the door slowly opened, and Jake stepped out.

He was breathing hard. His face was bright red, his jaw was clenched, and his eyes were hard and dark. He held out his hand. "He told me to give you this."

It was a wad of cash. Virginia reached out and took it out of his hand. "What's this for?"

"Follow me," he said, leading her towards a wooden table with benches a few yards away.

They sat across from each other, Virginia still clutching the wad of hundreds in her hand. "I don't understand, Jake. Why did he give me money?"

"Ginny...I know you don't know me very well, and I probably shouldn't be telling you this, but I just can't do this any longer."

"Do what? What are you talking about?"

"When Raine signed his record deal five months ago and hired me to be his road manager, I was so excited, because I thought he was a great guy with all this talent. I knew the first time I saw him perform, he was destined to be a star, and I was thrilled to be part of that ride." He looked across the table into her confused eyes. "I know I'm not making much sense, but please let me finish."

She shook her head and gave him a small smile. "Ok, go on."

"Ginny, you don't know me, but I know everything about you. Do you know how I know? Raine told me all about you, everything. I know you two grew up together, and you have been his girlfriend since high school...and I know you love him."

She lowered her head and whispered, "Yes, I do. I've loved him since the first day I met him."

"That's what makes this so hard. I wish you knew me better, so you would know for sure I'm telling you the truth."

"Jake, I'm a little confused right now, but I think I'm a pretty good judge of character. I've liked you since the first time we met. You've always been so sweet to me, so please just tell me what you're trying to say. Why did Raine give me this money? I think I know, but I need to hear it said out loud. Please tell me. I promise I'll believe you."

"Ginny...the money didn't come from him. It came from Susan Sharp. Unfortunately, she's in his ear now, and he's listening to her."

Virginia raised her eyebrows. "Who is Susan Sharp?"

"She is his Artist Representative from RCA. She's the one that discovered him, introduced him to the label, got him signed, and is in complete control of him. Susan is a real snake. She's telling him what to wear, what to say, and what to think. And trust me, she doesn't want her new star to be tied down to an old girlfriend. It's all about his image, and that doesn't include you, or anyone in his past. She is the worst part of this slimy business. The second Raine signed that record deal, she got her hooks in him. She's telling him exactly what he wants to hear, so he believes anything she says, and will do anything she wants, even if that includes leaving you behind. He's not the guy you grew up with anymore. He's drinking too much Jack Daniels and snorting too much coke. He's let all of this go to his head, everything, the fame, the screaming fans...the groupies."

She lifted her head. "Coke? Raine doesn't do drugs; he hates drugs."

Jake didn't respond. He just raised his eyebrows, shrugged his shoulders, and stared back at her.

She dropped her head and whispered, "Really? Isn't that illegal? Where's he getting the drugs?"

"I told you, Susan is the worst part of this business, and it's all part of her hold over him."

Virginia sat up erect in her chair. "Is she supplying the groupies too?"

"Nobody has to supply them; they're everywhere. Ginny, I know this is none of my business, but I have to tell you...there's been a lot of drugs, and a lot of women."

He frowned and looked her in the eyes, "I've been doing this a long time, for a lot of stars and...well, it's all part of the package; one of the perks that come with fame."

He took her hand again. "I've seen this so many times before. Everyone is telling him he's going to be a huge star, and that's exactly what he wants to hear. He doesn't care about anything or anyone but himself. I know it's a hard thing to accept, but Raine is showing you his true colors, who he really is now. If he truly loved you, he would choose you and tell Susan to go to hell! But that's not what he's doing."

He leaned back in his chair and stared into her eyes, "He doesn't deserve someone like you. Ginny, you need to run away, forget him, and go on with your life. If you don't...he will destroy you along the way."

She held up the money. "I want to know what this is for! What did he tell you, his exact words?"

Jake looked away and shifted in his seat. "I'm sorry, but I can't say those words to you, but please, Ginny...for your sake and the sake of your child, walk away from this jerk and never look back."

He stood up. "You need to go on home. I promise I will call you in a few days. Come on; I'll walk you to your car."

It took them late into the night to complete the video shoot. Although it was supposed to be a secret, Susan Sharp couldn't resist the free publicity, so she called a few local radio stations to tell them how well the CMT video shoot at Gruene Hall was going.

It was almost 1:00 a.m. when the musicians and the television crew walked out of the front doors. When the doors swung open, they were met with the sounds of the crowd. The street was packed with hundreds of Raine Waters fans, mostly women, hoping to get a look and maybe even get to touch the new rising country star. When Raine finally appeared in the doorway, the air exploded with deafening screams as the crowd rushed toward him.

Bertha jumped in front of him, holding out his massive arms, blocking back the crowd of screaming women. "We need a little help here," He yelled.

A few of the musicians and television crew ran up and created a human barricade, reaching from the front door of Gruene Hall to the open door of the tour bus.

Jake had pushed his way through the screaming crowd to the television production truck, jerked open the door, stepped inside, and plopped down in a chair behind the massive video control desk.

The producer looked over and smiled at him. "Can you believe this shit? You'd think he was Elvis or the Beatles." He said, motioning towards the bank of video screens mounted on the wall.

Three police cruisers had rolled up with their blue lights flashing. The officers quickly ran up and took control of the surging crowd, pushing them back away from Raine. The musicians ran to the open door of the bus and got on board. Raine, loving all of the attention, with a broad smile on his face, slowly made his way toward the bus, occasionally stopping to reach over the locked arms of the policemen to sign an autograph or shake the hand of a swooning fan.

The cameras were rolling, and in silence, Jake listened to the producer yelling orders to the engineer sitting next to him, and the cameramen outside in the crowd.

"Go to three," he said to the engineer. Then he picked up the headset and said, "Billy, work your way closer and try to stay with Raine, I want a full-body shot. Jason, I need a wide shot panning the crowd."

Jake stared at the screens taking in the chaos, shaking his head. "Are you gonna use this in the special?"

The producer shook his head. "Maybe a few frames of it, but the cable news channels are going to be all over this. And it won't hurt your boy there at all. You can't buy this kind of publicity."

Jake shrugged, leaned back in his chair, and continued watching the circus flashing in vivid colors on the screens. He watched a close up of

Raine's smiling face as he slowly made his way toward the open door of the bus. When the camera pulled back, showing the crowd surrounding the bus, Jake jumped to his feet and ran to the truck door. He jerked up on the handle and tried in vain to push open the door, but it was blocked by the crowd of screaming fans.

"MOVE OUT OF THE WAY!" He yelled, pushing on it again, but they couldn't hear him and didn't move. After a few more tries, he gave up and slowly walked back to his seat behind the video controller desk. He stared up at the image of Virginia, pushing her way through the screaming girls and ducking under the arms of a policeman. When Raine got close, she jumped in front of him. There was no audio signal, but Jake knew what she was saying.

"HOW COULD you do this to me?" Virginia shouted, "Why won't you talk to me?"

Raine set his guitar case on the ground and held up his hands. "Please, Ginny, don't do this, not here, not now."

He turned toward Bertha, standing behind him, and motioned with his head for him to do something, but he didn't move.

"I'm not one of your groupies that Bertha can just take away. Why won't you talk to me? What have I done?"

He dropped his head and stared down at his feet. "It's not you, Ginny. You haven't done anything wrong. It's me, and all this," he pointed at the crowd.

"What does all this have to do with us? You told me that you loved me. What about the plans we made together?" She put her hands on her belly and locked eyes with him, "What about this? Raine, it's your child!"

He shrugged. "Didn't Jake give you the money?"

She reached in her purse and pulled out the cash. "Are you talking about this?" She held it up in his face and threw it at him, "What is this supposed to be for?"

Bertha dropped to the ground on his knees, picking up the money.

"PICK UP YOUR GUITAR AND GET ON THE BUS, NOW!" Susan Clark yelled behind them.

Virginia jerked her head around and glared at her. Then she turned back to look at Raine. "Don't listen to her. She doesn't know you like I do. I know you love me, and you know I love you. Don't do this, please don't do this to us, to our baby!"

"RAINE, GET ON THE BUS!" Susan yelled again.

Raine picked up his guitar and shrugged his shoulders. "I'm sorry, Ginny, but I have to go. I hope you'll forgive me for this someday, but I have no choice. I do love you, but my life has changed since we made all those plans. This is what I want now. I'm so sorry."

She didn't try to stop him as he stepped around her and walked to the bus.

"Miss Virginia," Bertha said softly, holding up the money, "I think you need to keep this." He gave her the wad of cash and boarded the bus.

Susan Clark walked up and stared into Virginia's eyes. "Bertha's right. You need to keep that money and stop being so naïve. You know what it's for. It's time for you to realize that high school is over and this puppy love between you and Raine is over as well. Raine is destined to do amazing, great things in his life, and the last thing he needs is a pregnant girlfriend dragging him down, like an anchor around his neck. If you have any brains in that country bumpkin head of yours, you'll go back to Abilene or whatever hick-town you're from and use that money to fix your problem. You'll be fine. Marry one of the local rednecks and have four or five more kids. Then when you get old, you can brag to all your friends that you once had a fling with the world-famous Raine Waters."

Susan turned and walked up the steps as the door closed behind her. Slowly, the bus began to pull away from the curb, rolling down the street, followed by the screaming crowd of women running and waving behind it.

2

REAP WHAT YOU SOW

"Weren't you supposed to be on that bus?" The engineer sitting next to Jake asked.

"Yeah, but no big deal. I'll catch a plane tomorrow. I'll probably beat them to Tulsa."

In two of the video screens on the wall, Jake could see Virginia still standing in the same spot where she had confronted Raine. He couldn't tell if she was crying or not; she had her back to the camera. Jake watched her let go of the money in her hand and watched it blow down the street like confetti. He wanted to run to her and pull her into his arms, comfort her...but he didn't. He just sat there watching as she slowly walked away.

"I'd give anything to be him for one day," The engineer said, pointing to a video screen with a frozen image of Raine's smiling face, "You're so lucky to get to work with him. I can't imagine what it must be like to be him. With his looks and his talent...and all those women. This guy's got it made!"

Jake gazed at the screen and frowned. "Yeah, he's something alright...he's a real winner."

OVER THE NEXT FIVE MONTHS, at least once a week, sometimes twice, Jake called Virginia and talked to her for hours about her progress with her pregnancy, and he also filled her in on the latest developments in Raine's career. In all that time, he had not called her once.

She made Jake promise not to tell anyone that she was having the baby, and made him swear that he would never tell Raine about it. She didn't want him in her life or near her baby. As far as she was concerned, Raine had forfeited all his rights to his child the day he gave her that money for an abortion and left her standing in that street, alone and on her own.

In her third trimester in the 27th week of her pregnancy, by accident, she discovered the gender of her child when the nurse, looking at the latest sonogram, said, "She looks perfect."

Until that moment, Virginia had thought that she didn't want to know, but once she knew that it was a little girl, she was thrilled.

"It's a girl?" Jake shouted on the phone. "Ginny, I'm so happy for you. She's going to be so beautiful."

"Thank you, Jake. You are so sweet to say that."

"Just stating the obvious," He said with a chuckle, "Knowing the gene pool she comes from, it's a pretty good bet that she is going to be a stunner, just like her mama."

"I'm just praying for ten fingers and toes, and that she's healthy," she said wistfully.

"She's gonna be great, I just know it," Jake said, "Ahh...are you going to watch the CMA awards this Wednesday night? I guess you know he's up for the Horizon award."

"Actually, I didn't know it, but I'm not surprised. Who else could it be? But to answer your question...no, I won't be watching. Will you be there?"

"I have a ticket," He said, "but I'm not sure I'm going. I was thinking about going somewhere else that night."

"Really?" She said, surprised, "It must be somewhere important for you to miss the CMA's."

Jake chuckled in her ear. "I'm hoping it will be *very* important, but I won't know until I get there."

"Ohh, that sounds very mysterious. Let me know what happens," she said, laughing.

"I promise you will be the first to know."

THAT WEDNESDAY NIGHT, Virginia lost the argument with her parents, who were big country music fans.

"I'll change the channel when it's Raine's turn," her father said, but I don't want to miss the rest of the show just because of that asshole."

"Ok, ok," she said, giving up the fight, slowly lifting out of her chair, "I'll go watch something less stressful in my room."

Two hours later, her father knocked on her door. "Ginny, there's someone at the front door who wants to talk to you."

"At this hour?" She said, looking at her watch, "Who is it?"

"I don't know, I've never seen him before, but he said he needs to talk to you about something important."

She shook her head and sighed, "Alright, but you're gonna have to help me up." Slowly, she shifted her body to the edge of the bed and reached out her hand.

Her father lifted her off the bed and helped her slip on her robe that barely fit around her.

"Need some help putting on your house shoes?" He asked with a chuckle, "I used to have to help your mother because she couldn't see her feet after the fifth month."

She smirked at her father and said. "So, does mom help you now? How long has it been since you've seen *your* feet?" She said, laughing.

"Very funny," he said, grinning and patting his belly, "This is all muscle."

As he walked down the hall behind her to the front door, he said, "By the way, he didn't win."

She stopped and turned to look at him. "What?"

"Raine Waters didn't win the Horizon award," he said, "some other guy I've never heard of won. It was pretty sad."

"Sad? I thought you hated Raine."

"I do, I can't stand the bastard. I'm not sad he didn't win; that's not what I'm talking about. It was his performance that was sad to watch. He was so drunk and screwed up he could barely sing and almost fell off the stage. He was so drunk or stoned the network cut his performance short and went to a commercial. Mark my words, that boy is on the fast road straight to Hell."

When they made it to the front door and opened it, Virginia saw Jake standing there.

"Jake?" She shouted, shocked, "What on earth are you doing here?"

He grinned and held out his hands. He was holding a small box, and his hands were shaking.

Her mother walked up and stood next to her father in the doorway behind her. "What's going on?" She asked. "Ginny, who is this?"

With his trembling hands, Jake fumbled with the small box but finally got it open, exposing a glistening diamond ring and nodded at her parents. "Mrs. Harper, Mr. Harper, I'm Jake Taylor...if she'll have me...I'm the man who's going to marry your daughter."

He dropped down on one knee, looked up at her, and held out the ring. "Ginny, I know we haven't known each other very long, but, well...I can't really explain it." He took a deep breath and let it out slowly, "Ever...Ahh...ever since the day I met you, I've known that you were an extraordinary woman, and it didn't take me long before I fell completely and madly in love with you. I realize that you may not feel the same way about me, and that's OK because if you let me, I believe I can win you over."

"I'm off the road now. I quit my job with Raine three days ago. I found a job here in Abilene, and I start on Monday. Ginny, that little girl you are carrying needs a father, and although she may not be mine by blood and I haven't even met her yet, I'm already in love with her too."

His eyes filled with tears and his words began to choke back. "Ginny, I promise to cherish, honor, and to take care of you, and that little girl, until the day I die. Please, Virginia Camilla Harper...make me the luckiest man on earth! Will you marry me?"

She could hear her mother and her father sniffling behind her, trying not to cry. She reached down, took the ring box out of Jake's hand, and looked at the beautiful sparkling diamond. Smiling down at Jake, still on his knee, she said, "Before I give you my answer, don't you think we should at least go out on a date first?"

THE MORNING after the CMA Awards, Bertha was startled awake by the sound of someone banging on his hotel room door. When he opened it, he saw the enraged face of Susan Sharp glaring up at him.

"I can't believe you let that happen!" She yelled, pushing the door open, walking around him. "I need coffee. Do you have a coffee maker in here?"

Bertha turned and slowly followed her back into the room. "Miss Sharp, I just woke up, and I'm not in a very good mood. Why are you here?"

She rushed past him to the bathroom, searching. "Seriously, there's no goddamn coffee maker in this room? What kind of hotel is this?"

Bertha sat on the edge of the bed and lifted the receiver of the telephone. "It's a five-star hotel," He said, "If you want coffee, you have to call room service. You want cream and sugar?"

Frustrated, she shook her head and sighed. "No, don't order it. I won't be here that long."

"Ok," he said, hanging up the phone, "So why are you here? What do you want with me?"

"I want to know how the hell you could've let that happen! When I left Raine in his dressing room, he was fine. Thirty minutes later, he was so messed up he couldn't even walk. How did that happen?"

Bertha sighed. "Miss Sharp, I am his bodyguard, not his nursemaid. I tried to tell him, but when he gets that way, there's no talking to him and no way to stop him. If you hadn't given him the cocaine to start with..."

"Don't you dare try to put this off on me!" She snapped, "It wasn't just the cocaine, he was trashed, stumbling drunk. And if that wasn't bad enough, he lost the damn award to that prick on Capitol Records!"

Bertha had heard enough, so he stood up, towering over her. "Yes ma'am, he was really messed up, but as it says in the Bible, 'you reap what you sow.' I may get fired for saying this, but I've wanted to tell you this for a long time, and at this point, I really don't give a shit if you fire me or not."

He took a step closer and glared down at her. "All of this is your fault. *YOU* did this to Raine. He was a good guy until you got your hooks into him. You, with all your sneaky manipulations and that bag of candy, you always seem to have with you. You're nothing more than a high-class pusher wearing fancy clothes and expensive shoes. You got him hooked on that shit, and I think it's time you try to get him off of it before it kills him."

Her face flushed, and she clenched her jaw. "How dare you!" She yelled, taking a step back, "You can't talk to me like that! And you were right. You're fired!"

She walked to the door, then turned around, looking back at him. "Where is Raine? He's not in his room."

Bertha walked up to her, forcing her to back out the door with his huge presence. "Probably on the bus. He hates sleeping in hotels." He grabbed the door, and with all the strength he could muster, he slammed it in her face.

"Are you so stupid you can't see the damage you've done?" She yelled in his face, "Raine, you lost the friggin' Horizon Award! THE HORIZON AWARD!"

He took a step back and grinned, "Whoa, calm down. Come on, Susan, the votes were already cast. I'm sorry I got a little screwed up, but you know damn well my performance last night couldn't have had anything to do with me winning or losing that damn award!"

She glared up at him. "A little screwed up? You were pathetic. Of course that embarrassing performance had something to do with it! Are you that naïve? Wipe that stupid grin off your face! Your dimples and Southern charm don't work on me."

Raine lifted his eyebrows. "Are you telling me that the CMA Awards are rigged?"

"I did not say that!" She snapped, "And don't you ever say anything like that again, to anyone. All I'm trying to tell you is record sales are the lifeblood of this town. If you had won that award like you were supposed to, your sales would be soaring this morning, but they're not!"

Raine shrugged, stepped around her, and walked to the galley on the bus. He opened the door of the refrigerator and pulled out a beer.

"Want one?" He asked, still smiling.

"Of course not!" She said, "It's ten o'clock in the morning; I haven't even had breakfast."

"Your loss," he said, popping the tab and chugging the beer. When he finished, he crushed it on the counter, tossed it in the trash, and opened another.

She was disgusted at the sight. "Raine, you have a serious problem. You're an alcoholic, and if you don't get some help, you're going to blow everything."

He laughed. "Come on, Susan, this is just a little hair of the dog. The only problem I have is a raging hangover. I'm not an alcoholic! I can stop drinking anytime I want to, but today, I don't want to."

"What about all the drugs?" She asked.

"Well, you're the one that keeps showing up with em'," he said, grinning, "I figure if you'd quit bringing them, I could stop that too. But why would I want to do that now? I'm only having a little fun, what's wrong with that?"

Susan stared at him, slowly shaking her head. "You don't under-stand what you've done, do you? Raine, you humiliated me, your fans, and RCA on live national television last night. The cable news networks are playing that ridiculous, bumbling performance over and over and over. You have done irreparable damage to your career. Don't you see that? The only thing that might save you would be for you to own up to it, apologize to your fans, and check yourself into rehab."

Raine plopped down on the couch behind the driver's seat and looked up at her. "I can't do that. I'm booked solid, opening for Willie. Don't worry so much. This will all blow over, and I'm not going to rehab, because I'm not an alcoholic or a drug addict!"

3

NO RAINE TONIGHT

It only took four official dates for Ginny to say yes to Jake's proposal. On the second day of her 39th week of pregnancy, in a small ceremony in her parents' back yard, she officially became Mrs. Virginia Camilla Taylor. Unfortunately, they didn't get to go on a honeymoon, because 6 hours later, she gave birth to a healthy 6 pound 3-ounce baby girl. They named her Brooklyn Riley Taylor, Brooklyn, because that was where they had first met, and Riley, after her grandfather, Riley Harper.

Because Jake wanted nothing more to do with show business, he had taken a job selling heavy farm equipment, like tractors and combines. And although at first, he couldn't tell the difference between a cultivator or a rotary tiller, he was a quick study and worked hard.

It didn't hurt him at all that he had a lot of interesting stories to tell the local farmers about the days he was on the road with George Jones, Merle Haggard, and Johnny Cash. Of course, he didn't mention to them the fact that he was just a kid working as a roadie, loading in and loading out their equipment in those days. They all knew that he had been Raine Waters' road manager and assumed he had held the same position with all the other stars. It was the only part of the wild, crazy stories he told them that wasn't exactly true. Within a few years, Jake became one of the top producers for the company in the entire West Texas region.

When Brooklyn turned three, Jake had saved enough money to buy a few acres just south of Abilene and built a new house. He had let Ginny and Brooklyn design it and oversee the construction. When it was finished and decorated, it was the most beautiful house he'd ever seen.

Jake had known about all of Virginia's furniture and decoration choices, but she had kept one of the room's interior a secret. So when he opened the door to the room, he was shocked.

"What's all this?" He asked excitedly.

"It's your music room. I know you said that you didn't want to be part of the music business anymore, but Jake, music is part of you, it's in your soul."

Slowly he walked around the room, running his fingers over the electric piano, guitars, microphones, and speakers. "That's a Les Paul, I've always wanted one of those, and this is a great microphone. How did you know what to buy?"

"I called Bertha," she said grinning, "He talked to all the guys in Raine's band. They got together and told me what to buy and where to get it. Did you see this?" She said, pointing at a new Macintosh computer, "Bertha insisted that I buy this. It has a software on it called ProTools. I don't know exactly how it works, but he told me that it records on the computer memory instead of on tape. It's something brand new, and he said that it's supposed to be great."

He looked around the room, not talking for a long time.

"Jake, is it ok? Do you like it?" She asked softly, "I...I just thought..."

He threw his arms around her and whispered, "It's amazing, and I love it!" Then he bent down and gently kissed her on the lips.

When the kiss ended, he pulled back and stared into her eyes. "Ginny, I hope you know how much I love you. When I wake up every morning and look over and see you lying there beside me, I thank God. Then I ask him to please tell me what I've done to deserve someone like you. So far, he hasn't answered me, and I still don't know, but I *do* know that I'm the luckiest man on earth to have you in my life."

OVER THE NEXT FEW YEARS, Raine Waters' record sales began to slip. His second album only sold about half as many copies as his first. His addiction to alcohol and cocaine continued to progress, and he missed so many live performances, Willie kicked him off his tour. But the worst thing that could have happened to him was when he didn't show up for another concert, and Willie branded him forever when he walked on stage and said, "Well folks, it looks like it's gonna be no Raine tonight." All the cable news shows and several newspapers picked up on that line, and soon, *No Raine Tonight* became synonymous with his name.

After dealing with Raine's nonsense for several years, Susan Sharp had had enough. At the next monthly A & R meeting, in the RCA boardroom, she threw him under the bus.

"It's such a damn shame, Raine is so talented. I love his music!" Jim Ed, the President of RCA said, "Can't you do something? How about rehab?"

"I've tried, but he won't go. It doesn't matter anymore how talented he is. He's completely out of control," Susan Sharp said, "He's either stupid drunk or manic high on cocaine 24 hours a day."

"Well, Susan, you know how things work around here," Jim Ed said, "He's your guy, you brought him here and convinced me to sign him. Everything he's doing reflects on the label...and you. So, what do you suggest we do about him?"

PART II

THIRTY YEARS LATER

4

THE BOOKSTORE

As he pedaled past the large marquee in front of the bank, the digital screen flashed 98 degrees, humidity 100%. That was normal for Cocoa Beach, Florida, in August.

He was pedaling the old rusted bicycle as fast as his legs would let him, on his way to the bookstore in the Merrit Island Shopping Mall. To get there from the beach, He had to go over two long bridges. He was praying he could make it across the last bridge before the rain started pouring down again. But if he didn't make it, he was prepared for it.

After he made it over the first and longest bridge, the sky turned angry and dark so, in the Walmart parking lot, he stopped and took three of the black plastic garbage bags he had dug out of a dumpster behind a Publix grocery store and fastened them over him.

He tore a small hole in the bottom for his head, and two more holes on the sides for his arms then pulled it over him like a coat. He slipped the other two bags over his legs. They worked well, but they smelled terrible, so he took them off and turned them inside out. He figured that when it finally did rain, it would wash away the old food and gunk.

He had made it about halfway over the last bridge when the rain finally started pouring down. By the time he pulled up under the overhang of the mall, his long hair, beard, and shoes were soaked. When he pulled off the plastic bags, he was happy to see that his shirt and his pants weren't too wet.

As usual, the people walking by him stared and gave him dirty looks, like it was some kind of crime to be homeless. He guessed they didn't like him parking his bicycle on the sidewalk, or perhaps watching him drying his wet hair with an old tee shirt. Whatever their problem was, he didn't care. He was used to it, so he ignored the looks, finished drying his hair and beard, and then untied the rope to his brief-case. He had covered the leather satchel with two plastic grocery sacks to keep it dry. After he peeled them off, he opened it up and checked inside to see if anything had gotten wet, and thankfully, it was still dry inside. The old leather briefcase was all he had left, and It contained the only things of value he still owned.

After his hair and beard were dry enough and not dripping, he tied the plastic garbage bags to the frame and chained the bicycle to a steel rail.

When he opened the door to the bookstore, walked inside, and the cold air hit him in the face, it felt wonderful.

As he stood there in the doorway enjoying the air conditioning with his eyes closed, he could hear several audible gasps. He didn't have to open his eyes because he could feel the hateful looks directed his way.

He ignored the sneers and bad looks and slowly walked to the tall spinning rack displaying the reading glasses. When he found a pair he liked, he pulled them out and put them on. He held up his hand and looked at his fingers. He could see the dirt under his long fingernails clearly.

"These will work," he said out loud as he turned and walked toward the shelves of books. When he turned to walk down each row, the people in the isles would scatter, running away from him like he had leprosy or something.

He was looking for the fiction section. When he found it, he pulled out the new John Grisham novel, walked to the center of the store, sat down in one of the chairs, and began to read.

BETTY USUALLY WORKED the cash register at the Mall entrance to the bookstore, but today she was stationed at the register near the back door. She smelled the man before she saw him casually walk up to the reading glasses rack. The stench of body odor hung in the air around him.

She watched him carefully as he took a pair of reading glasses out of the rack, put them on, and walk away.

When he was out of her line of sight, she picked up the phone and punched in a number."Mr. Beasley, I need your assistance."

"Sure," He said, "What's up?"

"Ahh, I have a customer in front of me now, so I'd rather not say. I'm on the back register. I need to talk to you, and please hurry."

Jim Beasley stood up from behind his desk and walked out of his office, but he didn't have to walk all the way to the back register to understand the problem; he smelled it when he got to the reading area. A few rows away, he saw Betty holding her nose and pointing toward the obviously homeless man sitting in a chair, quietly reading a book.

Jim slowly walked up and sat down next to the man. "I see you're a John Grisham fan." He said.

The man looked up at Jim but said nothing.

"Hi, I'm Jim, Jim Beasly, what's your name?" He said, holding out his hand.

The man looked up and tentatively took his hand and shook it. "Raine...my name is Raine Waters."

Jim raised his eyebrows. "Did you say Rain Water?" He pointed at the ceiling, "Like thunder and rainwater?"

Raine smiled. No, there's an E at the end, R A I N E, and my last name is Waters. I'm not sure where the extra E came from, but apparently, my parents had a sense of humor."

Well, Raine, it's nice to meet you. Call me, Jim. I'm the store manager here and..."

"I have a right to be here!" Raine shouted, "It's a public place! Please don't call the cops!"

"Whoa...slow down. Who said anything about calling the cops? I just wanted to talk to you a minute."

Raine shrugged. "Well, that's what they usually do. I don't mean to cause any trouble. I was just trying to get out of the rain until it passes by."

Jim smiled. "I'm not calling anybody, but I wonder if you would mind coming back to my office for a minute?"

"Ahh...sure...I guess so," Raine said, picking up his briefcase and following him.

Jim led Raine back to his office and opened the door. "Have a seat. Do you want something to drink, Coke, or coffee?"

Raine smiled and nodded. "Sure, coffee would be great." He sat down in a chair facing the desk. "Jim, why are you being so nice to me? And why are we talking in here? Am I in some kind of trouble?"

Jim poured two cups of coffee, handed one to Raine, and sat down behind his desk. "No, no trouble, nothing like that. But can I be truthful here? Can I tell you the real reason?"

Rain shook his head. "Yeah, I wish you would. If it's about these glasses? I wasn't going to steal them, I promise."

"No, it's not about the glasses," He said, smiling, "Why don't you just keep those as a gift from me."

Jim shifted in his chair, searching for the right words, "To tell you the truth, Raine...we're talking in here because I needed to get you out of the store. You were chasing away all my customers."

Raine frowned. "I wasn't doing anything. How could I be chasing away your customers? I was just sitting there reading?"

I know, I know, but...I...I don't know how to say this to you without it sounding awful."

"Just say it, man. What is it? What'd I do?"

Jim took a deep breath. "OK...uh...uh...well, Raine...you stink, man. You smell God awful. You need a bath and some clean clothes. People were leaving because they couldn't stand the smell. I'm sorry, Raine...it's awful."

Raine set his coffee on the edge of the desk and looked up at Jim. His eyes were tearing up. "I smell that bad... really?"

"Yeah, It's...it's pretty bad."

Raine dropped his head and wiped his face with his sleeve. "I didn't realize it was that bad. I don't smell it. I guess I'm used to it or something," He was trying to hold back his emotions, but his voice cracked, "I'm so sorry. I don't have any soap or any other clothes. I try to wash every day in the ocean, but...I'm sorry, I'll go now."

"No, don't leave; it's still raining hard out there. Stay here until it stops."

Raine stood up, wiping his eyes. "No, I think I'd like to go now. You're a good man, and I appreciate you being so nice to me, but I think I need to leave."

"Come on, Raine, please don't go. Sit down, finish your coffee at least."

Raine thought for a moment and sat back down in the chair, picked up his coffee, and wiped his eyes again with his sleeve. "Thank you. Ok, I'll stay a few minutes more."

They both sipped their coffee in awkward silence a few minutes, neither one of them knowing what to say. Finally, Jim asked. "Raine, what happened to you? Please forgive me for saying this, but you seem...normal, an intelligent guy. How the hell could someone like you wind up like this?"

Raine looked down at his shabby, ragged then lifted his eyes back up to Jim. "What you see here is all self-inflicted. There was a time I had a future, a big one. At least that's what everyone told me, but I screwed it up. That's...that's what I do, over and over again. I screw it up, burn it to the ground and leave a trail of flames behind me."

He took another sip of his coffee and shrugged. "The worst part was, I knew what was happening to me, but I didn't try to stop it. I just let those flames surround me and burn up everyone and everything I've ever cared about, and I let those flames turn my life...into ashes."

Jim wasn't sure what to say to him, but he knew he had to try to help. "Raine, I know this is none of my business, but I'd like to help you get back on your feet. I don't have a lot of money, but I have a little saved. How about I take you to a hotel and rent you a room for a few days. That way, you could take a good shower and rest up. We're about the same size, so I could give you some of my clothes. And if it's OK, I'll take you to my barber. I believe if you trimmed that beard, got a hair cut, and with some new clothes, I'm sure you could find a job around here doing something. I'll be glad to talk to the other store managers. I know they're always looking for help unloading the trucks, and they come almost every day. And I'd like to take you to my church. I'm sure my pastor will want to help too."

When he said that, Raine turned his head and looked away, staring off into space. "Look at me, Raine! I'm serious about this. I believe God brought you here to meet me today so that I could help you. It's dangerous out there living on the street. Please let me do this for you. You need to do something with yourself or...or you're going to die living like this."

When Raine finished his coffee, he stood up, handed Jim the book and glasses back, then reached out his hand. "I want to thank you for the coffee and the company. Thanks for treating me with some dignity. That's something I haven't felt in a long time."

Raine walked to the door, opened it, and looked back. "I'm pretty sure God doesn't want to have anything to do with me because he gave up on me years ago, and I don't blame him. I do appreciate your offer, but I know that I'd only disappoint you in the end. I'm an alcoholic and a lost cause. Don't worry about me. I'll be OK. You see...I died a long, long time ago...I'm just waiting for the day when someone comes along, finds my corpse, and buries me."

WHEN HE WALKED out of Jim's office, he closed the door behind him and walked as fast as he could toward the back door. He could hear Jim yelling behind him not to go.

When he reached for the door, it suddenly swung open as two men entered. He was thrown off balance when the door hit him, and it knocked him backward falling onto a display table of books. He dropped his briefcase on the floor and the books scattered everywhere.

Raine started picking up the books and putting them back on the table. "It's OK, sir, it was just an accident," a woman said, rushing up to him, "I'll put them back."

He picked his briefcase up off the floor and turned around to walk out.

"I'm sorry, sir," one of the men said, "We should have been paying more attention. I didn't mean to knock you over. Are you ok? Are you hurt anywhere?"

Raine shook his head and stepped towards the door. "No, I'm not hurt, I'm fine, " he said.

When he passed the second man, his eyes widened. "Wait!" He yelled, "I know you! Are you Raine Waters?"

The other man turned around and stared at Raine's face. "Oh my God, It *is* you! I'm a huge fan. I used to come to see you perform at Billy Bobs all the time. I have both of your albums."

"Me too!" The other guy yelled, "I still play them all the time. They're like collector's items now. Could I get your autograph?"

Raine turned away and walked to the door. "I'm sorry, but you're mistaken, " he said, "I don't know what you're talking about. I'm not him. I've never heard of Raine Waters!"

He pushed the door open and ran to his bike as fast as he could. When he got to it, he unlocked the chain, put his briefcase in one of the black garbage bags, and tied it to the handlebar. Then he took off, heading back to the beach, pedaling as fast as he could, getting soaked in the pouring rain.

5

THAT WAS HIM

Wyatt Shaw and Owen Anderson bent down to help Betty pick up the scattered books off the floor.

"What happened here?" Jim Beasley asked, walking up, looking at the mess.

Owen straightened up and set a stack of books on the table. "It's all our fault. My friend Wyatt and I weren't paying attention, opened the door too quickly, and knocked this guy backward. When he fell, he knocked all the books off the table."

"What guy?" Jim said, looking around, "Was he hurt?"

"Some guy with long hair and a long beard," Wyatt said, "He looked like he might be homeless, but I don't think he was hurt."

Jim lifted his head. "Raine? You knocked Raine into this table?"

Owen and Wyatt looked at each other and then back at Jim. "That was Raine Waters?" Owen asked, "Damn, I can't believe it; that *was* him!"

"I told you so!" Wyatt said.

Confused, Jim raised his eyebrows and looked at them. "You know Raine? How do you know him?"

"Are you kidding? Of course, we know him," Owen said with wide eyes, "He's famous. Don't you know who he is?"

Jim shook his head. "No, I just met him. You said he's famous? For what?"

Owen smiled at Jim and asked, "How old are you?"

"I'm twenty-nine. Why?"

Wyatt and Owen shook their heads and grinned. "That explains it. You're too young to remember him," Wyatt said, "but about thirty years ago, he had the hottest band in the whole damn country, and his records were climbing the charts. He even did a couple of television specials. He was a great singer and songwriter."

"He was also famous for his eyes," Owen said, "Back then all the girls went nuts when he looked at them. You could barely hear him singing for all their screaming. That's how I recognized him. It was those piercing blue eyes."

"Yeah," Wyatt said, "he was a real lady killer back then, but man he looks like shit now. I wonder what in the hell happened to him?"

"Did you say Raine Waters?" A woman's voice said behind them. They turned around to see a tall, attractive blonde woman standing there.

"I don't mean to be eavesdropping," she said, "but I thought I heard you say something about Raine Waters. Was I right?"

"Yes, ma'am," Jim said, "we were talking about Raine."

Owen took a step closer to the woman and studied her face carefully. "I think I know you. You're Louise Coleman, aren't you?"

She nodded and smiled. "Yes, I am. It's Louise Parker now. How do you know me?"

Owen looked back at Wyatt. "Don't you recognize her?"

"Sure I do," he shouted, "You were in Raine's band, and in the TV specials!"

Her eyes twinkled with her smile. "That was such a long time ago. I can't believe you recognized me from that."

"It's much more than that, ma'am. Every time Raine's band got anywhere near Abilene, Owen and I would jump in our truck and go see you guys perform. We were huge fans; we loved you guys! You were great! I can't believe it, after all these years seeing *you* and Raine Waters on the same day!"

"You saw Raine?" She asked, stunned, "Where?"

"Right here, just a few moments ago," Jim said, "I had a long talk with him in my office."

"He was here? In this store?" She said, breathing rapidly.

"Yes, ma'am," Owen said, "He just left. He ran out that door, jumped on an old beat-up bicycle, and rode off in the rain."

"An old bicycle? Seriously? Why would he do that?"

"How long has it been since you've seen him?" Jim asked her.

She thought for a few moments. "A long time. I'm not exactly sure, maybe twenty-five years, why?"

The three men looked at each other. "Well, Mrs. Parker," Wyatt began, "ahh…he doesn't exactly look like you may remember."

"In what way?" She asked.

"Well ma'am…he looks pretty bad," he said, "He's got real long gray hair and a long shaggy gray beard. To be honest with you, Mrs. Parker, we're pretty sure that he's homeless, living on the street. He looks awful."

"You're telling me that Raine Waters…*THE*…Raine Waters is homeless and right this minute, he is riding an old bicycle out there in this lightning and torrential rain? Which way did he go?"

Owen opened the door and pointed. "He rode off in that direction."

Louise covered her head with her purse and ran out the door. She was soaking wet by the time she got to her car, but she didn't care. For over an hour, Louise drove up and down the highway, searching for him. Then she slowly drove down every other road that led to the beach. It was well past dark when she finally gave up and drove home.

RAINE GUESSED that it was somewhere around eight o'clock when the rain finally stopped. When Raine left the bookstore, it was raining so hard he couldn't see where he was going, so instead of riding over the two bridges to the beach in all the traffic, he pulled over, walked down the hill, and got underneath the bridge to shelter from the rain.

There were three or four other men under the bridge with him, but they didn't talk. No one had anything to say anyway, so they just sat there quietly, keeping their distance from each other, watching the rain pouring down.

Bridges were good places to shelter, but Raine always had to keep an eye out for water moccasins and alligators. He never slept under a bridge unless it was near the ocean. He didn't have to worry as much about alligators there, but in those waters, the Indian River, there were lots of snakes and giant, aggressive alligators. With the growing home-less population in Cocoa Beach and bridges being an excellent place to shelter, it didn't take long for the gators to figure out where to go for a quick snack when it rained.

For protection, Raine had put his bicycle over him, and he had the chain and lock in his hand just in case. Fortunately, he didn't see any snakes or gators that night, so when the rain stopped, he pushed his bicycle up to the highway and headed East towards the beach.

When he got there, he saw his friend Dave walking along the beach road looking in a garbage can. He got off the bike, put down the kick-stand, and sat on the curb watching him. Dave reached into the can and pulled something out Raine didn't recognize. Dave held it up to his nose, smelled it, and then took a bite.

He instantly spat it out, cursing. "Oh, man!" he yelled, "That tasted like shit!"

He looked over at Raine, who was laughing at him. "It ain't funny, man, that was God awful. You got anything to drink? I need something to wash this out of my mouth."

Raine opened his briefcase, pulled out the almost empty fifth of whiskey, and handed it to him. "Don't drink it all," he said, "that's all we have."

"Too late," Dave said, grinning, "Man, that was nasty!" He killed the bottle and threw it into the can.

"I keep telling you not to do that, you dumbass," Raine said, shaking his head, "Only eat stuff from behind a restaurant. That's fresh, and it won't kill you."

"Yeah, I know," Dave said, "but man, I'm starving. Let's go over to Grills and see what they've got to offer. We can listen to the band rock out. I think the Nash Cooper Band is there tonight. I really like them."

It took them almost an hour to walk the three and a half miles from the Cocoa Beach pier to Grills. Of course, they didn't go inside. Instead, they walked around back to the dumpsters, dug out some food, and walked across the street to eat it.

Dave was eating some fried shrimp and fish, and dancing around in the street, flipping his long hair, playing air guitar grooving to the music. Raine was also eating and smiling, watching him dance.

"Now, isn't this better?" Raine asked him.

"Yeah, It's great, man! Why would they throw something this good away?"

"They have to," Raine said, "If someone leaves it on their plate, they can't just scrape it off and re-sell it," he said, "They have to throw it out."

Raine finished his meal and leaned back against the building, watching Dave dancing around to the music. "You like this band?"

"Yeah, man! They rock! You don't like em'?"

"I like the band, but I don't like that Nash guy. I don't like the way he treats his musicians. Remember last time, when he came out and started screaming at them?"

"Yeah, he was pissed about something."

Raine shook his head. "Not really, he's just a certified dick! He's playing at a damn beach bar, and he thinks he's a friggin' star! He treats his band like crap! The truth is without them; he's not all that special!"

"Maybe so, but I still like em'!"

The music stopped, and a few minutes later, they saw the musicians coming out the back door on their break, lighting up cigarettes and talking.

"You guy's rock!" Dave yelled across the road.

They looked over at them, waved, then lifted their beers in a toast and said thanks.

One of the members walked across the road to talk to them. "Hi, I'm Billy Lang. Are you guys eating out of that dumpster?"

"Yeah, it's great! You want some?" Dave asked, smiling.

"No! God, no!" Billy said, "Hold on a second."

He walked back to the band for a moment, then returned with some cash in his hand. "Here, take this and go buy some real food. That stuff will kill you!"

"Thanks," Raine said, "That's nice of you guys. We appreciate it."

"Just promise me, you'll spend it on food, not drugs," he said.

"Hey man, we're drunks, not dope heads!" Dave said, grinning.

Billy laughed at Dave and then looked over at Raine. "I'm serious. Spend this on some real food. Ok?"

The back door slammed open, and Nash Cooper stormed out and started yelling. "What the hell was that? What chords were you playing?" He looked around the area, "Billy? Where the hell is Billy?"

"He's over there," One of the musicians said, pointing toward them across the street.

"Billy, get your ass over here! What are you doing talking to those bums! Come back over here before you catch some disease."

"Hey, Dude," Dave yelled, "We're homeless, not bums!"

Nash smirked and gave Dave the finger. "Hey, DUDE... Fuck you. Billy, get your ass over here!"

Dave held up both of his arms and gave Nash the finger with both of his hands. "Well, double back to you, Dude!"

Dave looked back at Raine and said, "You're right. This guy is a real dick!"

Nash jerked around and started walking toward Dave. "What'd you say asshole? What was that again?"

Raine jumped up and started walking toward Nash. "He said you are a DICK! A real penis. But he wasn't talking about a big penis. He was talking about a tiny little penis! You got a problem with that?"

Raine's sudden aggressive action shocked Nash, and he stopped in his tracks, but Raine kept walking toward him.

Billy jumped between them. "Whoa! Back off, guys. Come on, cool down."

Raine glared over at Nash. "You got a real problem with that ego of yours. One day it's going to get your ass kicked real good."

"Screw you, old man!" He yelled.

"Come on, guys," Billy said, still standing between them, "There's no need for this!"

Raine took a step back and stared at Nash. "You know, sonny, without this band, you're nothing. They are all great players, so instead of screaming at them, why don't you just tell them what you want? If they respected you, they'd give you whatever you wanted, but respect is something you have to earn."

Nash shook his head and laughed. "Great! I'm getting words of wisdom from a degenerate! I'll write that down on a piece of paper and then use it to wipe my ass! What the hell do you know about music?"

Raine smiled. "Much more than you think."

"Oh... I get it now," Nash yelled, "Boys, we have a musician in our midst. Well, sir, if you don't mind me saying, it looks like all that vast musical knowledge of yours hasn't worked out that well for you, now has it?"

Raine just looked away and didn't respond, because he had him there.

6

WHO IS RAINE WATERS?

For the past 29 years, on the 15th day of August, Virginia and Jake had thrown a big party at their house to celebrate their anniversary and Brooklyn's birthday.

So when August rolled around, even though Brooklyn begged her parents not to, Virginia sent out the invitations to their friends to celebrate their 30th year together.

On the day of the party, when Brooklyn turned onto the road that led to her parents' property, she could see the line of cars parked on each side of the road leading up to the house.

When she opened the door, the house was full, buzzing with people standing around holding their drinks, laughing, and talking in every room. She did a quick search but didn't see her mother anywhere, so she walked to the kitchen.

Virginia was standing over the stove, stirring a big pot. On her left was an IV stand with a small long tube running along the floor and up her body, attached to her left arm. On her right was the Oxygen tank with its plastic tube running up and over her shoulder to the nose piece, held in place by the two straps looped over her ears. The bright red sparkling party dress Brooklyn had helped her mother pick out two years earlier on a shopping trip they had taken to Dallas, hung loosely over her skeleton thin frame. It looked more like a loose sack than an expensive form-fitting designer dress. She was barefoot, her red heels sitting side by side neatly behind her.

Brooklyn walked to the stove and stood beside Virginia. "Mother, what are you doing in here? You promised me. Please stop. Let me do this."

Virginia frowned at her and continued stirring the pot. "Honey, I may be dying, but I ain't dead yet. If I stop stirring, it will stick to the bottom of the pan."

Brooklyn took the spoon out of her hand and began stirring. "I wish you wouldn't say things like that. Sit on the stool. I'll do this."

Virginia took the spoon back. "No! I don't want to sit down. I'm feeling fine. Please let me do this. I have to do something besides watching everyone out there looking at me with all those sad eyes! It's driving me nuts."

"Ok," Brooklyn said, frustrated, letting go of the spoon. "If you need any help, just yell."

As she made her way through the crowd, Brooklyn was stopped several times by people expressing their regrets about her mom's condition and telling her how much they loved hearing her sing in church the past Sunday. As politely as she could, she gradually worked her way through the party to the back porch. There was no one there, so she sat down alone in a deck chair watching the sunset on the horizon.

As she sat there quietly, she could hear voices, so she strained to hear where they were coming from and what they were saying. She recognized her father's voice and two of his friends. They were standing around the corner by the pool.

She got out of her chair and peeked around the corner.

Her father was standing behind the barbecue grill, turning pieces of chicken with long tongs with his right hand and holding a cigar in his left. Standing behind him was Owen Anderson and Wyatt Shaw, puffing on cigars as well.

I'm telling you, Jake," Wyatt said, blowing out a cloud of white smoke, "It was Raine Waters."

"No question about it," Owen added, "And man, he looked awful! He's gotten old, and he was wearing ragged clothes. I'm telling you, he's either off his rocker, or he's homeless or something."

Jake took a puff of his cigar and shook his head. "Raine Waters broke? Homeless? How could he be broke? Do you know how much money he was making?"

"Jake, that was 20, no 30 years ago," Owen said, "Trust me, the guy we saw in Florida didn't have a dime. I guess he blew it all."

"What were you two doing in Florida anyway?" Jake asked.

"Owen's father has a boat down there. So he took us out fishing, while the wives drove over to Disney World. All of this was an absolute coincidence."

Wyatt took a drag off his cigar and blew it out. "That's the first bookstore I've been to in years. It was raining real hard that day, and we couldn't go out in the boat. Since we had a little time, we drove over to that bookstore because I didn't know anything about the local fish. I wanted to get a book on it, so I'd know what I was catching."

"Talk about perfect timing," Owen said, "We drove to the mall, jumped out of the car, and ran to the bookstore. We pushed open the door just as he was coming out and knocked him back on his ass. But there he was, bigger than Dallas, looking up at me with those piercing blue eyes of his."

Jake flipped the chicken and puffed on his cigar. "I haven't heard a word from Raine in over 25 years. The last time I talked to him, he was out there still touring, living pretty fast and hard. It's just so difficult to believe that Raine Waters could be broke and living on the street. Wow!"

Jake reached in his pocket, pulled out his lighter, and re-lit his cigar. "For God's sake, don't mention any of this to Virginia."

"Who is Raine Waters? And why not tell mom?"

Jake turned around to see Brooklyn standing behind them. "Oh hi, baby," he said, reaching out, hugging her, "I didn't know you were here."

"I just drove up. I guess you know Mom is in the kitchen. I tried to make her stop cooking and rest, but you know her."

"You're fighting a losing battle there. Your mom may have cancer, but as long as she has the strength to fight, she's not going to let it stop her from doing what she wants to do."

"She looks so thin. Has she lost more weight?"

Jake looked down. "It's the chemo. She eats, but can't seem to keep it down."

"I know it's none of my business," Wyatt said softly, "but has she tried cannabis? I hear that's good for things like that."

Jake nodded, "Her doctor talked to us about it, but she refused."

"How long does she have?" Owen asked.

"We don't know at this point, Owen. It all depends on how this round of chemotherapy goes. If it doesn't slow it down," He looked down and shrugged, "well, there won't be much else we can do...maybe only a few more months."

"Let's not talk about that now," Brooklyn said, changing the subject, "You didn't answer my question, who is Raine Waters, and why are we not telling mom about him?"

"Ah... he's...ah...he's nobody," Jake stammered, "He's no one that concerns you."

Jake took the chicken breasts off the fire and stacked them on a plate. "Hey guys, we're missing the party. It's almost time to eat. How about another drink first."

"Yeah, sure," Wyatt said, "I could use a refill."

"Me too," Owen quickly added.

The three of them rushed away, disappearing into the house, leaving Brooklyn standing there alone.

She was confused with her father's answer to her questions. He had always been a terrible liar, and she knew his hasty retreat was his way of avoiding her questions.

She sat down on a chaise lounge by the pool and tried to make sense of what had just happened. *Who is Raine Waters?* She thought to herself, *And why is it so important to keep it from mother? What is going on?*

WHEN BROOKLYN finally walked back into the house, the party was in full swing. The dining room table was surrounded with friends filling their plates with food, talking, and swaying to the music coming from the speakers in the ceiling.

She was glad to see her mother finally sitting down on the sofa in the den, talking and laughing with two of her good friends sitting next to her. Although she was frail, she still had that radiant smile and her infectious laugh.

Brooklyn was hungry, so she worked her way around the guests to the dining room table and got in line behind two of her mother's old friends.

They were talking just above a whisper, but loud enough for Brooklyn to hear them. "Really? He's homeless?" One of the women said.

"That's what I heard."

"I can't believe it," the other one quipped, "Who told you that?"

"Wyatt Shaw. He said that he and Owen accidentally ran into him in a bookstore in Florida last week."

"Oh my! Does Virginia know?"

"I'm not sure, but I think she needs to know."

Brooklyn wanted to ask whom they were talking about but didn't want them to know that she was eavesdropping, so she kept quiet. When she finally made it to the table, she loaded her plate with some of her mother's famous potato salad and a piece of the chicken her father had cooked on the grill. Juggling her glass of ice tea in one hand and her plate in the other, she walked back to the den and squeezed in beside her mother.

As she slowly ate her food, she listened carefully to her mother as she laughed and talked to her friends. It was good to hear her laugh again. It had been a long time since she'd heard it. In the past year, there hadn't been many occasions to laugh.

It was only a few days after last year's party when the headaches started, and it was only a few months after that when they had received the frightening news. Brooklyn had insisted on going with them to MD Anderson Hospital in Houston to hear the tests' results, and it was a day she would never forget. Even though she had tried very hard to lock that memory away, every time she looked at her mother's disintegrating body, sunken eyes, and emaciated face, she remembered that day vividly and the shocking words the doctor had said to them...stage four inoperable brain cancer.

Brooklyn looked over at her mother and smiled, forcing herself to think of something else.

One of the women she had stood behind at the dining table slowly walked up and stood in front of her mother. It was Hattie May Johnson, one of her mother's oldest friends.

"Virginia, did you hear about Raine?" She said softly.

Virginia lifted her head and looked up at her, "About who?"

"About Raine Waters," she said in a loud whisper, "He's flat broke, homeless, and living on the street in Florida."

Even though Hattie was trying to whisper, everyone had heard her. The room suddenly fell silent, everyone staring at Virginia, waiting for her response.

Virginia's face flushed bright red as she glared up at Hattie and yelled, "NO HATTIE! NOT IN THIS HOUSE! DON'T EVER SAY THAT NAME IN THIS HOUSE AGAIN! NEVER AGAIN!" She looked around the room, "Where is Jake? JAKE!" She yelled, "WHERE ARE YOU?"

Jake pushed his way through the crowd and ran to her. "I'm here, what's wrong?"

"Help me up," she said, trying to stand, "I'm tired and want to go to my room."

With his arm around her waist, Jake and Brooklyn helped Virginia maneuver the IV stand and Oxygen tank through the silent and stunned crowd. When they reached the bedroom, Jake opened the door, took control of the IV stand, and the Oxygen tank from Brooklyn, followed Virginia inside and closed the door behind them.

ONE BY ONE, the guests began to leave the party after Virginia's abrupt and dramatic exit.

At the front door, telling them goodbye, Brooklyn and Jake shook their hands, and received their hugs and condolences as they filed out.

After the guests had all left, Jake poured himself two fingers of bourbon and walked outside to the pool.

After she picked up the paper plates and cups and put the dirty dishes in the dishwasher, Brooklyn walked out to the pool and sat down in a chair next to him.

"Dad, I think I'm going to leave now," she said, "But I wanted to say goodnight first."

"Ok, Baby," Jake said with a smile, "Please drive safe."

"I always do," She said, hugging him, "Is mom asleep?"

"I doubt it," he said, frowning, "she doesn't sleep much these days."

"Would it be Ok if I looked in on her? I'd like to tell her goodnight too."

He smiled and kissed her on the forehead. "I think she would love that."

When Brooklyn opened the door, Virginia was sitting on the edge of the bed, staring out the window and wiping her eyes with a Kleenex.

"Mom," she said softly, "I'm going home now. I wanted to say goodbye. Are you alright?"

Virginia turned and looked at her. "I'm fine, honey," she said, wiping her eyes, "I'm just tired."

"Ok...I just wanted to check on you before I left."

"I'm OK. You go on home now. I'll be fine."

Brooklyn walked to her mother's bed and sat next to her. "Mom...I have to ask. Who is..."

Virginia burst into tears and looked away. "Please don't ask me that. Not now. Please, Honey, just let this go. I'm begging you, Brooklyn. Please, don't do this now. Just go home."

7

AN OLD FLAME

Louise Coleman-Parker joined Raine Waters' band six months before he signed his record deal with RCA. When she joined the band, never in her wildest dreams did she imagine what was about to happen.

She was with him for the full rocket ship ride from total obscurity to nationwide fame, and it happened almost overnight. She was his backup singer for both of the CMT television specials, she stood behind him each night he opened for Willie, and she was there standing behind him when he almost fell off the stage at the CMA awards. She was also in his dressing room when they announced that someone else had won the Horizon award. She was with Raine for the summit of his career but fortunately wasn't with him for the fall.

She had met Bill Parker a few months before the fiasco at the CMA Awards show at a special corporate event in Orlando.

She was instantly attracted to him. Bill was a little older than she was, very handsome, and was a bit of a nerd. But the thing she liked the most about him was that he wasn't a musician or connected to the music business in any way. In fact, when she met him, he had no idea who she was and had never heard of Raine Waters.

They met standing in the breakfast buffet line at a hotel on the morning of the event. She had spotted the tray of cinnamon rolls the second she grabbed her plate and got in line. But when she made it up to the tray, the man in front of her, picked up the last one and put it on his plate.

"Shit!" She said to herself, or at least she thought she had. The man turned around and looked at her. "Having a bad morning, are we?"

"Did I say that out loud?"

He smiled and nodded his head. "Yes, ma'am you did. Loud and clear."

He looked down at his plate. "I guess if I was a true gentleman, I would just let you have this," he said motioning towards the cinnamon roll.

"That would be very sweet of you," she said.

"Yes it would," he stared down at the roll, "but the problem is...my mouth has been watering over this since I spotted it way back there by the plates."

She laughed. "I know exactly how you feel. My mouth was doing the same thing."

"Well young lady, we have quite the dilemma on our hands, don't we?"

"Yes sir, I think we do," she said with a giggle.

He lifted the plate and sniffed the cinnamon roll. "Oh my, that smells delicious." He lifted his eyes and looked at her. "How about a compromise?"

"What kind of compromise?" She asked.

"How about we share it?"

"That sounds fair."

"Ok that's a deal," he said, "but I have one condition."

She raised her eyebrows. "And what's that?"

"On the condition that you have breakfast with me now, and allow me to take you out to dinner tonight."

Before she could answer, a woman walked up to the buffet table, removed the empty tray, and set a full tray of cinnamon rolls down in its place.

He dropped his shoulders and frowned. "Just my luck."

Louise took the tongs, picked up a fresh cinnamon roll, and put it on her plate. "So, where are you sitting? And what time is dinner?"

She gave him her hotel room number and he told her that he would be there to pick her up at eight o'clock sharp, but the next time she actually saw him was that afternoon...from the stage.

The corporate event they were performing for was a group of scientists and engineers from NASA. As she learned later that night at dinner, Bill was one of the engineers responsible for the successful launches for the manned space program. He was an actual rocket scientist and she was mesmerized by him.

Unfortunately, she was back on the road with Raine the next morning and although they talked almost every night on the phone, she didn't see Bill again for six months.

They had opened for Willie in Jacksonville and she had just gotten back to her dressing room when Bertha knocked on her door.

"Miss Louise, there is a man out here that told me that he was your fiancé. Do you want me to bring him back?"

"My fiancé?" She said shocked, "Some man told you that he was my fiancé?"

Bertha smiled. "Well not in those exact words. What he said was...he was the man who was going to marry you, and if I would let him back to see you, he would invite me to the wedding."

When Bertha moved out of the doorway, Bill was standing there holding a dozen Roses in one hand and a diamond ring in the other. Six months later, Bertha wasn't just at the wedding, he was one of the ushers. All of the other members of the band were there as well. The only one missing was Raine.

For the next twenty-five years, Louise and Bill lived in a beautiful two-story, split level house located next to the 14th green on LaCita Country Club in Titusville, Florida. And other than singing at church, Louise never performed on a stage again.

LOUISE WAS SITTING on her couch in the living room, with her computer in her lap when she heard the front door open.

"Hello? Are you here?"

"Up here!" She shouted, "I'm in the living room."

Her friend Karen closed the front door, and climbed the five steps to the room. When she walked in, she gave Louise a hug and sat down on the couch next to her.

Louise turned back to her computer and started typing on the laptop.

"What are you doing?" Karen asked.

"I'm searching for someone."

"Who are you looking for?"

"Someone I used to work with a long time ago. But I can't find anything on him on the internet...It's like he never existed. Nothing, not one post about Raine."

"Did you say Rain?" Karen asked.

"Yes, Raine Waters. Raine with an e at the end. I sang with him years ago. He was amazing. Everyone thought he was on his way to becoming a huge country star."

"What happened to him? Why didn't he make it?"

"I don't really know what happened. I didn't leave the band under the best terms. So, when I left, he wrote me out of his life and I never heard from him again. It's been years since I've even thought about him."

"I knew you used to be a singer," Karen said, " but I didn't know you sang in a band. You sang with a country band? You? Really?"

"Oh yeah...it was actually a great chapter in my life. The Raine Waters Band was pretty big time back then. We were playing all the big country bars, we opened up for several big stars in huge concert halls. We even did a few TV specials on CMT and opened for Willie. Raine had just signed a record deal with RCA and was so good, really talented. He was on his way..."

Louise put her laptop down and walked to the kitchen. "Want some tea?"

Karen followed her. "I'd love some. So, what do you think happened to this Raine guy?"

"I don't know. He had the looks, the talent...he was really something. He had these amazing blue eyes. When he looked at you...well, you'd just melt."

"Sounds like you... ahh...might have had a thing for him."

Louise laughed. "Me and every other girl that ever heard him sing, or looked into those eyes. That was the problem. There were so many girls swarming around him..."

"Did you two ever... ahh... you know..."

"Oh yeah. Remember this was the late 80's, I was young and he was so friggin' hot. Oh, I was in love with him, but there were so many girls, I knew he wouldn't be faithful, so I never told him how I truly felt."

Karen took a sip of her tea. "Is that why you left? All the women?"

Louise nodded. "That was part of it. Watching him go from one girl to the next and then come back to me was...well, It was killing me. Then I met Bill."

"And he swept you up and took you away from all of that!" Karen said, "I know it's not really any of my business, but it sounds like Bill was your salvation. He was such a sweet man."

"Yes, he was what I needed then. He put stability in my life and gave me everything I could ever want...I miss him so much. Tears began to roll down her cheek."

"Oh no," Karen yelled, "none of that today. We just got you smiling again. We're not going to be sad about Bill today. More tea please."

Louise smiled and poured Karen another cup of tea. "I'm intrigued about this Raine character. Why are you looking for him now?

Before she could answer, the doorbell rang.

"Hello. Anybody here?"

"Hey, Melissa! We're in the kitchen," Karen yelled.

Melissa jogged up the stairs.

"Hey girl," Louise said, "We're having tea."Want some?"

"And we're talking about one of Louise's old flames!" Karen added.

Melissa pulled out a stool and sat down at the bar. "I'll pass on the tea. How about a Jack and Coke?"

Louise frowned at her. "Seriously? It's only 10:00 am!"

"Ok, then. I'll take coffee...with a shot of rum."

Louise rolled her eyes. She poured Melissa her coffee, set it in front of her, and poured in the rum.

Melissa took a sip and smiled. "So catch me up. Who is this 'old flame', and where is he now? Cause girl...you could use a little chiavata."

"Chiavata? What does that mean?" Karen asked.

Louise looked at her. "Karen, consider the source... That was Melissa talking."

Karen pulled out her phone. "How do you spell that?"

"C H I A V A T A," Melissa said with a smirk.

Karen typed the letters on her phone. "Oh my... I can't say that out loud."

"Don't be such a prude. It means sex, doing the horizontal mambo, you know...screwing! If there was anyone who needs some schtupping, it's Louise."

"Ah...ladies...I'm right here. You know I can hear you, right?" Louise said, laughing. "Schtupping? Where do you get this stuff?"

"It's Yiddish for you know-what-ing! Honey, you know we love you, but Bill died four years ago. It's time, and you are still young. You need someone and you know it!"

Louise sat down on the stool across from them. "I know, but..."

"No butts! It's been long enough. So tell me about this old flame. What's his name, and how big was his…"

"MELISSA!" Louise screamed.

BROOKLYN AND JAKE stood silent on each side of Virginia's hospital bed holding her hands, trying to ignore the loud beeps and blips

coming from the numerous video monitors and machines. Virginia's
breathing was labored and shallow. The doctors had let them know that
she was in her final days.

Brooklyn leaned down and kissed her cheek and whispered, "Mom,
Dad and I are going to get some lunch. We'll be back soon. OK?"

Virginia slowly nodded her head, but didn't open her eyes.

When they walked out of the room to the hallway, Brooklyn broke
down crying, reaching for Jake who held her in his arms as she wept.

When they got to the cafeteria, they each took a tray and slid it
along the rail, but nothing looked appetizing so they just got coffee and
found an empty table to sit down.

They didn't talk for a long time, both staring into space, lost in sad
thoughts about Virginia.

"It's not fair," Brooklyn said, breaking the silence.

"No, it's not," Jake said, "but we have to accept it and be brave for
her. You know your mother, she's more worried about us than
herself."

After a few minutes more of silence, Brooklyn looked at Jake and
said, "Dad, can I ask you something?"

"Sure honey, anything."

"Who is Raine Waters?"

Jake turned away for a moment, then looked back directly into her
eyes. "Honey, I know you won't understand this, but I can't tell you. I
made a vow to your mother to never tell you about Raine."

She frowned, "But dad..."

"Brooklyn, I can't...I promised. If your mother wants you to know
about Raine, she will tell you, but... I can't."

VIRGINIA OPENED her eyes and smiled up at Brooklyn. "Your father
told me that you asked about Raine Waters again."

Brooklyn gently stroked her mother's forehead with her hand. "You
don't have to tell me anything. It's not important to me anymore. You
just rest now."

Virginia slowly reached for her hand and squeezed it. "If I was a good Christian...I could forgive him...but..."

"Mom, please. You don't have to do this. I don't care anymore. Please just rest now."

Virginia took a few labored breaths. "I will never forgive him for what he did to me...and you."

"To me?" Brooklyn asked. "What did he do to me?"

Virginia's eyes filled with tears. "He didn't...want you...but...when he...found out."

Brooklyn squeezed her mother's hand. "What are you trying to say?"

"There is... a shoebox... the top of... my closet."

She was having trouble catching her breath. "Mom, please stop. Don't talk anymore. Just rest."

Virginia reached up, pulled Brooklyn close, and whispered, "Find...the box...his letters."

———

THE POLICEMAN WALKED UP to the bench and shook Raine awake. "Come on guys wake up! You know you can't sleep here during the daytime. Wake up! You have to leave now."

Raine sat up on the bench and wiped his eyes. "Yes, officer, we're going. Come on Dave, let's go see if we can find something to eat."

They gathered their few belongings and slowly walked away, Raine holding his leather briefcase in his left hand and pushing his bicycle down the beach road with his right.

———

THE LADIES HAD MOVED the conversation from the kitchen to the pool deck. "Homeless?" Melissa shouted from the pool, "Did you say homeless?"

Louise nodded her head. "I think so, but I don't know for sure. I'm not even sure if it was really him."

"How are you gonna find out?" Karen asked.

"What if it was him?" Melissa said, "What'll you do then? If you find him...what's next?"

Louise shrugged her shoulders. "I have no idea, but I think I have to at least try to help him if I can."

Melissa climbed out of the pool and dried off. "I don't care what time it is, I think we all need a drink."

Louise looked at her watch and smiled. "I've got wine in the fridge. A nice Pinot Grigio."

Melissa jumped up and ran to the kitchen.

"I'm not running," Karen said.

Louise laughed. "Me either."

They gathered around the bar as Melissa opened the wine and poured. She held up her glass. "I say... let's go find Raine Waters!"

Karen lifted up her glass. "Let's do it!"

Louise smiled at them and lifted up her glass in solidarity. "Ok, but where do we look? I don't have a clue where to start?"

Quietly, they sipped their wine, thinking.

"We've got to think like a homeless guy," Melissa said, "If you were homeless, where would you be right now?"

"Well, he was spotted at the bookstore in the mall on Merritt Island," Louise said, "And they told me that he rode off to the East, toward the beach. Maybe he stays somewhere close to there...it's a public place."

Karen looked at her. "Are there any shelters near the beach? Maybe he's there in a shelter."

"I guess it's possible," Louise said, picking up her keys. "I'll go get the car if you'll lock the front door on your way out."

Louise backed her car out of the garage and waited for Karen to walk down the steps and get in.

"Wait for me," Melissa yelled, running out of the front door and down the steps, holding the bottle of wine, "Let's do this! Raine Waters, here we come."

RAINE PUT the kickstand down on his bike, walked up, and looked in the pawnshop window. "Dave, come and look at this."

Dave walked over and looked in the window. "Cool looking guitars." He said.

"Yeah, they are. That black one in the middle looks like a vintage Les Paul. If it's real, it's worth a fortune. I used to have one just like it."

THE GIRLS HAD STOPPED at two of the shelters in Cocoa Beach with no luck, so they decided to just drive along A1A and see if they could see any homeless people there. If they saw any, they planned to stop and ask them if they knew him.

Louise pulled to a stop at the light, then turned down the beach road scanning the area, searching. Then suddenly, she slammed on her breaks, skidding to a stop. "Oh my God! I think that's him."

Karen looked up. "Where?"

"Right there looking in that window. In the pawnshop. I'm pretty sure that's him."

She pulled up in front of the pawnshop, put her car in park, and jumped out. "Raine!" She shouted, "Is that you?"

Raine turned around to see Louise standing behind him. "Dave, let's go!" He grabbed his bike and started walking away, ignoring her.

"Raine wait! Stop! Talk to me. I'm Louise Coleman. Don't you remember me?"

Raine started walking faster.

"Your name is Raine Waters, right?" She yelled.

"No, it's not!" He yelled back.

Dave looked at Raine, then back at Louise very confused. "Sure it is."

"Shut up Dave!" He yelled glaring at him.

"Sorry man, but that's your name...isn't it?"

Raine shrugged his shoulders, accepting defeat. He stopped walking and slowly turned around to look at Louise. "Hello, Louise."

Her face lit up. "It *IS* you! And you remember me!"

"Of course I remember you. I may not have much anymore, but I still have my memories."

Dave walked toward Louise's car. "Wow, cool car!"

When he noticed Karen and Melissa sitting inside, he smiled at them, walked up, and leaned in the window. "Well hello, ladies! Especially you, Blondie!"

In a panic, Karen quickly rolled up her window. "Oh my God! Go away, go away, go away."

"What's the matter, baby?"

"Leave her alone Dave. She doesn't want to talk to you."

Dave shrugged, "I was just trying to say hello." He walked back toward Louise and Raine.

"So, what do you want Louise?" Raine asked.

"What do I want? I don't want anything." She said.

"Then why are you here?"

"I'm here because I want to help you."

He shook his head. "Thanks, but I don't need any help."

"Raine, you are homeless, living on the street! Of course you need help! Please let me help you. I have money."

"Look, Louise, I know you mean well, but I'm a lost cause. I've burned my life down to the ground. Only God can make something from ashes, and he gave up on me a long, long time ago. I don't want your help. I'm not looking for a handout, especially from you! Go find another charity and leave me alone." He turned and walked away.

"Who said anything about charity? I was going to offer you a job, so you could earn some money, but I guess you are too far gone...a worthless bum, too lazy to even work!"

Raine stopped walking.

"I guess you were right after all. You're not Raine Waters...not the Raine Waters I remember anyway."

Raine turned around, looked at Louise, and grinned. "You sure haven't changed much over the years."

"What do you mean?" She asked.

"You are still a real pain in the ass, even after all these years. You know, you could always see right through me, always busting my balls."

"And you are still the same stubborn, hard-headed jackass! Please, Raine, let me help you."

He slowly walked back to her and smiled. "What kind of job?"

8

THE LETTERS

They couldn't have hoped for a better day. There wasn't a cloud in the sky and there was a constant cool breeze blowing to the East.

Overnight, the cold front had pushed the oppressive heat away and the temperature had dropped down to just above 60 degrees. Her mother called it sweater weather; not cold enough for a coat, but too chilly for just a long sleeve blouse.

Brooklyn smiled, remembering how excited her mom used to get when she would pull out her favorite sweater and hold it up in front of her in the mirror. "Your father surprised me with this one Christmas." her mother had said, every time she pulled it out of her closet. "It's the only thing he ever bought me that wasn't butt ugly and actually fit."

Brooklyn had picked out a beautiful blue dress for her, but when she woke that morning and felt the chilly weather, she stopped by the house on the way to the funeral and got the sweater.

Although her mother had insisted on a closed casket funeral, after everyone had filed out of the church, Jake had them open the casket, so he and Brooklyn could see her one last time wearing that beautiful blue sweater and say their final goodbyes.

After the funeral, and when their friends had finally left them alone in the house, Brooklyn put her arms around Jake and kissed him on the cheek. "How are you holding up?"

He shrugged. "Other than having a huge hole in my heart, I guess I'm doing alright. What about you?"

Brooklyn shook her head. "I'm going to be OK. It's a promise that I made to mom."

Jake smiled. "She made you promise stuff too, huh?"

"Yes. She made me promise her three things."

"Oh yeah? What were the three things?"

"Number one...that I wouldn't fall apart without her in my life and that I would follow my dreams."

"And number two?" Jake asked.

She smiled. "That I would look after you and not let you grow old alone."

He laughed. "That's the same thing she made me promise, but that's gonna take me some time to even consider."

She looked up at him and laughed. "That's exactly what she said you'd say."

Jake shook his head and walked into the kitchen. "Want some coffee?" He shouted out to Brooklyn.

"Maybe later," she shouted back, "I've got to go take care of number three."

When she opened the door to the bedroom, it was eerily silent. Slowly, she walked around the room touching things: her mother's hairbrush, a necklace in the open jewelry box, her favorite perfume, and the small silver pendant she had given to her mother years ago when she was a child.

She had saved her allowance for almost six months to afford it. She could still remember the big tears in her mother's eyes that rolled down her face when she told her how she had paid for it. She picked up a picture of her mother off the dresser, pulled it to her chest, and broke down crying.

Just outside the door, standing in the hall, Jake wiped his eyes with his sleeve as he listened to Brooklyn cry through the closed door. He reached for the doorknob, but stopped and backed away, leaving Brooklyn alone to grieve for her mom.

After a good cry, she wiped her eyes and walked toward the closet. She pulled out a stool, climbed up, and started searching the top shelf. When she found the shoe box, she climbed down off the stool and sat on the closet floor with the box between her legs.

Slowly, she untied the string that secured the box and opened the lid. It was stuffed full of letters. She pulled one out, turned it over, and discovered that it had never been opened. She took a deep breath, tore one open, and began to read.

Jake knew what she was doing, so he walked outside, sat down at the patio table, and slowly sipped his coffee.

He was on his third cup an hour later when Brooklyn walked outside and sat down next to him. She put one of the letters on the table in front of her.

"Did you find what you were looking for?" He asked.

She nodded. "I'm so confused. Why didn't she tell..."

"Why didn't she tell you?" He shrugged, "I know why she didn't at first...but I always assumed that she would tell you when you got older, but..."

She made eye contact with him. "If she couldn't...then why didn't you?"

"I told you, honey...I made a vow to her. I couldn't break that. I tried to get her to tell you, but she was adamant. What Raine did, just destroyed her. She was so young and loved him so very much. Eventually, I won her heart and I know she loved me too. She was the love of my life, but the truth is, she never got over Raine, not completely. And the damage he did never truly healed."

Brooklyn looked over the table at Jake. "So...you're not my father?"

Jake smiled and took a long sip of his coffee. "Biologically no, but that's not what makes a father. Love is what makes a father. Unconditional, never-ending, forever, and ever love. That's what I have for you. I am your father and I know in my heart, that you know that too. For years, I kept telling Virginia that, but she was so afraid of what might happen if you found out. But I've never worried about that."

Brooklyn took his hand, with tears rolling down her face. "I love you, dad."

"I know you do, Honey. Did you know that I was the first person on this earth to hold you? You were so tiny... about the size of my hand. And at that very moment, when I saw those blue piercing eyes staring up at me...you stole my heart. And you still have it today. I knew then and I know now, I was put on this earth to be your father. And no matter what happens with you and Raine I will always be your father, always."

They sat there holding hands in silence for a long time. Finally, Brooklyn said, "Dad, I want...no...I need to know the whole story. What really happened back then?"

WHEN RAINE OPENED the car door and sat down in the back seat, Melissa and Karen instantly jumped out of the car.

"I'll be right back," Louise said to Raine, walking over to Melissa and Karen.

"Why did you get out of the car?" She asked.

"Are you serious?" Melissa said, trying not to let Raine hear her, "Can't you smell him?"

Louise rolled her eyes. "Of course I can smell him, but he can't help that."

"I know that, but I have a weak stomach. I don't mean to be rude, but there's no way I can ride in that car all the way back to your house sitting beside him. I'll throw up."

"So how do you suggest we do this, strap him to the roof?"

"I have an idea," Karen said, "You guys go on, and we'll call an Uber to come pick us up."

"Ok," Louise said, "I'll see you there."

When Louise pulled into the driveway, Raine got out of the back seat and slowly walked around looking at the house.

"You live here?" He asked, staring up at her beautiful home.

"Yes," she said, "this is my house."

"Wow! This is beautiful. I think I understand why you quit the band and married Bill. How's he doing? Is he here?"

Louise looked down and sighed. "Bill died four years ago. He had a heart attack while he was playing golf."

"I'm so sorry. I had no idea. I was wondering what he was going to think about all of this. If I remember, he wasn't much of a Raine Waters fan."

Louise smiled. "Oh, he liked your music...he just didn't like *YOU* very much. He thought you were an arrogant jackass!"

Raine grinned and nodded his head. "The way I was back then, he'd be right. I was...well....you know."

"Oh yeah, I know how you were. I was there remember?"

Louise slowly walked around her property with Raine, showing him around the outside. "So what do you need done around here? What's that job you keep talking about?"

"It's in here," she said, opening the door to the pool screen enclosure.

Raine followed her inside and walked around the pool admiring it. "I don't see anything wrong in here. This is beautiful!"

He was standing near the edge of the pool. Louise walked up to him and said, "Well, actually there is one big problem we have to fix."

He looked around the room again and shrugged. "What's that? I don't see anything wrong."

She took a step closer. "We have to fix the way you smell!" Louise reached out and pushed him into the pool. When he hit the water, he made a big splash and came up gasping and coughing, swimming toward the ladder.

"Oh no you don't," Louise said, pushing him away from the ladder with the pool hook. "You are staying in there a while. Now off with those filthy clothes!"

Raine hit the water with his hand and tried to splash her, but she jumped out of the way. "I can't believe you did that!"

"The clothes...*NOW*!" She shouted.

"Ok, ok," he said grinning and stripping off his old clothes.

Louise picked them up with long BBQ tongs, stuffed them into a black garbage bag, and threw it into the trash can. When she got back she said, "Put on this robe and go take a very long shower, and wash that nasty hair and beard!"

She pointed toward the stairs. "The guest bedroom is up there! I'll put some of Bill's clothes on the bed for you. They should fit you fine."

LOUISE HAD JUST FINISHED CLEANING and disinfecting the back seat of her car where Raine had been sitting when the Uber pulled into her driveway.

"Where is Mr. Stinky?" Melissa asked.

Louise chuckled. "He's in the shower."

"Thank God!" Karen said, "Did you burn his clothes?"

"No, but I double bagged them and put them in the trash can."

"So what now?" Melissa asked, "You want us to stick around or leave you alone with him?"

Louise frowned. "I'm not afraid of him, if that's what you're asking," she said, "but please come in. I would like you to meet him and get to know him a little."

She turned and looked at Karen. "Could I ask you a big favor?"

"Sure, what do you need?"

"Would you give him a hair cut and maybe trim his beard? You always did such a good job on Bill's hair."

"I'd love to. I can't wait to see what he looks like under all that hair."

It was almost an hour later when Raine walked out of the bedroom. Louise noticed the smell of aftershave before he actually appeared in the doorway. Of course, Melissa was the first to react.

"Wow!" She yelled, "Muy Caliente!"

"Oh my!" Karen added.

Louise had seen Bill in the powder blue, collared polo shirt and the faded blue jeans many times before, but they didn't fit him like they fit Raine.

His long hair was still wet, but he had shaved off his beard, and the powder blue shirt enhanced the brilliant color of his eyes and they seemed to be glowing at them.

"What's wrong?" Raine asked, obviously uncomfortable from their intense stares, "What are you looking at?"

Louise grinned. "We're looking at *you* silly. You look...well, a lot better than you did."

"Thanks. Do the clothes fit OK?"

"Ohh yeah," Melissa purred, "They fit real, real good. What do you think girls? He's sort of a combination of Bradley Cooper and Sam Elliott in *A Star Is Born*."

Karen nodded her head. "Exactly what I was thinking."

Raine tilted his head confused. "I thought Kris Kristofferson was in that movie."

"That works for me too!" Melissa said.

"Just ignore them," Louise said motioning toward a barstool. "Come sit here, Karen's going to give you a hair cut. And please excuse Melissa. She's harmless, but just a little crazy."

He sat down on the stool and Karen went to work cutting his hair. "So who's Bradley Cooper?" He asked.

———

JAKE AND BROOKLYN were sitting at the dining room table. Brooklyn had been there for hours listening to Jake tell her a story she had never heard.

"Haven't you ever wondered where you got all that talent?" He asked, "Where that beautiful singing voice of yours comes from?"

She shook her head. "No, I just assumed that I got it from you because mom sure couldn't sing."

Jake's eyes sparkled as he laughed. "Honey, I can't sing a lick and can barely play guitar. Why do you think your mother built that music room?"

"She told me it was for you."

He leaned back in his chair and smiled. "Music was the only part of Raine she allowed inside this house. When you were maybe three or four years old, your mother heard you singing to the radio in your room. She called me and held the phone up to the door, so I could hear you too. That's when we knew. What we both heard that day, wasn't just the voice of a little girl singing, we heard the voice of a talented singer. You were singing in perfect tune and perfect time with a unique tone and style that couldn't be learned at your age. You were born with that voice and ability...and it came from Raine."

He leaned forward and looked her in the eyes. "I believe that's the real reason she never told you about him, and why she was so insistent about you going to college and getting a real job. Her biggest fear was your talent. She was so afraid that you would try to follow in your father's footsteps. She witnessed the results of what following that dream could do to someone, and she never wanted that for you."

She smiled. "She *was* a bit over the top about all of that. But it all makes sense now."

Brooklyn set the shoebox full of Raine's letters on the table between them and took off the lid. "How old was I when he found out about me?"

Jake took a sip of his coffee, leaned back, and sighed. "I'm not really sure, but it was sometime before your sixth birthday."

She tilted her head. "What happened on my sixth birthday?"

"He sent you a present."

"Really?"

"Oh yeah. When your mother saw it, she was enraged and immediately threw it in the trash. The letters started arriving that Christmas."

Her eyes widened. "He's been sending me letters for 24 years?"

Jake shook his head. "No, they stopped when you turned 18...but for 12 years, he sent one on your birthday and one every Christmas. There should be 24 letters in that box. You were in her closet a while...how many did you read?"

She looked down at the box. "Only three so far. I didn't realize they were in some kind of order. I just picked them at random."

He smiled. "They might make more sense if you started from the beginning."

Brooklyn slowly nodded her head. "Yeah, I think you're right, but I don't want to read anymore tonight."

She glanced at her watch. "I'm thinking about driving back to Ft. Worth, would that be OK? I'll stay if you want me to."

"If you're worried about me being alone, don't worry, Virginia hasn't been in this house for over two months. I tried, but I couldn't sleep in her room at the hospital, so I've been coming home every night. Don't worry about me, I've gotten used to being here alone."

"Are you sure?" She asked, taking his hand and squeezing gently.

"Actually, I would prefer being alone tonight so I can grieve for your mother," he said, wiping his eyes, "I think I did too good of a job preparing myself for this day. I want to cry a little...maybe cry a lot and...I don't want anyone to see me do that."

It was almost 10:45 when she backed her car out of her father's driveway. On her two hour drive back to her apartment in Fort Worth, she thought about everything Jake had told her.

As she drove, with the shoebox full of the letter's from her real father sitting on the passenger seat next to her, she wondered what he was feeling when he discovered that she was alive. Was he excited and happy to know he had a daughter?

She wondered where he was now. Was he really homeless, living on the streets somewhere in Florida? Should she try to find him, get to know him...or should she hate him like her mother did for what he had done?

She had no idea what to do about that, about him. But now that she knew the truth, she finally understood and had answers for so many questions that had bothered her, her entire life.

Now she knew why her mother never seemed to be impressed with her musical talent. Even when she received those standing ovations at all of her high school musicals, her mother never seemed to care.

When her friends would come to their house and go on and on about a song she had sung in church, or her performance in one of those plays, her mother would just clam up and do her best to change the subject. Never one time in her entire life did she tell her that she thought she was good or had any talent.

It was the one and only thing she ever resented about her mother. And even though everyone, since she was a little girl, told her that she was a great singer, deep down she never believed them. Of course Jake did, he raved about how special her voice was and had spent hours and hours in the music room teaching her how to play the guitar, piano and how to read music...but her mother could not have cared less.

Before she knew it, the two-hour drive had flown by and she was at the main gate that led up to her apartment building.

She rolled down her window and punched in the gate code and slowly drove through it. When she pulled into her parking space, she saw that Josh's car wasn't there.

"Damn," she said, picking up the shoebox and popping open her trunk to get her suitcase.

She sat the shoebox down next to her on the couch, pulled her cell-phone out of her purse, and punched in his number.

"I'm home, where are you?" She said.

She heard him sigh. "I'm at Stan's."

"Josh...I'm so sorry..."

"I really don't want to talk about it now," he said, "Maybe tomorrow, but not now." The phone clicked in her ear.

She instantly punched in his number again but didn't hit the call button. Instead, she turned her phone off and walked to the kitchen, and opened the refrigerator door.

It was almost 2:00 am, and she knew she should probably just go to bed, but she also knew her mind wouldn't let her sleep.

She grabbed the half-full bottle of Chardonnay from the refrigerator door, pulled out the cork, and filled the glass.

Back on the couch, she opened the box and counted the letters. When she finished, she counted them again, laying them out, one at a time on the coffee table in front of her. Again, she had counted 25, not

24. Slowly, she inspected each letter, looking carefully at the date of the postmark. When she picked up the last one, she realized it was different. There was no postmark and it wasn't from Raine Waters, it was from her mother.

To my darling Brooklyn,

If you're reading this letter, I know you must be feeling very sad, but I don't want you to be. This is not a time for that, it's a time to rejoice. I am in no more pain and I am with my precious Jesus in Heaven.

I leave you with only one regret. I wish I could have forgiven your father and told you about him sooner, but the flesh is weak and I can only ask God to forgive me for not telling you.

I have no idea what Raine has written to you in these letters, but I can only hope he is asking for your forgiveness. If he is, I will leave that up to you, but remember he was very young and foolish.

I want you to know that you were conceived in love. At that time, I know he loved me, and I loved him with all my heart. I can only pray that someday you will forgive me for keeping this secret from you all these years.

I thought I did it to protect you from the cruel realities of life, but I know now that I was wrong to keep you away from him.

You are so much like him and I saw it every time I looked at you. You have his beautiful eyes and his amazing talent. I know I never told you, but when I heard you sing, I heard the voice of an angel. I have always been so proud of you.

You may have inherited some of your musical talent from Raine, but your voice is a gift from God.

Promise me that you will follow your dreams where ever they may take you, and I hope you never forget how much I loved you.

I'll be watching

Mom

9

A PERFECT STORM

After Karen finished cutting Raine's hair, he walked to the bathroom to see what he looked like. Staring into the mirror he barely recognized the face looking back at him. It was a face he hadn't seen in many, many years.

When he walked back to the kitchen, no one was there. He heard Louise at the front door telling Melissa and Karen goodbye.

When she walked back up the stairs she smiled and asked, "You want something to drink?"

"Sure, how about a beer?" he said, "Did Melissa and Karen have to go?"

She took two beers out of the refrigerator. "Yes, Melissa had an appointment, and Karen decided that it might be better if she left us alone to talk."

She reached out and handed him a beer, "This is probably not a good idea, I was actually talking about a Coke, but I don't mind as long as you can control your drinking when you're around me. Do we have a deal?"

Raine nodded. "I'll do my best, but you know me, I've never been any good at that."

They walked to the living room and he sat in a chair while Louise curled up on the couch and stared into his eyes. "Raine, what happened to you? The last time I saw you, you were on top of the world."

He took a sip of his beer and shrugged. "Yeah I was, but if you remember correctly, I was also probably drunk and stoned. All this is self-inflicted."

"You were always drunk or stoned," she said, softly, "It had to be more than that. Everyone knew you were a little out of control, it was no secret in the industry. Something else had to have happened for you to fall so far and so hard."

She leaned over and took his hand. "You know I've always cared about you. We were always close. You can trust me. Tell me how this happened."

Raine stood up and walked to the fireplace. There was a large mirror over the mantel. He looked at his reflection and ran his hands through his now short hair and touched his clean-shaven face with his fingers.

"This feels like I'm touching the face of a stranger," he said, "The last time I saw that face, I didn't have all these wrinkles, but I guess I've earned every one of them."

"It's a good face," Louise said, "wrinkles and all. To tell you the truth, I've never seen that face before. It was always hiding behind a beard. You are so handsome, why would you ever cover that face up?"

He shrugged. "Susan Sharp convinced me to grow the beard a few weeks after I signed my record deal. I was only 26 then. She was also the one that suggested I grow long hair and wear all those leather clothes, even when I wasn't on stage. She told me it was all part of the outlaw image she was trying to promote. Of course, being the puppet I was in those days, I did everything she said or asked...except for one thing; I wouldn't sleep with her."

"Oh, lord!" She gasped, "I never liked that woman! Did she really come on to you? I can't imagine that. How old was she?"

He grinned. "Too damn old. I guess I was just too naïve to see it at first, so I laughed off her flirting. She was twice my age and honestly the thoughts of fooling around with her never once crossed my mind. I was writing songs for my third album and playing to sold-out venues opening for Willie when it all came to a head."

"What happened?"

"We were on a break from the tour and Susan showed up one night at my house in Nashville. She said that she wanted to talk about my new album, but she had something else on her mind that night."

"I think I see where this is going," Louise said, shaking her head.

"As usual she had some coke with her. After we did a few lines together, she excused herself and walked to the bathroom. When she came out, all she was wearing were her high heels and a smile."

"She was naked?" She shouted, "Oh no!"

"Yep, naked as a jaybird!"

"What did you say to her?"

"I didn't know what to say. I was so shocked. I yelled, '*Whoa,* 'when she tried to kiss me. '*What the hell are you doing?*'"

"She got closer and whispered. '*Don't you think it's about time you thanked me properly for everything I've done for you?*' I backed away from her and said, '*No, I don't! Not like this! Come on, Susan, you're old enough to be my mother!*'"

"Oh God! You didn't really say that, did you?"

He nodded. "Yeah, I'm afraid I did. I know it was a horrible thing to say, but I was stoned and it just sort of came out."

Louise frowned and shook her head. "That's like a knife to the heart to a woman, especially a woman like her. What did she say?"

Raine looked down and shrugged. "This is where things started to go south. She didn't say a word. She ran back to the bathroom, put on her clothes, and stormed out my front door. That was the last time I ever saw her or talked to her. A few months later, RCA dropped me from the label, and a few weeks after that I was kicked off of Willie's tour."

"She did all of that, just because you wouldn't sleep with her? What a bitch!"

"Susan Sharp was a powerful woman in Nashville back then,"

Raine said, "but I'm not sure she had that much power, maybe she did, but no one ever told me why. When I tried to call and talk to Jim Ed, the President of RCA, he was always in a meeting. When I called Willie's management company, they never returned a single call. From that point on, well...that's when sugar turned to shit."

"Did you try to go to another label?"

Raine laughed. "Nashville is a very small town and news travels fast. I knocked on every single door on Music Row trying to get another deal. I had sold millions of records, but no one would even talk to me or answer my telephone calls. Overnight I had gone from one of the hottest country acts in Nashville to a pariah. They even stopped playing my music on the radio. I called and got through to one of my friends who was a DJ for a big station in Dallas and he told me that his program director had received a call from someone at RCA. He said that he was sorry, but if he played any of my songs on the air, he'd get fired."

Louise gave him a gentle smile, "Raine, I'm so sorry, and please forgive me, I don't mean to pry, but what happened to all the money you had made?"

He laughed out loud. "When I signed my record deal, I didn't look at the fine print. Nobody looks at the fine print. Even if I had read it and understood it, I still would've signed. I wanted a record deal, it was my dream and I would've signed anything."

He sat back down in the chair and leaned back. "You're right, I made a lot of money for RCA, but before I got *my* share, first, they took out all of *theirs*," He held up his hands making air quotes, "Promotional cost."

"Promotional costs? What's that?"

He laughed again. "Well, let's see...things like every lunch or dinner Susan Sharp took me to, and every hotel room I stayed in while I was in Nashville cutting that first album, even though they had booked me in the most expensive hotel in town. I was charged with all of the production costs of my two CMT television specials and half of the costs of the promotional ads they ran. Every minute I spent in the studio, every studio musician, every roll of tape, the engineers, the producer, the arrangements, which by the way, were all mine, and on an on and on..."

"Was there anything left for you?" She asked.

"Not much. The only real money I got was from Willie's tour. He made sure I got everything I was owed."

"I'm so sorry, Raine. I had no idea. This must have all happened right after I left."

He nodded. "Yeah, that's why I didn't come to your wedding. I couldn't face you or the band."

"So where did you go from there?"

"Nowhere. For about a year, I just hung around the house feeling sorry for myself, drinking. I had no idea what to do next."

Raine finished his beer and set the can on the coffee table. "Would it be OK if I had one more?"

"One more," She said, jumping up and walking to the kitchen.

When she came back and handed him the beer, she looked him in the eyes and said, "But that's all for tonight. Ok?"

He nodded and took a sip. "My dad was still alive then. He begged me to come back home to Abilene, so I drove there and stayed almost a month, but I couldn't stay, I had to leave."

Louise tucked her legs under her and leaned forward. "Why, what happened?"

"I accidentally ran into Virginia."

"Who's Virginia?"

"Oh yeah, I forgot you never met her. She was...well, I guess the only woman that ever really loved me. We grew up together and started dating in high school. She was great, but I screwed that all up."

"Did you love her too?"

"Oh yeah, I was crazy about her, and always thought we'd get married eventually, but that didn't happen.

"So what did you say to her when you saw her in Abilene?"

"I didn't say anything. I hid behind a building and watched her."

"Why not? You should have at least said hello?"

He shook his head. "No, you're wrong there. She would not have been happy to see me. It's a long story that I don't want to get into, but the short version is…I did something awful to her, something she will never forgive me for, and I don't blame her."

Raine finished the beer and looked across the coffee table at Louise. "There was another reason I didn't talk to her."

"What was that?"

"She was with my daughter."

"You have a daughter?" Really? I had no idea you had a child."

He nodded his head slowly and frowned. "I had no idea either, not until that moment."

"Seriously? Then how did you know she was your child?"

He shrugged. "It has to do with that awful thing I did to Virginia, but the second I saw her…saw those blue eyes and black hair…I knew. Virginia was a blonde, with green eyes. I guess she would be about 30 now, but I really don't know, I've never met her."

"What?" Louise's eyes widened, "You've never met your daughter? Why not? Does she know you're her father?"

He shrugged again. "I don't know that either. I tried to connect with her. I wrote her letters and sent her birthday and Christmas presents, but she never wrote me back. I gave up and stopped writing when she turned 18."

They sat in silence for a few minutes, awkwardly staring at each other, not talking. Louise stood up, walked to the kitchen, and came back with another beer.

"Ok, one more, and then I think we need to call it a night. Tomorrow is going to be a big day for you."

He lifted his eyebrows. "In what way?"

"Tomorrow, you start that job I was talking about."

"Sounds good to me," he said sipping the beer.

"Are you sure you are ok talking about this?" She asked.

"Sure. It's alright, I don't mind."

She thought for a moment, searching for her words. "I don't really know how to bring this up, so I'm just going to come out with it. I can understand how devastated you might have been with everything that happened to you in Nashville, but, Raine, that was almost 25 years ago. What happened after that? What I'm asking is…how did you get here? I mean, here in Cocoa Beach...homeless, living on the street? How the hell did that happen to you?"

Raine sat silent for a long moment, then he looked her in the eyes and smiled. "It was a lot easier than you might imagine. I ran out of money, I didn't have a way to make anymore and couldn't think of anyone I could call for help."

He took another sip of the beer and shrugged his shoulders, "There was nowhere else to go, but the street. That's when I met Dave and he showed me the ropes. If it hadn't been for him, I'm not sure what would have happened to me."

Louise stood and began pacing the room. "Wait. What do you mean you had no way to make more money? What about your music? You could have gotten a gig at some bar. Why didn't you do that?"

"I did. I did that for years. I played every beer joint and dive bar that would hire me."

She stopped pacing and stared down at him. "Why did you stop?"

"It was a combination of several things that hit me all at once. A perfect storm of events. After that, I stopped caring about anything and just gave up on me...and life."

Louise sat back down on the couch. "What happened?"

He shook his head and frowned. "Brooklyn turned 18."

She wrinkled her forehead. "Brooklyn? Who is Brooklyn?"

"My daughter," he whispered, "Her name is Brooklyn."

Louise tilted her head. "I'm sorry, Raine, but what difference did that make? What's the significance of her turning 18?"

"I started writing her letters the day I first saw her in Abilene, but she never wrote me back. Somewhere in my twisted mind, I convinced myself that the reason she didn't write me back was because of Virginia. In my drunken screwed up head, I concocted the whole story. I told myself that she wanted to write to me, and wanted to get to know me and that she actually secretly loved me, but her mother forbid her from letting me know that."

Louise began to nod her head with understanding. "But in this story," she said, "when she turned 18, she would be old enough to make her own decisions and would finally write you back."

Raine began to smile. "I knew it was just a fantasy, but she was the only thing in my life worth living for, the only dream I had left."

"But she never wrote you back, right?" Louise whispered.

"No, she didn't," he said with a sigh, leaning back in the chair. "In my last letter I told her that if she didn't respond, I would stop writing and never bother her again. That was 12 years ago."

The room fell silent again as they sat there sipping their beers not talking. When Louise finally spoke her voice was quiet, "You said there was a combination of things. What else happened?"

He took a deep breath and leaned forward. "When I wrote her that last letter, I was living in this fleabag apartment complex in Jacksonville and singing, doing a solo act, in this bar. It was a pretty good gig actually. They were only paying me fifty bucks a night, but the tips were good and I was getting by. I had given Brooklyn the Jacksonville apartment address in my letter, so I didn't want to leave there until I heard from her."

He shook his head and grinned. "When I think about it now, I realize how foolish I was to actually believe she would finally write to me after all those years, but I just knew she would. In anticipation of her letter and finally getting to meet her, I had stopped drinking. Well, to be honest, I hadn't stopped, I was just not drinking as much. I didn't want to lose my gig, so I made sure I always started on time and watched my breaks. For the first time in years, I was actually sort of sober and enjoying singing again. The customers seemed to notice and my tips were getting better and better. With the extra money, I saved up enough to buy a plane ticket to Dallas and had it all planned out in my head. I even had a few dreams about walking off the plane and seeing her standing there, smiling and waving at me."

Louise sighed. "How long did you wait for her letter?"

"I checked that mailbox three times a day for six months, but it never came."

"Oh, Raine, I'm so sorry. You must have been devastated."

"Yeah, it was a hard thing to accept, but I don't blame Brooklyn. If my father had done what I did, I wouldn't want to meet him either."

"I'm sorry, but I'm confused," Louise said, "What could you have possibly done to her when you've never met her?"

Raine dropped his head, fighting back his emotions. "The last time I saw Virginia," his voice cracked. He wiped his eyes with his sleeve and took a deep breath, "I'm sorry, but I can't talk about this."

"Please, Raine, tell me. I think you need to talk about it, to get whatever this is out in the open. Holding it inside all these years sure hasn't helped you...it's killing you. Please, you can trust me."

Louise reached over and took his hand. "Raine, look at me. What happened the last time you saw Virginia?"

He turned and looked into her eyes. "Virginia told me that she was pregnant."

"With Brooklyn?"

"Yes, but..."

"So you did know you had a daughter!"

He shook his head. "No, no I didn't."

"I don't understand," She said confused, "If she told you that she was pregnant, then how could you not have..." Her words trailed off and her eyes flew open. "Did you think she had an abortion?"

He looked away. "I told you, it was an awful thing I did to her."

"Oh my God, Raine," she shouted, "You told Virginia to get an abortion...and you thought she had until you saw her that day with Brooklyn. Am I right?"

He nodded. "I'll never forgive myself for what I did that day, but yes...I actually gave her the money to pay for it and left her standing there crying."

Once again the room went silent as they sat there, staring at each other.

"I've thought about that day for thirty years," He said, just above a whisper, "I've dreamed about it, had nightmares about it, and tried to come up with some kind of excuse for doing it, but...there is no excuse and I'll never forgive myself for it."

Louise looked across the coffee table at him. "Is that why you've always been so self-destructive?"

He shrugged. "I don't know, maybe. My career was taking off like a rocket and it should have been the best times of my life...but all I could think about...was the look in Virginia's eyes that day. The only time I didn't think about it was when I was drunk or stoned, so I guess that could be why I drank so much and did all those drugs. I really didn't like myself much back then. I still don't."

"That's why you were so obsessed with meeting Brooklyn," Louise said, "so you could somehow make it up to her and ask her to forgive you."

He didn't respond.

"So how did you wind up here? Did you lose your gig in that Jacksonville bar?"

"Oh, that was another one of my brilliant decisions. I met this lady in the bar one night. She told me that she booked cruise ships and offered me a job. It was for a six-month contract. She said that they'd give me free food and a free cabin, so I jumped at the chance."

"That sounds nice, a perfect gig for you."

"Yeah, that's what I thought too, but it didn't turn out very well."

Louise rolled her eyes. "Oh lord, what happened? What on earth did you do?"

"What I always do...drink too much, make an ass of myself and treat everyone like shit."

"Did you get fired for drinking too much?"

He laughed. "No, it wasn't the booze. We were docked in Aruba for the day and I bought a joint off this guy on the beach. When I tried to get back on the ship that afternoon, security found it in my backpack."

"Did you get arrested?" She asked with wide eyes.

"No, nothing like that. All they did was fire me on the spot and kick me off the ship. They paid me for the days I had worked, left me with my passport, my luggage, and instruments on the dock, and sailed away. It took most of the money I had made to pay for a flight back to Orlando and the rest for the taxi cab ride back to the port to get my car."

He finished the beer, crushed it between his hands, and set it on the coffee table. "I looked for a gig, I really did, but I couldn't find one. I even called the bar in Jacksonville, but they didn't want me back. I was sleeping and living in my car and I didn't have any money, so for food and booze, I had no other choice...I had to start hocking my guitar and equipment one piece at a time. A few months later, the bank found my car and repossessed it. That was about five years ago."

Raine looked up at Louise and shrugged. "And, well...here I am."

10

A TAYLOR FAMILY TRADITION

W hen Josh Arnett opened the apartment door and walked inside, he found Brooklyn sound asleep on the couch. She was clutching a piece of paper in her right hand. There was an open shoebox sitting on the coffee table half full of white envelopes. The table was covered with sheets of paper and there were several lying on the floor in front of the couch.

Quietly, he walked up to the coffee table and picked up one of the pieces of paper. It was a handwritten letter to Brooklyn.

When he turned it over and looked at the signature, his eyes widened and he shouted, "RAINE WATERS?"

Brooklyn stirred on the couch and opened her eyes. "Josh? What are you doing here? You said you were gonna stay at Stan's for a while. I thought you were mad at me?"

He smiled at her, leaned down, and kissed her. "Yeah, I guess I was a little mad, but I couldn't stay away. I'm sorry if I acted like a jerk."

She sat up and swung her legs off the couch, patted the seat next to her, and smiled. "That's ok, you're always kind of a jerk."

Carefully, he stepped around the letters on the floor and sat next to her. "What's all this?" he said, holding up the letter, "How do you know Raine Waters?"

Her eyes opened wide. "You...you've heard of him?"

"Sure I've heard of him! He was a great singer and songwriter. I have both of his albums."

"Really? You have them here? In this apartment?" She said, excited, "Where?"

Josh stood and walked to the bookshelf. He searched for a few minutes, then pulled out two albums.

He sat back down on the couch and handed them to her. "These are very rare and worth a lot of money because Raine Waters only recorded two albums in his entire career. Then he just disappeared. It's a real mystery in the music business. Nobody really knows what happened to him, or why he stopped recording."

Brooklyn held up the albums and studied the cover. "Is that him?" She asked, pointing at his picture on the cover, "He was really handsome."

Josh nodded his head. "Yeah, that's him. Who knows what he looks like now. These are at least 30 years old."

She gently ran her fingers over his picture. "What kind of music did he play?"

"Country rock, I guess would be the best way to describe it, but more rock than pure country."

She looked at him and grinned. "I didn't know you liked country music. I've never heard you play any."

"I'm not a big country fan, but my father was. These were his albums and I grew up listening to them. My mom and dad loved Raine Waters' music, and actually so do I. His music wasn't complicated, but his lyrics were amazing. If you want to hear them, we could go to Stan's house. He has a great system there. He's into vinyl big time."

He took one of the albums out of her hands and looked at it. "How do you know him? Why did he write you this letter?"

She looked him in the eyes. "He didn't just write me that one, he wrote me 24."

"He wrote you all of these? Why?"

She raised up and kissed him. "We have a lot to talk about, but we need to talk about *us* first."

He dropped his head and looked away. "Brook, I'm sorry I blew up like that and walked out, but I love you and wanted to be with you, by your side, holding your hand, especially at your mother's funeral."

"I know you love me, and I would have loved having you there, but can't you understand...that day was all about my mother. If I had brought you there with me, it wouldn't have been about her...it would have been about us. We would have been the talk of the town. I just couldn't do that to my father. It was hard enough on him already. It was the wrong time for him to find out about us. Don't you see that?"

He gently touched her face. "Of course I see that, but sometimes I can't help but wonder...will there *ever* be the right time?"

"I promise you, it won't be long," she said. "Give my dad a few more months to adjust to living without my mom and we'll go there and I will introduce you to him."

She put the album down next to her and placed her hands over her belly and smiled. "By then, I'll be showing."

Josh grinned. "I hope he doesn't shoot me."

She laughed. "Don't worry, he's not gonna shoot you. My dad is the best. He's a sweet and wonderful man. I love him so much and he loves me too. When I tell him how I feel about you...he's gonna love you. And..." she rubbed her belly, "he's going to fall head over heels in love with *her*, too."

WHEN BROOKLYN LEFT to drive back to Fort Worth, Jake tried, but he could not fall asleep. He was exhausted, but he couldn't stop thinking about Virginia and the last words she had said to him.

She had been in and out of consciousness most of that last day. When she would come to, she was surprisingly clear, her eyes were bright and glistened in the light.

"Do you know that you were my hero?" She whispered, "My knight in shining armor. You saved me. Have I told you enough how much I love you?"

He leaned down and smiled. "I can never hear that enough," he whispered back.

"I love you, I love you, I cherish you," she said with a small smile, "Is that enough?"

He dropped the side rail of the hospital bed and laid down next to her. He pulled her into his arms and gently kissed her. "Do you know how much I love you? I love you, I love you, I cherish you," his voice cracked, and a single tear rolled down his cheek.

"Please don't cry," she whispered, "Not now. I need to tell you something."

Her breathing was getting slower and he knew she only had a few moments left.

"What do you want to tell me?" He whispered softly.

She opened her mouth and said something, but he couldn't make it out. "What did you say?"

He placed his ear next to her mouth. "You were...my true...love. Not...Raine."

His eyes filled. "I know," he whispered back.

She squeezed his hand and stared into his eyes. "Find...Raine," she was barely breathing, "Tell him...I forgive...him."

Her eyes suddenly opened wide, sparkling in the light. Then she said, "Oh, isn't it beautiful." She took one more shallow breath, closed her eyes...and she was gone.

Jake held her in his arms and cried for almost an hour. Finally, he kissed her one last time and let her go. He stood up, looked down at her beautiful face, and whispered, "Goodbye, Ginny." Then he turned and slowly walked out of the room.

BROOKLYN TOOK Raine's letters and re-organized them by date. "Start with this one," she said to Josh, "It was the first one he wrote to me. It will explain everything."

He took the letter and read it slowly. When he finished, he dropped it in his lap and looked up at her. "Oh my God. Raine Waters is your father?"

She nodded her head. "Apparently."

"They never told you? Why?"

She shrugged her shoulders and raised up her hands. "Dad said he tried to get mother to tell me for years, but she wouldn't do it."

Brooklyn looked up at him, "I guess keeping secrets is a Taylor family tradition. I don't feel so bad about us now."

"Have you read all of them yet?" He said pointing to the shoebox.

"No, only about half of them. I fell asleep reading this one last night." She handed him the letter, "I think you'll find this one interesting. He didn't want to quit recording. He lost his record deal."

"No way!" He shouted, "Why would they drop him?"

For the next three hours, they sat on the couch together, reading Raine's letters, mesmerized by his words.

"I'm hungry," she said standing up, stretching, "Let's go get something to eat. And after that, maybe we could go by Stan's and listen to these albums. I really want to hear his music."

———

JOSH HAD MET Stan Garrett in high school and they had instantly become best friends. Stan played drums, Josh played piano and they had formed their first band together a few months later. Stan was a serious musician and loved all kinds of music, and like most musicians, he was color blind. The fact that Josh was black and he was white, never crossed his mind. From the first day he met him, all he saw was a great guy that could play the hell out of a piano. He didn't care if he was green, he was a brilliant musician and a good friend.

The two of them had gone through too many guitar players and bass players to count, but after almost 15 years, they were still gigging together every night, making their music.

Actually, Stan had indirectly introduced Brooklyn to Josh, when he had stopped to talk to a table full of pretty girls on his break.

"You need to get her up there!" One of the slightly intoxicated girls said, "She can really sing!"

"Yeah, she's amazing!" They all said slurring their words.

Brooklyn had just enough courage from the two tequila shots to ask him, "Could I? I love your band and I really can sing."

Josh frowned and moaned when Stan asked him if he could bring up a girl singer to sit in, "Are you serious? Not another drunk, amateur chick singer!"

Stan insisted, so he finally agreed, "Sure, what the hell, bring her up. There's nobody in here anyway."

The bar had been half full all night and no one had been paying much attention to the band, so Stan waved to Brooklyn and motioned for her to come on stage.

He noticed her shaking hands and knees when he gave her the microphone. "Don't be nervous, you're gonna be great," he whispered in her ear.

"What do you want to sing?" Josh asked her with a rude, disinterested tone.

Brooklyn smiled and said, "Do you know any Aretha?"

Josh shot a hard look at Stan, obviously pissed that he had gotten him into this. "Yeah, I know some Aretha, but are you sure you want to start with one of hers?"

Brooklyn was just drunk enough to stare back at him and say. "What's wrong, you think I'm too white to sing one of her songs?"

Pissed, Josh shouted back, "Ok lady, how about *Respect* in A? Count it off Stan!"

Stan clicked his sticks and the band started playing the intro chords. He looked over at Josh who had one of his, "I'm gonna kill you" looks on his face. But the second Brooklyn sang the first note, everyone in the bar turned around and stared. She absolutely killed the song and when she finished, the crowd jumped out of their chairs yelling and screaming, "More! More!"

She sang three more songs to roaring ovations before she went back to her table. When Josh looked over at Stan behind his drums, he shot him the finger and burst out laughing.

From that night on, a few nights a week, Brooklyn would come to the bar and sing a few songs with them. Every time she showed up they tried to get her to join the band and sing with them every night, but for some unknown reason that she wouldn't divulge, she always turned them down, telling them that would be impossible.

Her relationship with Josh started out as just good friends, but the attraction between them was obvious to everyone.

"Are you ever gonna ask her out on a date?" Stan asked Josh one night after their gig.

"Who are you talking about?" He asked.

"Brooklyn, you moron. When are you finally going to take her out?"

Josh rolled his eyes. "We're just friends. And besides..."

"Besides what?"

"You know?"

"You know what?"

Josh frowned and glared at him. "Come on, Stan. Don't make me say it."

"Josh this isn't the 1960's. Nobody gives a shit about that stuff anymore."

"I wish that was true, but you're wrong. Her parents live in Abilene. They would never accept me and I would never put her through something like that."

"Come on Josh, every time she walks in the room you light up like a Christmas tree, and so does she. I know you man, and I know you've got it bad for her. Don't be so small-minded, just because her parents live in a small Texas town doesn't make them racist. If they love her, and you know they do, they will accept whoever makes her happy."

Stan put his arm on Josh's shoulder. "Trust me on this. You guys are perfect for each other. Don't blow it. Ask her out, what could it hurt?"

AFTER BROOKLYN and Josh had lunch, they drove to Stan's apartment and asked him to play Raine's albums.

"Who is Rainy Waters? I've never heard of him."

"It's Rain, not Rainy," Josh said, "and as weird as it may sound, he's Brooklyn's father."

"No shit?" Stan yelled, inspecting the album, "I thought her father sold farm equipment and lived in Abilene. This is an RCA Record. Why would he stop cutting records for them and start selling tractors?"

Brooklyn burst out laughing. "Not that father, it's my other one."

"What?"

"Will you just play the damn record," Josh yelled, "We'll explain it to you later."

When Brooklyn heard Raine sing the first note, cold chills ran through her body and she started to cry.

Josh put his arm around her. "I told you he was great."

The words to the songs were printed on the album sleeve and as she read the lyrics and listened to him sing, she cried uncontrollably through every song.

When the second album was finished, she looked at Josh and Stan. "Could I hear them again?"

Before they left that night, she had listened to both of the albums three times.

"Thank you, Stan. I really appreciate it."

Stan gave her a hug. "Don't thank me, I loved listening to your dad's music. If you want me to, I'll burn you two CD's so you can play them in your car."

She hugged him. "Thank you, Stan, I would love that."

When they got back to their apartment, Josh sat down on the couch and reached into the shoebox. "It's awfully late," Brooklyn said, "are you sure you want to keep doing this?"

Josh smiled and patted the couch beside him. "You know you won't be able to sleep until you read them all. Come on, sit down here with me. I've got to know the whole story."

It was a few minutes past one o'clock when Josh looked up and saw that Brooklyn had dozed off holding one of the letters.

He gently took it out of her hand and laid it on the table. He was fading too, so he dug through the shoebox and found the last letter Raine had written to her. When he tore it open and pulled it out, along with the letter, was a handwritten sheet of music. Carefully, he slid off the couch, walked to the piano, and began to play the song.

The music woke Brooklyn up. "Josh, what are you doing?" She looked at her watch, "It's two o'clock in the morning. You're going to wake up the neighbors."

He stopped playing and turned to look at her. "You've got to look at this."

She sat up and rubbed her eyes. "What is it?"

He walked over to her and handed her the music. "Is this a new song?" she asked.

He smiled, looking down at her. "Yes, and it's...it's amazing. I think he wrote this about you and your mother."

Brooklyn held the music up and read the words. When she finished, she pressed the music to her chest, close to her heart. Then she looked up at Josh and whispered, "I have to find him."

11

FROZEN WAFFLES

The job Louise had told Raine about was not actually working for her, at her house. It was a job working for the LaCita Country Club and Golf Course. At least, she hoped it would be.

Her late husband, Bill Parker, had been a founding member of the country club when it was built in 1982. It was designed by Ron Garl and Lee Trevino on 120 wooded acres that twisted and turned through some of the most beautiful homes in Titusville, Florida.

Louise had designed and decorated every square inch of their 4,000 square foot, two-story split-level home that sat only a few hundred feet from the 14th green.

Cooper Brennan, the General Manager and part-owner at LaCita, was Bill's best friend. Coop, as Louise had always called him, along with his wife, Mary, had taken several cruises with them and even a few extended trips to Europe. The four of them spent almost every weekend together, playing cards or going out to dinner.

When Bill died that day on the golf course, it was Coop who came to her house and gave her the devastating news. And from that day on, Coop had gone out of his way to take care of her.

Although she never asked for it, every Thursday morning, the ground crew for the country club showed up, cut her grass, weeded her flower beds, and edged her driveway and sidewalk.

If anything in her house broke or needed some repair, all she had to do was call Coop, and he would take care of it. He was much more than just a friend.

At 7:00 am, while Raine was still asleep in the guest bedroom, she dialed Coop's number and told him the story.

"So, how do you know this guy?" Coop asked her.

"I've known him a long time," She said, "I used to sing in his band."

"Was that the band you were singing with when you met Bill?"

"Yes, we were performing a corporate gig in Orlando, and Bill was staying at the hotel. We met at breakfast."

Coop laughed. "Oh yeah, I've heard the whole story," he said, "but I thought that guy was a big country star. At least that's what Bill always claimed."

"He was," she said, "At that time, he was pretty big."

"But now he's a bum, living on the street?" Coop said.

"Coop, I didn't say that," she chirped in his ear, "I said he was homeless, and I would like to help him."

"Ok...what have you got in mind?"

"Well...I thought that maybe you could hire him to work at LaCita, cutting grass or something. Any kind of a job to help him get back on his feet."

She heard him sigh on the other end of the phone. "Are you sure he's not a drug addict or a criminal hiding from the cops or something?"

"To be honest with you, Coop, I don't know anything about him now. I just know he needs help, and I'd like to try to give it to him."

"Where is this Raine guy now?" Coop asked.

"He's asleep in my guest room."

"He's in your house now?" Coop shouted.

"Yes, that's why I'm calling you so early. I wanted to bring him by so you can meet him."

"Oh, Lord," he said with a sigh, "Well, it's against my better judgment, but bring him on over this morning. I'll be in the office about nine. If he's not a crackhead or anything like that, I'll give him a job doing something around here."

LOUISE KNOCKED on the guest bedroom door. When Raine opened it, she handed him a pair of gray dress slacks, gray socks, a navy blue Polo shirt, a black belt, and black shoes.

"Put this on," she ordered, "I want you to make a good impression today."

A few minutes later, Raine walked into the kitchen with a slight limp. "I hope we don't have to walk very far, these shoes are killing me."

She grinned. "You look great! I'll buy you some shoes that fit you later, we don't have time now."

She picked up her purse and car keys and walked toward the garage.

"Where are we going?" Raine asked, following her.

"You'll see," she said, cranking the car.

When they walked into Coop's office, he jumped up and held out his hand. "You must be Raine Waters," he said, smiling, "it's nice to meet you."

Raine shook his hand. "Yes sir, I'm Raine. It's nice to meet you too."

"Now that the introductions are over," Louise said, "I'll let you boys talk business. Raine, I'll be downstairs in the pro shop. See you in a little while."

When Louise walked out, Coop pointed to a chair in front of his desk, "Have a seat."

Raine sat down, wringing his hands nervously. "I really appreciate this, sir, but I've known Louise for a long time and I'm sure meeting me here today wasn't exactly your idea."

He laughed. "Call me Coop, and you're right about this meeting. When Louise makes up her mind about something, well, there's not much you can do but listen to her. She's a good friend with a big heart."

Raine nodded. "She's always been a force of nature."

"Louise tells me that you were a singer," Coop said, "sort of a big deal."

Raine shrugged his shoulders. "That was a long time ago. I don't do that anymore."

"Yeah, I understand you've been a little down on your luck. I guess that's why you're here today," Coop leaned back in his chair, "You need to understand that I'm only doing this because Louise wants to help you get back on your feet. Her husband, Bill was my best friend and I love her like my own sister. Because of that, I'm gonna do just about anything she asks of me."

Raine didn't know how to respond, so he remained quiet.

"I'm going to give you a job and a good chance to pull yourself up out of this mess you've got yourself into. I don't know how you got there and I really don't care, but you need to understand that this is a one-strike deal. You screw up and I'll fire your ass and chase you off in a heartbeat."

"Thank you," Raine said, "I'll do my best, sir."

"I sure hope so, because I don't want to have to fire you," He grinned wide, "I'd never hear the end of that from Louise."

He stood up behind his desk. "I need you to fill out some paper-work. Come with me."

Raine followed him around the corner to another office. "Darlene, this is Raine Waters. He's going to work for us as a full-time employee. I need you to get him all signed up."

Coop turned and walked out of the office, but turned around and stepped back in, "Oh yeah, for his address, use the one for the little house behind the equipment barn. Raine, when you're done here, Louise and I will be in the bar. See you there."

AFTER HIS MEETING WITH COOP, Louise took Raine to the mall and bought him some work clothes, work boots, and new dress shoes; a pair of black ones and a pair of brown.

When they pulled in her driveway, Coop was sitting there in a golf cart. "Raine, If you've got a minute, I'd like to show you something."

"Sure," Raine said, sliding into the cart.

Coop drove them down two fairways, then took a hard right into the woods and stopped in front of an old worn down house.

"I understand this has been here for over sixty years," he said walking up to the front door, "My partners wanted me to tear it down, but I just couldn't do it. I believe that just because something gets a little old and beat up, doesn't mean it's useless." He opened the door and walked inside. "Come on in."

Raine walked through the door and looked around, wondering why Coop had taken him there.

"It's funny how things work out," Coop said, looking up at the ceiling. "As I said before, my partners wanted me to tear this place down. One of them is a damn lawyer and he was worried about the liability. He was afraid some kids might find it and use it as a clubhouse, maybe get hurt and their parents would sue us. I couldn't really argue with him, so I bought the place and the half-acre of land it's sitting on."

Coop walked through the tiny house opening the doors that led to the small kitchen, the bathroom, and the bedroom. "I had plans of fixing it up, but never got around to it." He looked at Raine. "What do you think?"

Raine smiled. "Well to be honest with you, I'm not sure what to think. Why are you showing me this?"

Coop's belly shook as he laughed. "I guess I haven't made myself very clear, have I?"

Raine laughed with him. "No sir, you haven't."

"I want to make you a deal," He said, "On your off time, weekends and evenings, if you'll fix this place up you can live here rent-free. The plumbing and electrical works good. All it really needs is a new roof, some new kitchen appliances, and a fresh coat of paint. I'll pay for everything if you'll do the work. What do you say? This beats the hell out of sleeping under a bridge, doesn't it?"

———————

JOSH LOOKED up from his computer. "There's nothing about him online. Not one thing! If you google his name, you only get links to his albums on e-bay. How can there not be one article or story about him online?"

Brooklyn grinned, "Well, it could be that he was famous way before anyone ever heard of something called the internet, or a PC."

"I know," he said, with a deep sigh, "but if we can't find anything about him here, how are we ever gonna track him down?"

"I think I know a way," she said, "but we'll have to go to Abilene."

Josh lifted his head and stared at her. "Did you say...*we* will have to go?"

She walked to him and sat in his lap. "That's what I said. You think you're up for it?"

"I thought you wanted to wait a few months, to give your dad some time to adjust."

"I did say that, but he called me this morning. He's doing ok, but he seemed so sad and lonely. I thought that maybe I would go there this Saturday and you could drive up after you finish your gig that night. It's only a couple of hours."

"Are you sure? I wouldn't get there until four or five in the morning."

She thought for a moment. "You're right, that's pretty late. Tell you what, why don't you just drive up Sunday morning and meet us for breakfast."

———————

JAKE WAS WASHING out his coffee cup when Brooklyn pulled into the driveway. He ran to the door and yanked it open. "Hey there! Why didn't you tell me you were coming?"

She opened her car door and ran up to him. "I wanted to surprise you," she said, hugging him.

"If you'd told me you were coming, I would have gone to the store and bought some groceries. There's not a damn thing to eat in this house."

"That's what I figured," she said, "We can go to the store later, but for now...when was the last time you went to The Shed? I've been thinking about their barbecue all the way here."

The entire time they were eating their brisket and ribs, Brooklyn's mind was spinning trying to think of a subtle way to tell Jake about Josh, but it never seemed to be the right time.

"Did you read all of Raine's letters?" he asked.

"Yes I did, and you were right, there were 24 of them."

"Mind me asking what they said?"

"No, I don't mind, but they may not be what you think."

He tilted his head. "What do you mean?"

"It's a little hard to explain. They're not really like personal letters. They're more like a diary of his life. I brought them with me. You can read them if you want to."

"If you don't mind," Jake said, "I'd love to read them."

She put down her fork and looked at him. "He told me the whole story about mom and him in the first one...and he talked about you too."

Jake raised his head. "Me? What'd he say about me?"

"He really liked you. He said that you were a great road manager and the only honest person he ever met in Nashville. He said you were the only one around him he trusted."

"Really, he said that?"

"Yes he did, he thought you were a great man, and he was happy that you married mom. He said that he knew that you would be a great father to me."

She reached across the table and squeezed his hand. "And he was right about that."

After their meal, they stopped at the store to buy some groceries. "Would it be Ok to buy these?" She asked, holding up a package of frozen waffles.

Jake put his hands on his hips and grinned. "Is this your subtle way of telling me after all these years, that you don't like my homemade waffles?"

She laughed. "No, I love your waffles, it's just that...ah...well...I've been wanting to tell you something all night."

Jake took the waffles out of her hand and dropped them in the basket. "All night? Humm...must be something important," he looked her in the eyes and grinned, "and it has something to do with frozen waffles...very mysterious."

After they put away the groceries, Jake opened a bottle of red wine and poured two glasses. "Let's go watch the sunset."

Brooklyn followed him outside to the pool and sat next to him at the patio table.

"OK young lady...spill it." He said. "I want to know about the waffles."

"Dad, someone is coming here tomorrow to meet you. Someone I love."

He jerked his head up and stared at her. "Someone you love?"

"Yes, I do."

He took a long sip of his wine and set the glass on the table. "Is...this someone...a man?"

"Of course it's a man! Who else would it be?"

"Well, you never know these days, with all this transgender, gay pride stuff. I'm just trying to keep up and adapt."

"Well, you don't have to worry about that. He's definitely a man."

"That's good," he said with a smile, "How long have you known this man?"

"We've been dating for over a year," she said, "and we've been living together for about three months."

He raised his eyebrows. "You're living together? Why the big secret? Why am I just finding out about this now?"

"It's not really a secret, but with mom being so sick this last year...well, I wasn't sure how she would react."

"Brooklyn, you're mother loved you more than anything on this earth. Why would you keep something like this from her? What's wrong with this guy?"

"There's nothing wrong with him. He's a great person and I just know you're going to love him, but..."

"Oh God, there's a but." He said with a chuckle, "So...but...what?"

"He's a musician."

"Oh no!" Jake grabbed his chest, faking a heart attack, "Not a musician! Anything but that!"

He burst out laughing and put his arms around her. "As long as he makes you happy and he's not a politician, I don't care what he does. A musician wouldn't be my first choice for you, but good thinking about not telling mom."

Brooklyn giggled. "She would have gone nuts and crawled out of her hospital bed and tried to spank me." They both laughed out loud.

Jake lifted his glass of wine and clinked it against hers. "Is he a good musician?"

"He's brilliant. He's a classically trained pianist. He graduated from North Texas University."

"Whoa, he must be good! I can't wait to meet him," he said, kissing her on the forehead, "So...what's the deal with the frozen waffles?"

She laughed. "What can I say, he loves them."

12

PINK TEXAS SUNSET

Josh's hands were trembling when he pulled into the driveway and turned off the ignition. He had the same sinking feeling inside his gut the day he told his parents about Brooklyn. But of course, they both instantly fell in love with her. Who wouldn't fall in love with Brooklyn? But this time, it was all about him. Before he opened the door and stepped out of the car, he said a small prayer.

Brooklyn opened the front door and ran down the steps to greet him. "Hey, you made it!" She said, smiling, "Did you have any trouble finding it?"

"No, I used the GPS on my phone."

He started to lean down and kiss her, but turned and walked to the back of his car to get his suitcase instead.

"Did you tell him?" He asked, rolling his suitcase toward her.

"Not everything," she said with a sheepish grin, "I wanted to wait for you before I told him about the baby."

"But you told him everything else, right?"

She lifted her eyes to his. "I told him you were a brilliant musician."

"Brooklyn, you know what I'm talking about," he said frowning, "Did you tell him I was black?"

She shook her head. "I'm sorry, I planned on telling him last night, but It never seemed to be the right time to bring it up."

He stopped walking and sighed. "You promised me."

"I know, but..."

He shook his head and walked past her, rolling his suitcase up to the door. "This is not the right way to do this. It's not fair to him...or to me," he said angrily.

Jake was standing behind the stove, cooking bacon when he heard the car pull into the driveway. He put down the fork, walked to the window over the sink, and watched the young man step out of the car. He tried to hear what he was saying to Brooklyn, but couldn't make it out behind the closed window. But after getting a good look at the handsome young man, he had a good idea what he was asking her.

When they walked into the kitchen a few minutes later, he had to bite his lip to keep from laughing. The young man was literally shaking in his shoes.

"You must be the damn musician Brooklyn was telling me about," he growled, glaring at him.

"Yes sir. I...I'm a musician," he said, stammering. He held out his shaking hand, "I'm Josh, Josh Arnett."

Jake took his hand and gripped it tight. "You're not one of those damn rappers are you?"

"Dad, stop that! Be nice!" Brooklyn said, "You're scaring him to death."

Jake looked him in the eyes and smiled. "You didn't answer my question. Do you play rap music?"

Josh smiled back. "No sir, but I'll learn some if you want me to."

Jake burst out laughing, pulled Josh into his arms, and hugged him. "It's nice to meet you, son! Brooklyn told me all about you. Well," he looked over at her and lifted his eyebrows, "she told me *almost* everything."

Brooklyn set the table, Josh poured the orange juice while Jake finished cooking the breakfast. When he sat Josh's plate down in front of him, there were two eggs, three slices of bacon, and four waffles on his plate. Two on one side and two on the other.

"Wow!" Josh said, "This is way too much food for me."

Jake leaned over the table and pointed at his plate. "The waffles on the right are those damn frozen ones Brooklyn made me buy for you last night at the store. Those on the left are *real* waffles, homemade. Just take a bite and I'm betting we'll be chuckin' those frozen ones in the trash."

AFTER BREAKFAST, while Brooklyn cleaned up the kitchen and put the plates and glasses in the dishwasher, Jake gave Josh a tour of the house.

Brooklyn heard the piano coming from the music room, so she put down the dish towel, walked down the hall, and stood in the doorway. Josh was sitting behind the piano playing and Jake was smiling, swaying to the music. When he finished, they both clapped and yelled, "Encore, encore!"

For the next hour, Josh gave them a private concert, playing everything from classical, to jazz, to rock. She had never heard him play better.

"We should play him the new one," Josh said.

"The new one?" She looked at him, confused.

"You know, the one Raine wrote for you and your mother."

Jake looked at Brooklyn. "He wrote a song for you and Ginny?"

"Yes," she said softly, "It was in his last letter. I was going to show it to you before I left, but we don't have to do it now if you don't want to."

"No, please. I'd love to hear it. Would you sing it for me?"

Brooklyn walked to her room, found the sheet music, and handed it to Josh. She didn't have to read the words because she knew them by heart.

Purposely, she didn't look at Jake while she was singing, because she knew if she did, she'd never make it through the song.

When she finished and turned around to look at him, he was crying. Wiping his eyes with his handkerchief he said, "I'm sorry. I don't know if it was the song or the way you sang it, but honey...wow, that was absolutely amazing. What a song!"

AFTER THEY HAD DINNER, Jake opened another bottle of wine and they walked outside to watch the sunset.

Josh was mesmerized and didn't say a word until the sun disappeared on the horizon. "I've never seen anything like that before," he said, with wide eyes, "I had no idea the sky turned pink like that. That was the most beautiful sunset I've ever seen."

"When it's clear like this," Jake said, "they're always beautiful, but this time of year, when we get that Sahara dust coming off the coast of Africa, they can be unbelievable. I try not to miss one if I can help it. It was one of Ginny's favorite things to do. She loved sitting here, sipping good wine, and watching God's show. That's why this house is wonky and doesn't face the road like all the others on this street. Ginny designed it this way, so we could sit here by the pool and watch the beautiful sunsets."

"Really?" Brooklyn said, "I never knew that. I always thought that the contractor had made a terrible mistake."

Jake laughed. "Oh no. She went round and round with that poor builder about it. But you know her, she eventually wore him down."

Jake had noticed it earlier during the sunset and then once more while he was telling them the crooked house story. Josh was doing his best to be subtle, so he wouldn't see, but it became obvious when he did it a third time.

"Are you going to tell me what's going on, or are you two just going to keep shooting each other signals all night?" He said smiling at them, "What's up guys?"

Brooklyn glanced at Josh, then turned and looked Jake in the eyes. "Dad, we have something else to tell you."

"No kidding?" He said with a smirk, "I figured that out about an hour ago. Am I going to need a shot of whiskey for this?" He said with a chuckle.

Josh and Brooklyn looked at each other and grinned. "That might not be such a bad idea," she said, reaching over and taking his hand.

Jake raised his eyebrows. "Oh boy! That bad huh?"

"No!" She exclaimed, "It's not bad news, it's great news!"

She let go of Jake's hand and stood up. Josh got out of his chair and stood beside her, holding her hand in his. "Dad," she said softly, "I'm pregnant. You're going to be a grandfather."

Jake lifted his head and stared up at them with a blank expression. Without saying a word, he jumped up and rushed into the house, closing the door behind him.

They looked at each other with shocked eyes. Brooklyn sat down in her chair and shook her head. "What on earth? I thought he'd be thrilled. We were all getting along so well...I guess he was just pretending."

Josh sat down next to her. "Brooklyn, he just lost your mother, the love of his life. If he was pretending about anything, it was that he was doing fine. Didn't you see the look in his eyes when he was talking about her? He's full of pain, still grieving and he's all jumbled up inside, barely getting through each day. Then *we* show up and throw all this at him. It's just way too much for him to handle."

They sat silent, holding hands looking at the stars. "What should we do?" She said, "We can't leave things like this."

"Do you want me to go talk to him?" Josh asked, "After all, I'm the one that got you into this."

"You didn't get me into anything. I love you, Josh. This is our baby, that we made together. I don't know what to do about dad. I'm just so surprised."

"Surprised about what?"

They both turned to see Jake standing in the doorway.

"Dad, I didn't tell you about Josh," Brooklyn said, "because...because I honestly thought that it wouldn't matter to you. That's what I'm so surprised about."

Jake frowned and walked up to her. "What the hell are you talking about? Do you think I'm upset because Josh is black? How dare you!" He yelled and stormed back inside the house.

Brooklyn jumped up and ran after him. "Dad! Where are you?"

She found him sitting on his bed, holding one of her framed baby pictures in his hand. She sat down beside him. "I'm sorry."

He held up her picture. "Ever since you were a little girl, I've tried to be the kind of man you would look up to, someone you could be proud of. The kind of man that judges people by their actions and character...never, ever by the color of their skin. That you could even think that of me..." His words trailed off, "I guess you don't really know me at all, do you?

"You're wrong dad. I never thought that! That's why I was so surprised by your reaction."

He turned and looked at her. "Honey...I wasn't upset because of Josh...it was because of you."

"Me? What did I do?"

He took her hand. "I want you to think about something. Do you ever remember your mother talking about our wedding day?"

Brooklyn thought for a moment. She slowly raised her head and stared at him. "No. I don't think I ever heard her say anything about it."

"You want to know why?"

"Of course. Why didn't she talk about it?"

"Because that was the same day you were born, and she was ashamed of herself."

"I was born the same day you were married?" Her expression slowly changed from total confusion to understanding. "Ohhh...yeah..." she whispered to herself, "Raine Waters."

Jake nodded. "Yep...Raine Waters. Do you understand now?"

"I think so."

"Your mother never wanted that to happen to you. She always dreamed of you having a big church wedding, and then maybe in a few years...you'd give us a grand baby."

He looked down at his hand and twisted his wedding ring on his finger, "Your mother was a little old fashioned, I guess. And because of what happened with Raine, well, you know...she never wanted you to do it any other way. She used to talk about it all the time when you were growing up."

"Really?" Her eyes sparkled up at him.

"Yes, she did, all the time."

He bit his lip, fighting back his emotions. "I realize that the world has changed and people these days have different ideas about marriage...and that's alright, but...on that last day she made me promise that someday you would have that big wedding." He lifted his eyes to hers, "So when you told me that you were pregnant..."

"Dad, I understand," She placed her hands on her stomach, "This messes up mom's dreams. And I'm sorry I jumped to the wrong conclusion and misunderstood."

"What about Josh? Did he think..."

"No sir I didn't," Josh said from the doorway. "not for a second."

He took a few steps into the bedroom. "Mr. Taylor, would you mind if I asked you a question?"

"About what?"

"It's about that big church wedding you were talking about. The one your wife always wanted for Brooklyn," he said, "I'm sorry, but I was listening to you guys."

"What do you want to know?" Jake asked.

"My father is a preacher in a church in Frisco. That's a small town about 50 miles north of Fort Worth. His church seats about six hundred,"

Josh walked up to Brooklyn and reached for her hand. "Do you think that would be big enough?"

13

WRONG ASSUMPTIONS

I t only took Raine a little over a week to get the house in good enough shape to move in. Coop bought him a bed, a couch, a chair, and a new stove and refrigerator.

On the second weekend, Coop showed up with a new air conditioner and together they installed it in the window.

After they got it running, Coop went to his golf cart and grabbed a couple of beers, and they drank them sitting on the front steps waiting for the house to cool down.

"Coop, I have something I'd like to talk to you about."

Coop leaned back against the door. "Fire away, what do you want to talk about?"

"It's about the roof," Raine said, pointing at the stack of shingles, "That's gonna be a big job, and I know you want to help but, I don't think it's a good idea for you to be up on that roof."

Coop smiled, "You sound like my wife. That's exactly what she said."

" I don't want to be rude, but I think she's right. You're too damn old to be up on that roof, and if anything happened to you...I'd never be able to forgive myself. And that's what I want to talk to you about."

Coop laughed. "To be perfectly honest with you, I was planning on hiring one of my crew to do that job."

"I think I have a better idea, but I'll understand if you don't agree. When I first found myself living on the street, I met this guy named Dave. He took me under his wing and showed me the ropes. If it hadn't been for him I'm not sure I would've survived. So, I was thinking that maybe I could get him to help me put on the roof, and in return, he could live here with me. He's really a great guy and I would love to help him get off the streets too."

The next morning, Coop and Raine drove to Cocoa Beach to look for Dave. "There he is," Raine said, pointing toward the pier.

"The guy with the really long hair and beard?" Coop asked.

"Yeah, that's him."

Raine walked up to Dave. "I told you to stop eating shit out of those dumpsters you dumb ass. It's gonna kill you someday."

Dave looked behind him. "Dude!" He yelled, "Is that you? What happened to your beard? Man, you look great!"

"Thanks. I feel great too. I've got a job and a good place to stay. That's why I'm here. I want you to come live with me."

Dave lifted his eyes. "Are you talking about a house? With a roof and everything?"

Raine smiled. "Well, that's another reason I'm here. My roof needs some new shingles and I was wondering if you could maybe help me nail them on, so the next time it rains we won't get wet. What do you say?"

They put Dave in the bed of the pickup and drove back to the little house.

Raine had known Dave for over five years but had no idea how extremely claustrophobic he was until he tried to get him to take a shower.

When he took him into the small bathroom, Dave started freaking out and hyperventilating. "No, no, I can't go in there!" He ran out and stood in the middle of the living room. "Sorry man, but I can't be in tight spaces."

"Really? I didn't know you were claustrophobic," Raine said. He looked at Coop. "Have any ideas?"

Coop thought for a minute, then smiled. "Yeah, I do. Follow me."

Raine and Dave followed him over to the equipment barn. "Stand over there by that drain," Coop said, "and take off those filthy clothes."

Dave stripped out of his clothes, while Coop untangled the hose. He smiled at Raine. "It works for the golf carts, it should work on him." He threw Dave a bar of soap, opened the hose nozzle, and pointed it at him.

Like it was something he did every day, Dave smiled and said, "Cool," and started scrubbing his body.

Raine ran back to the little house and grabbed the bottle of shampoo and some clothes. Like Louise had done, he took Dave's old dirty clothes, put them in a trash bag, and threw it in the trash can.

Dave was very skinny but tall, six foot three, so when he put on the clean clothes Coop and Raine couldn't help but laugh. The pants were way too short and the sleeves of the shirt only reached to his forearms.

"We're gonna have to do something about that," Coop said laughing, "He looks like Jethro from the Beverly Hillbillies."

After a quick trip to Walmart to buy Dave some clothes and shoes, they started working on the roof. It took them a little over two hours to rip off the old shingles and another three to carefully cover the roof with new tarpaper.

Although Coop didn't climb the ladder up to the roof, he supervised the clean up on the ground, having his crew pick up the discarded shingles and old tarpaper.

During those hot five hours of difficult work, Raine had climbed down the ladder four times to cool off and rest, but Dave never stopped. All he ever asked for was water, and after he chugged the bottle, he would start again.

When Dave and Raine finally finished for the day and climbed down the ladder, the sun was almost down and they were hot, thirsty, and hungry.

While Dave took his second shower of the day at the equipment barn, Raine took a long shower in the little house. When they had dried off and dressed, Coop pulled up in his golf cart loaded with hot food and cold beer.

They helped Coop unload the cart and laid out the food under the umbrella on the wooden picnic table that sat a few feet away from the front door.

"I can't believe you guys got that done in one day. Good job guys." Coop said, tapping his beer can against theirs.

"We had to," Raine said, "you never know around here when it might rain and we needed to get that tarpaper up before we stopped."

"It was hard work, but I liked it," Dave said, taking another bite of his drumstick, "Man, this chicken is great!"

"So what's your story, Dave?" Coop asked, "I've been watching you up there bust your ass all day and I can't imagine a man that works as hard as you do having a problem finding a job. How'd you wind up homeless and living on the street?"

Dave glanced at Raine but didn't answer Coop's question. "I'll be right back," he said, walking toward the woods.

"Dave, you don't have to go in the woods," Raine said, "Use the one in the house. Leave the door open if you need to."

Dave shrugged, "I don't know man, it's pretty small in there, but maybe...if the door is open."

When he walked inside the house, Coop said, "Has he always been that way?"

Raine shook his head. "I don't know. I had no idea he was claustrophobic. I don't mean to be gross, but the truth is when you're living on the streets there's not much access to things like bathrooms, or showers."

"What about in homeless shelters? They have bathrooms there, right?"

"Yeah, but Dave doesn't like shelters and never went to them."

"Why not?" Coop asked.

"Who knows? I think it's because one time they asked him for his name."

Coop lowered his eyebrows. "What's wrong with that?"

"Again, who knows, but he won't give anyone his real name. He's a little paranoid I guess. He always says it's because he wants to stay off the government's grid."

Coop frowned. "That's a little weird don't you think?"

"Well yeah, I guess it would be for anybody else except for Dave."

"What do you mean?" Coop asked confused.

"Dave's done a lot of drugs and drank a lot of alcohol in the past. He's been out here living this way for over 20 years. He's the sweetest guy you'll ever meet, but to be perfectly honest with you...I'm not sure Dave's all there. I think all that booze and drugs have fried his brains a little."

"Really?" Coop asked, "he seems all right to me."

"Just wait until you get to know him a little better and I think you'll see what I'm talking about."

"You don't think he's hiding from the cops or something, do you?"

"No way," Raine said laughing, "Dave wouldn't hurt a flea."

"I hope you're right because if he is hiding from the police I can't have him around here. They could shut me down for aiding and abetting a criminal."

Raine laughed again. "Come on Coop, Relax. I've known Dave for five years. He's a great guy and would never do anything like that."

"I sure hope not. Do you think he'd take a job if I offered him one? I could use a guy that works like that around here."

When Dave came back and sat down behind the picnic table, Coop said, "I don't suppose you'd want a job working here at the country club, would you? I could pay you minimum wage."

Dave grinned and looked at him. "Doing what?"

"I've got about 100 acres here that we have to keep landscaped and then, of course, there's the fairways and greens to keep up. I'm always looking for someone that's not afraid of work."

Dave thought for a moment. "How would you pay me? Could you pay me in cash?"

"Well, we could cash your paycheck at the clubhouse."

"No, no checks, but if you can just pay me cash I'll be glad to."

Coop shook his head no. "This is a corporation, so I have to put you on the payroll as an employee and write you a check. I can't pay cash off the books like that."

"I'm sorry," Dave said, "but I can't do that. I ain't going on nobody's payroll records."

———

WORKING a few hours each night after Raine got off work at LaCita, and all day Saturday and Sunday, they finally finished nailing the new shingles on.

While Raine and Dave worked up on the roof, Coop helped from the ground, handing them up the packs of shingles.

Trying not to be too obvious, Coop asked both of them questions about their past. He'd had several long talks with Raine and knew most of his story, but was very interested in hearing more about Dave. But after grilling him every day that week, he didn't find out much about him. He would either give him a shrug and say, "It just sort of happened," or, "I don't really remember," or he would ignore his question altogether.

With every passing day, Coop's suspicions of Dave grew. He didn't tell Raine but he was convinced Dave was hiding something. And he also didn't agree with Raine that Dave was not all there. He was a lot smarter than Raine thought and was very careful and elusive with his answers to his questions.

When they finished the roof on that Sunday afternoon, Coop had them stand in front of the little house and took their picture in front of it to celebrate. He also took a few close-ups of Dave.

The next day, he called one of his good friends, Alexander Rush, who was a Special Agent for the FBI in Orlando. "Alex, I was wondering if you could do me a favor."

"Sure," He said, "Who do you want killed?"

Coop laughed. "I think I'll save that favor for later when I really need it." He chuckled, "If you could, I need you to check up on someone for me. I know that's not necessarily what you do, but this guy is living with one of my employees and I think he may be hiding something."

"What's his name? " Alex asked.

"Well, that's one of the reasons I'm so suspicious. I only know his first name, it's Dave. When I asked him what his last name was, he got a bit nervous and said, 'Just call me Dave.' I do have a picture of him. I thought that maybe you could run it through your facial recognition software and find out if he's wanted somewhere."

"There's got to be more than that," Alex said, "Is he stealing from you or something?"

"No, in fact, I offered him a job. I finally got a new roof on that little house of mine in the woods, that's where this employee I'm talking about is living. It's his friend and he got him to help him nail the shingles on. This Dave guy is homeless, living on the streets for about 15 years, but he's not lazy, he worked his ass off on that roof. That's why I offered him the job, but he turned me down. He said that he didn't want to be on my payroll records, so he could stay off the government's grid."

"Hmmm, that does sound a bit suspicious. Email me his photo and give me a general description, height, weight, etc."

THE FOLLOWING SATURDAY, Jake drove to Fort Worth and checked into a hotel. He hadn't told Brooklyn and Josh that he was coming, because he wanted to surprise them. At least, that's what he told himself on the drive there, but the reality was that he wanted to hear Josh's band and see him in action in a bar.

He couldn't help himself, he had spent too many years around too many musicians not to have some suspicions about Josh. He knew first hand that the reputation assumed by most people about musicians was not unfounded.

His years in the music industry had shown him that of course, not all musicians were self-obsessed, egotistical, took drugs, drank too much, and were notorious womanizers, but the ones that were not were the rare exceptions. They almost had to have a giant ego to be able to believe in themselves against all odds. When they didn't have the ego, then they either took drugs or alcohol to have the courage to get on that stage night after night facing a crowd of strangers.

On his long drive there, he thought about the time he had sat backstage during a music festival talking to Waylon Jones.

Waylon had been known to drink a little too much alcohol or even snort a line of cocaine before he walked on stage.

"Waylon, could I ask you a question?" They were sitting on a black travel case just off stage watching the crew setting up for the next act.

"Well I guess that depends on the question," Waylon said with a chuckle.

Jake pointed at the crowd of 20,000 or so fans sitting in the auditorium. "You know most of those people out there are here to see you, don't you?"

He nodded. "That's what they're telling me."

"Well, they're telling you the truth," Jake said, "People have come from miles around just to hear and see you."

He nodded again. "Yeah, I guess so."

"They came here because they love you and your music. Please don't take this wrong, but the facts are, you could walk on that stage and do just about anything and get a standing ovation tonight. What I'll never understand is, with all those people out there who love you so much, why do you need to get high or drunk to face them?"

Waylon looked at him and grinned. "I was working in this little bar in Lubbock when this all happened. I had my chance in Nashville and kind of blew that, so I moved back to Texas. I found some gigs in a few small bars playing to a couple hundred of the local drunks each night, and like I said I was happy and doing ok. Then my friend Willie called me and asked me to record this song with him in Austin, so I did. The next thing I knew, it was the number one record in the whole damn world and I'm playing for thirty or forty thousand people."

Waylon leaned close to Jake. "And well, you know...I'm not really all that good," he laughed out loud, "so to keep my damn knees from shaking I drank a little and before I realized it, I was drinking a lot."

Jake never forgot that night. He was sitting there talking to a country music legend, one of the greatest singers and songwriters of all time, and even *HE* didn't think he was worthy of his fame.

JAKE ARRIVED at the bar early and took a seat in the back. Every time the waitress would come to the table to take his drink order, he would ask her a few questions about the band, especially about the piano player.

"Yeah," he said laughing, "I was here the other night and it looked like that guy was drunk as a skunk, or stoned on something. Does he do that a lot?"

The waitress frowned. "Are you talking about Josh?"

Jake nodded. "I don't know what his name is, but he was the black guy playing the piano."

"Josh doesn't drink when he's performing," she said, "Are you sure you're talking about the 'Josh Arnett band?' None of the members of that band drink when they're on stage."

"Come on now, I'm not trying to get him in trouble or anything, but all musicians drink. Oh, I get it, they're smoking some weed backstage before they come on. Is that what they're doing?"

The waitress didn't answer, spun around, and walked back to the bar. A few minutes later the bartender walked over to him. "Are you a cop or something, or maybe from the liquor control board?" He asked.

Jake looked up at him and smiled. "No, why would you think something like that?"

"Well, Judy was telling me that you were asking her all kinds of questions like, how much did the band drink, or if they were smoking dope. If you're not a cop, then what are all the questions for?"

"Do you know Josh Arnett well?" Jake asked ignoring his question.

"Yeah, I do. He's a great guy, one of my good friends. Why do you ask?"

"No real reason, just curious. I bet he gets a lot of girls, a good

looking guy like him. He probably has a whole harem full, am I right?"
Jake said laughing.

The bartender glared down at him. "Look Mr., I don't know who
you are, or why you're here, but you're talking about one of my good
friends. Josh Arnett is one of the nicest guys I've ever known. I think
it's time for you to leave."

Jake smiled up at him. "Do you know his girlfriend?"

"Yes, I know Brooklyn, why?"

Jake stood up and reached out his hand. "I'm her father and he just
asked her to marry him. I wanted to find out a little more about him. I
hope you understand."

The Bartender shook Jake's hand with wide eyes. "You're
Brooklyn Taylor's father? You were the road manager for all those
stars?"

Jake smiled. "A few. How do you know about that?"

"Josh told me all about you. You were with Raine Waters too,
right?"

Jake lifted his eyebrows. "You know about Raine Waters?"

"Yes sir, my parents are huge fans of his. I grew up listening to his
records. What was he like? I mean, in real life?"

Jake laughed. "Why do you think I'm here checking up on Josh?
All those stories you've heard about Raine Waters are true. I just
wanted to make sure Josh was nothing like him."

"Oh no sir, Josh is a serious musician and a terrific guy, you don't
have to worry about him."

"Please don't tell him I'm here. I just wanted to listen to his band
and not make him nervous, OK?"

About an hour later Josh and the rest of his band walked on stage,
tuned up, and started to play. It only took him a few songs of the first
set to realize that Josh *WAS* a great musician and his band was equally
good. He was especially impressed by the drummer. He never over-
played, had impeccable timing, and was a good singer as well. At the
end of the second set, he saw Brooklyn walk in the door. He pulled his
baseball cap down over his eyes and slid his chair back, so she
wouldn't see him.

When the next set started, Brooklyn got on stage and started singing. It was all he could do to keep from crying: he knew she could sing, but he had no idea she could sing like that. It wasn't just her voice, she had this magical stage presence, that had him, and everyone else in the entire bar staring at her. No one could take their eyes off of her. She was absolutely incredible and he was beaming with pride.

In the middle of their final set, Brooklyn suddenly stopped singing and yelled into the microphone, "Dad, is that you?"

THE ONE THING the Josh Arnett Band had in common with every musician Jake had ever known, was the instant desire after the gig to head to the nearest IHOP to fill up on coffee, pancakes, and omelets, and to swap stories and laugh, coming down from the indescribable high that comes with performing music in front of a live responsive audience.

One of Jake's biggest surprises of the night came when he discovered how much the members of Josh's band knew about him and his past, and until almost 4:00 am, he sat there answering all their questions.

"What was Johnny Cash like? Did Merle Haggard really go to prison? Is it true that George Jones didn't want to record He Stopped Loving Her Today?"

Jake did his best to answer them all, with most of his stories ending with roaring laughter. But the one question he couldn't answer came from Brooklyn.

"Dad, what really happened to Raine Waters?" She asked, "It doesn't sound like he was any worse than all those other stars. Why did RCA drop him and why did they stop playing his music on the radio?"

Jake shook his head and smiled at her. "I honestly don't know what happened to Raine because you're right, he wasn't any worse than a lot of them. It's a real shame too because he was incredibly talented. When I first met him, he was just like you guys. He was a serious musician, great songwriter, and had this voice and stage presence that just couldn't be denied."

Jake looked over at Brooklyn and smiled. "I saw that same magic when I was watching you sing tonight. It's something everybody wants but very few people have. It's called charisma and you got that from Raine. There's no way to deny it and everyone in that bar tonight saw it too."

"Really?" She said with bright eyes.

"Yes, really," he said looking at the members of the band, " Am I wrong?"

Josh smiled at her. "We've been trying to tell you that, but you just wouldn't listen."

IT WAS ALMOST 4:30 am when Jake finally made it back to his hotel and crawled underneath the sheets for a few hours of sleep. When the phone rang with his wake up call at 7:30, he moaned, crawled out of the bed, and jumped in the shower.

At 8:00, he checked out of the hotel, jumped in his truck, and drove North, 49 miles to the little town of Frisco, Texas. Fortunately, the traffic wasn't bad, so when he pulled into the parking lot of Grace Church, he had five minutes left before the service started.

He was there to check out the little church and listen to the sermon preached by Reverend Ansel Arnett, Josh's father. Jake was surprised by the size of the pew area. It was larger than he had imagined in his mind when Josh told him that it only seated 600. The chancel, the area behind the altar for the choir and band, was also much larger than he had envisioned.

He found a pew in the back row and sat down, studying the architecture of the ceiling. Then he glanced around the room looking at the people in the congregation. Again, he was surprised at the wide variety of ages and races. He was actually a little ashamed of himself for making the assumption that because Josh's father was black, his church's congregation would also be black. It was akin to the same stupid assumption he had made about Virginia's oncologist. For some archaic, ridiculous reason he had assumed that a doctor of oncology of that renowned status would be a white male. He was wrong, just like he was today...she was brilliant, a woman, and she was Asian.

A few moments later, he shook his head and laughed, realizing that he had a lot of work to do on himself with his thought process and his completely wrong assumptions. When the music started, sitting behind the large Hammond organ was Josh, and behind the drums was Stan Garrett.

He couldn't believe it. He had barely made it to the service that morning, not completely awake, driving with sleepy eyes from staying out way too late at the IHOP with Josh and Stan, but they had beaten him there.

That's when he knew that he had nothing to worry about when it came to Josh Arnett. Everyone he had met so far loved him and held him in the highest regard. Without a doubt in his mind, he knew that Josh was definitely *not* a typical musician and was going to make a good husband for Brooklyn, and a great father for his grandchild.

FOUR WEEKS LATER, when Brooklyn walked into the back of the little church wearing that beautiful dress and took Jake's arm for him to walk her down the aisle, he couldn't hold back his emotions.

She reached up, wiped his eyes with a Kleenex, and whispered, "Don't cry, Daddy."

"I'm sorry, baby. You just look so beautiful, I can't help it. I hope Ginny is looking down to see the way you look right now."

"She is," Her eyes glistened and sparkled with her smile, "I've been talking to her all morning. I can feel her...here," She held her hands up to her heart, "Don't worry, Dad, she's here with us...and she will probably be crying too, watching us walk down the aisle together."

14

MUSIC ROW

N ash Cooper's heart was pounding in his chest when he took the exit off the freeway to downtown Nashville. It had taken him years to get there, but his dreams of becoming a big country star were finally about to come true. It had taken him over two years to finish the ten songs he had written and recorded and he couldn't wait to see the look in the record company's executive's eyes when they heard them.

He had imagined that scene in his head many times and could hardly wait to see it in real life.

"You wrote all of these songs?" they would say astonished. *"Nash, these have to be the ten greatest country songs ever written!"* Then the bidding war would begin between all of the major labels to sign the soon to be world-famous, Nash Cooper.

After he was signed and his album was declared Platinum or even Diamond, he would buy a mansion on Old Hickory Lake in Hendersonville just north of Nashville where a lot of the other country stars lived. Or, he might even buy a small ranch near by. He didn't really care as long as it was a huge flashy looking house with plenty of room to park his tour busses. Of course, he'd build a studio there, so he could keep writing and recording his gold records.

He couldn't wait to see the look on the faces of his band members when he told them about his new record contract. After they all got excited, assuming he was going to take them with him... he would smile and tell them that they were all fired, being replaced by real Nashville musicians who believed in him and his music. That was going to be the best part of it all because they had never supported him. They had only criticized his original songs and never like playing them.

He smiled wide thinking about it. "Big mistake boys," he said out loud, "I can't wait to leave all your asses behind."

Nash checked into his hotel a few blocks away from Music Row, then quickly unpacked and got back in his car to drive around and check out the city.

He drove downtown and circled the old Ryman Auditorium a few times. *It won't be long until I'm on that stage*, he said to himself.

It was a Sunday evening in late August and the sky was turning angry and dark. He could see the rain coming, but instead of heading back to his hotel, he drove southwest and turned down 17th Avenue South to finally see the historic streets called Music Row.

He wasn't sure what he was expecting to see but after he circled 16th and 17th Avenue a few times he was disappointed because there really wasn't much to see. He had read that Music Row was considered to be the heart of Nashville's entertainment industry and knew it was centered on 16th and 17th Avenues South, which were also known as Music Square East and West.

He slowly passed the historic RCA Studio B, Columbia's Historic Quonset Hut, the first recording studio on Music Row, and Owen Bradley Park. There were several shops and upscale restaurants, but primarily the streets were lined with rather unimpressive small office buildings and restored historic houses where the record labels and publishing companies were located.

He had read that there were supposedly over 100 recording studios in that area, but he couldn't find any of them. There were no large signs, neon lights, or anything that would let you know that you were driving down some of the most historic streets in America.

After he jotted down the actual addresses of four of the largest record labels, he stopped at a Shoney's restaurant close to Music Row and had dinner.

As he ate his dinner, he constantly looked around the restaurant hoping to see someone famous, but he didn't recognize anyone.

He was in no hurry to get back to his hotel, especially in the pouring rain, so after he finished eating, he ordered a piece of pecan pie and a cup of coffee. On his way back from the restroom, he noticed four men sitting in the booth behind him. One of them was writing numbers on a yellow legal pad.

"Is that a Nashville number chart?" He asked, "Are you guys studio musicians?"

The man looked up and smiled. "Yes it is, and yes we are."

Nash stared down at the pad, then held out his hand. "Hi, I'm Nash Cooper."

The man shook his hand. "Nice to meet you, Nash. I'm Dino, that's Walter and Jim. This real ugly guy sitting next to me is Owen. Nash shook all their hands. "I've heard of the Nashville number charts before, but I've never seen one. How does it work?"

"Are you a musician?" Dino asked.

"Yes, but I'm more of a singer."

"Well, a number chart is really simple. Let's say that a song is in the key of E, that would be number one," Dino looked up at Nash and said, "So, if number one is E and the chords order on a guitar are E, F, G, A, B C, D…what do you think number two would be?"

Nash thought for a second. "F?"

"Right. F is two, G is three, A is Four, and so on. The reason we use the numbers instead of the letters is when we need to change the key up or down in the session. If we go down a step, then D would be one, E would be two, and so on. When you're in the middle of a session and the songs not working for the singer in that key, then we can move up or down and don't have to take the time to re-write the charts. Does that make sense?"

"Yes, it sure does, but I'm glad I'm not here trying to be a session player. I'm not sure I could make those changes in my head that fast."

Dino laughed. "Well trust me, Nash, being a session musician is no way for a grown man to make a living anyway. So why *are* you here?"

"I'm here to sign a record deal."

The four men glanced at each other. "Oh yeah?" Owen asked, "Who with?"

"Oh, I don't know yet," Nash said, exposing his naïvety, "but I was thinking maybe RCA."

They all shot each other glances but suppressed their laughter. "Good choice," Dino said, "RCA is a great label. So, when are you meeting with Joe?"

"Who's Joe?" Nash asked.

"Joe Galante. The president of RCA Nashville. He will be the guy that signs you."

Nash reached into his pocket, pulled out a notepad, and wrote down the name. "Thanks, Dino. I really appreciate that," he said smiling, "now I'll know who to ask for tomorrow."

They all burst out laughing. "What's so funny?" Nash asked confused.

Dino slid over and patted the seat next to him. "Sit down Nash. I think we need to talk."

He sat down. "Talk about what?"

"Is this your first trip to Nashville?" Owen asked.

He nodded his head. "Yeah. I was planning on coming earlier this year, but it took me longer than I had planned to finish my CD."

"Yeah, cutting a record always takes longer than you think it will," Dino said, "So...can I ask you a few questions?"

"Sure."

"Who produced your CD and where did you cut it?"

"I did," Nash said, "and I cut it in a studio in Melbourne, Florida"

"Who wrote the songs?"

"I did."

Dino glanced at Owen across the table, who was shaking his head. "Nash, do you know people here in Nashville with any connections in the music industry, like a music producer or an entertainment lawyer, something like that?"

"No, not really."

"So what exactly is your plan?"

Nash shrugged his shoulders. "I don't really have a plan, I was just going to get up tomorrow morning, drive to Music Row and start knocking on the doors of the labels."

"Good lord Nash, do you really think it's that easy? Do you have any idea how many singers arrived in Nashville today just like you? And, they are all here trying to do the exact same thing you're doing. What do you think is gonna happen when you knock on RCA's door?"

Nash grinned. "I don't have any idea, but I'm not worried about that, because when they hear me sing and hear my songs, they're gonna all be fighting to sign me up."

Owen grinned. "You're that good, huh?"

"Yes I am," he said arrogantly, "You'll be hearing about me soon, I promise you that."

Dino nodded his head and smiled. "Well, I'm glad you're so confident and I wish you all the luck in the world...you're gonna need it. Could I give you one small piece of advice?"

"Of course," Nash said, sliding out of the booth and standing up.

Dino took a deep breath and looked up at him. "There's a FedEx store a few blocks down. You need to go there with that CD and buy about 10 or 15 flash drives. Then you need to rent one of their computers and load your CD onto those drives. Nash, for God's sake, don't walk into a record label with a CD in your hand. We stopped using those years ago. Everything is on a flash drive these days."

Nash thanked them, went back to his booth, and ate his pecan pie. When he left, he thanked them again and waved goodbye.

Owen watched him walk out sipping his coffee and chuckled. "What an arrogant dumbass. You know, normally I feel sorry for guys like that, knowing that he's about to get his heart cut out by this city, but that guy is so full of himself I think he might deserve it."

"He *was* a little overconfident, I'll give you that," Dino said laughing, "but I don't think anybody deserves what he's about to get. Those label guys on Music Row are going to eat him alive and shatter every dream he's ever had. And if I remember correctly it hasn't been that many years ago when this arrogant little shit came to town named

Owen Green. He was knocking on all the same doors telling everybody how great he was too."

Owen grinned. "The difference was...I could back up my bullshit because I *AM* great!"

"No, you're wrong there," Dino fired back, "You just *THINK* you're great...just like Nash does."

They all laughed and began swapping stories about their experiences of the first time they arrived in Nashville.

"This city has changed a lot in the last 20 years, and not for the better. Most of the labels don't even have artist development departments anymore. It's all iTunes, YouTube, and entertainment lawyers these days. I doubt if any of us at this table could even book a session if we showed up today. It's not about the talent or the music, it's just about the business."

Dino pulled out his cell and punched in a number. "Let me speak to Scott," he said, "tell him this is Dino Zimmerman calling in one of the *many* favors he owes me."

"What are you doing?" Owen asked.

"Hell, I don't know what I'm doing. There's just something about that kid. I guess he reminds me of myself at about that age. I thought I was the greatest singer-songwriter that ever lived too. The only thing that saved me was my guitar playing. If I hadn't landed a few studio sessions, I would have been long gone years ago. The way it sounds to me, I don't think Nash is much of a musician, so I thought maybe I could pull a few strings and at least give him a shot. Have somebody that can actually do something for him at least take a meeting and listen to his songs. Who knows, he may be as great as he thinks he is."

"Who thinks he's great?" Scott asked on the other end of the phone, "and what's all this crap about me owing you a favor. The way I figure it, I don't owe you shit!" He said laughing.

"Come on, Scott, you know damn well if It wasn't for me, you'd still be delivering pizzas instead of being a hotshot record executive."

"Well, you did put down a damn good ride on that first record we did together," He chuckled, "Dino it's good to hear your voice. How the hell are you?"

"I'm doing great, crazy busy," Dino said, "I've only got a few more tracks to lay down on Amanda's new one, I should knock that out tomorrow. We start on the Trio's new one next week. Mark my words, I believe Amanda has three, maybe four number ones on this one."

"That's what I've been hearing," Scott said, "James was telling me he thinks it's her best one yet. So, what can I do for you today? What do you need?"

"I need a favor," Dino said, "and don't ask me why I'm doing this, because I don't really know myself. I guess I'm kind of missing the way it used to be around here when we both showed up. I met this kid tonight at Shoney's, and man, you talk about green, this poor kid hasn't got a clue what he's in for. He's got the looks and the ego for damn sure, but I haven't a clue whether he can carry a note in a bucket or not, because I haven't heard him."

"Oh Lord," Scott sighed, "Not another one."

"Yep, and I mean he's right off the bus, but there's something about him I can't explain. Actually, he's so damn egotistical he's a little bit of a prick. He kind of reminds me of you."

Scott laughed. "He's that good looking?"

"He *does* have the look, but I was referring to his incredible over-confidence."

"Very funny asshole," Scott said, "What's his name?"

"His name is Nash Cooper, and I think he's from Florida."

Scott wrote down his name on his pad. "Ok...so what do you want me to do with him?"

It was a little past 9 am when Nash walked up the steps and opened the door of the RCA Building.

He was immediately stopped by a security guard. "Can I help you?"

Nash smiled at the guard. "Yes sir. I'm here to see," he reached into his back pocket, pulled out a small note pad and started flipping the pages, "Hang on a second, it's here somewhere."

When he found the page, he looked up at the guard and said, "I'm here to see a Mr. Galante."

The guard raised his eyebrows. "You're here to see, Joe Galante? The President? Do you have an appointment?"

Nash shook his head. "No sir, but he's gonna want to see me."

"Oh really? And why's that?"

Nash held up the flash drive and smiled. "To hear this."

"Is that your album?"

"Yes sir and they're all hits, every single one of them. That's why I came here first, so Mr. Galante could have the chance to sign me to RCA before all the other labels hear it."

The guard smiled. "That's really considerate of you son. Is this your first trip to Nashville?"

"Yes sir."

"That's what I thought. Where are you from?"

"I'm from Melbourne, Florida. That's where I cut this," he said holding up the flash drive again, "but I figure when Joe hears it, he'll probably want to get me into a studio to redo it with Nashville musicians."

"Son, you seem like a nice kid, but let me give you some advice. First of all, this is Nashville and nobody comes to work around here untill after 10. And second, they hired me, to keep people like you, from getting through this door. I'm sorry, but Mr. Galante is not going to see you. He doesn't see anybody without an appointment."

Nash looked up at him with shocked eyes. "How do I get an appointment?"

"That's a good question. If I was you I would hire an entertainment attorney, they seem to be able to walk in and out of here pretty easy."

"I can't afford that. I barely have enough money to pay for my gas to get back home and my hotel room."

The guard smiled. "Why don't you give me the flash drive and I'll put it in that bucket over there on the receptionist desk with all the others. If they listen to it, and if they like it, they'll contact you."

"All the others?" Nash asked.

The Guard nodded. "Yeah, there's probably 200 of them in that bucket."

"That's not right!" Nash exclaimed, "200 others? How does anybody get signed around here?"

"Welcome to Nashville, son," the guard said with a grin, "People have been asking that question for years. If I was you, I would put a video of you singing those songs on YouTube. That's where they found the last three they signed. If you get a few million hits, trust me, they'll call you."

WHEN NASH WALKED out of the RCA Building, he was depressed, but he didn't give up. He drove back to the Shoney's restaurant, got a cup of coffee, and waited until after 10:00 am before he started walking up and down the streets of Music Row again. He wasn't stopped by any more security guards, but unfortunately, the receptionists asked the same question at each label, "Do you have an appointment?" All he was allowed to do was leave his flash drive with his name and phone number written on the side.

When he ran out of the major labels, he started knocking on the doors of the small independent labels but got the same story at each one of those as well.

He had loaded his CD on 15 flash drives. He was down to his last one when he knocked on the door of "Huge Records."

He had never heard of it before, but the receptionist at his last stop had suggested he try there.

"Have you tried Scott Hugley's new label?" She had asked.

"No, who's Scott Hugley?"

She frowned. "Seriously? You've never heard of Scott Hugley?"

Nash shook his head. "No, I haven't. Who is he?"

"He's only one of the biggest producers in Nashville. Have you ever heard of Amanda Jones?"

"Yeah, she's really good," he said.

"He discovered her when he was with Dream Works. When he left them last year, he started his own label called Huge Records. He's in the third house past the Writers Group building on 17th. It's worth a try."

Huge Records was located in a restored historic house at the end of Music Row. When he walked up the steps, opened the door, and told the receptionist why he was there, he was prepared for the usual question of, "Do you have an appointment?" But he was shocked when instead, she smiled and asked, "What's your name?"

"Ahh," he was so stunned he had to think about it for a second.

She laughed. "That's not really that hard of a question. Do you remember your name?"

"I'm sorry, I wasn't expecting you to ask me that." He said grinning, "I'm Nash, Nash Cooper."

She picked up a small handwritten note off her desk and looked at it. "Have a seat, Nash, I'll be right back."

A few minutes later she returned. "Scott will see you when he gets off the phone. Would you like some coffee or a Coke?"

"Scott Hugley will see me?" He said a bit too loud, with wide eyes.

She flashed him her smile again. "He's the only one back there. So, coffee or Coke?"

"Ahh," he stammered, "coffee please."

His hands were shaking so much, he could barely sip his coffee without spilling it.

"You must be Nash," he heard a loud deep voice say in the doorway.

He looked up. "Yes sir, that's me," He said.

"Hi, nice to meet you, Nash. I'm Scott Hugley, come with me."

On shaky legs, he followed Scott back to his office and took a seat in front of his desk.

"You have something for me to listen to?"

Nash reached in his pocket and pulled out his last flash-drive. "Yes sir," he said, handing him the drive, "There are 10 songs on here."

He wanted to tell him about the songs and the recording, but before he could say anything Scott stuck the drive into his computer and hit the play button.

Staring intensely into Nash's eyes, Scott listened to about 30 seconds of the first song, then stopped and listened to the next one. 30 seconds later, he stopped that one and went to the next. It took him less than five minutes to listen to all 10 of them, never once breaking eye contact with Nash. It was an extremely nerve-racking and uncomfortable five minutes.

Scott pulled out the flash drive, laid it on his desk, and leaned back in his chair, thinking.

"I understand you met Dino Zimmerman last night," he said.

"Who?" Nash asked.

"Dino Zimmerman. He told me he met you at Shoney's."

"Oh yeah, I met him while I was eating my dinner. He didn't tell me his last name, but he was a really nice guy."

Scott smiled. "Do you have any idea who he is?"

"No, not really. All I know is that he's a studio musician. He explained to me how a Nashville Number chart worked."

Scott leaned back in his chair and laughed. "Well, he definitely would know how those work. Nash, Dino Zimmerman isn't just a studio musician, he is one of *THE* studio musicians here in Nashville. He's played on more number one records than any other musician that's ever lived."

Nash's mouth flew open with wide eyes. "Really? He didn't act like he was anybody at all."

"When you get back home, dig through your albums and CDs, I guarantee you his name will be on nine out of 10 of them. Son, you met a true Nashville legend last night and you didn't even know it."

"Wow!" Nash exclaimed, "I wish I'd known."

"There's no way you could have unless you were part of the music business around here. Session guys don't get a lot of press, and honestly, they like it that way."

He picked the flash drive up off his desk and handed it back to Nash. "Do you know what makes a hit record?"

Nash shrugged his shoulders. "I thought I did. That's why I recorded those songs. I thought they were *ALL* hits."

"Dino called me last night and asked me to meet with you and listen to your songs. I'm not sure what you did, but whatever it was, it impressed him enough to make that call. That's why you're sitting here right now."

Nash smiled. "And I really appreciate it."

"When I asked Dino what he wanted me to do with you, he said, and I quote, 'Tell him the truth.' So here it is."

He leaned forward in his chair and made eye contact once again. "Nash, the truth is...no one really knows what makes a hit record, not me or anyone else in this town. But when we hear one...we know it instantly."

Nash held up the flash drive. "You only listened to a few seconds of each song. How could you tell if it was a hit or not? You skipped over the best parts."

"That's your problem, Nash," Scott said, "There are no 'best parts' to a hit song. It's obvious when you hear the first note. Of course, I may be wrong, it's just my opinion, but I didn't hear one hit song on that flash drive. Please don't get me wrong, you sing great, you certainly have the looks, and you have a few good songs here, but I'm not looking for a good song...I'm looking for a *GREAT* song, a song that hits you in the heart and takes over your emotions. A song you have to hear again and again...a song they'll be talking about 50 years from now."

He stood up behind his desk. "Dino Zimmerman is one of my dearest friends. For whatever reason, he sees something in you, and because of that friendship, I'm going to try to help you. So here's the deal...my door will always be open to you, all you have to do is call. Go home to Florida in the morning and don't come back until you have written that hit record. If and when that happens...I promise you...I'll make you a star."

He glanced at his watch. "What's your plans for the rest of the night?"

Nash shrugged. "I really don't have any, why?"

"Dino's doing a session right now down the street. Do you want to hear him play?"

15

THE PARTY

J ake jerked awake, startled by the ringing. In the dark, he fumbled for his cellphone, flipped on the light, and glanced at the clock. It was 3:39 am. "Hello." His voice was low and gravelly.

"Jake, we're on the way to the hospital," he heard Josh's voice say, "I think this is it."

Jake jumped out of bed and threw on his clothes. He ran to the bathroom, brushed his teeth, and rushed to his truck. Two hours later, he ran through the doors of the Methodist hospital in Fort Worth. Reverend Ancel and his wife Margaret waved at him from the lobby.

"How is she?" he asked, running up to them. "Has she had the baby yet?"

Margaret smiled. "No, not yet, don't worry you made it in time, but it won't be long now."

The three of them paced the room waiting and praying for almost an hour before Josh walked up to them smiling and crying at the same time.

"It's all over," he said wiping his eyes, "Brooklyn did great and little Ginny...she's...she's beautiful."

Jake raised his head. "Ginny?"

"Yes, sir," Josh said, smiling, "We named her Virginia Eileen Arnett. And if you don't mind...we'd like to call her Ginny."

Jake's eyes filled with tears. "I would love that. When can we see them? I can't wait to meet my granddaughter."

RAINE STOOD up from his folding chair and said the words out loud with the rest of the group.

"God give me the serenity to accept the things that I cannot change, the courage to change the things I can, and the wisdom to know the difference."

He held up his right hand, looked at the chip he had just received, and read the words that were printed on it out loud, "Nine months sober."

After he helped put away the chairs, he saw Louise's car pull up outside the front door and stop.

As they pulled away, she looked over at him and said, "Raine, I'm so proud of you. Not just for the A.A. thing, but for how you have turned your life around. Coop told me that he gave you a promotion today, and a raise. Is that true?"

"Yeah. He put me in charge of the fairway groundskeeping crew," he said, "and thanks, I'm kind of proud of myself too. I can't believe how much my life has changed, and so quickly." He looked over at her, "I owe all that to you. I'm not sure how, but someday I'm going to repay you for everything you've done for me."

She smiled. "You don't owe me a thing. I'm just glad I could help you."

"One day I'm gonna pay you back," he said, "Just wait and see."

"So how's Dave? I haven't seen him in a while. Is he still working with you?"

He nodded. "Yeah, every day he can get out of bed. Honestly, It hasn't been easy trying to get clean living with crazy Dave."

Louise laughed. "I can imagine, but he's so sweet. How could you ever get mad at Dave."

"Trust me, it's not that hard. Especially when I'm trying to get some sleep so I can go to work the next day, and he's up dancing around drunk, blaring music. He can be a real pain in the ass sometimes."

"But we all still love him, right?" She said laughing.

IT HAD BEEN over a year since that day on the beach when Louise found him. Since then, Raine had landed a good job, had a nice place to live, quit drinking, started attending Alcoholics Anonymous meetings, and had re-discovered church.

For most of his adult life, he had believed that God had forgotten about him, or had forsaken him for the things he had done. But with Coop and Louise's help, and a few long talks with his new pastor, he stopped thinking that way.

It did take him a while to understand and accept it, but he finally believed that there was nothing too big God wouldn't forgive him for if he would just asked Him. He had been lost and miserable for so many years, not realizing that the only one who had turned his back...was him. For the first time in almost 30 years, he didn't hate himself and was actually happy with his life and who he was.

His friend Dave was doing better as well. He wouldn't go to church and constantly refused to attend the A.A. meetings with him, but worked almost every day beside Raine doing whatever he asked him to do around the golf course. He wasn't an official employee, but every Friday when Raine picked up his paycheck, there was always $400 cash inside the envelope. The first time it happened, Raine walked into Coop's office and asked him about the money.

"400 cash?" Coop said giving him a phony astonished look, "I have no idea what you're talking about. But if that cash somehow made its way back to Dave, well, that would have nothing to do with me or the LaCita Country Club. It would be against the law for me to do that sort of thing."

Then he winked at him and said, "Got it?"

It didn't take Raine long to realize that giving Dave $400 cash was not a good idea. The first Friday he gave it to him, he took off and didn't return until Tuesday. In those four days, he had spent every cent of it and looked like hell when he finally showed up.

Raine wouldn't let him back in the house. "So this is the way it's gonna be?" he yelled, "You work a few days and then go on a binge and drink up every penny? That's not cool, Dave. This is no way to repay Louise and Coop for all their help!"

Dave dropped his head and shuffled his feet. "I didn't spend it all on booze," he said. He reached in his pocket, pulled out a plastic bag, and held it up. " I scored some killer weed too."

Raine slammed the door in his face and made him sleep outside that night. The next morning, he made him take a shower in the equipment barn before he let him back in the house. While Dave was taking his shower, Raine searched his clothes and found a half-pint of bourbon in the back pocket, but the marijuana was gone. He didn't really care about the whiskey, it was legal and because *he* didn't drink anymore didn't mean that Dave couldn't, but there was no way he was going to allow him to bring drugs inside Coop's little house.

"What did you do with the pot?" He asked him when he got back.

"Don't worry, it's all gone," Dave said with a grin.

Raine frowned and stared at him. "I don't think this is funny. We need to get something straight between us right now. I'm trying my best to clean up my life and you are not helping. You of all people know why I'm doing this; so that one day if I ever have a chance to meet my daughter, she won't be ashamed of me and maybe forgive me for what I did to her. You know that, right?"

Dave nodded and looked away. "Yeah. I'm sorry man."

"I want you to understand this, so look at me," Raine said. Dave lifted his head.

"Louise and Coop are great people who sincerely are trying to help us. That means me *and* you. They deserve more than this for everything they've done and if you want to keep staying here with me, they're going to get it. Do you understand what I'm trying to say?"

"I think so," he said, "No more weed?"

"Damn it, Dave," he yelled, "It's not just the weed, it's the booze too. You've been gone for four damn days and they've been worried sick about you, and so have I. If you want to keep receiving their help, and mine, you have to at least try."

Dave sat down on the couch and looked up at Raine. "Do you want me to go back to the street? I'll understand if you do."

"No. That's not what I'm saying at all. I just want you to try to clean up your act a little and act like a normal person. Do you think you can do that?"

He didn't respond for a long time. "I'll try," he finally said, "but I don't think I can stop drinking like you did. To be honest, I don't really want to. You have your daughter, something to live for...I have nothing."

"You're wrong! You have me, and Coop, and Louise...and we all care about you. Isn't that enough?"

He nodded his head slowly and smiled. "I promise I'll try to do better."

That was the last time Raine gave Dave the full $400. If he needed something, all he had to do was ask, but from then on Raine deposited his weekly cash into a savings account at his bank. Dave still got drunk two or three nights a week, but he never disappeared again.

THAT CHRISTMAS, Dave, and Raine helped Louise decorate her house and her property, and she invited them to attend her annual Christmas Eve party. It was a big blowout with all of her friends with lots of food and booze. It was difficult, but Raine made it through the night without drinking, and Dave surprised them all by pacing himself and not getting very drunk.

After all the guests left, Louise asked Dave and Raine to stick around, so she could give them their Christmas presents.

"I'll be right back," Dave said and ran out the door.

"Where is he going?" Louise asked.

"I'm not sure, but I think he's going back to the little house to get your Christmas presents," Raine said.

"So how are you doing?" She asked, curling up on the couch next to him.

"I'm doing good," he said with a smile, "how about you?"

"This is always the hardest time of the year. Bill loved Christmas, that's why I do all these silly decorations. It's my way to honor him and not feel so alone."

"Really, you're lonely?" Raine said, surprised, "I thought with all of your friends and everything you do around here...well... I guess I've never really thought about it."

She sighed."This is a big house and everywhere I look I see Bill. I wish he could've gotten to know you the way you are now. I'm sure you two would have become good friends."

"Me too," Raine said, "From what Coop tells me, he was the best. Have you thought about dating again?"

"Now you sound like Melissa and Karen," she said with a chuckle, " Before *you* showed up that was their life goal. They were always trying to fix me up with one of their friends."

Raine lowered his eyebrows. "Before I showed up? What does that mean?"

She sighed again and laughed. "They are both convinced that there's something between you and me," she said softly, looking into his eyes, "I keep telling them that they're wrong, that we're just friends."

She reached over and took his hand in hers. "We *are* just friends, right?"

He let go of her hand and stood up. "Louise, you know I love you, right?"

A bit surprised by his quick actions, she looked up at him and tried to smile. "I sure hope you do," she said softly.

"Well, I do. And because I love you so much, I have to tell you the absolute truth. I've thought about it a lot. Louise, I think that you are one of the most beautiful women I've ever met. I'm not just talking about your obvious physical beauty, but you are the most beautiful person on the inside I've ever known. The only one I can think of that even comes close is Ginny. I hope you know how wonderful you really are."

Raine sat back down beside her. "And if we were together, as a couple...that would make me the happiest and the luckiest man that ever lived."

Her eyes glistened in the light. "It would make me happy too." She said.

Raine looked at her and gave her a gentle smile. "But I can't do that. Not to you. Oh, I would love it, but deep down inside, you have to know that I'm the wrong guy. I don't deserve someone like you. You need someone that's as beautiful as you, inside and out, and we both know that's not me."

Before she could answer, they heard Dave open the front door, climbing the steps.

"HO HO HO!" He shouted, "Santa Claus is here, Merry Christmas!"

Raine had hesitated when Dave had asked him for $2,500 of his money a few weeks earlier because it was almost all he had, but that night he found out why he wanted it.

Dave walked into the room with one huge long box and three small ones. Two of the small ones were Raine's gifts, one for Louise, and one for him.

Dave played Santa Claus and started by handing Louise their presents. Raine handed Dave his, and Dave pushed the large box over in front of him. "That's for you, Dude," he said with a wide grin, "but don't open it yet."

They sat anxiously watching Louise open the two presents from them. Raine's present was a beautiful emerald necklace. Dave's was the matching earrings.

"Guys!" she exclaimed, "This is beautiful!" She jumped up and ran to the mirror over the fireplace mantel and put on the necklace and earrings. "I love them." she said, throwing her arms around their necks.

"Who's next?" Dave asked excitedly.

"Open yours from me," Raine said.

Like a little kid, he grabbed the box, tore off the bow, and ripped it open. It was a new iPhone. "DUDE!" he shouted, taking it out of the box, "This is so rad! Very cool!"

Raine smiled at him. "Now I'll be able to find you next time you disappear."

He held the phone up to his ear and said, "Hello. Yes, this is David Baker, what can I do for you today?"

Raine didn't react to his slip of the tongue, but in the five years he had known him, that was the first time he'd ever said his last name.

"Now open your presents," Dave said, almost giddy, "but open Louise's first."

She pointed at a large box sitting behind the tree. "It's that one."

Dave jumped up, took hold of the huge box, and slid it up in front of Raine. "It's kinda heavy," he said grinning wide.

Carefully, Raine removed the big red bow and laid it on the coffee table, and ripped the wrapping paper away from the top of the box.

When he looked inside, he saw several black canvas bags with BOSE, printed in white letters on them. He reached in the box, pulled out one of the smaller bags, and laid it on the floor in front of him.

"What is this?" he asked, completely confused.

Not able to hold back his excitement any longer, Dave ran to the box and started pulling out all of the black bags, laying them out on the floor. "It's a Bose tower. You won't believe how good it sounds. Louise and I heard it at The Guitar Center in Orlando. It totally rocks, man. You're gonna love it."

It took them about 15 minutes to get all the pieces out of the black bags and the system hooked up. "Isn't it cool?" Dave shouted.

"Yeah, it's way cool," Raine said, "but what's it for? I don't have anything to plug into it."

Dave looked over at Louise and burst out laughing. "Now open mine!"

Inside of Dave's box was a microphone, a boom stand, a small mixing board, and a black guitar case. Raine pulled out the guitar case, laid it on the coffee table, and opened it.

"It's the one you were always looking at in the window of that pawn shop. The guy said it was an authentic 1975 Les Paul. It cost a fortune, but Louise helped me pay for it. You're gonna need to give her that $400 for the next couple of years," he said laughing, "Come on, plug it in. I want to hear you play."

When Raine got the guitar tuned up and plugged in, Louise asked, "How long has it been since you held a guitar in your hands?"

He shook his head, strumming the strings. "I don't remember, maybe six or seven years."

"Is it a good one? "Dave asked.

Raine smiled at him. "It's a great one, buddy, maybe the best electric guitar ever made. It's the best gift I've ever received from anyone. Thank you...you are a great friend."

He bent over and hugged Raine. "You're the best friend I've ever had. I love you, Bro."

"I love you too, you big dumbass," he said with a tearful chuckle, "I can't believe you spent all your money on this, on me."

Dave leaned back and used his sleeve to wipe the tears out of his eyes. "Well, you won't let me buy any good weed anymore, so I might as well spend it on something cool. Come on, Dude, turn it up. I want to hear you rock out!"

Raine played for a few minutes then put it down because his fingers were killing him. "It's gonna take a while to build my calluses back," He said rubbing his fingertips.

It took them two trips in the golf cart to get the BOSE tower and the rest of the equipment from Louise's living room to the little house in the woods.

It was almost 11 o'clock when they finished unloading it. "See you in a little while," He said to Dave.

"Where are you going?"

"To my church," he said, "They're having a midnight service."

"Can I go?"

That was the first time Dave had ever asked Raine to go to church. "Sure, hop in. If we hurry we'll just make it."

Dave didn't say a word during the service but three times, Raine saw him wipe tears from his eyes with his sleeve.

On their ride back from the church, Dave was unusually quiet. "Did you like it?" Raine asked.

"Like what?"

"Going to church, the service."

Dave shrugged his shoulders. "I guess so."

"You guess so? What is that supposed to mean? Don't you believe in God?"

"I don't want to talk about it," he said looking away, "But I did like your church. There were a lot of nice people there. I see why you like it so much."

The next morning, Christmas morning, they found a good place to set up the equipment and Raine played for almost two hours. The fingertips on his left hand were raw and throbbing, but he didn't care. He was loving playing music again after all those years.

At one o'clock they got into the golf cart and drove to Louise's house and had a big turkey and dressing Christmas lunch with all the trimmings. Louise and Raine marveled at how much Dave could eat. After his third full plate of turkey, ham, dressing, mashed potatoes, candied yams, green bean casserole, and sweet creamed corn, he started on the desserts. One piece of pecan, one piece of pumpkin, and one piece of coconut pie. After that, he laid down on the floor by the television and fell sound asleep.

"Well, at least I don't have to worry about finding room in my fridge for the leftovers," Louise said laughing.

"You want to hear the worst part?" Raine asked, with a chuckle, "He had a big breakfast this morning a few hours before we came over here. He is an eating machine."

They stepped over Dave and settled on the couch. "We didn't finish what we were talking about last night," she said.

Raine nodded. "I guess not, but there's really not much more to say. I love you, Louise, but you know damn well I'm the wrong guy."

She frowned. "Why do you keep saying that?"

"Because it's the truth. You just don't understand. One miss-step and I'm back to square one. I'm barely hanging on. It was all I could do not to drink last night at your party. That's not what you need in your life, Constantly wondering if I'm gonna fall off the wagon and go crazy again."

"Raine, I'm not worried about that. If it happens, you'll just start over again. I know it's not easy, but I believe in you and I know you can do it."

He shook his head and frowned at her. "You're wrong. If I fall off the wagon this time, I know that I'll never make it back. This is my final chance, my last shot. If I blow this...it's over for me."

"That's why I want to be there for you," she said, "So you can lean on me."

"And I want you here...as my good friend. But that's all it can be," He took her hand and looked into her eyes, "Louise, I do love you, but you need someone that's stable, someone that *you* can lean on. And you know that's not me."

EVERY NEW YEAR'S EVE, for the last 18 years, Coop filled his golf cart with a few cases of champagne and drove down the fairway passing out the bottles to his good friends, reminding them about the New Year's Eve party at the club. On his way down the 14th fairway, he heard music. It was coming from the little house in the woods.

He pulled up close to the house and listened. He had heard Louise talk about how great Raine was many times in the past, and he assumed that he must have been pretty good when he was young, but the longer he sat there listening to him sing and play, he realized what she had been trying to tell him. Raine wasn't just good, he was great, and apparently, the years hadn't taken away any of his talents. After listening for almost an hour, he grabbed a bottle out of the box and knocked on the door.

"Hey Coop, what's up?" Dave said when he opened the door.

"I'm just driving around passing out a little bubbly for New Year's Eve. I know Raine doesn't drink, but I thought you might like a little champagne to celebrate the New Year."

"Thanks, Dude!" Dave said, taking the bottle out of his hand.

"Are you guys coming to the big party tonight?"

"What party?" Dave asked.

"The New Year's Eve party at the club. We got a band coming and everything. It's gonna be fun. You two should come."

Raine walked up to the door. "I really appreciate the invitation, Coop, but that party is for the members and I wouldn't feel right being there."

"Are you sure?"

"Yeah. We're just gonna hang around here and watch the ball drop on television, but thanks anyway."

NASH COOPER WAS NOT LOOKING FORWARD to playing a New Year's Eve party. Especially one at a damn country club full of old people, but he needed the money so he packed his guitar in his car, and started driving to the gig.

Ever since he had gotten back from Nashville, things had not been good between him and his band. When he told them about Scott Hugley, and what he said, instead of getting excited for him, they just rolled their eyes and walked away. Over the past months, each gig had gotten worse. He could actually hear them moaning, laughing, and snickering at him behind his back. At their rehearsals, all they did was complain and barely play, when he tried to get them to learn one of his new original songs.

Almost every day since he had arrived back from Nashville, he had spent his time trying to come up with that magical hit song Scott had talked about, but so far he had nothing. He had spent hours staring blankly at his piano trying to think of something unique. He had written almost 20 new songs and there were three or four that he thought were pretty good, but nothing great. Of course, the band didn't like any of them.

On his way to the New Years' gig at the La Cita Country Club, he came up with a plan. After all, he was just weeks away from signing a major record contract, and it was a bit beneath him to be forced to play all those worn-out songs to a bunch of old drunk people like he was some kind of a nobody.

He decided to let the band start the night and play the first set without him. Then on the second set, he would come on stage and do a real show, performing only his original songs. He was sure it was a great idea, giving them a small taste of one of his future concerts that they would all be paying big bucks for soon.

When he arrived and told the band his plan, they all moaned and tried to talk him out of it. "Nash, please, this is a New Year's Eve party and these people came here to dance! They don't want to hear your original songs," They all told him, but it was his gig, he had signed the contract and if they wanted to get paid, they had to do what he said.

"You guys just don't get it," he said, "I'm doing these people a favor. In a few years, they'll all be telling their friends about the night they got to see Nash Cooper live and up close."

The crowd started clapping when the band walked to the stage and began tuning up. The air was filled with sounds of laughter and conversations. Occasionally someone would blow one of the small horns that were laying on each table alongside the silly looking hats, noisemakers, and paper streamers.

When the band started playing the first song, the temporary wooden dance floor in front of them immediately filled and stayed that way until they took their first break.

The volume of the room had increased with the hum of the people talking, shouting, and laughing. The waitresses looked like a swarm of bees working their way around the packed room, carrying their trays of bright, multi-colored drinks above their heads. You could almost feel the excitement in the room.

When the band walked back into the room and got on stage, the crowd actually started cheering and clapping, anxiously waiting for the music to start up again.

When the musicians were all tuned up and ready to start, reluctantly, Billy Lang, the guitar player, walked up to the microphone and read the words on the piece of paper that Nash had written and given to him backstage.

"Ladies and gentlemen," he began, "tonight we have a very special treat for you. Please welcome to the stage, direct from Nashville, Huge Records recording artist, Nash Cooper!"

Obviously surprised, the crowd began looking around and applauding politely.

Nash was standing in the back of the room by the sound man and the mixing board when Billy made the announcement. He broke into his best, well-rehearsed smile and began walking up the dance floor toward the stage, waving at the crowd.

The applause dwindled down to a smattering and had actually stopped before Nash made it all the way to the stage. But that didn't stop him from waving his arms in the air and shouting, "Thank you, thank you!"

When he reached the stage he slipped on his guitar and walked up to the microphone. "I am so happy to be here in Titusville tonight to perform my show for you. To tell you the truth, I really enjoy performing to small crowds like this, rather than in the big concert halls. It's so much more intimate. I would like to start my show tonight with a song I wrote a few weeks ago. By the way, this song will be on my new album coming out on Huge Records soon."

He looked around the room and gave them his best smile. "You can tell all your friends that you heard it here first."

Coop was in the kitchen when he noticed the silence coming from the ballroom. He rushed out of the kitchen and leaned against the wall, only a few feet away from the stage.

The dance floor was empty and the room was eerily silent except for the music coming from the singer who was sitting on a stool in the middle of the stage. When the song ended, the crowd applauded politely, but they were not smiling.

One of his friends who was sitting at the table a few feet away got out of his chair, walked up to him, and whispered, "Who the hell is this guy?"

Coop shrugged. "I don't know. How long has this been going on?"

"This is his fourth or fifth song. I think he said his name was Nash something. I've never heard of him, but he's acting like he's some kind of a fucking star," his friend said frowning. "Coop, I love you, but I didn't pay 200 bucks tonight to hear this shit!"

Coop waited until Nash finished his song, then walked up to the stage. "What's this?" he asked. "When we talked on the phone, I told you I wanted you to play dance music," he pointed at the empty dance floor, "and they're not dancing."

Nash smiled. "Yeah, I know, but I thought I'd do something extra special tonight and let them hear some of my original music."

Trying to keep his cool, Coop smiled back at him and said, "I appreciate the effort, but this is New Year's Eve and these people paid a lot of money to come here tonight to dance. Tell you what, I'll have you back for a special night someday, so you can play them your original songs, but tonight I need you to play some rock 'n' roll that they recognize. How about that?"

Nash's expression dropped and his smile faded. "I don't think so. I would prefer to finish my show now, so would you please step away from my stage."

It was all Coop could do to keep from grabbing Nash and jerking him off the stool. "It's not *YOUR* stage, you arrogant little shit, it's *MY* stage. So either start playing songs these people came to hear, or pack up your crap and leave!" He yelled.

Nash stood up and looked down at him from the elevated stage. "We'll be happy to leave, just as soon as we get our check."

Coop's face flushed. "If you leave I'm not paying you a fucking dime!"

Nash turned around and looked at the band. "Take a break. We may be through for tonight."

He took off his guitar, stepped down off the stage, and looked Coop in the eyes. "I suggest you go read your contract. There's nothing in there about what songs I have to play. I could sing Happy Birthday all night if I wanted to."

Coop looked back at one of the musicians. "Could you at least put on some break music?"

When he got to his office he pulled out the contract and read it. Nash was correct, there was nothing specific about the songs they were required to perform. The only thing specific was the amount they were earning and the hours they were required to play.

When he walked back into the ballroom, the dance floor was packed. The sound man had put on some classic rock and the party was back in full swing.

Coop found Nash and the band sitting at a table on the outside patio. "You're right, it doesn't say anything about the songs you have to play, so you've got me by the balls. All I can do now is to appeal to you out of common courtesy."

He looked past Nash to the band. "Here's your Check. Do what you want. But you guys know damn well what I hired you to do, so please don't do this to me. Please don't ruin this night for everyone in that room."

Nash took the check out of Coop's hand and put it in his pocket. "You guys can do what you want, but I'm done for the night," he said, walking away.

Billy Lange looked up at Coop. "Don't worry, sir. We're not going anywhere. We'll finish out the night, but Nash sang most of the songs. None of us are really good singers, but we'll do our best."

"Thank you guys," Coop said, "you saved my life and I really appreciate it."

He turned to walk away, then got an idea and stopped. "If I could find a singer, would you guys be willing to back him up?"

They all nodded. "Sure," Billy said, "that would be better than having to listen to me sing all night."

Coop ran down the steps, jumped into his golf cart, and drove to the little house.

The second Dave opened the door, Coop said, "Raine, I need your help bad, I'm in real trouble and I need a huge favor."

Raine could see the stress in his eyes. "Sure, anything, what do you need? What's wrong?"

Dave held on to the roof of the cart, standing on the back rack where the golf clubs were usually kept, and Coop and Raine rode in the seats as they flew down the fairway back to the clubhouse.

When they arrived, the band was playing and the dance floor was packed. Dave, Raine, and Coop stood in the back and listened to the band a few minutes.

Although the crowd didn't seem to notice how bad the singer really was, it only took a few verses before Coop looked at Raine and shouted over the music, "See why I need you?"

The band was playing Van Morrison's Brown Eyed Girl, a song Raine had sung about a million times, so he walked to the stage and took over singing the song. The crowd may not have noticed how bad the first singer was, but they definitely noticed the improvement when Raine started singing.

When he finished the song, the room filled with the sound of applause and cheers. As soon as the country club members began to realize that it was their groundskeeper on the stage doing the singing, they applauded even louder.

Fortunately, the band had some lyric sheets, so Raine was able to fake his way through the rest of the sets. After the big countdown at midnight, Raine led the room singing Auld Lang Syne.

Right before they started the countdown, a waitress walked up and handed him and the rest of the band a glass of champagne. While they all sang Old Lang Syne, he held the glass in his hand and fought with himself not to drink it. After he finished the count down, the sound man put on a slow song, so everyone could dance.

He handed the glass of champagne to the drummer. "You want this? I don't drink." Then, to avoid any more temptation, he stepped off the stage and walked outside to the patio and leaned against the rail.

It was a beautiful clear night without a cloud in the sky. Below him, he could see the putting green and the number one tee box, lit up by the bright moon glowing through the trees.

Raine couldn't stop smiling. He had that feeling inside that he hadn't felt in years. It was the afterglow from the rush of a performance. He loved that feeling and had forgotten how much he missed it.

Gazing up at the moon, he said a quick prayer, thanking God for putting him back on a stage.

"There you are," he heard a voice say behind him, "Wow, you were great tonight. Did you have fun?"

Raine turned around and smiled. "Thanks, Louise. Did I sound Ok?"

"Are you kidding? Didn't you hear them? Everyone loved you."

He grinned. "It felt like old times and yeah, I loved it."

Coop opened the door and walked up to them. "Will you look at that?" He said pointing toward the ballroom.

Through the glass, they could see the tables and the people sitting around them. Coop looked at his watch. "It's 12:20, by this time last year that room was completely empty, but they're all still here."

"Why aren't they leaving?" Raine asked, "What are they waiting for?"

Coop smiled at him. "They're waiting for you to come back and sing some more. Are you up for one more set?"

When Raine stepped back on the stage, everyone in the room started clapping, including the band. Sitting next to the sound man behind the mixing board, Nash Cooper fumed. "I don't get it," he said, "what's so wonderful about this old guy?"

But what really angered him the most, was when Raine began singing again, nobody danced. Instead, they just sat there listening to him intensely. And when he finished, they actually stood and cheered.

"I thought this was supposed to be a dance and they didn't want a show." Nash growled.

When Raine finished the song he looked around the room and smiled. "Thank you, I really appreciate it. It's been a long long time since I've stood on a stage like this, and that's my problem. It's been so long I can't remember any more songs to sing for you."

From the back of the room, he heard Dave's voice yell, "Sing one of your songs! Sing em' something you wrote!"

The crowd started clapping again. "Are you sure?" He said, looking around the room.

"Yes!" He heard several people shout.

He turned around and looked at the guitar player. "Could I borrow your axe?"

Sitting on the same stool in the exact same spot Nash Cooper had sat in a few hours earlier, Raine began to strum the strings of the guitar and sing.

When Nash heard the song, he looked at the sound man and said, "Record this."

"Why do you want to record him?" He asked.

Frowning at him, Nash didn't answer. Instead, he leaned over him and hit the record button.

Raine sang seven more original songs that night. Six of them were supposed to be on his third RCA album that was never released. Each of them received thunderous applause and cheers.

"I'd like to finish tonight with a song I've never performed before," he said, smiling at the audience. "It's not a new song, in fact, I wrote this song almost 15 years ago. I wrote it for someone I've loved my whole life but have never met. It's called, From Ashes."

The moment Raine played the first chord of the song, cold chills ran down Nash Cooper's spine and he instantly knew what Scott Hugley had been talking about. And, he also knew that he had finally found that elusive, magical song he had been searching for that would make him a star.

PART III

16

IMITATION OF LIFE

J ake's father was brilliant. He was always amazed when he would go to him with questions about his homework, no matter what the subject was, he would instantly know the answer.

His father's favorite subject was American History and almost every night after dinner, Jake would take long walks with him around their small town square listening to him tell stories about the forefathers and how the United States began. He was a true patriot and loved his country.

During the '60s and the civil rights movement, his father became very unpopular with most of the locals, because of his outspoken stance. The local chapter of the Ku Klux Klan even burned a cross in their front yard, but that didn't stop him or slow him down. He lost many of his long time friends because he believed in the Golden Rule and almost every day of Jake's life his father would say it.

"Jake, if you always treat people, no matter who they are, what color they are, or what they have done to you, the way you would like them to treat you, God will reap great blessings over you."

Then he would always wink at him, laugh, and say, "Now, of course, this doesn't apply if you're playing poker."

As Jake grew up and witnessed hatred and bigotry around him, his father's words in a speech he had given to the local City Council always came to his mind:

> "In America, my America, a man is only judged by his character, not by the color of his skin.
>
> In the Constitution, my Constitution, it says that all men are created equal.
>
> And in the Bible, my Bible, it says God made man in his own image and he didn't mention any specific color.
>
> However, it *DOES* say…that it's not our job to judge, and that we are supposed to love each other and not hate."

Jake was there that night, and even though his father was booed and shouted at from his small-minded neighbors in the audience, Jake was proud of him and beamed with pride.

The best advice his father ever gave him, the advice that he had tried to live his life by, came the day he left for Nashville.

His father helped him load the last cardboard box in his trunk and leaned against the car. "Jake, it's a cruel world out there and I can only pray that I've raised you to be strong enough to handle what is about to be thrown at you. Son, there are a lot of stupid people in this world… try not to be one of them."

He handed Jake his Bible. "I want you to have this, to read whenever you can. When you're faced with something you're unsure of, maybe a difficult decision, an unpopular decision, trust your heart and do what you know is right, even if it causes you great pain and trouble. Because those feelings in your heart is God talking to you. If you'll listen to him, he will guide you down the right path every time."

JAKE HAD READ that when a child is produced by a black father and a white mother, it was not uncommon for the child to show no signs of the mixed race. It was possible for the child to have blonde hair, blue eyes, and white skin, or brown eyes, black curly hair and brown skin. It was also possible for the child to have a mixture.

Jake didn't care what little Ginny looked like, but he was hoping that she would share traits from both of her parents, so the world would be able to see who she truly was, and hopefully allow her to cherish both sides of her heritage.

Of course, he had learned that his father had been right, the world was full of stupid people and he knew that she would be rejected by a few idiots because she wasn't black enough or white enough.

One of Virginia's favorite old movies that she made him watch with her every time it aired on cable television, was called, Imitation Of Life. He couldn't count the times they had watched it, but ever since the day Brooklyn had told him that she was pregnant with Josh's baby, that movie had been on his mind.

Virginia's favorite version of the movie was the one made in 1959, years before the civil rights movement. It starred Lana Turner and was a story about a movie star that hired a black housekeeper to take care of her house and help raise her daughter while she was away on her movie shoots. The black housekeeper also had a daughter about the same age, but she was fair-skinned and easily passed for white. The movie star was very generous and not prejudiced at all, and as a result, the two girls were raised together in the same beautiful house experiencing the same life of privilege. Because she could, the housekeeper's daughter rejected her African-American heritage and grew up living her life as a white girl.

As an adult, she becomes famous herself and completely rejects her mother in public and hides her true identity from her friends and the rest of the world. It has to have one of the saddest endings of any movie ever made, when her mother dies alone and her daughter finally admits who she truly is, begging for forgiveness as she follows behind the horse-drawn carriage carrying her mother's casket.

That movie and the title, Imitation Of Life, was incredibly ironic. The last time they had watched it together, only a few months before Virginia had died, she had looked at him with tears in her eyes and said, "If Brooklyn ever has a black child, promise me you will never let that happen to her." It was as if she had a premonition of what was to come.

He realized that the world had changed since that movie had been made, but not for everyone. He hated the thoughts of that but planned to vow to little Ginny that as long as he was alive he would be there for her, to protect her, and to do his best to shield her from that kind of ignorance.

———

JAKE HEARD her the second he stepped off the elevator, and like her mother, she was born with two powerful lungs. Her crying echoed down the halls at a deafening volume.

He followed the sound to Brooklyn's room and stepped inside. When Brooklyn saw him she smiled and said softly, "Hi daddy."

Jake grinned wide, "I think we may have another singer in the family," he said, walking up to the bed, "I could hear her all the way down the hall."

"I can't get her to stop," Brooklyn said, frustrated, "What am I doing wrong?"

He laughed. "That's the problem with having babies, they don't come with any instructions. There is no right or wrong," he said reaching down to pick little Ginny up, "Don't worry, honey, you'll get the hang of it."

The second he cuddled Ginny in his arms, she stopped crying, looked up into his eyes, and smiled at him. His mind instantly flashed back to the day he had first held Brooklyn when she had done the exact same thing.

"Well hello there, Ginny," he said softly, rocking her in his arms, "I'm your Grandpa Jake. What do you think about that?"

She smiled again and cooed. She had Josh's golden brown skin, Brooklyn's shiny black hair, and her beautiful blue eyes. "Young lady, you are a real looker. Your daddy's gonna have to get a big stick to keep all the boys away from you."

"Isn't she beautiful," Josh said, looking down at her.

"Yes, she is," he said, touching her face, "especially when she's smiling like this and doesn't have her face all red and wrinkled up."

Ginny smiled up at him again, reached out her tiny hand, and grabbed his finger. When she did that, Jake's heart instantly melted in his chest…and he fell madly and completely in love.

WHEN RAINE RECEIVED his one-year sober chip from Alcoholics Anonymous, Louise threw him a big party to celebrate his success. She had planned on not serving any alcohol at the party, but he insisted that she did.

"If this chip means anything," he told her, "and if I'm going to survive in this world sober, I have to be around people that drink. What kind of life would that be, if I can't even go to a party?"

"You're right," Louise said, "I'm just so proud of you, I wanted to celebrate your sobriety, not test it."

"And I appreciate the thought, but like we say, '*One day at a time*' and I will do my best to get through this one."

It turned out to be a wonderful party with great food that everyone seemed to enjoy, but only a few of the guests drank alcohol out of respect for Raine. The only one that drank too much, was Dave.

Actually, he had started drinking hours before the party and showed up drunk. That angered Louise and infuriated Coop.

When Dave drank, he was either Jekyll or Hyde—happy and funny, or dark and angry. That was the one thing about him that always confused Raine. When Dave turned dark, he was not the sweet guy everyone loved, he was a completely different person. He could be rude, loud, unpredictable, and easy to anger.

Raine had only seen his dark side a few times in all the years he had known him. The first time happened a few months after they had met when he was still living on the streets. That night Dave actually got into a fight with another homeless man and had beat him senseless. It was all he could do to pull him off the guy. He was in such a rage he was afraid he was going to kill the man.

When he asked him about it the next day, after he had sobered up, Dave acted like he didn't know what he was talking about, like it had never happened.

As far as Raine knew, that was the only time Dave's dark side had resulted in physical violence, because from then on, when he saw the anger in his eyes, he walked away and left him alone for the night. In the year and a half they had lived together in the little house, it had only happened once. When Raine saw it, he went into the bedroom and closed the door. A few minutes later, he would hear the front door slam and Dave wouldn't return until the following afternoon.

Raine had tried to talk to him about it a few times over the years, but each time he brought it up, he acted like he didn't know what he was talking about.

RAINE SAW the look in his eyes, the second Dave walked into the room at the party.

He pulled him into the kitchen. "Are you already drunk?" He said.

Dave smirked. "Who cares if I am?"

"I think you need to go before you do something stupid. Please, Dave, don't cause a scene. Not here at Louise's house."

Dave looked down at him. "Well, I think you need to fuck off and mind your own damn business."

"What's going on?" Coop asked, walking up to them.

"I'm trying to get Dave to go home and sober up."

"I just got here, man!" Dave shouted.

"Keep your voice down!" Coop said, gripping his arm, "I think Raine is right, you need to go home and sleep this off."

When he tried to jerk his arm away, Raine took the other one, and they forced him back through the door into the garage and down the driveway.

"Get in!" Coop said firmly, pointing at his cart.

Dave glared at him, shrugged, and sat down in the cart.

"I'll be right back," Coop said, driving away.

Neither one of them said a word as they drove down the fairway toward the little house. When Coop turned off the fairway down the path through the woods, Dave suddenly yelled, "SCREW THIS!" He smashed his fist against the windshield of the golf cart, jumped out, and ran away into the woods.

Coop slammed on the brakes and stared at the cracked windshield in shocked disbelief of what had just happened. It was the first time he had ever seen Dave show any signs of anger or violence.

When he carefully inspected the broken windshield, he saw specks of red. When he realized what it was, he turned the cart around and drove directly to Alexander Rush's house, his FBI friend.

"Sorry to bother you, Alex," Coop said when he opened the door, "but I need you to look at something."

Coop led him out to the cart and pointed at the cracked windshield. "Is that blood?" Alex asked.

Coop nodded, " Yes. It's Dave's. You said they couldn't get anything from what I gave you before, but what about this? You can get DNA from his blood, right?"

OVER THE NEXT SIX MONTHS, little Ginny gained six pounds and grew almost four inches. According to the pediatrician, she was very healthy and doing great.

Unfortunately, Ginny's body clock seemed to be turned upside down. She slept well during the day but constantly woke up crying during the night, keeping Brooklyn and Josh awake taking turns feeding her, or holding and rocking her trying to get her back to sleep.

The only time she slept through the night was when Grandpa Jake came for a visit. It was one of those unexplained mysteries of life, but all Jake had to do was let her know that he was there and she would sleep through the entire night.

To help them out and let them catch up on sleep, almost every weekend, Jake drove the two hours to Fort Worth and slept on a blowup mattress on the floor next to Ginny's crib.

"Thank you, Daddy," Brooklyn said when he showed up, "I hope you know how much we appreciate this."

"Are you kidding? This is the highlight of my week," he said, "I love being here. Where's my girl?" The minute Ginny saw him, she started smiling and giggling, and Jake did the same.

The next morning, while everybody was still sleeping, Jake slipped out the front door and drove to McDonald's to buy breakfast for everyone. As he drove back to Brooklyn and Josh's apartment, he flipped on his radio but wasn't really listening to the music.

As he drove, he let his mind wander, thinking about how blessed his life was. "Virginia, I sure hope you're up there looking down seeing all of this," he said out loud, "I've never seen Brooklyn happier, and that little girl, well, she's sure got me wrapped around her fingers."

His eyes filled with tears, "Ginny, I sure wish you were here, I miss you so much."

When he pulled into the parking lot of the apartment building and reached for the key to turn off the ignition, he heard the DJ say, "That was a brand new song by *Nash Cooper* called, *From Ashes*. What a great song! I have a feeling we're going to be playing this one a lot."

When he turned the key, the radio went off. He reached down, unbuckled his seatbelt, and grabbed the sacks of food, but when he reached for the door handle, he stopped and looked down at the radio.

"Did he just say, From Ashes?" He put the key back in the ignition, started the truck again, and listened.

The DJ was still talking about the song to someone who had called into the station. "I've never heard of him before," he said, "I believe this is his first one."

"Can you play it again?" The voice on the phone asked.

"I'll have to check with my program director," the DJ said, "but the way these phones are lighting up, I'm pretty sure I'll be playing it again real soon, so don't turn that dial and stay tuned."

Jake ran up the steps to the apartment and opened the door. Josh was in the kitchen pouring a cup of coffee.

"Morning, Jake," he said, "Is that breakfast?"

Jake's mind was on the song and he had forgotten about the sacks full of breakfast he was holding in his hands. He smiled and set the sacks on the kitchen cabinet. "Yeah, I thought I'd cook breakfast this morning," he said laughing.

Jake waited until after they had eaten breakfast before he brought it up. "Do you have a way to listen to FM radio in here?"

"Of course," Brooklyn said, "Why?"

"Could you turn it on KSCS, I think it's 96 point something."

Brooklyn walked to the bookshelf, turned on the stereo, and tuned the dial until she found it. "I think that's it. Why do you want to listen to it now?"

Before he had a chance to explain, the DJ said over the air, "OK folks, we can take a hint. You can stop calling now. Our phone lines have been jammed for the last hour, so we're going to play it again. You might want to write down this name because I think we have a new rising country star. His name is Nash Cooper and the song is called, From Ashes."

Brooklyn froze and stared up at Jake. "From Ashes?" She murmured, "Is it the same song?"

Jake shook his head. "I'm not sure yet."

It only took a few notes of the intro before Josh said, "That's Raine's song!"

Brooklyn and Jake sat on the couch, staring at the speakers listening. When it was over she walked to the bookshelf and turn down the volume. "Who is Nash Cooper, and how did he get that song?"

Jake shrugged his shoulders. "I've never heard of him before."

They heard Ginny crying, so Brooklyn jumped up and ran to get her out of her crib. "I'll be there in a minute," She yelled from the back, "I need to change her diaper and feed her."

While she changed her diaper, Josh looked over at Jake and asked, "You think Raine is back in the business? Maybe he sold his songs to a music publisher or something?"

Jake nodded. "That's what I'm thinking."

"If that's true," Josh said excitedly, "the publishing company would have his address to send his royalties. We could track him down that way. How can we find that out?"

Jake stood up, walked to the kitchen, and poured another cup of coffee. "First, we need to find out the name of the publishing company," he said.

"How do we do that?" Josh asked.

Jake thought for a second. "I guess we could call the radio station and asked them? They have to have that information for their reports to ASCAP and BMI."

Brooklyn walked into the room holding Ginny in her arms. When she saw her grandpa Jake, she reached out her tiny arms for him and giggled. Jake took her from Brooklyn and cradled her in his arms.

"What were you guys talking about," Brooklyn asked.

"I think we know how to track down Raine," Josh said.

Her eyes lit up and sparkled. "Really? How?"

"Jake and I believe that Raine is back in the music business," he said, "We think that he sold that song to a publishing company in Nashville. If he did, they will know how to contact him."

"How do we find the publisher?" She asked.

"The radio station will know," Jake said.

Brooklyn picked up her cell phone off the coffee table. "What were the call letters of that station?"

Jake shifted in his seat trying not to disturb Ginny who was sound asleep in his arms. "KSCS," he said softly, "But before you call them, there's something I'd like to talk to you about."

Brooklyn stopped typing on her phone and looked over at Jake. "Sure, what is it?"

He handed Ginny to Brooklyn and stood up. "There's more to Raine's story that you don't know. I've been struggling over this ever since your mother died and you discovered his letters. It's something I wasn't sure you needed to know...something I thought I would never have to tell you because honestly, I never believed you would find him."

"It must be something awful for you to have kept it a secret," Brooklyn said, "If it is, why tell me now?"

"It's because of her," Jake said pointing at Ginny, "The moment I saw her, everything changed. I realize that none of my blood is running through her veins, but blood has nothing to do with the never-ending, unconditional love I have for her. It's exactly the same way I feel about you."

"What are you trying to say, dad?"

Jake sat down next to her, dropped his head, and sighed. "This is so hard for me to say to you because you just barely found out about Raine. I know why you want to find him and get to know him...he is your biological father and Ginny's biological grandfather. I completely understand why you feel the need to do that."

He took a deep breath, let it out slowly, and stared into her eyes. "I hope he has changed, but the truth is...even if he has, I'm not sure he deserves to meet you...and honestly, I'm not sure I want him around my granddaughter."

"Why not?" She asked confused.

"Because if it had been left up to him...you and Ginny would have never been born."

Choosing his words carefully, he told Brooklyn and Josh the truth about what had happened and exactly what Raine had said to Virginia the last time she had seen him at Gruene Hall.

When he finished, Brooklyn didn't say a word. She just stared down at Ginny, rocking back and forth.

"In his defense," Jake said, "he was very young, naïve, and he was getting terrible advice from very bad people. They were not interested in Raine, just the money that he could make for them."

"Do you think he thought she would actually do it when he gave her the money and walked away?" Josh asked.

"Josh, I don't know what he was thinking. All I do know is that he never called her after that. Not once."

"So what do you think I should do?" Brooklyn asked, "That doesn't sound like the man who wrote me all those letters."

Jake nodded, "I know, I read those letters too and they were full of remorse. I'm sure he regrets what he did now, but has he really changed? Can a leopard truly ever change his spots?"

Jake gently stroked Ginny's head with his hand. "That's why it's been so hard for me to decide whether or not to tell you. It's why your mother kept Raine a secret from you all those years and why she could never forgive him. But I do think you need to know that the last words your mother said to me were…tell Raine that I forgive him."

Brooklyn wiped her cheek with her hand and looked Jake in the eyes. "Really? Those were her last words?"

"Yes," he said, "And because of that, I can't let my personal feelings influence you on what you do. I believe you needed to know the truth, but what you do from here on has to be your decision, not mine."

"Can I say something?" Josh asked.

"Of course," Jake said, "This is about you too."

"I think we need to call the radio station and ask who published that song, and at the very least, find out how to locate Raine," he said, "Once we know how to find him, we can make the decision to contact him or not. Until we actually know where he is, this is all a moot point and not really a decision one way or the other. But if we *COULD* contact him, whatever we decide will be a form of closure to all of this, and hopefully, be something we can all live with."

Jake smiled at Brooklyn. "You didn't tell me that he was smart too!"

Brooklyn picked up her cell, googled the radio station, and got the phone number.

"I only have one more thing to add before we talk to the radio station," Jake said, "We all know what an incredible song this is, and apparently the rest of the world is about to find out as well. From now on we don't have to worry about Raine Waters being broke, homeless, and living on the beach. He's about to become a very wealthy man. He's going to make millions from his writers' royalties alone."

"I already thought about that and I'm happy for him," Brooklyn said, "but I'm a little sad at the same time. In his last letter, he told me that was *my* song, that he wrote it for me and mom and that it was mine to do whatever I wanted to do with it. He even said that he was giving me all the rights and royalties to it."

Jake smiled. "Well, as I said before, sometimes, even if they want to, a Leopard can't really change his spots, and apparently, neither could Raine."

17

RIPPED OFF

I t was Summer, but one of those rare July afternoons for Central Florida. It was hot, about 88 degrees, but the humidity was low with a strong cooling ocean breeze blowing across the golf course. Raine pulled his cart to the top of the hill overlooking the number six fairway and looked down at the majestic sight below. The dark blue water in the lake was rippling gently from the strong breeze, as the sun slowly began its descent behind the giant trees that lined the fairway. He sat there quietly watching the sky turning golden with streaks of pink and purple.

He pulled his now, warm Coke out of the holder and lifted it up. "Good job, God," he said, toasting him, "This is one of your best sunsets."

As he sat in his cart, drinking the Coke, watching the show, he let his mind wander thinking about his daughter. Doing the math in his head he calculated her age. *She's 33*, he thought to himself, *probably married and might even have a few kids*.

When he realized that he could be a grandfather he smiled but had to fight back the reoccurring pain that usually came when he thought about Brooklyn.

He looked up at the sky and said, "How am I doing, God? I sure hope it's good enough, I'm really trying. You've given me so much. My life is good and for the first time in a very long time, I believe I'm going down the right path. I'm not sure how much longer you are going to give me, but I hope you know how grateful I am. I don't mean to bother you but none of this is going to mean anything if Brooklyn's not in my life. I really do appreciate everything you've done, but you know that's really all I want. If nothing else, please at least let me meet her and talk to her before I die. I know that may not be in your plans for me, but until I know for sure, I'm going to keep bothering you and praying for it."

Along with his pay raise and new responsibilities, Coop had also given him a brand new work golf cart. It was street legal, with tail-lights, headlights, blinkers and it even had a radio.

When the sunset was over, he turned the key, flipped on the headlights, and headed back to the little house in the woods. It was such a beautiful night, he decided to take the long way home, so he turned on the radio and sang along with the songs as he drove down the streets, looking at the beautiful million-dollar homes along the way.

His mind had wandered and he wasn't paying much attention to the radio when the song started. When he realized what he was hearing, he jerked the cart to the side of the road and slammed on the breaks. He could feel his blood boiling and his heart pounding in his chest as he listened. He had instantly recognized the singer's voice and of course, he knew every word he was singing, because they were his...he had written them, and every single note of the music echoing through the air.

"THAT ROTTEN SON OF A BITCH STOLE MY SONG!" he yelled.

He sat there gritting his teeth waiting for the song to end. When it was over, the DJ said, "That was a brand new smash hit from, Nash Cooper. And I'm very happy to say that he's one of our own. Nash is from Melbourne, Florida, and I guarantee you will be hearing a lot from him."

Raine turned off the radio and stared out the windshield in shock.

He was furious and needed to hit something, so he slammed his hands down on the steering wheel, screaming, "NO, NO, NO!"

When he regained control he had no idea what to do next, but his first instinct was to drive to a liquor store, buy a bottle of bourbon and get very, very drunk.

On his way to the liquor store, he saw blue lights flashing in the woods near the little house. He turned off the street and drove as fast as the cart would go down the fairway toward the house.

His first thought was a fire, but when he turned down the path, he saw that the little house was surrounded by seven or eight police cars, with their blue lights flashing. Coop was standing near one of the cars, talking to a policeman when he pulled up.

"What the hell is going on?" he asked, "Why are the cops here?"

Coop frowned. "I'm so sorry, Raine, but they're here for Dave."

"What? For Dave? What did he do?"

Before he could answer him, the front door opened and Dave was led down the steps, with his hands cuffed behind his back by two men wearing black FBI jackets. His head was down and he was crying.

Raine jumped out of the cart and ran up to them. "WAIT! HOLD ON A SECOND!" he yelled, stepping in front of them, blocking their way, "this is my friend. Why are you arresting him?"

"Because he is a wanted fugitive," The agent said, "Please sir, you need to step out of the way."

Raine didn't move. "Wanted for what?"

"Sir, I'm warning you. Step out of the way!"

Standing his ground, he glared back at the agent. "Well, Sir, this is my house and my property. I'm not going anywhere until you tell me why you are arresting my friend."

"Please, Raine, don't let them put me in a cage," Dave mumbled through his tears, "I'll die in there. It's too small. Please, please don't let them put me in a cage."

Raine felt someone take his arm. "You need to get out of their way," Coop said, pulling him back, "It's murder. Dave is wanted for murder."

Stunned, he stepped out of the way and watched the two FBI agents walk Dave to a black SUV. Dave continued begging them, "Please don't put me in a cage."

When they tried to put him into the backseat, he started yelling and screaming, resisting, trying to kick them with his feet.

They struggled with him a few minutes, yelling for him to stop fighting, then one of the agents grabbed a taser off his belt, held it to Dave's side, and hit the button. Dave screamed and fell to the ground.

Raine ran up to them and dropped on top of him, putting his body between him and the taser. "You don't have to do that, just let me talk to him. He will listen to me. He's extremely claustrophobic. Please, let me talk to him."

The agents backed away and he helped Dave sit up, leaning against the SUV.

Raine tried to get him to look him in the eyes, but he turned his head. "Look at me, Dave. It's me, Raine, and I really want to help you, but I need you to tell me the truth. Did you do this? Did you kill someone?"

Dave dropped his head. "My father," he whispered, "I killed my father."

Raine was stunned when he said those words and wasn't sure what to say next. "Was it an accident? Because if it was an accident I'll hire you a good lawyer and..."

"It wasn't an accident," Dave said, interrupting him, "I did it."

"Dave, I know you. You're not a killer and don't ever say that again, to anyone. None of this makes any sense, there has to be some explanation, but I can't stop them from taking you now. You have to go with them."

"Please, Raine, don't let them take me. They'll put me in a small cage. I can't do that. You know I can't do that."

"Calm down and breathe. You have to go with them. I'm sorry, but there's nothing I can do about that right now, but I promise I'll talk to them and tell them about your claustrophobia."

Dave looked up at him. "Please tell them."

"I promise I will, but you need to let them put you in the backseat. You've done that before many times. I'll try to get them to roll down the window, but you can't fight them anymore. Do you understand?" Dave nodded and Raine helped him up to his feet.

The agents actually listened to him and rolled down all of the windows before they slowly pulled away with Dave handcuffed in the back seat.

When Raine turned around he saw Coop standing behind him. "I'm really sorry about this, but I had no choice," he said.

Raine frowned. "What are you talking about?"

"This is all my fault," Coop said, "I did this"

"You turned him in? How did you know he was wanted?"

Coop shook his head. "I didn't know that until tonight, but I've always had a feeling about him. He wouldn't tell me his last name and refused to sign any paperwork. That never made any sense to me. I knew he was hiding something, but I had no idea it was murder."

JAKE FROWNED across the table at Brooklyn and Josh, as he wrote down the information on the yellow pad in front of him. "Are you sure that's all of the information?" he asked, "what about a co-writer?"

"No sir," the radio station program director said. "We just got the song in a few days ago and I'm looking at the information that came with it. It says: From Ashes, artist Nash Cooper, written by Nash Cooper, produced by Scott Hugley, published by Big Dog Publishing, released by Huge Records. That's all it says, nothing about a co-writer. Why are you asking?"

"No real reason," Jake said, "it sounds a lot like a song I'd heard before. I was just wondering if it was the same one. Thanks for the information."

When he hung up, he stared across the table at Brooklyn. "Raine didn't sell your song. I don't think he had anything to do with this record at all. It sounds to me like this Nash Cooper guy somehow stole his song and ripped him off."

"That's not right," Brooklyn shouted.

"Yeah, I know. Welcome to show business. This sort of thing happens all the time."

"Seriously?" Josh asked, "And there's nothing we can do about it?"

"Sure, Raine could sue them, but to do that, we would first have to find him, and even if we did, I'm pretty sure he wouldn't have the money to hire a lawyer."

"Hang on a second," Brooklyn said, rushing out of the room.

When she came back she had one of Raine's letters in her hand. She carefully opened the envelope and flattened the papers out on the table.

Silently, she read the letter for a few moments, then pointed down at it. "Listen to this. I give all ownership profits, and any publishing and writer's royalties, to my daughter, Brooklyn Riley Taylor for the song, From Ashes, written by me, Raine Waters. I have also dated and signed the handwritten sheet music as proof of the origin of this song."

When she finished reading the letter, she looked up at Jake and smiled. "Raine may not have the money to hire a lawyer, but I do."

Jake grinned. "I'd be willing to kick in a little on that myself, but before we do that, let me make a few calls."

That afternoon, with Josh's help on the computer, they were able to track down a few of Jake's old friends that still lived in Nashville, and he started calling.

"Are you serious?" he said on the phone with a chuckle, "That's who owns Big Dog Publishing? Do you have his number handy?" He wrote down the number on the pad, "Hey man, I really appreciate this. I may be in Nashville soon. I'll look you up and buy you a beer when I'm there."

When Jake hung up the phone he jumped out of his seat and started dancing around the room.

"Dad," Brooklyn laughed, "What are you doing?"

He ran to Ginny's room and came back with her in his arms. "We're dancing. That's what we're doing," he said, laughing and kissing Ginny on the cheek.

Brooklyn glanced at Josh and shrugged. "I see that," she said, "and why exactly are we dancing?"

Jake stopped, sat down on the couch next to Brooklyn, and put Ginny down on his lap. "Because of someone named Bertha Brooks."

"Bertha Brooks? Who is she?" Josh asked.

Jake grinned at him. "It's not *SHE*, it's *HE*...and *HE* just happens to be the owner of Big Dog Publishing. Do you want to guess who the radio station said was the publisher of From Ashes?"

"Do you know him?" Brooklyn asked, "Is he one of your old friends from Nashville?"

Jake wiggled his eyebrows. "You could say that. He also knew and loved your mother."

"He knew mom?"

"Yep, and he also knew your father. Bertha was Raine's road manager and personal bodyguard for years."

Josh searched the internet, but couldn't find a home telephone number for Bertha. The only one they had was his office number at his publishing company.

"Damn," Jake said, "I'm pretty sure I have his number at home. Nobody works on Saturdays in Nashville, but I'll leave him a message anyway. He probably won't get it till Monday."

Jake dialed the number and listened to the rings waiting for the answering service to connect. The phone clicked in his ear and he heard a deep male voice say, "Big Dog Publishing, this is Bertha how can I help you?"

Jake grinned and looked over at Brooklyn when he answered. "What the hell is a big-time publishing executive like you doing answering the phone?"

Jake heard him laugh. "Somebody's got to answer the damn thing. Who is this?"

"A voice from the past," he said with a chuckle, "Are you still eating those green popsicles every day?"

"You bet your ass I do, I love em. Seriously, who is this?"

"I'm not saying, you have to guess, but I'll give you one more hint. 1984, Cabo San Lucas and a dead worm."

"You promised you'd keep that a secret!" Bertha yelled, "Jake Taylor, is this really you?"

"In the flesh," he said, "I'm so proud of you, Bertha. You own a publishing company? How long have you been doing that?"

"Almost 10 years now. I don't have to deal with those egomaniac stars and groupies anymore."

Jake laughed. "I understand about the stars, but don't you lie to me, I'm pretty sure you miss the groupies a little."

"Of course I do, but I'm so damn old now, I wouldn't know what to do if one of em' walked in my door."

Jake had forgotten how much he loved hearing Bertha's roaring, infectious laugh. "How is Miss Virginia and little Brooklyn doing these days?" he asked.

Jake sighed. "Bertha, Ginny died last year from brain cancer."

"Oh no, Jake. I'm so sorry to hear that," he said softly, "I loved that woman. She was such a sweetheart."

"Yes she was, and she sure thought a lot of you. You were always her favorite of all my friends."

"So how are you holding up?"

Jake and Bertha talked for almost an hour, catching up on old times. Jake also told him about Brooklyn, Josh, and his new grand-daughter.

"I bet she's beautiful and has you wrapped around her finger already," Bertha paused, trying to find the right words, "Ahh...I don't really know how to ask this...does Raine know? I mean about Virginia dying, and the baby? I've often wondered about what happened to him."

"No, he doesn't. Actually, we don't know where he is, but he's the reason I called you tonight."

"You're calling me about Raine? I don't know anything about him either. I haven't heard hide nor hair from him in over twenty years. The last thing I heard, was that he was broke and playing in some beer joint in Florida. Talk about a waste of talent."

"I know a little more," Jake said, "and it got a lot worse for him. Bertha this is a long story. Did I interrupt you, do you have time to hear this or do you want me to call you back later?"

"Well actually, I was just about to walk out when you called. Let me lock up and go get something to eat."

Bertha gave him his cell number and told him to give him a call around 10 o'clock when he got home. That call lasted an hour and a half.

"Oh, shit, Jake," Bertha said, "If this is true, I really screwed up this time. It never occurred to me that Nash didn't write that song. It's one of 15 songs I've published for him. I wonder how many of those he stole?"

"Who knows?" Jake said, "but I wouldn't doubt that there are two or three other Raine Waters songs in that batch. What do you know about this Nash Cooper guy?"

"Not much. Scott introduced him to me and told me I needed to sign him."

"Scott who?" Jake asked.

"Scott Hugley. You remember him, don't you? He was one of the studio musicians on Raine's albums. He played piano, don't you remember the real young-looking kid that we used to joke about being barely tall enough to reach the pedals?"

"The kid from Juilliard?"

"Yeah, that's him. He was a monster player and became a damn good producer. He was a VP for DreamWorks Nashville until a few years ago when he opened up his own label."

Jake grinned. "Yeah, I think I know him, and if I remember he was a bit of a prick. Let me guess, his label is called, Huge Records."

"That's him, and yeah he was a bit hard to take back then, but he's mellowed through the years. He's actually a pretty good guy, but he's gonna shit bricks when he hears about this. His label isn't all that big and he's sunk a ton of money on this Nash Cooper guy."

"Bertha, what do you think we should do?"

He thought for a moment. "I think you need to come up here to Nashville and bring Brooklyn and those letters with you. I'll set up a meeting with Scott, but I'm not gonna tell him what it's about. I'll let *YOU* break the news to him."

"You think I need to bring a lawyer with me?" Jake asked.

"Hell no, not yet," Bertha said, "We don't need any of those blood-suckers around. They've just about ruined Nashville. If you can't cut some kind of deal with Scott, you can call one then, but as I said, he's a pretty straight-up guy. I think we can all get through this without anybody getting hurt too bad. Well, everyone but Nash Cooper. His ass is toast."

When Jake hung up, he looked at Brooklyn and Josh. "Looks like we're going to Nashville."

"When?" Josh asked, "I just signed a six-week contract with the House of Blues in Dallas, we start next week. I've been trying to get in there for years."

"I don't want to go without you," Brooklyn said, frowning.

He looked over at her and smiled. "Honey, you need to go take care of this and soon. He left you the song, you don't really need me there."

Jake could see the disappointment in his eyes. "No, Josh, you're wrong. We may need you and Brooklyn to play the song from the original sheet music. No way are we going there without you. We're in this together and we're going to Nashville as a team."

Josh and Brooklyn smiled at him. "Thank you, daddy," she said.

"You are welcome. It's only six weeks," Jake said, "What could happen in six weeks?"

OVER THE NEXT SIX WEEKS, *From Ashes*, broke all the records. It was the fastest rising song on all the charts in history. It reached number one on the Billboard, and iTune charts in only 11 days, and it was certi-fied as a Gold record, meaning that it had shipped, sold, or streamed over 500,000 units by the end of the first month. By the sixth week, it was certified Platinum, selling over 1,000,000 units. You couldn't turn on the radio without hearing it, and almost overnight, Nash Cooper had become a major country star.

18

LIKE SALT ON A LEECH

Bertha told Jake that he would meet them in the baggage claim area at the Nashville airport, but when they walked up to the baggage turnstile, he didn't see him.

When the turnstile started rolling and the baggage began to appear, he turned around and scanned the area again, but still didn't see Bertha anywhere. A few minutes later, he saw a tall man walk through the automatic glass doors and wave. For a second he thought it was him, he was about the same height, at least six foot six, but he was thin, almost skinny. The last time he saw Bertha, he wasn't what you would call morbidly obese, but he wasn't even close to skinny, so he ignored the wave, turned around, and watched for his luggage.

"Holy crap, what happened to you? You're old as shit," he heard Bertha's voice say behind him.

When Jake turned around his mouth flew open. "Bertha? You're skinny!"

"Yeah, I've shed a few pounds. I figured you didn't recognize me when I waved at you."

"Well, I may look like hell, but you look great!" Jake said, hugging him, "How'd you lose all the weight?"

"Doctor's orders," he said, smiling, "I had a heart attack a few years ago and they took me off sugar, salt, beef, hell almost anything worth eating. He made me start exercising and before I knew it, I'd dropped 125 pounds. Since it ain't no fun to eat and drink anymore I just sort of lost interest in it. I've kept it off about five years now and I have to admit I feel a hell of a lot better."

Jake motioned toward Brooklyn and Josh, who were standing a few yards away waiting to grab their luggage. "Do you recognize her?"

Bertha squinted his eyes and looked down the turnstile. "Remember who?"

"That's Brooklyn," he said, "and that's her husband, Josh holding the baby."

"No friggin' way," he yelled, "That's little Brooklyn?" He ran up to her and lifted her off the ground with his bear hug. She was still laughing when he put her down and looked at Josh.

He put his arm around his shoulders and shook him. "Jake tells me that you're one hell of a musician. I'm Bertha. It's really nice to meet you. If we get some alone time while you're here, I'll tell you some wild stories about your father in law."

"Oh no you don't, that's not gonna happen," Jake said, "Josh, don't believe a word this man says."

"Could I hold her?" Bertha asked, reaching toward Ginny. When he picked her up, he swung her around high in the air and laughed with that loud infectious laugh.

Ginny's eyes were wide open and for a second Jake thought he had scared her with his loud laugh and quick movements, but a few seconds later she started giggling, which caused Bertha to start laughing louder, and soon everyone in the baggage claim was laughing too.

Bertha drove them to the hotel and after they checked in, he took them out to dinner and insisted on paying for it.

On the ride back to the hotel, Bertha looked at Jake and said, "I guess you know it just made Platinum, right?"

"No, I didn't. Wow, that was fast. Where is it on the charts?"

"It's gonna be one of those rare songs we talk about for decades.

It's going on the fifth week at number one on all of the country and pop charts."

"We saw Nash Cooper on the Tonight Show a few days ago," Jake said, "Actually, he's pretty good."

Bertha shook his head. "Yeah, for a thief he ain't all bad. The bastard keeps calling me wanting to know when he's going to get paid his royalties. It was all I could do not to tell him, but hopefully, this will all be over soon."

"How's he handling his new found fame?"

Bertha looked over at him. "Do you remember how well Raine handled it?"

"Oh yeah. Is he that bad?"

"He's kind of like Raine on steroids. His damn ego is so pumped up he can barely fit his head through a door."

"Do you think that's going to complicate things with Scott Hugley?"

Bertha shrugged. "To be honest with you Jake, I don't know how Scott's gonna react. He is no dummy and understands that he's got a once in a career song on his hands. I have no idea how dedicated he is to Nash Cooper, but I will tell you that he's all in, lock stock and barrel. If this blows up in his face, and I don't see how it couldn't, he's gonna lose everything. He's not a rich guy, so I'm pretty sure he's got every dime he has riding on this, including his house."

"Josh and I were talking about that on the plane," Jake said, "He did some research on Scott and Huge Records and told me that he only has one or two other artists doing well on that label, Amanda Jones and someone else I didn't know. Is that right?"

Bertha nodded, "Yeah and that's the shame of all of this. Nash Cooper, that little prick, deserves everything that's about to come to him, but Scott does not. He's worked his ass off to develop his label, but when all this shit hits the fan and Nash Cooper becomes the next pariah in this very small town...all his big gigs go away and they stop playing his records on the radio, I'm afraid poor Scott, his label and everyone on it, is gonna get sucked down the drain with him."

"Could that really happen?" Brooklyn asked from the back seat,

"This could affect Amanda Jones? Mr. Hugley could lose the label and a lot of money? What about you? Will you lose money too?"

"Well, to be honest, since you control the rights to the song, it all kind of depends on you. If you make them take Nash's record off the air, yeah I'll lose a little," Bertha said, "but don't worry about me. This is one of those songs that's gonna live forever. If you'll let someone else cut it, it'll take off and the money will start rolling in again."

SCOTT HUGLEY HID his frustration when Bertha called to set up the appointment. Nash Cooper was in town working on his new album and he really didn't have the time to spare, but Bertha was one of his few friends in Nashville, so he reluctantly accepted.

Scott had always had trouble fitting into Nashville. Most people there found him a bit arrogant, abrasive, and rude. He had always found it difficult making friends with the slow-talking, laid-back Southern boys on Music Row.

He was raised in Boston, was a child prodigy, and had graduated from Juilliard at 19 years old. His parents discovered his prodigious ability to play the piano when he was only five, when they heard music coming from the living room and discovered him sitting behind the piano playing a song he had just heard on the radio.

Of course, after he graduated Juilliard, his parents and everyone else that knew him expected him to become a concert pianist, but that music never really moved him. Although he could play it very well, to him, classical music was too restrictive. Having to play every note exactly as written suppressed his personal creativity.

When he told his parents that instead of pursuing a career as a concert pianist he was moving to Nashville to become a studio session player, they went berserk and refused to support him and cut him off financially. When he arrived in Nashville, three days after his 20th birthday, he had exactly $327 to his name. When he began knocking on the studio doors trying to land a job and told them about his music degree from Juilliard, instead of being impressed, they actually laughed in his face.

The only job he could find was delivering Pizza. Fortunately, a few months later, he got to deliver three pizzas to one of the recording studios on Music Row. When he walked into the studio booth, the musicians were recording a new song. When they finished, the engineer and producer grabbed a few slices and told him to take the rest out to the musicians in the main studio.

"Where do you want these?" He asked when he walked in.

"Put them on the piano," One of the musicians said, handing him some cash.

"These are already paid for," he said.

"That's your tip, kid."

Scott smiled and handed him back the cash. "I appreciate it, but what I'd rather have for a tip is to play this Steinway a few minutes."

"You play?" The musician asked.

"Yes sir, and I'd love to play this one. It's really old, right?"

The musician nodded, "Yeah, it's been here as long as I can remember," he pointed at the piano bench, "Have a seat kid, have at it."

When he sat down behind the piano and placed his hands on the keys, he paused trying to decide what to play. He did a few difficult classical passes showing off his skill. Then he closed his eyes and from memory, started playing the new song they had just recorded, adding a few minor changes to the chord structure.

When he opened his eyes, all five of the musicians were standing around the piano staring at him. "How'd you know that song?" One of them asked shocked.

"I don't know it, but that was what you guys were playing when I walked in, wasn't it?"

"It damn sure was," he said laughing, "What were you playing there toward the end?"

Scott played the song again and explained the minor changes he had made. "You don't have to keep the changes, but I think it feels a little better to me."

"What's your name kid? And what the hell are you doing delivering pizzas if you can play like this?"

That was 27 years ago, and it was the last pizza delivery he ever made, and his first paying session.

BERTHA BROOKS WAS the only person in Nashville that seemed to get him. Scott assumed it had something to do with the years he had worked with all those crazy egomaniac stars. When he would fly off the handle, exposing his arrogance, or say something stupid, Bertha would just grin at him. He never seemed to take it personally. Bertha was the only one in town he trusted and the only friend he had in the music business that he could confide in.

Scott had no idea why Bertha had called and asked for the meeting, but when his receptionist opened his door and they walked in, he was pretty sure he knew what it was all about; Bertha had discovered someone he wanted him to sign.

When they sat down and Bertha introduced them, he had to admit that he was instantly taken by the young girl. She was absolutely stunning, with long shiny black hair and the most beautiful blue eyes he had ever seen.

He missed the older man's name who was holding the baby, as well as the black guy's, but he caught hers. Brooklyn Taylor Arnett.

His mind instantly began to whirl. Why on earth would a beautiful country singer like her choose Brooklyn as her stage name, he thought to himself. Taylor was OK but, Brooklyn? Why not Dallas, or Austin, or even Jackson, but not Brooklyn.

He was looking at Bertha and he was saying something, but he wasn't listening. He had just noticed that the beautiful little baby with dark skin had the same amazing blue eyes as Brooklyn. Obviously, it was her baby and the black guy was the father. *They must be a duo,* he thought, his mind still spinning. *That's something I can deal with, something new and different. The first black and white duo in country music.*

"And they have undeniable proof," he heard Bertha say, finally listening to him. Bertha laid an envelope on his desk in front of him, "Read this."

Trying not to act like he hadn't been listening and had no idea what he was talking about, Scott picked up the envelope and opened it.

Inside, he found a one-page handwritten letter and two pages of handwritten sheet music. He picked up the music and scanned it. "What is this?" He asked, staring at Bertha.

"Read the letter," he said, frowning, "it will explain everything."

Scott leaned back in his chair, put his feet up on the desk, and read the letter slowly. When he finished, he took his feet off the desk, leaned forward, and looked at Brooklyn. "You're Raine Waters' daughter?"

"Yes I am," she said softly.

Scott could feel his blood pressure, along with his anger rising. "When did he write you this letter?"

"It's on the postmark," she said, motioning toward the envelope on his desk.

He picked it up and studied it carefully. "Oh my God," he said, staring at Bertha, "Nash didn't write it, he stole it!"

He picked up his phone and dialed a number. "Excuse me, but I think I need to talk to my lawyer. Would you mind waiting outside in the lobby?"

Bertha walked up to his desk, took the phone out of his hand, and put it back on the receiver. "You don't need to call your lawyer yet, let's just talk for a few minutes first. They are not here to sue you."

Scott took a deep breath and let it out slowly. "That's good to hear."

He looked at Jake, studying his face, "I know you, right? You were with Raine Waters. What's your involvement in this? Are you here representing Raine?"

Jake shook his head. "No, Brooklyn is my stepdaughter. I've raised her since birth. I'm not in the music business any longer, but I couldn't let something like this go."

Scott nodded and frowned. "I can understand that," he said leaning back in his chair, "So, here we are...what do you want?"

"Mr. Hugley," Josh said, "I'm Brooklyn's husband, and to be honest with you, we don't want anything from you. We're not here to put you out of business. Bertha has told us how heavily invested you are in this Nash Cooper guy, and to be honest with you we don't really know what we want. All we *DO* know is that it doesn't seem fair that Nash Cooper could steal Raine's song and reap all of the rewards."

"Scott, I believe we are all on the same page," Jake said, "We'd all like to see Nash Cooper crash and burn, but if that happens, you're going to feel the heat as well, and none of us want that. If we just put our heads together, I think we can come up with a good solution for all of this. Something that's fair for everyone."

Scott rocked in his chair and thought for a few minutes. "I don't see how I can do anything here without looping in my lawyer. I need to make sure that what I do to Nash is legal, but don't worry, my lawyer isn't one of these money-grubbing shysters that have taken over this town. I would understand if you want to call a lawyer as well, to protect your rights, but I'll give you my word that anything I do will be in your best interest too."

Scott looked at Brooklyn and smiled. "I don't suppose you're a singer, being Raine Waters's daughter? Who knows, I may be looking for a new act."

"She's a great singer!" Josh said.

"And Josh is a brilliant musician as well," Jake added, "He's classically trained like you."

"Oh really?" Scott raised his eyebrows, "Where did you go to school?"

"North Texas."

"Great school. I went to Juilliard, but North Texas is pretty damn close."

His eyes suddenly widened with an idea. He picked up the sheet music, held it up, and looked at Brooklyn. "Do you know this song, can you sing it?"

THAT AFTERNOON they met Scott at a small recording studio, one street off of Music Row. When they walked into the control room, Scott took Brooklyn and Josh into the main studio and set them up with mics and headphones.

In the control room with Jake, was Bertha and Jack Johnson, Scott's lawyer. When Scott walked back from the studio, he sat down behind the board and started flipping switches. A few minutes later, the door opened and Amanda Jones walked in.

"Hey, Amanda," Bertha said, "What are you doing here?"

Her smile lit up the darkroom. "Hey there Bertha," she said hugging him, "I don't really know why I'm here. I'm just following Scott's orders. And who is this?"

"This is my friend Jake Taylor. That's his daughter and son-in-law in the studio," he said pointing through the glass, "Jake was with Raine Waters. He was his road manager before he quit and left *ME* with the damn job."

Jake took her hand and shook it. "I'm a huge fan, I loved your last CD. I play it in my truck almost every day."

Suddenly, they heard the piano blasting in the speakers and a few minutes later, Brooklyn's voice came through, as Scott punched buttons and turned dials on the board.

"Can you hear yourself Ok?" Scott asked them. They both shook their head yes. "Ok, I'm gonna mute you in here, so you guys can run it a few times. I'll let you know when we're ready to start."

"Hey Scott," Amanda said, smiling at him, "What's up? What am I doing here?"

He sighed. "There's been a development that I can't tell you about right now, but I wanted you to hear a different version of Nash's song, a female version. I may want you to cut it."

"From Ashes? You want me to re-cut From Ashes? Are you crazy? It's the number one song in the world! Why on earth would you want to do that?"

Before he could answer, the door opened and Nash Cooper walked in. Scott leaned over and whispered in Amanda's ear, "Just hang around. You're gonna like this, and you'll figure it out."

When Amanda saw Nash she rolled her eyes and looked away.

"Well hello there, Nash," Scott said, "I'm glad you could make it. Have a seat." He pulled back a chair behind the board next to him, "There's something I want you to hear."

"Who's that?" Nash said, pointing at Brooklyn and Josh in the studio.

"They are my latest discovery, they brought me a song this morning that her father wrote for her almost 15 years ago and it is a real killer. It's one of those rare songs we talked about, something people will be singing and talking about for years. I thought you might want to hear it."

Nash pushed back the chair and stood up. "No thanks, I don't want to hear it. You know I only record *MY* songs," he said arrogantly, "I'll see you later. I've got an interview with a radio station in Birmingham in an hour."

Bertha stood up and blocked him. "Sit your sorry ass down, now!" He yelled staring down at him.

Nash sat back down in the chair and looked at Scott. "What's going on?"

Scott pushed the talkback button on the board and said, "Are you guys ready?"

Then he turned and looked Nash in the eyes. "Now remember, this song was written 15 years ago, by her father. And she has proof."

When Josh started playing the intro, Nash's face turned white and he began fidgeting in his seat. When Brooklyn started singing the words, he actually moaned and dropped his head.

"Sound familiar?" Scott asked him, but Nash didn't respond.

When they finished the song, Scott hit the talkback button. "Wow! That was unbelievable. Come on in and I'll play it back for you."

Nash looked over at him. "I...I was going to tell you, but..."

"Shut the fuck up, you thieving bastard!" Scott yelled, "I don't want to hear a word from you. You need to get out of here before I kick your ass. Meet me at my office at 4 o'clock sharp. We have a lot to talk about."

Nash slowly stood up and quietly walked out of the control room with his head hanging down, showing no signs of the cocky, arrogant jackass that had walked in earlier.

When Brooklyn and Josh walked into the control room, she screamed when she saw Amanda Jones standing there. "Oh my God, you're Amanda Jones! I love you!"

Amanda laughed, walked up to her, and gave her a hug. "Well, to be honest, I love you too. You're an amazing singer. And you," she said to Josh, "Are great too, so tasteful."

She picked up her purse and smiled. "I'm so sorry, but I have to go, I'm late for my own session."

She motioned to Scott, "Walk me to my car, we need to talk."

"Sure, but hang on a second." He pulled back the chairs behind the board and said, "You guys sit here and listen to this." He hit the play button and then followed Amanda out the door.

When it finished, Josh hit the play button again and they all listened to it one more time.

"Now, that's what that song is supposed to sound like!" Bertha said, "Damn Girl, I think you sing better than Raine."

Scott was grinning when he walked back into the control room. "What does Amanda think about all of this?" Bertha asked.

He laughed. "She told me that, although she thoroughly enjoyed watching Nash's complete humiliation, she doesn't want to cut the song."

"Nash Cooper was here?" Brooklyn asked, "While we were playing? I'm sorry I missed that. What did he do when he heard the song?"

Bertha laughed. "Have you ever seen what happens to a leech when you put salt on it? It sort of shrivels up and melts. It looked a lot like that."

"Why doesn't Amanda want to record the song?" Jake asked, "It might be a little weird at first, but with her fan base, I'm sure it would be a huge hit for her too."

Scott looked at Jake and smiled. "Are you sure you're not in the music business anymore? That's exactly the same thing I told her."

"What did she say?"

"She said that there's only one person she could think of that

should re-cut that song. And, she also told me that if I didn't immediately sign that person to a record contract, she was going to put sugar
in my gas tank."

"Who was she talking about?" Brooklyn asked.

Scott grinned and looked at Brooklyn. "She was talking about
YOU."

BROOKLYN AND JOSH finally got to meet Nash Cooper at the Huge
Records office that afternoon at four o'clock.

They met in the conference room with his lawyer and a court
reporter to take down the transcript of the meeting.

"I'd just like to say how sorry I am," Nash began, "I'm not really a
bad guy, it was just..."

"Nash, nobody wants to hear your bullshit excuses," Scott said
stopping him, "You're a freaking thief and because of that, you've got
my company in a world of shit. I want to drop your ass off this label so
bad, but right now I can't do that. So, from this day on, never, ever say
that you wrote that song. And every time you sing it, you tell the crowd
that it was written by Raine Waters. You got that?"

"Yes," he said.

"I need you to sign some papers giving up all your claim to this
song and any others of Raine's that you ripped off."

When he signed the papers, Scott said, "There is one more thing I
need you to do."

"Sure, anything," he said.

"We want to know where you got the damn song?"

ALTHOUGH THEY ALL hated that Nash Cooper was going to remain a
star and keep his record deal with Scott at Huge Records, Brooklyn,
Josh and Jake left Nashville satisfied with the deal they had cut.

Bertha changed the writer's name on all the publishing information on From Ashes to Raine Waters, and all of the current and future royalties earned would be deposited into a Nashville bank account in Raine Waters' and Brooklyn's names.

Scott had also insisted on giving Raine and Brooklyn a percentage of the profits on all sales of the Nash Cooper version of the song.

As unbelievable as it sounded when they boarded the plane, Brooklyn left Nashville, with almost $2,000,000 in the bank, and a three year, three-album recording contract with Huge Records. And they also, finally, had a really good lead on where to find Raine Waters. That would be the next step. They needed to find Raine, so they could tell him that he was a very, very rich man.

19

COINCIDENCE

When Raine didn't show up for work the morning after Dave's arrest, Coop wasn't surprised. He knew that Raine was angry at him for turning Dave into the FBI, and it was going to take him some time to cool down.

He wasn't looking forward to having a confrontation with Raine, but decided the sooner they had it out, the sooner they could both get back to some form of normalcy. Coop drove to the little house to talk to him, but when he pulled down the path, Raine's work cart wasn't parked in front of the house as he had expected.

It was only 7:30 am, and although that made him an hour late for work, it was still very early for him not to be there. Coop thought he might be at Louise's, so he drove down the fairway to her house, but Raine's cart wasn't there either. He decided that it was too early to knock on her door to ask her if she had seen him, so he headed back to his office at the clubhouse.

It had been a very busy morning and before he realized it, it was one o'clock and he was starving. When he walked into the clubhouse café, he saw Louise sitting with two of her friends at a table.

"Mind if I join you ladies?" He asked.

"Well of course, please join us," Louise said smiling, "You know

Karen and Melissa don't you?" Coop nodded, shook their hands, and sat down.

Louise shook her head and frowned. "We were just talking about Dave. I still can't believe it."

"Me either," he said.

"Did he really kill someone?" Melissa asked.

Coop nodded. "You guys know Alexander Rush, right?"

"Yes, but I had no idea he was an FBI agent," Karen said.

"He doesn't talk about it much around here, but he's been in the FBI for almost 20 years. He told me that Dave had been on their wanted list for over 22 years."

Louse looked at hm. "What exactly did he do?"

Coop sighed. "According to Alex, when Dave was 18 or 19 years old, he showed up at his parent's house unexpectedly and killed his father. He beat him to death with a crutch, locked him in a closet, and walked away. Then he stole the neighbors' car and drove it across the state line, that's when the FBI got involved."

Melissa frowned. "What does unexpectedly mean? If he was only 18 or 19, wasn't he living there?"

"No, he ran away from home when he was only 15 and they hadn't seen him in years. I figure he was probably living on the streets way back then."

Karen shook her head and looked at Coop, "Did he have any brothers or sisters?"

"No sisters, just one younger brother. I think Alex said that he was 12 or 13. He said that the brother was there when Dave showed up and killed his father."

"Oh God," Louise said, "That poor kid." She lifted her glass of tea and took a sip, "Does Alex know why Dave did it?"

"No, he has no idea. It was the first time he had ever been in trouble. He had a clean record up till then. That's the biggest mystery of all."

Coop leaned back and shrugged his shoulders. "I guess he just snapped and lost it for some reason."

The waitress arrived at the table and set their lunch plates down in front of them. They sat in silence, no one talking while they ate their food.

After a few minutes, Louise put down her fork and looked at Coop. "How is Raine dealing with Dave's arrest?"

Coop shrugged. "Honestly, I don't know. He didn't show up for work this morning and when I went to his house, his cart wasn't there. I was about to ask you if you had talked to him."

Louise shook her head. "No, I haven't seen him in two or three days. Did you check at Alcoholics Anonymous or his church?"

"No I didn't check there, it was too early for an AA meeting, and I doubt anybody would've been at his church. I'll give them both a call later and see if they've seen him."

"Do you think he's all right?" Melissa said, "They were really close and that had to be devastating for him."

Coop nodded. "He was pretty pissed off at me the last time I saw him, but he'll show up when he's cooled down. We just need to give him a little time until he does."

WHEN THEY FINISHED LUNCH, Coop jumped in his cart and took another drive out to the little house, but there were still no signs of Raine. When he got back to his office, he called the church and asked if anyone had been in contact with him in the last few days, but they told him the last time they had seen him was at the Sunday services. Next, he called the Titusville chapter of Alcoholics Anonymous, but they hadn't seen him since the last A.A. meeting five days earlier. They gave Coop the phone number of Raine's A.A. sponsor, so he punched in the number and called him.

"Hi, I'm, Cooper Brennan, Raine Waters' boss, and he didn't show up for work today. I checked at his house, but he wasn't there and I was wondering if you had talked to him in the last couple of days."

"No, I'm sorry," the man said, "but I haven't talked to Raine since our last meeting."

"Is that normal?" Coop asked.

"We usually talk at least twice a week, but not hearing from him in four or five days is not unusual. Why, has something happened?"

Coop sighed. "Unfortunately yes. One of his good friends has been arrested and he was very upset about it. No one has seen him since that happened. We can't find him and I'm beginning to get a little worried about him."

"Have you tried calling his cell?"

"Yeah, several times but it just goes to message. I think he has it turned off."

When Coop hung up, he sat behind his desk trying to think of someone else to call, but he couldn't think of anyone. He dialed Raine's cell one more time, but it went straight to voicemail again.

"Where are you, Raine?" He said out loud.

"Are you looking for him too? I've searched all over this damn course and I can't find him either."

Coop looked up and saw his golf cart mechanic standing in his doorway. "Hey, Tom. Why are *YOU* looking for him?"

"When I got to work yesterday morning his cart was sitting there in my shop. I figured there was something wrong with it or it wouldn't have been there, so I took it for a spin. Coop, I can't find a damn thing wrong. That's why I'm looking for Raine, so he can tell me what to fix."

Coop stood up behind his desk. "Raine's cart is in your shop, right now?"

Tom nodded. "Yes sir, it's been there for two days."

"Don't worry about it, Tom. When I find Raine I'll let you know. Just park it back outside for now."

Coop ran down the stairs, jumped in his cart, and took off. On his way, he called Louise on his cell. "I think Raine is gone," he said when she answered.

"What do you mean, gone?" she asked.

"I'm heading to pick you up now. I think we need to go look inside the little house because I'm pretty sure Raine has packed up and disappeared."

When they got to the house, Coop walked up the steps and knocked on the door. "Raine, are you here?" With his master key, he opened the door and walked inside, "Raine?" He shouted, looking around.

He looked back at Louise and frowned. "He's not here."

Louise walked into the bedroom and looked in his closet. "Most of his clothes are still here," She yelled from the bedroom, "but he's taken some shirts and pants, and his work boots are not here either."

She walked out of the bedroom a few minutes later and looked at Coop with sad eyes. "His razor, toothpaste, toothbrush, and shampoo are missing too. I'm afraid you're right."

"Yeah, I know I am," he said, grimly, "take a look at this."

He pointed at five envelopes laying on the kitchen counter. "It looks like he's left us all letters."

Louise walk to the counter and inspected the envelopes. There were five of them. One for her, one for Coop, one for Virginia, one for Jake and one for Brooklyn."

They took their letters, sat on the couch, and opened them.

Dear Coop,

I know why you turned Dave in and I'm not mad about it anymore. I sure wish you hadn't, but I understand that you didn't have a choice.

I'm writing you this letter to thank you for everything you've tried to do for me. You are a good Christian man and I sincerely wish that I was more like you, but I know now that I am not.

I wish I had your faith and belief in God. I know you said that HE will forgive anyone if they just ask. I sincerely tried to believe that, but I realized now that the things I've done in my past must be unforgivable, even for HIM, because once again he's taken it all away.

There are no words to express how much I appreciate what you've done for me, but I can't accept your amazing generosity any longer, so I have to leave. I don't know where I'm going, so please don't try to find me. Just let me disappear and live the life that I deserve.

Your grateful friend,
Raine

Coop folded the letter and put it back inside the envelope. "I guess losing Dave was his last straw," he said wiping his eyes, "He's gone for sure this time, and he's not coming back."

FOR ALMOST THE entire plane ride back to Nashville, Brooklyn, Josh and Jake talked about what they needed to do next.

"What was the name of that country club in Florida where Nash Cooper said he saw Raine performing?" Jake asked.

Brooklyn reached under her seat and pulled out her purse. "Hold on," she said, "I wrote it down."

She dug through her purse a few minutes then pulled out a small notepad. "It was called La Cita Country Club in Titusville, Florida."

Jake looked at Josh and said, "When we get back home, you need to Google that place and see if we can find a phone number. If he was singing there, somebody's bound to know where he lives, or at the very least, have some contact information for him. If you can get me a number I'll make the call and see where that takes us."

Josh nodded. "Good idea, it should be easy to find."

"I know this has all happened fast, but have you guys thought about *your* plans yet?"

Brooklyn wrinkled her forehead and looked at Jake. "Our plans?" She said, " what are you talking about?"

He smiled at her. "It hasn't hit you yet, has it? Honey, you just signed a record contract and your life is about to change big time. You two have a lot to talk about, like what are you gonna do when you're on tour promoting your new album? Who's gonna watch little Ginny when you're on stage? Is Josh going to be up there on stage with you playing, or is he going to be in the dressing room watching Ginny?"

They looked at each other with wide eyes. "We...we haven't thought about that. What do you think?"

Jake laughed. "Oh no, you're not getting me tangled up on that decision. That's something you guys have to talk about seriously because whatever you decide, you need to start planning for it now.

You met Scott Hugley, trust me, this is all going to happen really fast. Once your album is completed, you're gonna need a band, a road manager, a personal manager, a publicist...it's a big list."

Josh turned in his seat and looked at Brooklyn. "Unless there's some reason you don't want me to, I want to be on the stage with you, playing. We can use my band."

Brooklyn smiled at him. "Of course I want you there, but what about Ginny? Who's gonna look after her when we're on stage? We can't just grab a roadie."

"What about hiring a professional nanny?" Jake asked.

Brooklyn thought for a moment. "I guess that would be OK, but I'm not sure I'd feel comfortable leaving my child with a complete stranger."

"That's why you need to hire one soon, so you can get to know her and she can get to know you and Ginny. There's a lot of stars doing that right now out there on the road. I'm sure Scott could help us find one."

The flight attendant rolled her cart by and they all ordered a drink. Jake held his up. "To good nannies and gold records!" he said, grinning.

No one talked for a few minutes as they sipped their drinks. "Daddy, can I ask you a question?"

"Sure, honey," Jake said, "About what?"

"Do you really like selling combines and tractors?"

He smiled. "Well, let's just say it wasn't my life long passion but it sure came in handy when we needed it."

"I'm serious dad, do you still like what you do? Do you ever miss the music business?"

He shook his head. "Some of it I do, but most of it I don't. I do miss the traveling, that was a lot of fun. And I always enjoyed being around the backstage of the concert and making sure everything went smoothly during the show, but I don't miss all of the other crap that went along with that."

"Like what?" She asked.

"I'm hoping that it has changed, but that remains to be seen. Back then, the worst part was all of the drugs flying around backstage. I saw that destroy some good people. Then there were the groupies, hanging around like a pack of hungry animals, and of course all the stupid show business politics that came with working with a star. But I guess what I hated the most was being on call at the whim of those egotistical maniac stars."

"They were all that way?" Josh asked.

"No, they weren't all nuts, but most were completely out of control." He looked at both of them. "You guys are about to find out what it's like to be revered as royalty. And that's exactly what it is. Everyone will treat you differently. They put you up on a high pedestal and almost bow to you."

He shook his head and frowned. "I've always thought it was sad because most people are willing to do just about anything to be near a star. And, if you're that star, it's easy to lose touch with reality, and start believing that you really *ARE* special. I just pray that doesn't happen to you."

Brooklyn looked Jake in the eyes. "That's why I was asking if you liked your job. I don't want that to happen to me, and I was thinking that maybe if you were around you could help keep me grounded."

"What are you asking me, Brooklyn? Do you want me to be your nanny?"

She burst out laughing. "No, of course not. I want you to come with us and be our road manager, and maybe that other manager you were talking about."

Jake leaned back in his seat, sipped his drink, and thought about what she had said.

"Well, what about it?" Brooklyn asked, "You already know all about this. You could really help us, and keep us out of trouble. What do you say, Dad? Please?"

Jake grinned. "Let me get this straight...you want me to quit my job, go on the road with you as your road manager, and be at your beck and call? Let you order me around. Is that what you're asking me to do? Seriously, that's what you want me to do?"

"Yes sir," she said, with a big smile, "And I especially like that ordering you around part."

―――――――――

WHEN THEY LANDED, they drove back to Brooklyn and Josh's apartment. It only took Josh a few minutes to find the La Cita Country Club's website and get the phone number.

"Josh, can you pull this place up on a map? I'd like to see where it's located in Florida. There's something about this that sounds very familiar."

"It looks like it's about 40 or 50 miles east of Orlando," Josh said pointing at the map on the screen, "It's just north of Cocoa Beach."

"That makes sense. When Owen and Wyatt first spotted Raine in that bookstore, it was only a few miles away from there."

"Looks like it's real close to the Kennedy Space Center," Josh added.

"Wait, go back! Titusville is close to the Kennedy Space Center?"

"Yes sir, Cocoa Beach and Titusville are within 15 or 20 miles of it. This area is called "the Space Coast.""

Jake started shaking his head up and down. "I remember now. I've been to this area of Florida before, 25 years ago, at a wedding. How long has the La Cita Country Club been there?"

Josh types on the computer keyboard and moved his mouse. "It says that it was built in 1983. This is what it looks like," he turned the screen toward Jake. "It looks beautiful."

Jake bent over and looked at the pictures. "Well, I'll be damned!" he said, "I've been there too. That's where they had the wedding, in that building, and it *WAS* beautiful."

"Whose wedding?" Brooklyn asked.

"Her name was Louise Coleman, she was a singer in Raine's band. Louise was beautiful and a great singer, but she quit to marry some guy that was a rocket scientist or something. All I can remember is that he worked at NASA. As you can imagine, Raine was pretty pissed about her leaving."

"Do you remember the scientist's last name?" Josh asked.

Jake shook his head. "No I don't, why?"

"I just pulled up the members, looking for a Louise Coleman. Could his last name be Parker? There's a Bill and Louise Parker listed as members. Does that ring a bell?"

"No, I'm sorry it's been way too long. Are there any other Louise's there?"

"No," he said, "she's the only one on this list. Hang on a second." Josh began typing on the laptop again.

After a few seconds, he started reading the screen. "Bill Parker wasn't a rocket scientist, but he must've been a hell of an engineer. He was part of the original team for the first manned space project. It says here that he was also a big part of the space shuttle team."

He scrolled the page down and read more, "Here it is," he said excitedly, pointing at the screen. "Bill Parker married Louise Coleman-Parker in 1989. That has to be her."

"Yes, I'm sure that's her. Can you get me her phone number?"

20

SMITTEN

W hen Coop dropped Louise off at her house, she opened the door, kicked off her shoes, and settled on her couch. Then she took out Raine's letter and read it again. It was short and sweet.

Dear Louise,

Thank you for trying to be my guardian angel. I know you did your very best, but I was too far gone to save. I hope you will find it in your heart to forgive me for leaving, but it was time for me to go. I don't deserve your goodness.

I pray that you will never change who you are. I'm convinced there is the perfect guy out there waiting for you. Someone who deserves your love...someone that can love you back.

Don't worry about me, I will be fine. I will never forget you.

Love,

Raine

AFTER SHE WIPED her eyes and put Raine's letter back in the envelope, she was tempted to open up the other three, but instead, she stacked them up on the coffee table with plans to contact Brooklyn, Virginia, and Jake soon.

Louise was hoping that Virginia and Jake still lived in Abilene and was planning on trying to call them first thing in the morning when her phone rang.

"Is this Louise Coleman?" She heard a deep male voice say.

"Yes, this is Louise Coleman-Parker," she said timidly, "Who is this?"

"This is Jake Taylor. I'm not sure you remember me after all these years, but I was Raine Waters' road manager. Do you remember me?"

She was so stunned, she dropped the phone.

The phone cracked and snapped in Jake's ears. "Hello? Are you still there?"

"Yes," she said breathing hard, scooping up the phone, "I'm sorry, I dropped the receiver. Yes, I'm here."

"Do I have the right Louise Coleman?"

"Yes, Jake, it's me," she said, "and of course I remember you. I'm just so shocked to hear from you, this is quite a coincidence."

"Coincidence?" Jake asked puzzled, "what do you mean, a coincidence."

He could hear her laughing. "What's so funny?"

"Believe it or not, I was planning on calling you in the morning. That's what so amazing about this. Just minutes ago I was thinking about how I could find your phone number, and you called me. Isn't that what you call a coincidence."

Jake laughed out loud. "I'm pretty sure that's the exact definition. Why were you going to call me?"

"Well, actually it's about our old boss, Raine Waters."

"NO FRIGGIN' WAY!" he shouted, "Are you serious? You were calling me about Raine? This is getting damn right spooky. Louise, the reason I'm calling you is about Raine too!"

"Oh my God! How weird is this?" She said with a chuckle, "Hold on a minute. I think I need a drink."

"Now that's a great idea. I'll get one too."

Jake ran to the refrigerator and grabbed a beer, while Louise poured herself a glass of wine. "OK, I'm back," she said, "You first. Tell me why you're calling me about Raine after all these years."

"Before I get into that, I want to say how good it is to hear your voice again," Jake said, "The last time we talked was at your wedding. How is Bill these days?"

He heard Louise sigh on the other end of the phone. "I'm sorry to have to say this, but I lost Bill four years ago. He had a heart attack. I miss him a lot, but I'm doing Ok, How about you, how is your wife?"

"Oh my God," he said, shaking his head, "Can this get any stranger. I lost my wife, Virginia, a little over a year ago to cancer."

Not knowing what to say to each other, they both sat quietly not talking for a few minutes.

"Louise," Jake said, breaking the silence, "I'm so sorry about Bill. Honestly, I'm at a loss for words here, I don't really know what to say next."

"I'm sorry about your wife as well, I completely understand what you're feeling. And like you, I'm a little speechless myself," she said softly, "and if you remember...that's not like me."

"Oh Yeah, I remember you firmly telling Raine exactly how you felt a few times." His laughter echoed through the phone.

"I didn't change much after I left the band. I've been known to give Bill a piece of my mind a few times too."

They both laughed and the mood lifted. "So what about Raine?" She asked, "Why are you calling me today?"

For the next hour, Jake told her the whole story, starting with the letters Raine had written to Brooklyn. Then he told her about how Nash Cooper had stolen the song he heard him sing at the country club, and finally, he told her about the two million dollars sitting in a bank in Nashville.

"I've heard that song on the radio a hundred times," Louise said, "I can't believe I didn't recognize it. Jake, I was there that night when Raine sang the song, but I never put the record on the radio together with the song Raine sang that night in the club. It was the first time he had performed in front of a crowd in years, and it was unbelievable. It was after the countdown for New Year's Eve and everyone wanted him to sing more, so he sat on a stool with his guitar and sang a few of his original songs and it was absolutely mesmerizing. Of course, now that I know, it's obvious to me. I remember it clearly. It was the last song he sang that night."

"Apparently, Nash Cooper was recording his set," Jake said, "that's how he got the song."

"What a terrible thing to do." She said.

"Yes it was terrible and stupid on his part, but at least, now, Raine will get all the royalties. I assume you know how to get in touch with him, right?"

"Well…not exactly," Louise said.

"What does that mean?"

"I think it's time for me to tell you my story and why I was planning on calling you tomorrow," she took a sip of her wine and leaned back in the couch, "Raine was living here, working at the country club, but disappeared a few days ago."

"What do you mean he disappeared?" Jake asked confused.

"It's a long story, but something bad happened to one of his close friends, he was arrested by the FBI and Raine packed up and walked away the following day. We all thought the arrest was the reason he left, but now, knowing about his song getting stolen, it makes more sense."

She set her empty glass on the table. "Oh God, Jake, he must have heard it on the radio, and then when they arrested his friend, that was all he could take."

"Who was his friend, and why did they arrest him?"

She glanced at her watch. "What time is it there? It's almost 11:00 here. Are you Ok to keep talking? Like I said, this is a long story."

"It's only 10 o'clock here," Jake said, "So yeah I'm good for another hour or so, but I need to hit the head and get another drink. Hang on, I'll be right back."

Louise took advantage of the break and did the same. When she got out of the restroom she poured another glass of wine and settled back on the couch.

When he got back he said, "Ok I'm back, and I feel a lot better.

Why don't you back up a little and tell me how Raine Waters got a job working at a country club cutting grass. That doesn't seem like a good fit to me."

IT WAS WELL after midnight when they finally said goodbye and hung up. The next morning, Jake booked three seats on a flight to Orlando.

When Louise walked into the baggage claim area, Jake recognized her immediately, she hadn't aged at all and was as beautiful as the last time he had seen her almost twenty-five years earlier.

When she saw him, she ran up and gave him a hug. "Jake, it's so good to see you again," she said, "You look great!"

"Thanks," he said blushing, "But you're the one that looks great. I'm serious, you haven't aged a day."

Brooklyn nudged Josh and whispered. "I've never seen Dad blush before."

"Me either," he whispered back, smiling.

"Louise, this is my daughter Brooklyn and her husband Josh."

"And who is this?" She said leaning down to the stroller, gently touching Ginny's face with her fingers.

"That's my granddaughter, Virginia, but we call her Ginny," Jake said.

Louise squatted down close to her, "Well, hi there, Ginny. You have the most beautiful eyes."

"She got those from me," Brooklyn said.

Louise stood up and smiled at her. "I can see that," she said.

Brooklyn looked her in the eyes. "What does he look like now?"

Louise glanced over at Jake. "It's OK," he said, "You can talk about him."

"Raine is showing his age a little," Louise said to Brooklyn, "but considering everything he's been through, he looks good. He's a bit thin, but in good physical health and he still has those amazing eyes, just like you."

Louise drove them back to her house and helped them settle into the guest rooms. She had told them to bring their bathing suits, so while she watched Ginny, the three of them took a swim.

After they had showered and dressed, she took them to the La Cita Country Club for dinner. Coop dropped by their table and invited them to meet him later in the bar for an after-dinner drink.

"I can't tell you how glad I am to meet you," Coop said to Brooklyn, "I have spent so many hours in this bar talking about you with Raine."

"Really?" She said shocked, "You talked about me?"

Coop laughed. "Actually, all I did was listen to him talk. You were all he ever thought about, his only inspiration in life."

"What could he say about me? We've never even met."

"That's what he talked about. He talked about what it would be like if and when he ever got to meet you someday. All he really wanted was to finally get to hold you in his arms."

Brooklyn's eyes filled with tears. "That's so sad. I didn't even know he existed until a year ago. That's when I found his letters."

Louise tilted her head. "I don't understand. Raine told me that he had sent you a letter every year until you turned 18."

Brooklyn looked at Jake. "He *DID* send them," Jake said, "but Virginia hid them from her. She could never find it in her heart to forgive Raine for what he had done to her. She swore me to secrecy, so we never told Brooklyn anything about him. But on her death bed, she asked me to tell Raine that she forgave him, and finally told Brooklyn about his letters."

"And those letters and his song is why we're here," Brooklyn said, "and why we have to find him."

"ARE YOU A RELATIVE?" The man behind the desk at the Orlando Central Florida Federal Reception Center said.

Raine shook his head. "No I'm not, but I am his friend and I want to see him. Please, I just want to talk to him and make sure he's OK."

The man picked up the phone and dialed a number. "Hold on a

minute," he said, "Let me see what I can do to get you back to see him."

A few minutes later, a different man dressed in a guard uniform walked out and told him to follow him. "How's Dave doing?" Raine asked.

The man frowned. "Not good. When we put him in the holding cell when we first received him, he went crazy, yelling and screaming. We finally had to sedate him and move him to isolation. We were afraid he was going to hurt himself, or the other prisoners in the cell there with him. We thought that after whatever drug he was on wore off, he would calm down, but he hasn't."

"He's not on any drugs," Raine said, "You said that you have him in isolation? What does that mean?"

"It's a small padded room, so he can't hurt himself, but that's not working well. He keeps banging into the door trying to open it, and he never stops yelling and screaming at the top of his lungs...and I mean never. We're hoping that when he sees you, a friendly face, he'll calm down."

Raine could hear Dave yelling through the massive 10 foot tall, steel doors before they opened them. The guard led him down the middle corridor, passing numbered cell doors on each side. When he got to Dave's, he stopped and slid back a panel that was covering a small plexiglass window with several holes in it.

"If you talk through the holes, he can hear you," the guard said, "If he calms down, I can open the door and let you see him."

He put his mouth next to the window and said, "Dave, it's Raine. Can you hear me?"

Dave instantly stopped yelling, walked up, and peeked through the window. "Raine. Is that really you?"

"Yes, it's me. I came here to see you, but they said that they won't open the door if you keep yelling. You need to calm down, so we can talk."

"PLEASE GET ME OUT OF HERE!" Dave yelled, "I CAN'T STAND IT, IT'S TOO SMALL! PLEASE, RAINE, HELP ME! GET ME OUT OF HERE!"

"Stop yelling! You've got to calm down. I can't help you if you don't stop this."

He felt the solid steel door move against his hand when Dave crashed into it. "PLEASE GET ME OUT OF HERE!" He screamed. Then he slammed into the door again with all his weight.

Raine turned around and looked at the guard. "He's not coming down off of drugs. He has severe claustrophobia, and he's never going to calm down in that small space. You've got to move him out of there into a bigger room. If you don't, he's going to hurt himself slamming into this door. Please, help him." He begged the guard.

The guard ran back down the corridor and came back a few minutes later with four other guards. One of the guards was holding a syringe in his right hand.

They made Raine move back, jerked the cell door open and three of the guards rushed into the room, trapping Dave down on the floor. When they had him secured, the fourth guard stuck the needle into his arm. He slowly stopped struggling against them and finally got still.

They pulled him out of the cell, loaded him onto a gurney, and strapped him down. He was groggy, mumbling something, so Raine walked up to him and grabbed his hand.

His face was bruised, with several cuts and scrapes, and it was covered in blood. "What the hell happened to his face?" He yelled.

"We didn't do that," one of the guards said, "he did it to himself, in holding. He kept slamming against the bars. That's why we put him in here because everything is padded."

"Where are you taking him to now?" He asked, following them down the corridor.

"To the hospital, the psych ward. We can't handle him here. They can keep him sedated and also check him out. I wouldn't doubt he's broken a few bones slamming against this door."

Raine followed the guards outside and watched them load Dave into an ambulance. "Can I come with you?" He asked.

"No sir, I'm sorry, but you can't."

"Where are you taking him? What hospital?"

"Orlando Regional Medical Center," the driver shouted to Raine, as he pulled away.

AFTER THEY FINISHED THEIR DRINKS, Coop took them to see the little house where Raine had been living.

"Is this his guitar?" Josh asked.

"Yes," Louise said, "I gave it to him for Christmas."

Brooklyn walked out of the bedroom holding up a shirt on a hanger. "Are you sure he's not coming back? His closet is full of his clothes."

"He only took his jeans and work boots," Coop said.

"And his toothbrush, toothpaste, and his razor," Louise added, "but that's not the reason we know he's not coming back."

"How do you know for sure?" Jake asked.

Louise glanced at Coop. "Because of his letters." she said, "We found them over there on the kitchen counter. He wrote one to each of us. He even wrote one to Virginia."

Louise ran her hand over the counter. "That's why I was planning to call you, to get your address, so I could mail them to you. If you'd like to read them, I have them at home."

When they got back to Louise's house, they all settled in the living room, and she passed out their letters. To give them some privacy, Louise and Coop took Ginny out to the pool deck and left them alone to read.

After 15 or 20 minutes, they walked back to the living room to join them. She could tell that all three of them had been crying. " I know it's none of my business, but I'm dying to know what he said."

"One thing for sure," Jake said wiping his eyes, "Raine has a way with words."

"What did he say?" She asked.

Jake lifted up the letter and read.

Dear Jake,

You were the best road manager I ever worked with. One of the biggest regrets of my life is that I never told you how good you were, and how much I appreciated what you did for me. I know it's a little late, but thank you.

The real reason I'm writing you this letter is to let you know how happy I was to hear that you had married Virginia. You are the kind of man she deserved, and I also knew that you would be a great father to my daughter. I know I have no right to call Brooklyn my daughter, but I hope you will allow me to say it this one time.

She is the only good thing I've ever done in my entire life and I'm so thankful that she had a man like you to raise her and to call her father.

Please take good care of her. She is the only thing left of me on this earth. I hope you and Virginia have a long and happy life together.

Raine

"I KNOW IT'S LATE, but does anyone care for a nightcap?" Coop said, "I think I need one after that."

"I've got two bottles of great red wine I bought last year on my trip to Italy," Louise said, "I've been saving them for a special occasion and I think this just might be the night. Does that sound good to everyone?"

Jake jumped up off the couch. "You need some help opening those bottles?" He said following her into the kitchen.

Brooklyn looked at Josh and grinned. "What is up with Dad?" She whispered.

Josh smiled. "Was he skipping?"

She laughed. "Almost."

"I was wondering if it was just me who had noticed it," Coop whispered to them, "but I think they are both a bit smitten with each other."

"Smitten?" Brooklyn said with a chuckle, "What does that mean?"

Coop grinned and held his finger up to his lips. "Shhhh, they'll hear us. That's old people talk that means they like each other."

They all sat there silently, smiling listening to Louise and Jake laughing and flirting with each other in the kitchen.

When they came back carrying the wine glasses, Jake said, "What are you all smiling about?"

"Oh, nothing," Brooklyn said, with a wide grin.

THEY DIDN'T READ any more of Raine's letters that night. The mood had lifted and no one wanted to get sad and cry again, so they changed the subject and talked as they drank their wine.

"So how are we going to find Raine?" Jake asked, "Does anyone have any ideas?"

"Well, I found him walking down the street near Cocoa Beach last time," Louise said, "That's as good a place to start as any, I guess."

21

BUTTERFLIES

The next morning, Brooklyn and Josh rode with Coop, and Jake rode with Louise on their search to find Raine. They split up and Coop searched the beaches near Titusville, and Louise and Jake searched the Cocoa Beach area.

"Where are we going?" Brooklyn asked.

"Canaveral National Seashore," Coop said, turning onto the bridge road, "It's the closest beach around here, but I doubt seriously if Raine's there."

Josh turned and looked at him. "Why do you say that?"

"It would be a hell of a long walk, about 15 or 20 miles from LaCita, and there's not much there. It's a national park with 24 miles of beautiful untouched pristine beaches, but there are no restaurants or any businesses out there."

Brooklyn's eyes widened. "Really? I didn't realize there were still beaches in Florida that haven't been developed."

"It's a national park, that's the only reason it hasn't," Coop said. "It's a wildlife preserve as well, and hopefully it'll stay that way. It's untouched by humans and absolutely beautiful."

Josh stared out the window as they drove through the tall bushes and trees lining the highway. "This looks like a good place for a man to get lost. That sounds like what Raine planned to do, so you never know...he might be here."

"Maybe on the beach," Coop said, "but not out here. This area is all wetlands, 58 acres of it and it's full of alligators and snakes and everything else you can imagine. A man wouldn't survive a week out here."

Brooklyn gasped and looked at Coop. "You don't think that's what he has planned, do you? Disappearing out here...dying here?"

Coop frowned but didn't respond. No one talked for a few minutes, all of them thinking about what she had said.

After a few minutes, Coop shook his head and said, "God I hope not. That would be a horrible way to die and no one would ever find his body."

Coop had planned on driving directly to Playalinda Beach to start their search but decided to take a few detours driving into the marsh areas along the way just in case.

"I don't mean to be nosy," he said to Brooklyn, "but did Raine say anything like that in his letter to you? You know, about ending it all?"

She turned her head and looked out the windshield. "No, nothing specific but it was the tone of the letter that has me worried."

"What did he say?"

She frowned and said, "In all of his other letters he always ended them with, *I hope we will meet someday.*"

"How did he end this one?"

Brooklyn turned her head and looked Coop in the eyes. "He just said...*goodbye.*"

———

It took them almost 4 hours to search the 24 miles of beach. They stopped at each public parking area, walked over the wooden walkways that went up and over the high dunes, and searched the beach. It was a Wednesday, so the beach was relatively empty and easy to scan.

It was 95°, without a cloud in the sky. By the time they reached the last parking lot with no signs of Raine, they were sunburnt and exhausted, so they gave up and drove back to Louise's house.

When Coop pulled up and let them out, he said, "Tell Louise I'll be back in about an hour. I need to take care of some business in my office and then I'm gonna go home and take a cold shower. If I was you, I'd go jump in that pool."

30 minutes later, Brooklyn and Josh were laying by the pool when they heard Louise's car pull up. They couldn't make out what they were saying but could hear them laughing and giggling like two kids.

Josh grinned and said, "Sounds like they're having fun."

Brooklyn smiled at him, "I really like her and I don't wanna jump the gun, but I think they're perfect for each other, don't you?"

"Hey, guys." Jake yelled, opening the pool screen door for Louise, "Did you have any luck?"

Brooklyn shook her head. "No, we searched the Canaveral National Seashore, all 24 miles of it, but he wasn't there. How about you?"

"We drove down every beach access road from Cocoa Beach Pier to the port, but no sign of him." Jake walked up to the edge of the pool. "Is the water cool?"

"Yeah, it's great," Josh said, "You should go put on your bathing suit and..."

Before Josh could finish his sentence, Jake turned around and fell backwards into the pool, clothes and all.

When he surfaced, wiping the water from his eyes, Louise burst out laughing. "You are such a nut!" She yelled, laughing louder.

Brooklyn leaned over and whispered into Josh's ear, "Who is this guy and what has she done with my father?"

Josh grinned. "I think this is what Coop called smitten?"

After they showered and dressed, Coop took them to *Dixie Crossroads*, a local seafood restaurant. "This place opened the same year we opened LaCita. It's world-famous and their specialty is Rock Shrimp. Everything's good here but my favorite is Royal Reds. That's the best tasting shrimp you'll ever eat."

Jake wrinkled his forehead and asked, "There are different kinds of shrimp?"

"Oh yeah," Coop said, "All different kinds. It depends on the season and where they catch them, but trust me, if they have Royal Reds, order a dozen or two. They're delicious."

Throughout the meal, tending to Ginny in the high chair, Brooklyn did her best to ignore her father as he blatantly flirted with Louise like a high school freshman. Although it was exactly what her mother had wanted for Jake, it was causing her to have conflicting emotions. She was happy for her father, but at the same time, sad for her mother.

"So what do we do now?" she asked, "Where do we look next?"

Coop looked across the table at Louise and shrugged. "Do you have any ideas?"

She slowly shook her head. "No, not really."

"What about this Dave guy," Jake asked, "Do you think he would have any ideas where Raine may have gone?"

"That's a good thought," Coop said, "The problem is, I'm not sure where they took him. But if we could find out and they would let us in to see him, maybe he would know something."

Coop pulled out his cell phone and dialed Special Agent Alexander Rush's number. "Hey Alex, this is Coop. I'm still trying to track down Raine Waters and thought that maybe you could pull some strings and get us in to see Dave. It's possible he might have an idea where Raine may have gone."

They all stared at Coop as he listened to Alex on the phone. "Really?" He said, "Raine was there?"

"WHERE?" Louise shouted.

Coop held up his hand for her to be quiet as he listened. "That bad, huh? On no. Was he hurt bad?"

"WHO WAS HURT BAD?" Louise shouted again.

Coop glared at her. "It was Dave. Now shut up, so I can hear,"

"Did he go with them?" Coop said, looking across the table at Louise, "Really? Do you think he's still there? What hospital?"

When Coop hung up, he reached for the check and slid out of the booth. "I think I know where Raine is, but we have to hurry."

"Where is he?" Brooklyn asked as she followed him to the cashier.

"They have Dave in a hospital in Orlando. Alex told me that Raine has been in the lobby all morning, waiting to see Dave."

After Coop paid the check, they ran to his car and jumped in. Coop flew down the road running two red lights to the I-95 freeway. 10 minutes later he turned on the 528 Beachline toll road to Orlando.

"So, what exactly happened to Dave?" Louise asked.

"He freaked out with his claustrophobia when they first put him in the jail cell, so they moved him to isolation, to a padded cell. Apparently, that didn't work either. Dave kept screaming and yelling and crashing his body against the door trying to get out. I'm not exactly sure how it happened, but Raine showed up and apparently convinced them to move him to a psych ward in a hospital."

Brooklyn leaned forward, so Coop could hear her. "Do you think Raine is still at that hospital?"

"I don't know, but that's where he was a few hours ago."

WHEN THEY ARRIVED at the Orlando Regional Medical Center, they jumped out of the car and ran inside, but Raine wasn't in the lobby.

Jake ran up to the reception desk and asked, "Is there a visitor waiting room for patients in the psychiatric ward?"

The receptionist looked up. "What's the name of the patient?"

"Dave," he said, "I don't know his last name. He's a prisoner. I think the FBI brought him here."

She frowned and said, "Oh, that Dave." She looked back down at the paperwork on her desk. "Since you don't know his last name I'm assuming you're not family. I can't let you up to that area if you're not family."

"I'm not here to see him," Jake said, "I'm looking for a friend of his. He's supposed to meet me here in the lobby. He's not in this one, so I thought maybe there was a different lobby somewhere else."

The receptionist lifted her head and smiled. "Are you talking about Raine?"

"Yes, Raine Waters. Have you seen him?"

She looked around, scanning the room. "He's been here all

morning sitting right over there." She pointing to a couch on the back wall, "Have you checked the cafeteria?"

He waved at Coop and they ran down the hall, but he wasn't in the cafeteria either.

Back in the lobby, Jake said, "I'm gonna go check the front parking lot. Josh, give Ginny to Brooklyn and check the men's rooms. There's probably one on each side of this building."

Louise looked at Coop and asked, "What should *we* do?"

"One of you needs to stay here in case he comes back." Coop looked at Brooklyn and asked, "Do you know what he looks like? Could you recognize him if you saw him?"

She shrugged. "I've only seen his pictures on the albums, with the long hair and beard, so I don't think so."

"OK then," he said, "Louise, you stay here with Brooklyn. I'm going to check out the parking garage."

Louise and Brooklyn walked to the couch where the receptionist had pointed to and sat down next to each other. "Does he look anything like those pictures on the albums?"

"Not much," Louise said, "Honestly, I didn't recognize him without the beard when I first saw him. I think he looks a lot better without it. He's very handsome."

Brooklyn lifted Ginny out of the stroller, sat on the couch, and put Ginny on her lap. "When you were singing with him back then, were you two...ah...dating?"

Louise nodded her head and grinned. "We were very close and we went out a few times."

"What about now? You said he was living with you for a few weeks. Did you two..."

Louise shook her head. "No, we're just good friends. He made that very clear from the beginning."

Brooklyn smiled. "Ok," she said, "That's good to know."

Louise lowered her eyebrows. "Are you asking me this because of your father?"

"To be perfectly honest with you...yes I am. I'm just concerned about him."

"Concerned about what?"

Brooklyn stared into Louise's eyes. "He likes you, he likes you a lot. I've never seen him act this way before, and I just wanted to make sure..." she paused, thinking of how to phrase it, "well, to be honest, I don't know what I'm trying to say."

"I think I know," Louise reached down and took her hand in hers, "You love your father, and you want him to be happy, but at the same time, it has to be hard seeing him with someone else. It's a natural reaction. Am I right?"

Brooklyn nodded and squeezed her hand. "Mom made me promise to help Dad find someone to live the rest of his life with, someone to fall in love with. Her biggest fear was that he would never remarry and grow old alone. I guess I just didn't expect it to happen so soon."

Louise let go of Brooklyn's hand, leaned back against the couch, and looked away. "When Bill died, I honestly thought that part of my heart had died with him. Over the past few years, my friends have set me up with a few very nice men and I've had a few dates. I enjoyed the company, but after each date, I felt nothing for them, and I never called them back. I had resigned myself to believe that I would never have those kinds of feelings again for anyone else but Bill, and I was OK with that...then Raine showed up."

"I thought you said that you and Raine were just friends?"

"We are," she said, "and that's all we will ever be. But when I found him on the street that day, brought him home, cleaned him up, and got a good look at him...well, I have to admit he gave me butterflies."

Louise turned her head and smiled at Brooklyn. "There's just something about him..."

"Did you tell him that you were interested?" Brooklyn asked.

"I hinted a little, but he quickly let me know that he wasn't, so I stopped thinking about him that way. I know now that he was right and we were never meant to be anything except friends. However, having those butterflies that day, made me realize that I *DO* have room in my heart for someone else."

Brooklyn shook her head. "Louise, you're beautiful. Why wasn't

Raine interested? That doesn't make any sense to me. What did he say to you?"

"He told me that he was interested, but that he was the wrong guy. He said that he knew there was someone out there that would love me the way I deserved to be loved."

"Do you think that's my dad?" Brooklyn asked with a grin.

"I really don't know. I guess we'll just have to see how things work out," Louise grinned back at Brooklyn, "but I will tell you...the butterflies are back."

THEY HAD SEARCHED every public place they could find at the hospital, but there was no sign of Raine anywhere.

"I'm not sure what to do next," Coop said, "but I could sure use some coffee."

They all got coffee and gathered around the table in the cafeteria.

"I guess he's gone. We missed him," Coop said, sipping his coffee.

"Did he ever get to see Dave?" Jake asked.

Coop shook his head. "I don't know."

"I'll be right back," Jake said, rushing away.

Ten minutes later he came back and sat down at the table. "No, Raine never got to see him," he said. "The receptionist told me the only people they can legally let up there are family members or his attorney."

"Poor Raine," Louise said, softly. "He came all this way and they won't let him see him."

"He had to have known that he couldn't see him," Josh said, "So why did he stick around in the lobby? Why was he there all day if they weren't gonna let him up there? That doesn't make any sense."

"I guess it was because he didn't have anywhere else to go," Brooklyn said, sadly.

"If that's the case," Josh said, "then why did he leave? Why isn't he still here?"

Coop lifted his head and stared at Louise. "Is there a chapel in this hospital?"

Louise jumped up, walked back into the cafeteria, and asked the cashier.

"Yes," she yelled, waving for them to follow her.

The tiny chapel was located on the first floor, just off from the lobby. When they found it, Coop held his finger up to his lips, motioning for everyone to be quiet and to wait outside.

When he slowly opened the door, his shoulders dropped with disappointment when he realized that Raine was not there. He walked into the small room and looked around. It was a tiny room, maybe 6 foot wide and 8 foot deep, with three rows of 2 chairs, facing a wall with a painted mural of Jesus Christ on the cross, covering it. He walked to the first row and took a seat and said a small prayer. When he stood up to leave, he saw something laying on the floor behind the second chair.

It was a Bible, but not just any Bible. It was the Bible Coop had given to Raine the night he had been re-baptized at his church. It was open, so he reached down and lifted it off the floor, careful not to lose the place.

He assumed that Raine had been reading where it was opened, so he scanned the page. When he realized what the passage was that Raine had been reading, a cold chill ran through his body, because Raine had been reading 1 Corinthians 3:16. "Oh no." He said, sitting back down in the chair.

Tired of waiting, Louise opened the door and looked around the room. Coop looked up at her with sad eyes and shook his head.

"What's wrong?" She asked.

He held up the Bible. "Raine was here, but he left this behind."

"Isn't that a good thing?" she said, "When he realizes that he left it here, he'll come back for it."

"No, I don't think so," Coop said, solemnly, "I'm pretty sure he's not coming back."

The door opened again and Brooklyn, Josh, and Jake walked into the room.

"What's going on?" Jake asked.

Coop looked at Jake and said, "He was here, but I'm afraid we may be too late."

"What are you talking about?" Brooklyn asked.

Coop held up the Bible again. "This is Raine's Bible. He's carried it with him every day since I gave it to him. He wouldn't have forgotten it, he left it here on purpose, because he won't need it anymore."

Louise frowned, "Why would he do that?"

"Did you know that Raine's father committed suicide?" He said.

Jake nodded. "Yeah, I heard about that. They found him in his barn, apparently, he had shot himself with a shotgun. But what's that got to do with this?"

"Raine came to me one night very upset," Coop said, "He needed to talk to someone about his father's death. This was a few weeks after he had been re-baptized. He wanted to know what the Bible said about suicide."

"Was he worried about his father getting into heaven?" Louise asked.

"Yes he was, so I told him what I thought about it."

Jake sat down in the chair next to him. "And what was that?"

"You need to understand how upset he was. I was just trying to make him feel better. I told him that most Christians are taught that it is a sin to commit suicide, but as far as I knew, there was nothing in the Bible that talked about it specifically. The only part that could be interpreted that way is One Corinthians 15-16.

Coop lifted the Bible and read. "Don't you know that you yourselves are God's temple and that God's Spirit dwells in your midst? If anyone destroys God's temple, God will destroy that person; for God's temple is sacred, and you together are that temple."

"I always thought that's what that meant," Josh said, "I know that's what my father preaches."

Coop nodded, "Me too, Josh, but there's a lot of Biblical Scholars that don't believe that's what it means."

"I don't mean to be rude, but why are we talking about this now?"

Brooklyn asked, looking around, confused, "What does this have to do with Raine?"

Coop sighed and locked eyes with her. "I found this Bible on the floor, right about where you're standing. It's Raine's Bible. When I picked it up it was opened to Corinthians."

He stood up and closed the Bible. "I believe he's been sitting here reading about this because he's contemplating suicide."

"We have to stop him!" Brooklyn shouted.

"How?" Coop said, "We don't even know where he is?"

"We need to tell the hospital security about this," Jake said, "get them involved in the search."

They rushed to the elevator and then ran down the corridor to the hospital security office. When Jake said, "We think our friend is going to commit suicide somewhere in this hospital," the security officer jumped out of his chair and said, "Follow me."

They ran behind him to the service elevator. When they were all inside the cab, he took out a key, inserted it, and turned it to the right. "We've had three jumpers this year," he said.

When the doors opened he used another key to open the door that led up to the roof.

They ran up the stairs and stepped out. Coop looked back at them. "Let me go alone. If he's up here, near the edge, we don't want to startle him."

Coop walked slowly around the giant air conditioning units scanning and searching the roof. When he saw Raine standing near the northern edge, he turned around, looked at Jake, and motioned for everyone to be quiet, stop and stay where they were.

Slowly, Coop inched his way toward Raine. "Not a bad view," he said.

Raine jerked around. "Go away, Coop. Leave me alone. This is none of your business."

"I'm sorry, Raine, but you know I can't do that, so why don't you just back away and talk to me. You know this isn't the solution to anything. We've talked about this...about your father."

Raine didn't move. "Maybe not for someone like you, but for me, it's the perfect solution. And just like my father, after a few months, no one will care, or remember I ever lived. One less loser in the world, good riddance."

Raine took a step closer. "You are so wrong Raine, you're not a loser. A lot of people will miss you, especially your music. You can't do this Raine. Don't deny the world your gift, your music. It's from God and you need to share it with the world."

Raine laughed. "He gave me the gift to write the song only to take it away." He slid his foot closer to the edge. "Coop, God let him steal her song!" he yelled, "Why would he do that? It was *HER* song. The only thing I ever gave her. Why would he stand by and let that happen? I know I was bad, but I've tried so hard to change. Why won't he forgive me? Why does he hate me so much?"

Raine collapsed, dropping to his knees, crying only inches from the edge.

Coop took a step toward him. "NO! MOVE BACK!" He yelled, "Please just go away and let me do this."

"God *DID* forgive you. And he didn't let anyone steal your song. I still have it."

Raine heard the words but didn't recognize the voice. Slowly, he lifted his head and stared into the stranger's eyes. "Who are you?" His voice was barely audible, just above a whisper.

Brooklyn didn't answer, but smiled at him and began to sing,

> *"God I know I have no right to even pray,*
> *because I turned my back on you and looked away.*
> *But I'm begging you before my whole life passes.*
> *Let me hold her in my arms,*
> *resurrect me from these ashes."*

He slowly pulled himself up to his feet, moving away from the edge and walked toward her. "Brooklyn? Oh my God!" Tears were rolling down his face. "Dear God...Is it really you?"

She reached out her hands and pulled him back to her, hugging him for a long, long time.

When they finally pulled back, Brooklyn took her sleeve and wiped her father's eyes. She smiled wide and said, "There's someone else I'd like you to meet."

Josh walked up to them, holding Ginny in his arms. "Dad, this is Josh my husband...and this...is Virginia but we call her Ginny...she's your granddaughter."

22

THE SHOP

Dave was on the FBI's wanted list because he had committed a crime in Colorado and then drove across several state lines to escape. Because his crime was not a federal offense he would not be tried in a federal court, so three days later, under heavy sedation, Dave was flown back to Colorado to stand trial in a state court.

Before they moved him, as a favor to Coop, Special Agent Alexander Rush called his friend, James Archer, the Special Agent in charge of the State of Colorado, and explained the situation to him.

"Do you have any influence over the Colorado Springs prosecutor?" Alex asked.

"No, he's new, so I haven't had much contact with him. I understand that he's a bit of a prick, but don't worry, my brother is very close to the Governor. I'll give him a call," James said, "What do you want me to tell him?"

"He needs to know how severe Dave Baker's claustrophobia is, and the doctors here believe he is possibly also schizophrenic. Honestly, I've never seen anything like it. Tell your brother I'm not asking for any favors for this prisoner and I realize this is an unusual request, especially for a murder suspect, but I wanted to give everyone a heads up. We've had a hell of a time with him, trying to stop him from bashing his body and head against the cell door trying to get out. This man cannot be locked up with the standard procedure. When he's in a large room he's fine, but if he's not, he is a danger to himself, the guards, and anyone around him. He needs to be held somewhere else with more space, like a hospital or a special holding center."

"How much time do I have?" James asked, "When does he arrive?"

"We are waiting on a judge to sign the extradition papers now," Alex said, "We should get that some time today. Our plans are to heavily sedate Mr. Baker and fly him there on Thursday. Are three days gonna be enough time?"

"Yeah, that should be more than enough. Will you be on the plane?"

"Yes, I was the arresting agent and this also involves a good friend of mine, so I'm personally handling the transport to make sure he gets there safely."

"Great," James said, "I'll meet you at the plane. When we get Mr. Baker settled in, we'll grab a beer and catch up."

Sam Greene, the new District Attorney for the Teller and El Paso counties was not happy when he hung up the phone with the governor, because he didn't like being told how to do his job.

"Special treatment for a murderer?" He said to himself, "That's bullshit!"

He punched the intercom button on his phone and said, "Nancy, have we received any paperwork from the FBI about a David Baker?"

"Yes sir," she said, "I just received the email. Do you want me to forward it to you?"

"No, print it out and bring it to me when it's done. Also, call records and see what they have on this Baker guy. Tell them it's a 20 something-year-old cold case."

After Sam scanned the files he quickly realized that this case would lead to nothing but grief for him. And even though the governor apparently had an interest in the case and was expecting him to handle it personally, he knew it was a lose, lose situation for him with nothing to gain. Plus, it would be the lowest of a low profile case and he decided not to waste his time on a case that probably wouldn't even make it in the papers. Especially one that was going to take special handling.

He hit the intercom button again, "Nancy, what's the name of the new girl again?"

"Everly Moore," she said.

"Tell her I need to see her, now."

A few minutes later Everly knocked on his door. "You wanted to see me, Mr. Green?"

"Yes, have a seat," he said, stacking some files on his desk, "How long have you been here now?"

"Six months," she said meekly.

"Think you're ready for your first murder trial?" He asked, smiling. Her eyes lit up. "Yes sir."

He handed her the files. "David Baker killed his father when he was 19 years old, stole a car, and fled across several state lines. He's been a wanted fugitive by the FBI for over 20 years. They caught him last week and are bringing him back to us to prosecute in two days."

Everly flipped through the pages as he talked. "I'm not sure how, but this case has the attention of the governor. I just got off the phone with him and he tells me that this Baker guy has a few problems. He has severe claustrophobia and is possibly schizophrenic. He can't be held in a standard jail cell, so you need to find someplace we can stash him until his trial. After the trial, he'll be the department of correction's problem, and out of our hands. Think you can handle that?"

"Yes sir, I'll get right on it," she said excitedly.

For the rest of the afternoon, Everly made calls to the surrounding hospitals, but none of them were willing to take a severe claustrophobic, possible schizophrenic prisoner. She called all of the rehabilitation centers within 100 miles and even tried a few secured halfway houses, but could find no one willing to take the prisoner.

She had called every possible facility in the state she could think of and had just gotten off a very unhelpful phone call with the Colorado

Department of Corrections when Sam opened the door of her office. "How are you coming on the Baker case?"

She looked up at him and frowned. "Not so good. I can't find anyone willing to take the prisoner."

Sam glared down at her. "That's not what I wanted to hear," he barked, "The prisoner arrives tomorrow at noon. I just hung up with the governor's office for the second time today. I don't know how, but this guy has got some juice. I want the governor off of my back, so find someplace to stash this guy where he can't escape and won't freak out. I don't care where it is. Everly, I gave you this case because I thought you could handle it. Don't let me down."

When Deputy Assistant District Attorney Everly Moore opened the front door of her house, Buster Moore, her father, instantly read the obvious stress on her face. "What's wrong, Honey?"

She looked at him and shook her head. "Work stuff," she said dropping her overstuffed briefcase on the floor.

"Anything I can do to help?"

"I don't think so, daddy," she said plopping down on the couch, "But thanks anyway."

He smiled, sat down next to her, and put his arm around her shoulders. "Come on now, it can't be that bad. Tell me what's going on."

After she told him the story, he sat back on the couch and thought a few moments. "Is this guy crazy or violent?"

She shrugged. "I'm not sure. I don't really know anything about him other than what was in the current FBI arrest records that say he's severely claustrophobic. I pulled up his old police records, but couldn't glean much from those either, because there was nothing there. He didn't even have a parking ticket on his record before he supposedly killed his father."

"What's going to happen if you can't find a place to put him?"

She shook her head and frowned. "I'll have no other choice than to put him into a regular cell in the county lock-up. If I do that, he'll go nuts and hurt himself or one of the guards, the governor will come down hard on my boss and I'll probably get fired off my very first murder trial."

Buster sat up and looked at her. "We could keep him in the shop."

She wrinkled her forehead and looked at him. "The shop? Dad, are you crazy? That's not a secured lock-up facility? The D.A. would never go for something like that."

"Honey, just because I'm a retired cop doesn't mean I've forgotten how to do the job. I've watched hundreds of prisoners in my day. We could clear everything out of the shop and put it in the garage. There is only one entrance and the building is rock solid. It has a bathroom and we could set up that old rollaway bed. Just think about it. It would be as secure as any damn hospital and it's a big open space. I'll call Joe and Art. They're both retired cops and as bored as I am. We could watch him in shifts."

Everly leaned back on the couch and thought about it. "Dad, we're talking about a wanted fugitive that has just been captured by the FBI. They'll never go for something like this."

He started laughing. "Oh to be so young and naïve again."

"What are you talking about? I am not naïve." She said angrily.

"I love you baby girl, but that's where you're wrong," he said taking her hand, "All the FBI wants is to turn him over and get him out of their hair. Your boss said he didn't care where you put him, so I'm pretty sure he'll go for it. Why do you think he gave you this case in the first place?"

She frowned at him. "Because I'm one of his deputy assistant district attorney's working in his office."

"Everly, I've been around DA's for my entire adult life. I've seen them come and I've seen them go. I've never met your boss, District Attorney Sam Green before, but I've heard plenty of stories about him to know exactly who he is and what he's thinking."

She shook her head and smirked. "Oh, you do, do you? Tell me, what's he thinking?"

"He's thinking that he doesn't want any part of this case. He knew damn well our local hospitals aren't equipped to handle a prisoner. That's why he didn't want to do it, because when he couldn't find any place to put him, just like you couldn't, and he was forced to lock him up in county, he knew this guy would go nuts and the governor would be all over his ass. That's why he gave it to you, the rookie. That way you take the heat for dropping the ball and he's off the hook."

"You think he wants me to fail?" She asked.

He shook his head. "No, of course not. I'm sure he'd love it if you found a place to keep the prisoner and everything on this trial goes smooth. If it does, trust me, he'll take the credit for it, but if it doesn't, he has a scape goat...and that's you."

He stood up. "Just think about it. Give me five minutes. I'm gonna call the chief. If he'll sign off on it, we're home free."

―――――――

THE NEXT MORNING, Ralph Walters, the Colorado Springs Chief of Police, showed up to check out the shop.

Buster had called Joe and Art, and they had worked late into the night cleaning out the place and were there next to him standing at attention in front of the shop door when the chief's driver pulled up in his black SUV. When the Chief slid out of the back seat, he was followed by a man they didn't know.

"At ease gentlemen," Chief Walters said, "I would like to introduce you to Special Agent James Archer. He is the FBI agent in charge of the state of Colorado. Since we are receiving this prisoner from their custody, I wanted him to inspect the facility with me." James reached out and shook their hands.

"James, before we inspect this facility, I want you to understand that these men standing before you, were three of my best officers before they retired. If it wasn't for these three men, I wouldn't have even considered this."

Slowly, the chief and Agent Archer inspected the shop. The chief ran his hand along one of the walls. Then he reached into his pocket, pulled out a pocket knife, and made a small cut in the paint.

"What's under this?" He asked. "Is it drywall or cinderblocks?"

Buster smiled. "Steel reinforced cinderblocks. I laid those blocks myself, every one of them," he said, "I guarantee you these walls are as strong as the walls at the county lock up."

"What about the doors?" Agent Archer asked.

"There's only two, the one side door and the big roll-up," Buster said, "The side door is solid steel and I'm going to bolt the roll-up door in place. It would take a blow torch to cut through either of them."

Chief Walters grinned. "Damn, Buster, did you build this with something like this in mind?"

"No sir," he said laughing, "I built it like this to keep people from getting in, not to keep em' from getting out, but I guess it works both ways."

Chief Walters looked at Agent Archer and asked, "What do you think, James?"

He sighed and nodded his head. "I think it's as secure as any of our safe houses," he said, "but if he escapes or something goes wrong..."

"I know," Chief Walters said, "We're gonna get our asses handed to us."

"For extra security," Buster said, "what if we stretched a steel cable across the room, bolted from that far wall to the bathroom. Then we could connect the chain from the prisoner's ankle shackles to it. He could still move around, but couldn't possibly escape."

Agent Archer opened the bathroom door and looked inside. "You'll need to keep this door open at all times. From what I understand, this prisoner is extremely claustrophobic."

"I can do that," Buster said, "Is there anything else I need to do?"

Agent Archer looked at the chief. "I like the cable and shackle idea. Also, until we get to know this prisoner, can you keep two officers in a unit in the driveway?"

The chief nodded. "Sure, I can do that." He looked at Buster. "How are you planning on doing the watches?"

"Two of us always here, alternating 8 on 8 off."

He smiled. "That should work."

"How long do you think he'll be here?" Buster asked.

"I guess that depends on your daughter since she's the prosecutor," he said, "but it could be several months."

The chief looked at Joe and Art, and then back at Buster. "Are you guys OK with that?"

WHEN CHIEF WALTERS and Agent Archer delivered Dave to the shop, he could barely walk from the heavy sedation and fell sound asleep in the bed the second he laid down.

Buster and Joe were sitting in wooden folding chairs on the other side of the room watching him sleep. "He's a lot bigger and stronger than I thought he'd be." Joe whispered, "I hope we haven't bitten off more than we can chew here."

Buster grinned and looked at Joe. "That's exactly what I was thinking, but I guess it's too late to back out now."

Buster was beginning to wonder if he had made a big mistake when Dave opened his eyes and looked around.

"Where am I?" He asked, with a hoarse, gravelly voice.

"You're in Colorado Springs," Buster said.

"I know that. What is this place? It doesn't look like a jail or a hospital."

"It's not a jail," Buster said, "It's my workshop. Is it big enough for you? They said you had severe claustrophobia."

Dave sat up, dropped his feet over the side of the bed, and looked around. "Yeah, this is plenty big, it's great, thanks. What kind of shop is it?"

"I build handmade furniture—chairs, tables, cabinets, things like that."

"Dude, that's cool. Did you make those chairs you're sitting on?"

Buster smiled. "Yes, I did."

"Cool man, they look great," Dave glanced behind him, "Where are all the saws and stuff?"

"We had to clear them out to make room for you."

Dave took a deep breath. "It smells good in here. Like some kind of wood, maybe pine or something. It smells a lot better than a hospital."

Buster grinned. "That's not pine, it's Colorado Blue Spruce. I was making a cabinet with it."

"Whatever it is, it smells good." Dave said, "So, are you guys prison guards are something?"

Buster shook his head. "No, we're both retired police officers."

"Cool, how long were you cops?"

"35 years for me and 36 for Joe," Buster said, "We were both lieu-tenants out of the same precinct."

"Well, it's nice to meet you, Buster, Joe," he said nodding at them, "I'm Dave."

He tried to stand but fell back on the bed. "I'm not sure what they gave me, but I'm really dizzy."

Holding onto the bed, Dave slowly stood up on shaky legs. "Is there a bathroom here? I really need to go."

Joe pointed to the opening. "The bathroom is in there," he said, "We took the door off so it wouldn't be so confining. You think you can go in there?"

The chains connected to the shackles on Dave's ankles and the steel cable running across the floor clanged and rattled against the concrete as he shuffled toward the bathroom.

When he made it to the opening, he looked inside the room. "It's pretty small," he said.

"I can get you a bucket," Buster said.

Dave shook his head. "Naw, that's nasty man. It's Ok, I think I can do this."

While Dave was in the bathroom, Joe glanced over at Buster and whispered, "He seems pretty normal to me, actually he's sort of a nice guy."

Buster nodded, whispering back, "Yeah, he seems alright. Let's just hope he stays this way. Don't forget he's a murderer."

23

LANCE MCCAIN

It didn't take Raine long to realize that Brooklyn was just as stubborn and hardheaded as he was.

"It's your money, not mine," Brooklyn said, firmly, "You wrote the damn song."

He smiled at her. "Yes I did, but remember, I gave it to you and all of the royalties, so technically it's *your* money."

Brooklyn was sitting in a chair in Louise's living room. Jake and Raine were sitting next to each other on the couch across from her. "This is very confusing," she said, "I don't want to hurt anybody's feelings."

"What are you talking about?" Jake asked, "What's so confusing?"

Brooklyn sighed and smiled. "I'm sitting here looking at you, my father, who is sitting next to someone who is also my father. I don't know what to call anybody now."

Jake glanced at Raine and grinned. "How about, Dad?"

"For both of you?" She asked.

"Well, I don't want you calling me Jake, and I'm pretty sure he doesn't want you to call him Raine," he said with a chuckle, "Personally I like Dad, how about you?"

"Dad works for me too," Raine said, laughing.

She grinned and shook her head. "Gee, thanks for the help, Dad's."

"So, we're all clear here, right?" Raine said, "You're keeping the money."

"No, we are not clear!" She shouted back at him," I am not keeping that money. Think about it, Dad. You're going to need money to hire a good lawyer for your friend, right?"

He nodded. "Yeah, I guess so."

"And you're going to need money to pay for your trips to Colorado to visit him. You need to buy a car and a house. There's a lot of reasons for you to keep this money. I don't need it, but you do."

"I guess you're right," He said with a shrug, "How about this? Why don't we share it? There's a lot of it now and a lot more coming. I'll use what *I* need, and you use what *you* need. Do we have a deal?" He held out his hand.

Brooklyn reached out and took it. "Ok, but before we shake on it, I have one condition."

"What's the condition?"

She smiled. "That you agree to help me produce my new album and write some new songs for it."

"Now we're talking," he said," I'd love that."

RAINE SPENT $200,000 of the money to retain Lance McCain, the best defense attorney in the state of Colorado. He wrote the check, even though Lance told him that more than likely, Dave would be convicted and have to do some time.

"The only question is," Lance said, "how much time? We know Dave killed his father, but we don't know why he did it. Was it an accident, or did he plan it? That will make a huge difference in how I present his case."

"When you met with him," Raine asked, "what did he tell you?"

Lance leaned back in his chair and shrugged. "Well, I haven't actually seen him yet. He's being held in a rather unusual place due to his claustrophobia and I'm not allowed to visit him there. I have talked to him twice on the phone, but he wouldn't tell me much. I'm not sure he trusts me. He was not very forthcoming with information."

"Is there any way I could go there and talk to him?" Raine asked, "I think he'll talk to me."

"You can't go there, but let me see what I can do. It's certainly worth a try," Lance said, "How long will you be in Colorado?"

"I can be here until Friday. I have to be in Nashville for a recording session with my daughter on Saturday."

"Is your daughter a singer? Have I heard of her?"

Raine grinned. "Not yet, but you will soon."

"What's her name?"

"Brooklyn Taylor Arnett. She just signed a record deal," Raine said proudly, "and we're recording the first couple of songs for her new album Saturday. That's why I have to be there."

BECAUSE OF THE unique circumstances surrounding Dave's incarceration, the judge agreed to have Dave transported to Lance McCain's office for their meetings.

With his hands cuffed to a chain around his waist and his ankles shackled, the two police officers slowly shuffled Dave down the hallway, and into the meeting room.

When he saw Raine sitting behind the table, he yelled, "Dude, good to see you!"

"Please remove the handcuffs," Lance said.

The police officer frowned. "I'm not sure that's a good idea."

"We're on the eleventh floor," Lance said pointing toward the window, "What's he gonna do, jump out? Please remove the cuffs and wait outside."

When the officers left the room, Raine walked around the table and gave Dave a hug. "How are you doing buddy?"

Dave smiled. "I'm Ok, I guess."

"Do they have you in a good place? Is it big enough? Are they treating you OK?"

"Oh yeah, it's really big and a pretty cool place. It's at Buster's wood shop."

"Who's Buster?" Raine asked.

"Oh man, he's the best. He and Joe and Art are retired cops and they take turns looking after me and bringing me food. I really like it there. So...what are you doing here?"

"What do you think, dumb ass? I'm here trying to help you. That's why I hired Mr. McCain. He's supposed to be the best lawyer in Colorado, but he can't help you if you won't talk to him. He needs to know what happened, the whole story, every detail. Do you understand?"

Dave dropped his head. "Yeah, I understand, but I don't like talking about it."

"I know you don't, but you're gonna have to tell him what happened that day. It's very important he knows every detail. Please, Dave, tell him everything you can remember, so he can help you."

THE NEXT DAY on his plane ride to Nashville, Raine couldn't stop thinking about the meeting with Dave in Lance McCain's office, but he wasn't thinking about the sad, horrible story that Dave had told them. That story explained so much and although he knew Lance McCain had heard thousands of stories like it before, Raine believed that even he was touched by it a little. But that story wasn't what he was thinking about.

What was on his mind was Dave's amazing transformation he had witnessed before his eyes. He kept asking himself how he could not have realized before, that the slightly dense, cool dude, hey man persona Dave had always presented, was just an act. He was not the brain fried, dumb, dense guy everyone thought he was. In fact, Raine learned that day that he was far from that. Dave was very intelligent and had calculated his every move. That was how he had been able to elude the FBI all those years.

Raine discovered this when Dave asked Lance his first question.

Dave's facial expression actually changed to something he had never seen before when he leaned over the conference table and said, "Mr. McCain, after you called me the second time, Buster let me use his laptop and I did some research on you. You received the *Distinguished Graduate Award* from the Air Force Academy, basically *summa cum laude*. That's very impressive. Why Yale, not Harvard? I assume you had the choice of either one?"

Lance smiled. "Harvard produces future politicians, Yale produces great lawyers."

Dave grinned. "Exactly," he said, leaning back in the chair, "So, are you as good as they say you are?"

"Better," Lance said.

Dave looked at Raine. "How the hell did you come up with the money to retain Mr. McCain? Is Louise paying for this?"

Raine shook his head no but didn't say anything for a few seconds. He was in a slight state of shock from Dave's sudden transformation and had to think about where the money had actually come from. "It's a long story I'll tell you about later, but it's not Louise's money. I paid for this."

Dave tilted his head. "That has to be one hell of a story," he said, "How much was his retainer?"

"Let's not worry about that now, trust me, I can afford it," Raine said, "Just tell him what happened, so he can earn it."

Dave smiled, leaned forward toward Lance, and asked, "Where do you want me to start?"

"I don't care where you start," he said, "I just need to know why you killed your father?"

24

THE CLOSET

The story he told them that day was difficult for him to tell and equally difficult to hear.

Dave's father was an angry and violent man. He was a veteran of the Korean War, where he had lost his left leg and three fingers on his right hand. To get around, he used a wooden crutch under his left arm. Due to his disability, he received a small check each month from the government, but it wasn't enough to pay the bills.

Because of his father's uncontrolled anger and rage, combined with his disability, he had trouble keeping a job, so eventually, he gave up and stopped looking. To pay the bills, his mother went to work at a small local hotel, cleaning rooms in the mornings, and washing and folding towels and sheets until late in the night. Because of the long hours she worked, Dave and his younger brother, Max were left alone with his father most of the time.

As the years past and Dave and Max grew older, his father became more and more disgruntled with his life, angry at everything and everyone.

When Dave and his brother would play and make noise, his father would scream at them to be silent. Soon his screams turned to physical violence, but it was only directed toward Dave, hitting him with his fist.

But one day, his father went after Max and Dave jumped in between them. When he did this, his father used his crutch and viciously beat him until he was unconscious. When he woke up he was locked inside of a dark closet. He screamed and cried for hours, but his father wouldn't let him out. Hours later, frightened out of his mind, his mother finally came home from work and unlocked the door.

From that day on, when his father went into one of his drunken rages, he would beat Dave with his crutch and force him back inside that dark closet.

"How old were you when this started?" Lance asked.

Dave shifted in his chair and stared past him out the window. "I was seven."

"How old was your little brother?"

He frowned and slowly shook his head. "He was just a baby, only four years old."

"Did he beat Max after he locked you in the closet?" Raine asked.

Dave looked at him with tear-filled eyes. "Yes, a few times."

"Why didn't your mother try to intervene, stop him, call the police or something?" Lance asked. "There is no record of any domestic violence calls from that house."

"You just don't get it, do you?" Dave said with a smirk, "He beat the hell out of my mother almost every day anyway. If she had called the police, he would have killed her, and probably me and my brother too, as soon as the cops pulled out of our driveway...and she knew it."

Lance glanced at Raine and shook his head with disgust. "How long did this go on?"

"Until I was 16," he said.

"What happened then?" Lance asked.

Dave leaned back and wiped his face with his sleeve. "I ran away."

"Where did you go?" Raine asked.

Dave looked at him and grinned. "You know where I went."

"You were on the streets at 16?" Raine said, shocked, "Dear God, didn't they look for you, try to find you?"

Dave frowned, and shook his head no.

Lance started flipping through a stack of papers on his desk. When he found what he was looking for, he pulled it out and held it up. "If you were living on the street, homeless, how do you explain this?"

He handed Dave the paper. It was a copy of his high school transcript. "How could you have graduated from high school in the top five percent of your class?" Lance asked, "Didn't your parents have to sign any paperwork? How did you pay for your school supplies?"

"Mr. Johnson." He said.

Lance lowered his eyebrows and leaned toward him. "Who is that?"

"He was my only friend," Dave said, with a smile, "In the woods behind the high school there was an old abandoned shack. I had discovered it a few months before I ran away, so that's where I went the night I left. It was really cold and it was the only place I could think of to get out of the weather. Mr. Johnson was the janitor for the high school. A few weeks later, after school, he saw me walking into the woods and followed me to the shack."

"What did he say to you when he found you?" Lance asked.

"He didn't say anything. I didn't even know he had followed me, but the next day after school, I found some food and blankets inside the shack. A few days after that, I found more food and some money. I didn't figure out who was doing it for almost two weeks."

"How did you find out?" Raine asked.

"I got called to the principal's office and when I got there, Mr. Johnson was there too. To this day I don't know for sure, but I believe he had told the principal about me living in the shack, but neither one of them ever said anything about it."

"Why did they call you there?" Lance asked.

"To offer me a job. They told me that it was a new special program for underprivileged students with a high-grade point average. I had always made good grades and had been moved up a few years, so I was a senior. I guess it was their way to help me graduate."

Lance smiled. "What was the job?"

"Helping Mr. Johnson with his janitorial duties. It paid minimum wage and three meals a day from the cafeteria."

"Wait," Lance said, "I thought the cafeteria only served lunch."

"That's what I thought too, but every morning there was a sack waiting for me with breakfast in it, and every afternoon there was a sack with a hamburger, a sandwich, soup or something for my supper. I found out later that Mr. Johnson's wife worked in the cafeteria, so I guess she was doing it for me."

"So you're telling me," Lance said, "for that year, you lived in that shack in the woods with no running water or electricity."

"No," he said, "I didn't stay in the shack. Mr. Johnson gave me a key to the back door of his office, and he made a point to tell me how comfortable his couch was. He told me that was where he took his naps during the day."

Dave looked across the table and smiled at them, "Mr. Johnson didn't take naps, he didn't have time for that, but I knew what he was doing. He sort of gave it away with his wide smile when he showed me where he kept the sheets, blankets, and pillows. I slept there every night, and took my showers in the boy's dressing room every morning before school started."

"Wow," Lance said, shaking his head, "that's quite a story. So you were only seventeen when you graduated high school, right?"

"Yes sir," Dave said.

"And you were nineteen when you killed your father," he continued.

Dave dropped his head and stared down at his hands. "Yes, I was."

"What happened during those two years to make you want to kill him?"

Dave lifted his head and glared at Lance. "I hated him, but I didn't want to kill him."

Lance looked down and wrote something on his yellow pad. "So, tell me what happened."

Dave took a deep breath and slowly let it out. "After I graduated high school, Mr. Johnson helped me get a job with a friend of his doing construction in Boulder. That's about a hundred miles north of

Colorado Springs. I didn't have a car, so Mr. Johnson drove me there and helped me find a cheap apartment close to the construction site. We were building houses. It was a great job and paid really well, so that's where I was until we built all of the houses."

Dave reached for the water pitcher on the table, poured himself a glass, and took a long sip. "The man that owned the company was a Gulf War veteran and most of the crew were also vets. They all smoked like chimneys and drank like fish. Before I knew it, I did too."

"All day long while we were working, they talked about their experiences in Vietnam and being in the military. They all loved their time in the military and were constantly encouraging me to join up. 'It'll make a man out of you,' they said, "and give you a real future.'"

Dave shrugged his shoulders and sighed. "After a while, it began to sound pretty good to me, so I decided that when we finished building all of those houses, I would join the Air Force and try to get into the Air Force Academy and maybe become an officer."

"With your grades, you probably could have made it," Lance said.

Raine looked over at him. "That sounded like a good plan. Why didn't you do it?"

He looked away and shook his head. "I was going to," he said, "I took a bus from Boulder and then a cab to a hotel within walking distance of the Air Force Induction Center. My plan was to walk there the first thing the next morning and sign up. It was about 6 o'clock pm when I finally made it to the hotel and got checked in. I was a little nervous about the whole thing and certainly wasn't sleepy, so I went downstairs to the bar to have a couple of drinks to relax. The bar was packed, so I sat down at a table next to a group of men. When they realized I was alone, they invited me to join them. They were nice guys in town for some kind of sales convention and were drinking hard, and before I knew it, I was pretty drunk. When I told them what I was doing the next morning, one of them asked me if I had told my parents that I was leaving? When I said no, they couldn't believe it and every one of them insisted that I tell them so they would know where I was. When I explain to them my relationship with my father, they convinced me that I should at the very least tell my mother and my brother."

"Oh, no," Raine exclaimed, "you went there drunk that night?"

He shook his head and looked him in the eyes. "I know it was stupid, but yeah I was real drunk."

"Dave," Lance said, "I realize this is very difficult for you to talk about, but I need to know exactly what happened that night, every single detail. Start with how you got from the hotel bar to your parent's house."

Dave poured another glass of water and took a sip. "I took a cab. Then I walked up and knocked on the door."

"What time was it," Lance asked, "and who opened the door?"

"It was about ten o'clock, I guess, and it was my father that opened the door. When he saw that it was me, he just cursed at me and limped back inside. I looked around, but my mother wasn't home from work yet. When I asked him where Max was he didn't answer. I walked back to his bedroom, but he wasn't there. So I went back and asked my father again where he was."

"He lifted up his crutch and pointed at the hallway closet door, 'The little bastard is in there, but don't let him out.' I ran to the closet door, unlocked it, and jerked it open. When the light filled the room, I saw Max looking up at me, with frightened eyes and a bloody, swollen face."

Dave stopped talking, staring forward over their heads, looking through the window.

"Was Max hurt bad?" Lance asked him.

Dave slowly lowered his head and looked at Lance. "I honestly don't know. The only thing I remember clearly was looking down at his bruised, bloody, swollen face, and the look of fear he had in his eyes. That's when I heard my father yell, 'I told you not to let him out,' and felt his crutch hit me across my back. I sort of lost it after that."

"What do you mean, lost it?" Lance asked, "Try to remember, it's very important."

The expression on Dave's face dropped and grew gray and dark. As if he was in a trance, his eyes began to flicker rapidly side to side as he forced out the buried memory.

"I turned around to see him swinging the crutch at me again," His voice was soft, just above a whisper, "but I jumped out of the way and jerked the crutch out of his hands. I pulled it back and swung it as hard as I could. When it connected, his eyes flew open with shocked surprise as he cursed at me at the top of his lungs. When I hit him the second time, the old wooden crutch broke in half and he dropped to the floor. I turned back around and helped my brother get out of the closet, then I walked to my father, grabbed his collar, and dragged him to the dark, cramped, cold place he had put me in so many times before. I wanted him to feel what that was like, so I stuffed him inside and locked the door."

The room grew quiet and nobody talked for several minutes.

"Did your mother let him out when she got home from work?" Lance asked him, "And when she did, did he come after you a second time?"

Dave sighed, shaking his head. "It was a little after midnight when she finally got home. When she saw me sitting in the living room next to my brother, bandaging his wounds, and saw the broken crutch on the floor, she let out a shriek. 'Oh God, what happened here? Where is your father?'"

Dave looked over the table at them. "I hadn't seen her in three years and she didn't even say hello. All she wanted to know was what had happened and where my father was. She didn't give a shit that I was back."

"I'm so sorry, Dave," Lance said, "I know this is hard, but you need to finish the story. What happened when she let your father out of the closet?"

Dave sighed again and said, "When I told her, she ran to the closet, unlocked it, and knelt down over him, trying to revive him. When he didn't come around, she lifted his arm and felt for a pulse, but he didn't have one. He was dead."

"He was dead?" Lance asked shocked, "That's how he died? Why did you run? It was self-defense. Your brother was a witness!"

Dave shook his head and shrugged. "I don't know. I was still a little drunk and she was crying and screaming at me, calling me a murderer. When she picked up the phone and called the police, I panicked, jumped up, and ran out the door. When I saw the keys in my neighbor's car, I jumped in it and sped away," he lifted his hands and shrugged, "and I've been hiding ever since."

Lance frowned. "Running away was a terrible mistake. You should have turned yourself in. Especially after all these years. You could have had all this behind you by now."

"I know. I've thought about doing it many times, but I was afraid they would put me in a small cell and I can't do that."

Lance nodded, "I can certainly understand why, after hearing your story. Have you considered getting professional help with your claustrophobia?"

"No, I never have," he said, "maybe someday I will if you get me out of this."

"Do you have any idea where Max is?" Lance asked, "We need to locate him. He's your only witness."

"No, I have no idea. I was always afraid to try to contact him because I assumed the FBI had him under surveillance. I didn't want to get him into any trouble, so I never tried. I called my mother once, a few years before she died and she told me that he had gotten married and moved to Texas, but that was 15 years ago."

"Was she happy to hear from you?" Raine asked.

"No, she wasn't. She told me to never call her again, and I never did."

"Don't worry," Lance said, "we'll find him."

Dave gave him a small smile. "If we can find him and he testifies, do you think they'll believe him?"

Lance grinned. "Oh, I'll have my work cut out for me, but that's what I do and I'm damn good at it. Dave, I believe if you will tell a jury exactly what you told us today, and your brother backs you up...I don't see them going any other way. Just trust me. I'm going to get you out of this mess."

25

BLESSED

When Raine's plane landed in Nashville, he jumped in a cab and gave the cabbie the address to the studio. On the ride there, his stomach was in knots and his heart was racing in his chest. He took several deep breaths trying to calm down, but he was really nervous. He hadn't been in a studio in 28 years and he had no idea if they were going to like any of the songs he had written for Brooklyn's album.

No one had heard his new songs because he had kept them all a secret, even from Brooklyn. He had hoped to have a chance to sit down with her in the studio and play them for her, so she could at least hear them first, but when he walked in the control room, it was packed. The only ones he recognized at first, were Brooklyn, Josh, Bertha, Jake, and Louise. When Scott Hugley walked up to him, he vaguely remembered him from his old sessions, but when Dino Zimmerman walked up and gave him a hug, it felt like old times.

Scott had lined up the best studio musicians in Nashville, but other than Dino, he didn't know any of them. They were all there waiting to hear the songs, so with shaking hands and his heart pounding in his chest, he walked into the main studio, put on the headphones, and adjusted the microphone. Then he picked up a guitar, checked the tuning, sat down on the stool, and started playing and singing the songs, one at a time.

Recording studios are soundproof, so he couldn't hear their reactions from the control room while he was playing. When he finished the last one, stood up and took off the guitar, he honestly had no idea what they thought of them. He assumed they wouldn't like them all, but he was hoping one or two would make the cut.

When he opened the door to the control room, everyone was eerily silent, staring at him. He glanced around the room, a little shocked at the cold reception, looking for Brooklyn. When he saw her and made eye contact, she burst out crying.

"What's wrong?" he said.

When she ran to him, wrapping her arms around his neck, the room exploded with the sounds of applause. Everyone was smiling, laughing, and clapping.

Still a little confused, he looked down at Scott, who was sitting behind the board and asked, "Were any of those worth a shit?"

When he said that, everyone started laughing and clapped even louder. Apparently, they had liked them all.

FOR THE NEXT YEAR, he spent most of his time on airplanes, flying to Colorado Springs to check on Dave, or back to Nashville working on Brooklyn's new album.

Lance McCain had been successful postponing Dave's trial for almost ten months to develop Dave's case, but it was finally scheduled to start in less than six weeks. Unfortunately, so far, his private detective had not been able to track down Dave's younger brother, Max.

He could hear the concern in Lance McCain's voice the last time he had talked to him.

"Without Max's testimony," he told me, "we don't have much of a case and I want to warn you that this may not go well for Dave."

Raine finally got permission from the Colorado Springs Assistant Deputy District Attorney to visit Dave at the small building where he was being held, and he seemed to be happy and doing well.

Raine flew there every weekend to see him. When he would visit Dave never wanted to talk about his upcoming trial. All he seemed to be interested in was hearing about Brooklyn's new album, and Raine's suddenly exploding renewed music career.

"Buster was too shy to ask you, so I told him I'd get you to sign this," Dave said, holding up three vinyl copies of his album.

Due to the worldwide success of Nash Cooper's recording of his song, *From Ashes*, without Raine's approval, because they didn't need it, RCA had quickly released a new Raine Waters Greatest Hits album. Once again, his old songs were placed in regular rotation on all of the country music radio stations around the country. Sirius XM even had a special Raine Waters channel for two weeks playing the 28 songs from his old albums over and over. Soon, stories about Raine and his songs started trending over social media and showing up on the iTunes download charts.

Suddenly, Raine Waters was a big deal in the music industry again. Interestingly, even though he was famous again, no one recognized him. The only pictures they had of Raine were from his old album covers when he was much younger with long hair and his face was hidden by a beard. For Raine, that was the best part of it all, he could walk around in public incognito.

Being a good businessman, taking advantage of Raine's new publicity, Scott Hugley leaked to the press and social media that his newest future star, Brooklyn Taylor Arnett, was Raine Waters' daughter and that the songs on her new album were new original Raine Waters' songs.

When the first single off of Brooklyn's album was released, it quickly zoomed up the charts and by the fourth week, Brooklyn Taylor Arnett had her first top ten record, on its way to number one, and she was the talk of the town around Nashville.

During all of this, Nash Cooper's recording of *From Ashes* had remained at number one on all the charts for 23 weeks, getting close to breaking all of the previous records. It was nominated for two Grammy's and was also nominated for Song Of The Year by the CMA Awards. Although Nash Cooper had recorded it, he was snubbed by the entire music industry and received no nominations.

When Raine found out that Nash had not received one nomination, he honestly felt a little sorry for him, because he knew first hand what it felt like to rise to the top of the world and then come crashing back down.

AT THIS POINT in Raine's life, he could have easily bought a fancy new house, but he had grown to love the little house in the woods at the LaCita Country Club, so he bought it from Coop.

When he was in Nashville, he stayed with Brooklyn, Josh, and Ginny in their new beautiful house Raine had forced her to buy with some of the royalties they had received in their joint bank account.

Jake had agreed to be Brooklyn's manager and had also moved to Nashville. His house in Abilene had sold quickly for his asking price and he used that money to buy a small ranch in Hendersonville, about 25 miles northeast of Nashville.

In the past year, Jake and Louise's relationship had grown. Every weekend he would either fly to Orlando to see her, or she would fly to Nashville to see him.

When they were all in Nashville, Jake and Louise would come over on Sunday, so they could all go to church together and spend the rest of the afternoon cooking, eating, and talking together as a family.

On those Sunday nights, after Jake and Louise had left, Raine would go to little Ginny's room, sit in the rocking chair, and watch her sleep. As he watched, he also prayed, thanking God for finally forgiving him, and for the life he had led him to. There was only one word that described the way he felt, sitting in that chair, watching his granddaughter sleep...and that was...blessed.

WITH BROOKLYN'S album finished and doing well, Raine's hectic life of travel calmed down a little, giving him some rare time for himself. One of the things he had discovered when he was working as a groundskeeper at LaCita, was the peaceful solitude he felt when he was cutting the fairways. The mower was very loud, so he always used earplugs from his cell phone when he was cutting the grass. He couldn't really explain it, but when he was out there in the sunshine, driving that mower, listening to the low rhythmic hum of the engine, he went into a slight trance letting his mind wander. It was a special time and place for him that seemed to turn on all of his creative juices. All of the lyrics of Brooklyn's new album came to him out there cutting that grass and some of the tunes as well.

Coop looked up at him from his desk. "You want to do what?"

"Cut a few fairways," Raine said, grinning, "What's wrong, you think I forgot how to do it already?"

"Of course not," he said frowning, "but, Raine, it's hot as hell out there and you are a damn star, you don't have to do that shit anymore."

"I like doing that shit," he said.

Coop shook his head, "Alright, I'll run you out there, I think they are cutting 14 now."

Coop was right, it was about 95° and Raine was soaking wet with sweat when he finished number 15. When he turned around to start 16, his cell phone rang in his ears.

He pulled up under a tree in the shade, killed the engine, and hit the button. "Hello?"

"Dad!" He heard Brooklyn scream in his ear, "You're never going to guess what just happened."

She was excited and talking so fast he could barely understand her. "Slow down," he said, "I can't understand a thing you're saying. Take a breath and tell me slowly."

"Scott Hugley just called and told me that they want us to sing, From Ashes, at the CMA awards. As a duet," she said, "Isn't that amazing?"

"Who is *us*?" He asked.

"Me and you, silly. Who else would it be?"

"Well, to be honest," he said, "I thought that maybe since you and Amanda Jones are both on Scott's label and you two have become such good friends, I thought it might be you and her. Actually, that makes more sense to me."

"No," she said, "Scott wants you and me to do it. What do you think?"

"Has he checked with the folks at the CMA awards?" He asked, "After my last performance on that show, I thought they banned me for life."

Brooklyn laughed in his ear. "Scott said that he had to argue with the producer, but he finally agreed if you promise to show up sober this time."

"Did they say anything about being stoned?" He said with a chuckle.

"Dad, that's not funny," she said, "So, seriously will you do it?"

"What day is the award show?"

"September the 16th. I think that is a Wednesday night."

"Oh shit!" he said, "Dave's trial starts on Thursday, September the 4th. I'm not sure it will be over by then. Brooklyn, I promised Dave that I would be there, every day. I'm sorry honey, but I don't think I can do it." He could hear the disappointment in her voice when she said that she understood and hung up.

45 minutes later his phone rang again, this time it was Scott Hugley. "Raine, I like your idea of having Brooklyn and Amanda sing the song, but it won't have the same impact without you."

"I appreciate you saying that," he said, "and I'd love to do it, but I have to be in Colorado Springs during that time and I can't guarantee I can make it there for the show."

"Yeah, Brooklyn filled me in about your friend's trial," he said, "I hope you don't mind, but I just hung up with Lance McCain. He tells me he can't imagine the trial lasting longer than seven days. The only thing he can't predict is how long the jury will be out. I'm willing to take the gamble if you are. If you'll agree to do the show with Brooklyn, I'll pay for a charter jet to fly you here when it's over. Just in case, I'll have Amanda and Brooklyn rehearse the song. That way Amanda could jump in if she has to. What do you say?"

26

AMANDA

R CA had discovered and signed Amanda Jones when she was only 13 years old. She was one of those rare child prodigies, that stood a little under 5 foot tall, but had an amazing, mature voice that no one could deny. She may have been tiny, but when she sang, she sounded like she was 10 feet tall.

Even though they were on the same label, Raine had never actually talked to her but had said, "Hello," to her several times when they had walked passed each other in the RCA building. Although she was a pretty young teenager, there was nothing really striking about her looks.

Unlike most child stars, she had survived the business without going nuts and had continued to be a major Nashville star charting number one hits for almost three decades.

Raine hadn't seen her in over thirty years, so when she walked into the studio with Brooklyn to work on their duet, he could barely form words to speak. The last time he had seen her, she had freckles, pigtails, and knobby knees, and although she still had those freckles, everything else had changed.

"Amanda, this is my father, Raine Waters," Brooklyn said when they walked up to him.

He stood, shook her hand, and planned on saying hello, but what came out was, "Oh my God, you're so beautiful."

Her eyes sparkled as she smiled up at him and said. "Well, honey, you ain't real hard on the eyes either."

He held on to her hand, staring into her beautiful blue eyes trying to think of something else to say, but his mind was blank.

"Would you two like to be alone?" Brooklyn said, laughing, breaking the spell.

"Well now that you brought it up," Amanda said, still smiling and staring back into Raine's eyes, "I wouldn't mind that one bit."

Brooklyn reached over and pulled their hands apart. "Come on guys," she said, laughing, "break it up, we have work to do."

During that rehearsal, every time *she* looked up, he was looking at her, and every time *he* looked up, she was looking at him. There was an instant and obvious attraction between them, and he was feeling emotions inside of him he thought had died years ago.

After Brooklyn and Raine shot the promo, Raine took Amanda out on their first date. He couldn't believe how easy she was to talk to, and that's what they did for hours and hours.

After they were kicked out of the restaurant, Raine drove her to her house, but he didn't go inside. Instead, they sat in his rental car and talked until the sun came up. The next day, she invited him to come to her recording session, and again, they couldn't seem to keep their eyes off of each other.

After her session, Raine drove her back to her house and she invited him inside for the first time. Her house was not what he had expected. It was beautifully decorated, but it was not the mansion you would expect a superstar like Amanda Jones to be living in.

"What's wrong?" She asked, handing him a Diet Coke. "Don't you like my house?"

"No, I love it. It's beautiful," he said, "but where are the maids and the butler?"

She laughed. "I gave them the year off."

"Don't tell me a superstar like you cleans your own house?"

"I even clean the windows." Her eyes twinkled as she laughed.

"Seriously," he said, "you don't have help? Why not?"

Amanda sat down on the couch and he sat next to her. "When I'm out on tour, which is most of the time, I have a service that comes in and cleans it every other week, but when I'm home, this is my sanctuary and I don't want anyone around."

Raine smiled and nodded. "That makes complete sense. I can still remember what it felt like to finally have some time at home alone, away from all the chaos of a tour."

"I was born and raised in Raywick, Kentucky," she said, "I had four brothers, I was the only girl. It's funny now thinking back, but I can remember hating having to do all those chores. Between my father working in the fields and my four brothers, me and momma never seemed to quit cleaning the house or washing clothes. When I started making money, the first thing I bought was a brand new washer and dryer for my momma's house."

He smiled. "I bet she loved that."

She had a beautiful smile, and every time she flashed it, his heart fluttered. "Yeah, momma loved that washer, but she still hung out her clothes on a line in the back yard. She thought they smelled better when they dried in the sunshine." They both laughed.

She leaned back and put her feet up on the coffee table and looked at him. "Can I tell you something?"

Raine leaned back and put his feet up too. "Sure, you can tell me anything."

"I had a huge crush on you when I was about 15. I even had a picture of you hanging on my wall."

He grinned. "Are you trying to remind me of how old I am?"

She raised her left eyebrow and frowned. "I know exactly how old you are. I knew it then and I know it now. When I was madly in love with you at 15, you were 28. I'm just about to turn 48, so...that makes you 61, right?"

He nodded. "Unfortunately, that is correct."

She grinned, raised up, and started looking around the room.

"What are you looking for?" he asked.

She flashed her beautiful smile at him again. "For your walker. How the hell did you get in here without it."

Her laughter filled the room. "Very funny, smart ass."

She turned, tucking her legs underneath her, and looked at him. "Can I ask you something serious?"

"Oh no, are you sick of me already?"

She gave him the one eyebrow lift/frown again. "Stop that. Come on, Raine. I really want to ask you something serious."

He took his feet off the coffee table, sat up, and looked at her. "Fire away."

"Am I just fantasizing here, like I used to do when I was 15?" She asked, "I'm too old to play games, so please tell me the truth. Am I just imagining this, or do we have something going on between us? Are you feeling what I'm feeling?"

Raine raised his head and looked her in the eyes. "Are you talking about my heart fluttering in my chest every time I look at you, or about the cold chills that run down my spine when we kiss?"

She took his hand and gently squeezed it. "Mine is more like butterflies when you touch me. It's almost like the feeling I get right before I walk on stage."

He leaned over, took her face in his hands, and kissed her gently. Her lips were soft and wet, and he held her there for a long time.

When he pulled back she said, "Now that's what I call a kiss kiss!"

"A kiss what?" He asked, "What are you talking about?"

"Well," she whispered, "there are kisses, and then there are kiss kisses. Those are the kind you can't stop thinking about."

Raine pulled her close and whispered back, "Is that a good thing?"

She snuggled closer, raised up, and whispered in his ear. "They're the best kind. The kind I dream about."

THE NEXT MORNING, while Amanda slept, Raine slipped out of bed and cooked breakfast. When she walked in the kitchen barefoot, wearing his shirt with her hair pulled back in a ponytail, she looked maybe 20 years old.

"Do you really have to leave today?" She said, rubbing her eyes, still waking up.

"Yeah, I have to go to Colorado Springs to tell my friend Dave the bad news about his brother," he said, "Remember? I told you about it."

She nodded. "Yes, I remember. It's so sad. How do you think Dave will take it?"

Raine shook his head. "Honestly, I have no idea. I thought I knew Dave well, but now I realize that I really don't know him at all."

"Could I go with you?" She asked, smiling, "You've talked so much about him and I know how much you care about him. If you don't mind, I'd really like to meet him."

AMANDA PACKED a bag while Raine called and tried to book another seat on the plane. Unfortunately, there were no more seats, so he changed and booked them on a flight to Denver. He also reserved a rental car, so they could drive it down to Colorado Springs. On the way to the Nashville airport, they had stopped at Brooklyn and Josh's house, so Raine could pack his bag.

In the past few days, Raine had seen the CMA awards promo he had taped with Brooklyn several times on TV, but he hadn't really thought about what he had done until they stepped off the plane at the Denver airport. The anonymity he had been enjoying was gone.

At first, he thought the gaggle of paparazzi were there for Amanda, but when they all started yelling his name too, he knew they were there for both of them.

"Raine," One of them yelled, snapping their picture, "What are you doing in Denver?"

"Are you and Amanda doing a concert here?" Another one yelled.

Raine tried his best to ignore them, as they rushed to the baggage area, but the paparazzi just seemed to yell louder and multiply.

When they got to the luggage turnstile, he looked down and

frowned at Amanda, but she just smiled up at him. "You should tell them why we're here," she said, "Tell them about Dave. They're not gonna go away and if you don't say something, they'll follow us all the way there."

He thought about what she had said for a moment, then turned and walked up to them. "Amanda and I are here to visit one of my best friends. His name is David Baker. He is in jail, accused of committing murder 22 years ago when he was only 19 years old. He's been charged with first-degree murder, of planning and killing his drunken, abusive father. He did kill him, but it was in self-defense. We are here to offer him our support and hopefully shine a light on his case. We're hoping to get the Colorado Springs District Attorney to drop the charges against him."

They were only about 20 minutes south of Denver on their way to Colorado Springs when Raine's cell phone rang. It was Lance McCain and he was pissed.

"Why in the hell would you hold a press conference and talk about my case?" He yelled in Raine's ear, "Do you have any idea what you've done?"

"Calm down and stop yelling at me," Raine said, "I didn't hold a press conference I just got surrounded at the airport by a bunch of paparazzi and I told them why I was here. That's all it was. What's the harm in that?"

He could hear Lance's rapid breathing in his ear. "What's the harm?" He yelled, "The harm is...you just blew a deal I've been working on for a month with the Deputy District Attorney that was prosecuting Dave's case. She believed that Dave was acting in self-defense and was just about to present our agreement to her boss, the District Attorney."

"What was the deal?" Raine asked.

He heard Lance sigh. "No trial. She was going to drop the charges to involuntary manslaughter and give him time served against three years at a psychiatric facility of our choice.

"Wow, that's great," Raine said, "but I don't understand. What did I say to the press that would possibly make her change her mind?"

"She didn't change her mind, but when she took the deal to her boss, he rejected it."

"Why did he do that?"

"Because he had just seen your performance at the Denver airport. It was breaking news on all the local channels. He's a registered prick and wants to take advantage of all the press you and your girlfriend will bring to this case. He has taken over Dave's case and unfortunately, that means a trial. If that happens, we'll have no choice but to put Max on the stand and hope he can make it through the DA's cross examination without losing it. If he can't do that, we're gonna lose, and Dave is going to prison for a long, long time."

27

THE PRESS CONFERENCE

"I feel horrible," Amanda said, "I was the one who convinced you to talk to them. I should have kept my mouth shut, this is all my fault."

"No, It's not you're fault," Raine said, "I'm the one who talked to them, and I meant everything I said. If it pissed off the D.A. so be it. That doesn't change the fact that it was self-defense and Dave shouldn't be charged with first-degree murder."

Lance had told them that Sam Green, the Colorado Springs District Attorney was going to hold a press conference talking about Dave's case at 3:00 pm.

When they made it to their hotel and checked into their room, Raine turned on the television to see what the D.A. had to say about Dave's case.

"Ladies and gentlemen of the press," he began, "I am Sam Green, the newly elected District Attorney of Teller and El Paso Counties. I am here today to talk to you about a case that I will be personally prosecuting. 22 years ago, a healthy, strong, muscular, 19-year-old man named David Baker, killed his father. His father's name was Arnold Baker. Arnold was a war hero, a veteran who was wounded so severely in the Vietnam War fighting for your freedom, he lost his left leg just above the knee and three of his fingers. To walk, Arnold used a wooden crutch that he could barely control because of the loss of his fingers. One night his oldest son, David Baker, who had run away three years earlier, came home unexpectedly, took Arnold's crutch away from him...and beat him to death with it, shattering it into pieces as he smashed it across Arnold's body."

He paused for dramatic effect and looked around at the crowd of reporters. "But the story doesn't end there. After David killed Arnold, he dragged his body to a closet, stuffed his lifeless corpse inside of it, and locked the door. Then he stole his next-door neighbor's car and ran away. David Baker has been on the FBI's most-wanted list for 22 years. But the FBI finally tracked him down, arrested him, and brought him back to the scene of his crime, here in Colorado Springs to answer for his brutality."

He took out his handkerchief and wiped his eyes. "This morning on one of your channels I saw a disgusting display. It was an interview with a famous celebrity. I'm not going to repeat his name, because he's famous enough, but this man had the audacity to suggest that this brutal crime I have just described to you was done in self-defense. A six-foot three-inch tall, muscular 19-year-old boy, killed his father with his own crutch, breaking it in half over his crippled one-legged body...in self-defense? I'm sorry, but even by Hollywood standards, that's a little hard to believe. I'm here today to tell the citizens of this county who elected me that as long as I am the District Attorney, this office will not be swayed or influenced in any way by negative publicity, especially when it comes from a celebrity."

He looked up, stared into the camera, and said, "Mr. Waters, you and your opinions are not welcome or needed here. Go back to Nashville, sing your little songs, and leave justice up to me."

Raine turned off the television and smiled at Amanda. "I don't think that guy is one of my fans, he doesn't seem to like me much."

WHEN DISTRICT ATTORNEY Sam Green showed up at the shop to remove Dave and lock him up in the county jail, he wasn't there. He was sitting in the back seat of Special Agent James Archer's black Cadillac Escalade in the driveway.

"You can't do this!" Sam Green yelled.

Agent Archer smiled at him. "Sure I can. His federal charges have never been dropped and he is now back in my custody." He leaned in closer and said, "That's federal custody, Mr. Green, and that trumps state every time."

Infuriated, Sam turned around and stormed back to his car. "And by the way," Agent Archer said, "you might want to call the Governor. I don't think he was very impressed with your, shall we say, 'performance' you put on for the press today. I think the problem was that you forgot to use the word 'alleged' anywhere in your rant. He wants to ask you if you have somehow forgotten the part in our judicial system that talks about innocent until proven guilty."

"I do not answer to the Governor!" Sam yelled back. "I only answer to my constituents in this county!"

"Maybe not," Agent Archer said smiling, "but Governor Bailey is the leader of your political party in this state and if you plan on having the continued financial support of that party for your future elections to those constituents, you might want to give him a call and hear what he has to say."

An hour later, Special Agent Archer received a call from the governor's office, letting him know that the district attorney had changed his mind about moving the prisoner to the county lock-up. He was also told that the governor would appreciate it if he would once again return the prisoner to the custody of the State of Colorado and see to it that Mr. Baker is returned back to the shop to continue his incarceration until his trial is completed.

———————

THE CHAIN of events that had led all the way up to the governor started when Special Agent Archer had watched the district attorney's press conference. As he watched, he couldn't believe what he was seeing. Although what the DA was saying wasn't actually against the law, he had stepped so far over the line, it was at the very least unethical and simply wrong.

After that press conference, Agent Archer had anticipated that the DA, to prove his authority over the case would try to move Dave to the county jail, and he knew he had to do something to prevent it, so he made the call to the governor.

After he had turned Dave back over to Buster at the shop and watched him reconnect the shackles around his ankles, he headed back to his office. On his way, he made one more call to Lance McCain.

"Mr. McCain," he began, "I wanted to call and let you know that I have transferred custody of your client back to the State, and he is now locked back up in the Shop. I also want to make it clear, that I will have nothing more to do with this case. Personally, I believe your client is probably guilty. With that said, as an attorney myself, guilty or not, I believe your client deserves to have a fair trial. It's my opinion, after watching the District Attorney's press conference today, receiving a fair trial will be impossible in El Paso county. I also realize that you certainly do not need my advice, but if this was my case, I would immediately file for a change of venue."

"I thought about that," Lance said, "and I think the judge would agree, especially if he's heard about the DA's press conference, but I don't see how that could help us much. It would just piss off the DA more, and make him dig in further."

"I'm sure it would," Agent Archer said, "but if the reason for the change of venue was somehow leaked to the press, maybe by some famous celebrity...the embarrassment and utter humiliation to Mr. Green and his career...might be worth it."

The following day in the judge's chambers, after listening to Lance's plea and then to a long and loud rebuttal from District Attorney Sam Green, the judge granted the change of venue to Jefferson county, one of the seven counties in the Denver Metropolitan area

The next morning, when Amanda and Raine walked out of the

hotel on their way to visit Dave, they were once again surrounded by the paparazzi and several official members of the press.

"Raine, do you have a response to what District Attorney Green said about you yesterday in his press conference?" A reporter from the CBS affiliate, KKTV asked.

Raine smiled, trying to remember exactly what Lance McCain had told him to say. "That was a press conference?" he said grinning, "I thought I was listening to his opening statement. I'm not a lawyer, I'm an entertainer, just a singer, and a songwriter, so I don't really know what to tell you, but after watching Mr. Green's pathetic performance yesterday, I'm not sure he's much of a lawyer either. What he did yesterday may not have been illegal, but it was wrong and certainly unethical. I'm not sure I'm supposed to talk about this, because it just happened this morning, but apparently I wasn't the only one who thought Mr. Green stepped over the line in his press conference, because the judge on David Baker's case has granted a change of venue. This case will now be tried in Denver."

It was obvious that was the first the press had heard about the venue change because when Raine said it, they all instantly started peppering him with questions.

He held up his hand, motioning for them to stop. "I don't know any of the details, so I suggest you ask Mr. Green about why the judge felt the need to do it. And while you're there, you might want to ask him if it's true that he graduated in the bottom 25% of his law school, and if he really had to re-take the bar exam three times before he passed it."

Raine grinned and shrugged at the reporters. "It kind of makes you wonder how he ever got elected, doesn't it? Tell him I think that it might be a better idea for him to turn this case back over to his Deputy Assistant District Attorney Everly Moore, because Miss Moore gradu-ated at the *top* of her class, and passed the bar on her first try. Perhaps Everly Moore should run for district attorney next time. I think she'd be a hell of a lot better choice for the citizens of Colorado Springs than Mr. Green."

Raine smiled and looked into the cameras. "Mr. Green, if you're watching this, I wanted you to know that after my visit today with my friend Dave, I *will* be going back to Nashville to sing my little songs, as you called them. But before I left, I wanted to suggest to you that maybe you should move to Hollywood because you're quite an actor. I especially liked the bit with the handkerchief, when you wiped away your tears." Raine gave an exaggerated thumbs up to the cameras. "Sam, now that was Oscar-winning stuff, very effective."

AMANDA AND RAINE spent almost 3 hours visiting with Dave. While they were there, Buster, Joe, and Art showed up with their Amanda Jones CDs and had her autograph them. Between the three of them, they had almost everything she had recorded.

Raine waited until the end of their visit to bring up Max. "Dave, we finally located your brother."

"Really?" he said, with excited eyes, "Where is he? Is he going to testify?"

Raine looked him in the eyes and shook his head. "He wants to, but I'm not sure he should."

Dave frowned. "Why not?"

"He's not well. He's in a nursing home in Oklahoma."

"A nursing home? What is he doing there? Max is four years younger than me!"

"Dave," he said softly, "I'm sorry to have to tell you this, but Max has early-onset dementia. I understand that it started about five years ago."

"Oh God no," he said, "How bad is he? Does he even remember who I am?"

"Yes he remembers you," Raine said, nodding, "but only when you were young. He's lost most of his short term memory, but like a lot of dementia patients, he remembers the past well."

Dave looked at Raine. "He remembers that night?"

"Yes he does, he remembers it vividly. But Lance is worried that he'll fall apart during the DA's cross-examination. Lance believes he will try to expose his obvious dementia to the jury."

"What kind of person would do something like that in a trial?"

"A decent person wouldn't," Raine said, "but apparently, this DA is a real son of a bitch and Lance believes that he'll go after Max hard."

Dave shook his head. "No way!" he shouted, "Tell Lance that he cannot put him up there on that stand. I won't allow it. I'm here because I was trying to protect Max and there is no way I'm going to put my brother through something like that just to save my ass."

He locked eyes with Raine. "Do you understand me? Call Lance, now. Tell him I said absolutely not! No fucking way!"

28

LIGHT OF TRUTH

The CMA Awards were drawing near, so when Scott Hugley received the show rehearsal schedule ,he drove to Eric Stark's office. Eric was the Executive Producer and Director of the CMA Awards Show. When he got there, he tried to explain the reason for needing an extra rehearsal time for Brooklyn and Amanda as a backup, in case Raine Waters was held up with Dave's trial and couldn't make the show.

When he told him that, he went crazy, jumping out of his chair. "From Ashes is probably going to win the Song Of The Year award!" He yelled in Scott's face, "THE GOD DAMN SONG OF THE YEAR!"

Eric forced himself to take a few deep breaths to calm down. "And you're standing here calmly telling me that you have a backup singer just in case '*No Raine Tonigh*t' doesn't show?"

He sat back down behind his desk. "Oh yeah, I know all about '*Mr. No Raine Tonight Waters.*' I've heard all the ugly stories. Scott, I was here the night he was so fucked up he almost fell off the stage, LIVE on national television. I was just an assistant director back then, but I will never forget that night and I promise you, he's not going to do that to me."

"Raine's not like that anymore," Scott said, "He doesn't even drink."

Eric smirked. "Yeah, sure he doesn't."

"Eric, I'm serious. Raine Waters is not the same guy he was back then. He may not be able to make the show because..."

"I don't want to hear it!" Eric shouted, interrupting him, "Listen close, Scott, because I'm only going to say this one time. If Raine Waters isn't in this building, completely sober, four hours before the broadcast, I'm pulling the duet with his daughter and letting Nash Cooper, the man who recorded the damn song in the first place, sing it. Are we clear about that?"

UNFORTUNATELY, due to the change of venue, and some conflicts with the Jefferson County courtroom's availability, Dave's trial didn't start until Monday, September 7th. That only gave Raine seven days before he had to fly to Nashville for the CMA Awards show. Unless something unusual happened, he was pretty sure that he would never make it to Nashville in time, but he decided not to call and tell Scott until the end of the first week of the trial.

As Lance McCaine had expected, District Attorney Sam Green showed up angry and prepared for war. When he walked into the courtroom, he turned and glared for several moments at Raine, who was sitting in the first row of the gallery behind the defense table.

When Raine smiled and waved at him, he jerked back around, slamming his briefcase down on the wooden table.

His opening statement was good and very damning to Dave's case. Raine could tell that even Lance McCain had been impressed by the grim look he gave him when he turned around, locked eyes with him, and shook his head.

WHEN SAM GREEN finished his opening statement and sat down behind the table, Lance stood up, walked toward the jury, and smiled. "Good morning," he began, "My name is Lance McCain and I am here representing the accused, David Baker. My job is to shine the light of truth on this case. As you all know, there are always two sides to a story. I'm here to make sure that you hear both of those sides, not just our esteemed district attorney's. I'm here to tell you David Baker's, and after you hear his side, you will have all of the information you need to make an informed decision."

He raised his hand and motioned toward Sam Green, sitting behind the large wooden table. "Before I start, I want to congratulate Mr. Green on his opening. Wow, that was *SOME* opening statement."

He smiled, "If I didn't know better, I would have thought that Sergeant Baker, Dave's father, deserved to win The Congressional Medal of Honor by the way he described his heroic actions in the Vietnam War. Honestly, I was expecting to see a drum and fife brigade come marching down the center aisle, waving Old Glory."

He turned back and faced the jury. "I'll admit, it was an impressive show. But like most good shows, the actual story behind it is exaggerated to make it more than it really is."

He scanned the faces of the jury. "I'm not saying that our esteemed district attorney didn't tell you the truth, because it is true that Sergeant Baker served in the United States Army during the Vietnam War. And tragically he did lose his left leg right above the knee and three fingers on his right hand." He nodded his head at the Jury, "Yes, that part is all true, but the *whole* truth, the small details that Mr. Green conveniently left out of the story, explains how Sergeant Baker actually lost his leg. I think it's important for all of you to know that Sergeant Baker did not lose his leg fighting for your freedom in combat, as Mr. Green so eloquently led you to believe, but rather, he lost his leg, and his fingers in a tragic shipping accident that took place on the Long Binh Post in, Saigon. Actually, Sergeant Baker was one of the lucky ones, because, in that tragic accident, seven other soldiers were crushed to death."

He paused, backed up, and frowned. "Of the eight men injured, Sergeant Baker was the only one that survived. I also think it's important for you to know that this accident took place three months after Sergeant Baker arrived in Saigon. So you see...he never actually fought in combat."

Lance shook his head. "Don't get me wrong, it was a terrible thing to have to live through. To paraphrase what the district attorney said...can you imagine, suddenly not having a leg to walk on, and not having your fingers to use to tightly grip a crutch so you could simply walk around."

He stopped, lowered his brow, and looked at the jury. "Wait a minute, I need to back up," he said, "Mr. Green just told us that Sergeant Baker lost his left leg and three fingers from his right hand."

He looked at the jury and asked, "Have anyone of you ever had to walk on crutches?"

One of the jurors nodded and said, "Yes sir, I broke my left ankle playing football."

Lance smiled. "Whoa, I bet that hurt," he said wincing, "To get around, did you use both crutches or just one?"

"I started out with both," he said, "but only used one after a few weeks."

"You said you broke your left ankle, correct? Which arm did you put the crutch under?"

The juror thought for a moment. "I used it under my left arm, to keep the weight off my left ankle."

"Thank you," Lance said, backing away. "So, if Sergeant Baker lost his left leg, it's logical to assume he used his crutch under his left arm." He turned and glared at Sam Green. "If that was the case, Sergeant Baker would've gripped the crutch with his left hand, *not* with the right hand that was missing the fingers as Mr. Green led you to believe."

Lance quickly turned back, facing the jury. "Now do you see why I'm here? Once again our esteemed district attorney has exaggerated the story. How did he say it again? Oh yeah, I remember, he said, and I quote, 'Can you imagine the incredible difficulty Sergeant Baker had to go through each day of his life, just trying to grip the handle of his crutch with those missing fingers.'"

"Objection!" Sam Green yelled, jumping to his feet.

"Sit down Mr. Green," the judge shouted, "I am not a fan of objections during opening statements. But for the record, your objection is overruled. Everyone in this courtroom can remember you saying those exact words."

The judge nodded at Lance. "You may proceed counselor."

Lance smiled at the jury again. "I'm not going to take much more of your time today, but before I go, I want to tell you what to expect when it's my turn to present my case. I promise to tell you the whole truth, not just the parts I want you to hear, as the district attorney has done. There is no question that David Baker killed his father, Sergeant Baker, but I will prove to you that he did it in self-defense. I will also prove to you that Sergeant Baker was *no* hero, in fact, he was a disgruntled, broken, angry man that released his violet anger against his wife and both of his children almost every day."

He turned to walk away, but stopped at the defense table, turned back around, and faced the jury. Then he held out his arm and pointed at Dave. "After Sergeant Baker beat this man senseless, he forced him inside of a 3-foot by 4-foot dark closet and locked the door."

He shook his head and frowned at the jury. "I would also like for you to imagine something."

He walked behind the table and put his hands on Dave's shoulders. "First, I want you all to take a good look at this man. Now I want you to imagine him as a young child, maybe seven or eight years old."

He paused for a long beat. "Can you see him? Now I want you to imagine what that little boy was feeling when he was bruised and bleeding in that dark closet, trembling with fear and crying for hours, begging his father to let him out."

He lifted his head and stared at the jury. "Does Sergeant Baker sound like a war hero to you? I sure hope not because to me...he sounds like a monster."

BERTHA STOOD and waved at Amanda Jones when she walked in the front door of the restaurant. It took her a few minutes to make it to his table because she had to stop several times to take selfies with her fans or to sign autographs.

When she finally made it to the table and sat down, Bertha said, "Do you ever get tired of that?"

She smiled and said, "Sometimes, but my biggest fear is that someday they'll stop asking me for autographs."

The waiter walked up to the table and took their order. When he left, Amanda looked at Bertha and asked, "So why did you want to meet me today? What's up?"

Bertha took a sip of his water, set the glass down on the table, and leaned forward, staring into her eyes. "I heard something yesterday about you and Raine Waters, and I wanted to ask you if it was true. Are you guys dating?"

Amanda lowered her eyebrows. "Yes," she said softly, "We've been out a few times."

Bertha leaned back in his chair and frowned. "How long have we known each other?"

"Since I was a little girl," she said. "Bertha, what's wrong? Why are you asking me about Raine?"

Bertha shrugged his shoulders and gave her a smile. "When you first came to this town, you were so young and innocent. The reason I made a point of meeting you and getting to know you was because I was afraid for you."

Amanda frowned. "Afraid? Afraid of what?"

"Of what could happen to you here. I'd seen it so many times before, and I didn't want that to happen to you."

"Bertha, what in the hell are you talking about?"

"Come on Amanda, don't be naïve. Thank God it didn't happen to you, but you have seen it, you've seen how this town can destroy good people, and turn them into something that they're not."

"You're talking about Raine, aren't you?" she asked.

He nodded. "Him and a thousand others just like him. Amanda, I watched Raine change from a nice kid to an out of control alcoholic and drug addict before my eyes."

"But he's not like that anymore," she said, pleading to him,

"Bertha, he's changed. He's gone through hell and back, and doesn't even drink beer anymore."

"Are you absolutely sure?" he asked, "How long have you really known him, two or three weeks? That's not enough time to know anyone, especially someone like him. Amanda, I know Raine Waters. I know who he is and what he has done, and I sincerely hope he has changed, but..."

"He's not that guy anymore," she said, smiling, "And I'm not that little girl you met all those years ago. Bertha, I know how much you love me, and I know you are just trying to protect me, but you are wrong about Raine this time. Trust me...I know what I'm doing."

Bertha smiled. "I'm glad you know how much I love you. I guess I've always thought of you like you were my own kid. All I'm asking is, what's the rush? I sincerely hope I am wrong about Raine, and if I am, time will tell. I'm just asking you to give it some time. There's nothing wrong with you two dating but I'm begging you, slow down a little, and don't rush into anything."

SAM GREEN'S entire case was based on Dave and Max being raised under strict almost military rule by their father. He tried to head off the possibility of their father's violence as being misunderstood, and he even referred to locking Dave in the closet as a similarity of putting a soldier in the brig. Of course, he had no actual evidence to back any of this up, but after two days of listening to several members of Sergeant Baker's old platoon that had served with him talking about what a great soldier he was, he changed his tactic and put two psychologists on the stand.

The first one explained post-traumatic stress disorder (PTSD), sometimes known as shell shock or combat stress, that occurs after someone experiences severe trauma or a life-threatening event.

"In your professional opinion, Doctor," Sam Green asked, "did Sergeant Baker suffer from PTSD?"

"Objection!" Lance yelled, "In all due respect to the doctor, there's no way he could possibly know if Sergeant Baker suffered from PTSD because he has never met the man?"

"Sustained," the judge said, "Mr. Green, what on earth does this have to do with the case before us? Please move this along."

Sam clinched his jaw. "Of course, Your Honor. I was trying to enlighten the jury to Sergeant Baker's mental state while he was..."

"I know what you were trying to do counselor," the judge said, "and I've already ruled on that so move it along."

From the beginning of the trial, the judge had made his distain for the district attorney obvious, sustaining almost every objection that Lance had made. In fact, it was so obvious, that Lance was worried that if he did win, the district attorney would have grounds for an appeal.

As a result, Lance did not object as often as normal, but couldn't stop himself during Sam Green's cross examination of his last witness. He was a Child Psychologist, and Sam Green kept trying to lead him to explain why Dave actually could have planned to murder his father.

After the barrage of sustained objections by the judge, Sam finally gave up and asked one last question.

"Doctor, in your opinion, based on the years you have spent dealing with your young patients, is it possible for a child to misunderstand the difference between strict parenting and parental abuse?"

The doctor nodded. "Yes, it's quite common."

"Only one more question, Doctor," Sam said, "If a child had misunderstood this his entire life," he paused for effect, "When this child grows up to be a man, a very strong man... is it possible for that lifelong misunderstanding to turn to rage and murder?"

"Objection!" Lance shouted, but it was too late. The jury had already heard the doctor's answer.

On Tuesday afternoon, the second full day of the trial, Sam Green rested his case and turned it over to Lance to present his defense.

29

MANSLAUGHTER

Raine turned off his cell phone when he finished his call with Amanda and looked out his hotel window at the twinkling lights of the Denver skyline. He sat there for almost an hour trying to figure out what he had done or said that may have upset her. He couldn't think of anything, but he knew something was wrong. He had called to invite her to spend the weekend with him in Aspen.

"Dave's trial is moving fast," he had told her. "Lance is starting his defense tomorrow and said he believes the closing statements will probably begin Friday morning. Then it will be up to the jury. He's confident they'll have a verdict by no later than Tuesday. If you come we can hang out in Aspen Saturday and Sunday and then come back to my hotel here in Denver until the jury's back. I know Dave would love for you to be here when they read the verdict. Don't worry, we can fly to Nashville Wednesday morning to make the CMA show on the private jet Scott chartered for me."

Raine was shocked because he thought Amanda would love the idea but without giving him any real reason why...she said no. Since she didn't seem to want to explain, he didn't press her and told her that he would see her at the CMA Awards show the following Wednesday.

AMANDA WAS STILL HAVING lunch at the restaurant with Bertha when Raine called. And although she would have loved to have spent the weekend with him in Aspen, she had just made a promise to Bertha, a few minutes earlier, to slow down their relationship.

"I'm sorry, Raine," she said looking across the table at Bertha, "it sounds like a lot of fun but I just can't do that right now."

When she hung up, she sighed and said, "I hope you're happy, I just turned down a weekend in Aspen and a plane ride on a private jet."

Bertha grinned. "You fly on private jets all the time, and you can't ski in Aspen in September."

She wiggled her eyebrows. "I don't think Raine was planning on doing much skiing."

Bertha frowned at her. "T.M.I. young lady," he said.

"What?" She asked confused.

"Too much information," he said, "I don't really want to hear about your sex life."

"Don't be such an old prude," she said laughing.

"Seriously, I think you did the right thing. Just take it slow with Raine, and if it's meant to be it will work itself out."

She smiled. "Yeah, but Aspen? I love Aspen."

"I sure hope I'm wrong about him," Bertha said, "and even if I am, someday...you'll thank me for this."

LANCE TRIED one more time but Dave refused to allow his brother Max to testify on his behalf. Instead he began his defense with two psychologists who gave the jury their expert opinions that contradicted the two psychologists that had testified for the State.

The following day on Thursday morning he called Raine to the stand as a character witness.

Of course, as expected, Sam Green did his best to destroy Raine on his cross-examination exposing his years of alcoholism and drug addiction to the jury.

"Did you actually perform intoxicated and high on drugs on national television?"

"Objection!" Lance yelled, "This man is not on trial!"

"That's ok," Raine said, "I'd like to answer that question, Your Honor."

The judge nodded. "Overruled. Go ahead, Mr. Waters."

Raine glared at the DA. "It was at the CMA Awards. I drank a full pint of Jack Daniels and snorted four or five lines of cocaine before I walked out onto that stage. It was the biggest mistake of my life. That one performance destroyed my career and is the reason why I wound up homeless and living on the streets. That's when I met David Baker and he saved my life. If it wasn't for him, I wouldn't be a recovering alcoholic today, I would be dead."

"Your Honor!" Sam Green yelled, "Will you please instruct Mr. Waters to address me and not the jury!"

"Mr. Waters, you must direct your answers to the district attorney," the judge said, "How long have you been sober?"

Raine reached into his pocket and pulled out his two year A.A. pin and held it up so the judge could see.

"Good for you, son. It's been 23 years for me."

"Your Honor, Please!" Sam Green yelled, "You're interfering with my cross-examination."

The judge glared down over his desk. "Mr. Green, I'm not sure what law school you went to, but mine taught me that a judge can talk to any witness sitting in that chair whenever he wants."

Once again, the judge's obvious bias toward the district attorney reared its ugly head.

Accepting defeat, Sam Green said, "No more questions for this witness."

On the lunch break, Lance was notified that the judge wanted to see him in his chambers.

When he arrived, Dave was sitting in the chair in front of the judge's desk still wearing his handcuffs and ankle shackles, and Sam Green was standing a few feet away, leaning against the wall.

"I called you here today to let you both know that if this jury comes back with a guilty verdict of first-degree murder, I will set aside their decision."

"You can't do that," Sam yelled, "this is a criminal case, not civil."

"Once again you are wrong," he said, "This is my courtroom and I can do anything I damn well please. Of course, that will give you grounds to appeal to a higher court, but after they review your inept prosecution, I don't think you'll get very far."

He looked at Lance. "Mr. McCain, I also want you to know that if the verdict comes back not guilty, I will set aside that decision as well."

"Why would you do that, Your Honor?" Lance asked.

"Because Mr. Baker is not innocent of this crime. He did kill his father, just not in the first-degree. And that's why we're all here today, to try to find a solution but before we get into that I would like to talk directly to Mr. Baker."

He looked over his desk and made eye contact with Dave. "May I call you Dave?"

He nodded. "Sure."

"Dave, you didn't go to your father's house that night with the intention of killing him, did you?"

"No sir, I didn't mean to kill him."

"I know you didn't but it also wasn't self-defense, like Mr. McCain is arguing, was it? Dave, I want you to look me in the eyes and tell me that when your father hit you on the back with his crutch, you believed that he was trying to kill you. What I'm asking is, did you sincerely believe at that moment he would have killed you if you hadn't have fought back?"

Dave took a few moments to respond. "He was too weak," "He couldn't have killed me."

"I know that's what you believe now," the judge said, "but I want you to think back carefully and tell me what you were thinking the moment you took his crutch away and hit him with it...were you fearing for your life?"

Dave lowered his head. "No sir. The thoughts of him killing me never crossed my mind. He had hit me with that crutch a hundred times before. All I was thinking was that I wanted him to feel what it felt like. That's why I put him in that dark closet, so he'd know what that felt like too."

The judge leaned back in his chair and shrugged. "I rest my case. This was not a first-degree murder, and it was not self-defense; it was involuntary manslaughter.

"What are you suggesting we do about it now?" Sam Green asked, with a frown.

"What I'm suggesting is that we all come to an agreement, and settle this case right here and now."

"You can't force me to lower the charges and make a settlement!" Sam Green shouted, "With all due respect, Your Honor, you are way out of bounds here."

The judge glared at Sam. "With all due respect to you counselor, I'm not trying to force you to do anything. I'm just merely suggesting that, in my opinion, you have not proven your case of first-degree murder, and I believe you are going to lose this case. I do not want to overturn the jury's verdict one way or the other, but I will if this case continues. All that will do, is keep Mr. Baker in limbo for several years while it goes through the appeals court process. If we can all agree that this is really a simple involuntary manslaughter case and come to a settlement now, we can save ourselves a lot of trouble, and the taxpayers a lot of money."

"Does that mean I have to go to prison?"Dave asked.

"No, Dave, it does not. If you will agree to settle this case and accept the charge of manslaughter, I can put you in a psychiatric hospital, rather than a prison. I believe you have several psychological problems that you need to deal with, the first being your severe claustrophobia. If you will agree to this I can put you into a safe large hospital, and when the doctors tell me that you are well and not a danger to yourself or anyone else, I will let you out."

"Are we talking about an insane asylum," Dave asked, "like a nuthouse? I'm not crazy."

The judge laughed. "We call them psychiatric hospitals these days. Dave, you eluded the FBI for 22 years. I don't believe we have to worry about whether you're crazy or not. I *do* believe, however, that you need some professional help to get you past your traumatic childhood. Will you agree to this and let me help you?"

———————

UNFORTUNATELY, it took another day and two phone calls from the governor to convince Sam Green to accept the plea deal. On Friday afternoon, the judge dismissed the jury and accepted Dave's plea, guilty of involuntary manslaughter.

"Mr. Baker," the judge asked Dave, "are you comfortable where you are being held now?"

Dave nodded. "Yes sir, it's great."

"Very good," he said, "I would like to spend a little time, a few weeks, investigating where I want to place you. Until I decide, you will continue your incarceration where you are being held now."

After it was all over, Raine hugged Dave and promised to come to visit him over the weekend before he left for Nashville on Monday. When he got back to his hotel, he tried to call Amanda but her phone went straight to voicemail. Next, he called Brooklyn to tell her the good news about Dave.

"How can three years in a mental institution be good news?" She asked.

"Well, it beats the hell out of a prison cell, and that's where he could have gone for a lot longer if he'd been convicted of first-degree murder," Raine said.

"Yeah, I guess you're right," she said, "but I just can't imagine having to live in a place like that for three years."

"Actually," Raine said, "Dave's got a lot of psychological problems he needs to deal with, so I believe it will be good for him in the long run."

"What does Amanda think about it?" Brooklyn asked.

"She doesn't know yet. I haven't talked to her in a few days. I just tried to call her but she didn't answer."

"Two days?" she said, shocked, "Why haven't you talked to her? I thought you two were...well, you know."

Raine sighed. "That's what I thought too, but apparently I was wrong."

"Oh, I'm sorry, Dad."

"Yeah, me too," he said, "but hey, that's show business. Tell Josh hello, and give little Ginny a big kiss for me. I'll see you next week at the CMA show."

He tried to call Amanda one more time before he went to bed that night but again her phone went straight to voicemail, so he left her a message. "Hey there, this is Raine. I just wanted to call and let you know that Dave's trial is finally over. It would be a little difficult to explain all the details to you on the phone, but I think he's gonna be OK. My plans are to head back to Nashville on Monday morning, and hopefully, when I get back we can talk. Amanda, I don't know exactly what's going on. If I've said something or done something wrong I can only hope that you accept my apology for whatever that may be. I would really like to see you again, so when I get back I'll give you a call."

THE NEXT MORNING, Raine packed a small bag and drove his rental car three hours on the winding mountain roads to Aspen. When he got there, he checked into the Little Nell Hotel. He realized that it didn't make much sense for him to go there, but he had already paid the non-refundable $1,200 per night rate for the room for Saturday and Sunday, so rather than waste the money he decided to use it, hoping it would help him finally relax. According to the concierge of his Denver hotel, it was the only five star, five diamond hotel in Aspen. Of course, he didn't really care much about that, he had booked the room hoping to impress Amanda.

Over the weekend, he took advantage of a few of the summer

adventures offered by the hotel and went on an off-road Jeep tour on Saturday, went fly fishing Sunday morning, and had two incredible four course meals. On his long drive back to Denver, through the beautiful mountains, he couldn't stop thinking about how much more fun his time in Aspen would have been if Amanda had been there with him. For almost the entire drive he racked his brain trying to figure out what he had done.

When he approached Interstate 25, he glanced at his watch. It was 4:30 pm. He had planned on driving to Colorado Springs to visit Dave, but the thoughts of that four-hour round-trip drive changed his mind. Instead, he called him. "Dave, I'm sorry but I'm not gonna make it there today. Aspen was a lot further away than I thought, and driving on these winding mountain roads have worn me out."

"That's cool, dude," Dave said, trying to hide his disappointment, "How was Aspen?"

"Very expensive," Raine said, "I just paid $45 for breakfast."

"No way," Dave said, laughing, "Are you serious?"

"I wish I wasn't. It's absolutely ridiculous. You wouldn't believe what the hotel cost."

"So, will I get to see you before you head back to Nashville?" Dave asked.

"Absolutely. I've decided to stay in Colorado a few more days and take Scott up on his offer to fly me back on a charter jet Wednesday. I'm going to check into a hotel there in Colorado Springs tomorrow. When I get there, I'll come to see you."

"That would be great," Dave said, excited, "See you tomorrow."

THE NEXT DAY, Monday, Raine spent almost four hours visiting with Dave talking about the crazy times they had spent together living on the streets.

"What'd you do for food?" Buster asked.

Raine shrugged. "Some of the locals brought us food or gave us money, and there were a few shelters that had hot meals. Dunkin

Donuts always had some day-old donuts they would give us, but most of the time we found what we needed to survive from the dumpsters behind the good restaurants."

"Oh Lord," Buster said, "you ate food out of the trash?"

"Oh yeah," Dave said, "and sometimes it was really good, and all you could eat for free!"

"Oh my God," Buster said, "That's disgusting."

"It's not so disgusting when you haven't eaten in a few days," Raine said, "It's funny we're talking about this now because when I was in Aspen this weekend eating in those amazing restaurants, I seriously had an urge to go outside and peek in their dumpsters just to see what was there."

When Raine got back to his hotel that night, he took out his cell to call Amanda but changed his mind and set it back down on the dresser. He was exhausted from his long visit with Dave and didn't feel like eating alone again in a restaurant so he called room service.

The next morning, he called room service again and ordered breakfast. While he was eating his phone rang. Hoping it was Amanda calling he jumped up and ran to his phone.

"Hello?" he said.

"Raine, this is Scott. I just wanted to call and give you the information for the charter jet that will be there tomorrow. The pilot's name is James Elliott and he will be picking you up at your hotel around 11 AM. Is that going to work for you?"

"Yeah," he said, "that's perfect. How long is the flight to Nashville?"

"The pilot said if you guys takeoff by noon you should make it here by 2:30 or 3:00 at the latest," Scott said.

"That's great," Raine said, "Will I need to get a cab from the airport or will there be a car there for me?"

"I'll be there waiting for you," Scott said, "That will give us some time to talk about a few things."

"Like what?" Raine asked.

"Well, I guess we could talk about it now if you have a few minutes," Scott said.

"Sure, I don't have much going on today. I have plenty of time. So what's up?"

"How would you feel about signing a record contract with me," Scott said, "I'd love to have you on my label, and I think we can make a lot of money together."

Raine sighed and sat down in the chair. "I'm not sure what I think about that, Scott. Honestly, money isn't something I'm needing these days. If I signed with you would you expect me to tour to promote the album?"

"Well yeah, of course."

"Scott, I've got a lot more unpublished songs I've written that I would love to cut, but it's the touring, being out there on the road again with all that pressure that worries me. I'm not sure I could hold up."

"I understand," Scott said, "but I wish you'd consider it. Raine, you're a hot property right now, and I'd hate to see you not take advantage of it. Just think about it, we'll talk about it more tomorrow."

When he hung up, Raine tried to eat the rest of his breakfast but he had lost his appetite. "What do I do, God?" he said, "Should I sign the record deal, and go back on the road? Am I strong enough to do that?"

He wanted to talk to Amanda about it so he picked up his phone and punched in her number.

She answered on the first ring. "Raine, " she said, "I was just about to call you."

"Really?" he said, "What were you calling me about? Is everything OK with Brooklyn?"

"Yes, she's great," she said, "I was calling you to apologize for being so rude. I wanted to call you back last night when I listened to your message but..."

"But what?" he asked, "Amanda, what have I done?"

"You haven't done anything it's…it's Bertha."

"Bertha? What does he have to do with this?"

Raine sipped his coffee and listened quietly as Amanda told him what Bertha had said during their lunch. "I shouldn't have listened to him," she said, "I should have flown up there and gone to Aspen with you. Will you forgive me?"

"Don't blame Bertha. He's probably right about me."

"No, he's not. Raine, you are not that person anymore. You have changed, grown up. I'm so sorry if I hurt you."

"Don't worry about it. We can talk about it later," he said.

"What time will you be here tomorrow?" She asked.

"Around three I think."

"You want me to pick you up?"

"No," he said, " I just got off the phone with Scott, and he's going to be there waiting for me. Look I'm sorry but I've got to go see Dave. We'll talk tomorrow at the show."

He didn't let her answer him and hung up. He sat quietly in the chair thinking about the words Bertha had said about him to Amanda. The more he thought about those words, the lower he sank.

"Who am I trying to kid," he said out loud, "Bertha's right. I'm the wrong guy. I'll destroy Amanda like I destroyed Virginia."

Raine stood up and reached into his pocket. He pulled out his two years sobriety A.A. pin, threw it in the trash, and walked out the door.

30

OMINOUS SKY

When Buster unbolted the shop door and opened it, he saw Sam Green standing on the other side. "I'm here to see the prisoner," he said firmly.

"I thought the case was over," Buster said, "What do you want to see Dave about?"

"I don't see how that could be any of your business," Sam shouted. "I am the district attorney of this county, and you are just a hired prison guard. Back out of the doorway, let me in, and leave us alone. You can resume your guard duty when I leave."

Buster let him in, closed the door behind him, and walked to his car. He took out his cell and called Raine's number but he didn't answer. He tried again thirty minutes later but he still didn't pick up.

When he saw the door open and the district attorney walk out, he ran to the shop to check on Dave.

"What did he say to you?" He asked.

Dave shrugged his shoulders. "He's still pretty pissed that the judge made him settle my case."

"What a jackass," Buster said, "Are you alright. Do you need anything?"

"No, I'm fine," Dave said, "I'm a little tired, that's all."

"Are you sure you are OK?" Buster said, "You seem a little off."

"Don't worry about me, I'm fine, Dave said, rolling onto his side and closing his eyes. "I'm gonna try to get some sleep."

IN THE WEEKS that Buster had guarded Dave, the only time he was out of his line of sight was when he was sleeping. A few times during his watch, he would step just outside of the front door for a quick smoke.

Buster lit his cigarette and took a long drag wondering what the district attorney had said to Dave to get him so depressed. He looked at his watch. It was only 9:30 pm. It wasn't like Dave to go to sleep so early. After he thought about it a few minutes he realized that Dave probably didn't actually want to go to sleep, he just wanted him to stop asking questions and didn't want to talk about it anymore. The poor guy just wants some time alone to think, he thought to himself.

Usually, Buster only smoked one cigarette but decided to smoke another one to give Dave a little more time to sort things out.

When he finished his second cigarette and stepped on the butt, he opened the door as quietly as he could, trying not to disturb Dave. When he stepped inside, Dave wasn't laying on his bed as he had expected. He assumed he was in the bathroom so he sat down in his chair and picked up a magazine to read. When he opened up the magazine, he suddenly realized that something was wrong. The bathroom door was closed.

He jumped up and ran to the door, "Dave? Are you alright in there?"

He waited a few moments but he didn't answer. "Dave, ANSWER ME!" He yelled, "ARE YOU OK?"

When he didn't answer the second time, he grabbed the doorknob and tried to turn it but it was locked. "DAVE!" he yelled, "OPEN THIS DOOR!"

When he didn't answer, Buster ran to his car, popped the trunk, grabbed the tire iron, and ran back inside. He jammed the tire iron in between the bathroom door and the frame and pulled with all his might.

When the door popped open, he saw Dave on the floor with his bed sheet wrapped around his neck. The other end was tied to the towel rack. Buster leaned down and shook him but he was unconscious, and he wasn't breathing.

WHEN RAINE GOT out of the taxi and staggered into the lobby of the hotel, the man behind the front desk said, "Are you Raine Waters?"

Assuming he was one of his fans, Raine smiled and said, "Yeah, I'm Raine Waters. You want an autograph?"

"No sir, well actually I would," the young desk clerk said nervously, "but that's not why I stopped you. You've got about ten emergency messages here."

Raine walked up to the desk, picked up one of the messages, and read it.

Raine held up his arm and tried to focus on his watch, it was 4:15 a.m. "When did the last call come in?"

"About 15 minutes ago," the desk clerk said, "He told me to have you call him back the second you returned."

"Do you have a phone around here I can use?" Raine asked.

"Yes sir," he said, "I'll call the number and put it through to that phone over there by the couch."

"Where the hell have you been?" Lance McCain yelled in his ear, "I've been calling you since 10 o'clock!"

Raine cleared his throat, trying not to sound drunk. "You don't want to know, " he said.

"Why didn't you answer your damn cell phone?"

"I left it in my room," he said, slurring his words, "Why have you been calling me? What's wrong?"

"It's about Dave. He's in the hospital, in the emergency room at The St. Francis Medical Center."

"What?" Raine yelled, "What happened?"

He heard Lance sigh over the phone. "I don't know all of the details but apparently when Buster went outside to smoke a cigarette..." he paused and took a breath, "Dave tried to commit suicide. Buster found him with a sheet tied around his neck. He hung himself."

Raine lowered himself down on the couch. "Oh, God no! How bad is it? Is he going to live?"

"I don't know," Lance said, softly, "The last time I heard from Buster was about two o'clock and he didn't know much, but he did say that he wasn't sure he was going to make it."

"Lance, I just talked to Dave yesterday. I spent four hours with him. He was fine, happy, and in great spirits. What the hell happened?"

"I'm sorry but I just don't know. I didn't want to go anywhere until you called me. I'm leaving now on my way to your hotel to pick you up. I think Buster will still be there. Maybe he can tell us why he did it."

It was almost 5 a.m. when they finally made it to the hospital. They found Buster in the lobby and ran up to him. "How is he?" Raine asked.

Buster dropped his head and looked down at his feet. "It's all my fault, Raine," he said, "it was on my watch and I went outside for a smoke and...I'm so sorry."

"Come on, Buster," Lance said, "You are an experienced police officer, and you know as well as I do that if someone wants to kill themselves there's nothing you can do to prevent it. You've done nothing wrong. He's here in a hospital with a chance to survive, and that's all because of you and your experience. Nobody is going to blame you for this. All I want to know is why he did it. Do you have any idea?"

Buster frowned and looked at Lance. "Yes, I do. I'm pretty sure it has something to do with Sam Green."

"Lance glanced over at Raine. "What the hell does he have to do with this?"

Buster told them about Sam Green's unexpected visit and how Dave's mood had suddenly changed after he left.

"I'm not sure what that little bastard said to Dave to make him want to do this," Buster said, "but I know how to find out."

"How?" Raine asked.

Buster smiled. "There are three video cameras hidden in the walls and ceiling at the shop. I flipped them on before I walked out. We have him on video."

At 10 a.m. they finally got to talk to a doctor.

"All I can tell you is that he is stable, he's breathing on his own, and that he does have brain waves. Unfortunately, he's still unconscious. The big questions are how long was he hanging there with the blood supply cut off from his brain, and will he ever wake up?"

At 11 a.m. Raine's cell phone rang. "Hello?"

"Mr. Waters, this is Jimmy Elliott, I am your pilot that will be flying you to Nashville today. I just wanted to let you know that I'm here in the lobby."

"Oh shit!" Raine shouted, "You're in the lobby of my hotel?"

"Yes sir, that's where I was told to pick you up."

"Yeah, I remember now," Raine said, "but I'm not at my hotel right now. Are you in a taxi?"

"No sir, I'm in a town car with a driver."

"OK, that's good. Tell him to bring you to the St. Francis Medical Center. I'll meet you in the lobby and explain what's going on when you get here. I'm sorry for all the trouble but I can't leave right now."

"OK, I'll get him to take me there," he said, "but you need to know that there's some bad weather coming our way, and we need to get out of here before it shows up."

Raine sighed and asked, "How long do we have?"

"I'm not sure," he said, "but my guess is maybe three or four hours at the most."

Over the next few hours, they all waited in the lobby as the minutes ticked by. Every thirty minutes, James Elliot took out his cell and called the tower at the airport to check on the weather.

"How are we doing?" Raine asked.

James shook his head. "Not so good, the window is tightening. If we don't get out of here in the next few hours we'll be grounded."

SCOTT HUGLEY HAD MADE arrangements for Raine's private jet to land at the John C. Tune Airport, just west of Nashville. Although it was still public, it was considered a 'reliever airport' for the Nashville International, only used for times they needed it for overflow extra capacity. It was where most of the stars kept their planes, and because of the well-trained security, it was the easiest place for a famous celebrity to fly in and out.

At 3:30 Scott got tired of waiting in his car so he got out, walked inside, and asked the pretty young woman behind the terminal counter about Raine's plane.

"They should have been here by now," Scott said, "could you check on it for me?"

He gave her the tail number of the jet, and she typed the numbers into her computer. "It looks like that plane has been delayed, " she said, "It hasn't taken off yet?"

"Oh crap!" Scott said, reaching for his cell phone.

When Raine saw Scott's name on the caller ID, he walked outside before he answered. "Hey, Scott," he said, "I'm so sorry, I forgot to call you and tell you what's going on."

"No shit!" he said, "I've been waiting outside this damn airport for over an hour. Why haven't you left Colorado Springs? What's the holdup?"

Scott listened to the story as he walked back to his car. "I'm sorry, Raine," he said, opening his car door, and sitting down behind the wheel, "I know how close you were to him. What are the doctors saying?"

"They won't know anything until he regains consciousness."

"So, I'm assuming you're not coming, right?"

"Scott, I'm sorry, but I can't give you an answer yet. I really want to be there for Brooklyn. I understand what our performance together could do for her career, and I'm going to try my best to get there for her, but I can't leave here like this. I have to know, one way or the other about Dave."

"I'm headed to the theater now," Scott said, "I'll let Brooklyn know what's going on, and tell the director to plan on Amanda to sing the song with Brooklyn."

"What time is the song scheduled?"

"Hold on," Scott said, "I've got the broadcast schedule on my phone. Let me look it up."

Scott held up his phone and scrolled through the schedule. "Amanda does her song first at 9:14, and Brooklyn does her song at 10:05," he scrolled down further. "Here it is. Looks like From Ashes is scheduled for 10:38 but you know how these shows go, they always run late."

Raine walked back inside the lobby and waved at Jimmy Elliot. When he walked up, Raine asked him, "How long will it take us to get to Nashville?"

"A little over two hours," he said.

"How far away is the airport to the theater," Raine asked Scott. "I'm guessing about 30 minutes, but if I know when you're landing I'll have a police escort waiting for you."

When Raine hung up, he glanced at his watch, it was 4:43. He looked at Jimmy Elliot who was staring up at the dark, ominous sky and asked, "Is there a chance this might blow over?"

Jimmy shrugged. "I doubt it," he said, holding up his phone for Raine to see, "All we can do now is pray."

Raine stared down at his phone and read the weather alert that said, All flights grounded until further notice.

When Raine walked back into the lobby, he saw Lance and Buster talking to a doctor...and they were smiling.

31

A PROMISE

Dave gave Raine a sheepish grin when he saw him walk through the curtains surrounding his hospital bed. His handcuffs rattled and clattered against the bedside rail when he tried to wave.

"What the hell, dude!" Raine said, walking up to him.

Dave shrugged and looked down. "I know it was stupid. I'm sorry."

Rain frowned down at him. "I'm sorry is not gonna cut it this time. Dave, you tried to kill yourself, and I want to know why. What in the hell were you thinking?"

Dave lifted his head slowly and looked at him. "I was thinking that I didn't deserve to live."

He took a deep breath and looked away. "Raine, I have been lying to you. When I hit my father with that crutch...I *was* trying to kill him. I wanted him to die."

"Dave, you were only 19 years old. You were just a kid."

"No, you're wrong. I was a grown man, drunk and angry, and I knew what I was doing."

Dave turned his head and looked Raine in the eyes, "You know what I'm talking about. You've seen me when I was that kind of drunk before."

"You know about that?" Raine asked, shocked, "All these years, you've lied to me about that too?"

Dave nodded. "I remember every time it happened and everything I did. I wish I knew what triggered it so I could stop that side of me from ever coming out, but I don't know why. I was afraid if I told you the truth, you wouldn't be my friend anymore."

Raine stared down at him, not talking for a few minutes. "So why would you do this now?" he asked, "Dave, the judge was placing you into a psychiatric hospital. A place where they might have been able to find out why this happens to you. I just don't understand. Why did you try to kill yourself now?"

"There's nothing I can say that could ever make you understand," Dave said.

Raine frowned. "What makes you think that?"

"Because I know you, and what you believe. Someone like you would never even consider killing yourself. So there's no way I could ever explain to you what I was feeling."

"Someone like me? What the hell are you talking about?"

"God. You believe in God," he said, "That's what I'm talking about. And you have a life, a daughter, a granddaughter, and a career. I have nothing...no one."

Rain took a chair and pulled it close to his bed and sat down. "Do you remember the day I came to see you when you were freaking out in the jail cell, and they finally took you out of there to the hospital?"

Dave nodded. "Yeah, I was going crazy in that padded room."

"I tried, but they wouldn't let me see you in that hospital," Raine said, "I was afraid that maybe I would never get to see you again, and at that point in my life, you were all I had. I was so tired of fighting myself, trying not to drink, I had just discovered that Nash Cooper had stolen my song, and I was angry at God for not answering my prayers. I found the chapel in that hospital and tried one more time to talk to God, but when he didn't answer, I finally gave up."

"What did you do?" Dave asked.

"I made the same stupid decision you did. I thought there was nothing left for me to live for, so I went up to the roof."

"To jump off?" Dave said, "Why haven't you told me about this before?"

"I had always planned to tell you about it, but things started happening fast in both of our lives, and I just never got around to it."

"What stopped you from jumping?"

Raine smiled wide and said, "God."

"Really? God finally talked to you? What did he say?"

"He didn't say a word; he let Brooklyn do the talking. That was the night I met her and my granddaughter. And the night I finally got to hold her in my arms."

Dave raised up in his bed. "You think he sent her there to save you?"

"I *KNOW* he did," Raine said, "and that's why I'm telling you this now. Dave, I know you don't believe in God, or at least don't want to for some reason, but please just think about this. If I had jumped that night, I would've never realized that he *HAD* answered my prayers. Don't you see, all the time I thought he had forsaken me and wasn't listening, he was actually working behind the scenes putting it all together."

Raine took Dave's hand and squeezed it. "According to the doctors, you should have died last night, but you didn't. They honestly don't have a medical explanation of why you are still alive, but I think I know. God saved you. And I believe he did it because you have something he wants you to do. And it must be something big for him to go to all this trouble."

"Do you know what it is?" Dave asked.

Raine laughed. "No, buddy, only He knows what that is. But if you will just let him into your heart, he'll lead you there. I believe we all have a reason to be here, some purpose for our lives. I think maybe He put me here because of Brooklyn."

"Not your music?" Dave asked. "He gave you that talent for some reason, don't you think?"

"Perhaps," Raine said, with a smile, "But I honestly believe He gave me my talent to pass on to Brooklyn. That girl is going to do great things in her life. Maybe I had to go first to show her what *NOT* to do."

Dave laughed. "Well, I can't argue with you about that. You certainly showed her that."

They both laughed for a while, then sat silent for a long time.

"I've always believed in God, " Dave whispered, "I'm not an atheist. But after I killed my father, I didn't think I had the right to believe."

Raine nodded. "I know exactly how you feel because that's what I thought for years...but I was wrong. Dave, there's nothing he won't forgive you for if you just ask."

The curtain slid back, and a nurse walked up to the bed. "Are you Raine Waters?" she asked.

"Yes, that's me."

"I have a note for you."

Raine unfolded the paper and read it. "Who's it from?" Dave asked.

"It's from my pilot. He's been waiting with me in the lobby to fly me to Nashville all day."

"What did he say?"

Raine looked at his watch. "I'm supposed to be on the stage at the CMA Awards in exactly five hours and 15 minutes. He thinks we could make it to Nashville in time for the show if we hurry."

"Well, go then!" Dave yelled, "hurry up!"

Raine stood and looked down at him. "I'm not going anywhere until you look me in the eyes and promise me that you'll never do anything like this again."

Dave smiled. "I promise," he said, "You got me interested in what that big purpose God has in store for me is all about."

"I'm serious, Dave. No one but God knows what's in store for us, so I want you to promise me that no matter what happens to you, or me, in the future, good or bad, you will keep your faith and follow His lead. Promise?"

"Never again," Dave said, "I promise."

"Good," Raine said, smiling. "And I promise you this. If you go to that psychiatric hospital and get well. When you get out, I'm going to buy you a beautiful house that sits right on Cocoa Beach. Do we have a deal?"

"I DON'T GIVE a shit *WHEN* he gets here," Eric Stark yelled in Scott's face, "Raine Waters is not allowed on that stage tonight. I told you he had to be here stone sober four hours before the show started. That didn't happen, so he's out, and so is the damn duet with his daughter."

After Eric stormed off, Scott looked at Brooklyn and grinned. "Don't worry, I've already talked to Nash Cooper. If he wants to keep his record deal with me, he won't sing the song. I've talked to Amanda, and she's ready just in case Raine doesn't make it. Trust me, It's all going to work out. I want you to stop worrying about this and concentrate on your performance. He'll be here."

BEFORE THEY TOOK OFF, Raine called Scott. "It's 5:23 here. The weather is still pretty bad, but James is confident he can get through the clouds. We should arrive in Nashville in about two and a half hours. That should get us there at about nine o'clock. I think that the police escort might not be a bad idea, either."

When he hung up from Scott, he called Brooklyn. "Hey, Dad," she said, "are you gonna make it?"

"I'm trying. Hopefully, I should be at the theater by about 9:30. When we get there, maybe we can find someplace backstage to run the song. If for some reason, we don't get out of here, and I don't make it, promise me, you'll go out there and sing that song and tell everyone that I wrote those words about you. I love you. See you soon."

"I promise, and I love you too, Dad," she said.

WHEN RAINE HAD NOT MADE it to the theater by 9:30, Brooklyn walked through the backstage area and opened the back door. She stood there listening for the sirens of the police escort but couldn't hear any.

Scott saw her standing there with the door open, so he walked over to her and put his arm around her shoulders. "Don't worry," he said, "he'll make it."

The cohosts for the CMA awards show were Brad Paisley and Carrie Underwood. The broadcast was going unusually smooth and on time. At 10:37, Brad Paisley walked to the microphone and began his announcement, "Well, here it is, the one everyone has been waiting for all night. Nominated for song of the year. Recorded by Nash Cooper, written by Raine Waters...From Ashes."

The house lights went down, the music started, and the stage began to flicker with streaming lights of every color in the rainbow. Then hundreds of long streams of brilliant blue lights started to move across the stage.

You could feel the anticipation and the excitement in the air, everyone waiting for Raine and Brooklyn to walk on the stage to sing the song that had touched so many hearts around the world.

At first, only the musicians knew that something was wrong when they finished playing the intro, and no one had walked out. But they were professionals and simply began playing the intro from the top once again. But when they finished the second time..: everyone knew, so they stopped playing.

Inside the television control room was complete mayhem. Eric Stark was screaming at the top of his lungs. "Where the fuck are the singers! Tell the band to keep playing. Where the fuck are the damn singers!"

"Who is that?" Someone yelled, pointing at a video monitor.

Eric stared up at the screen. "That's Nash Cooper. What the hell is he doing out there? He told me he wouldn't sing the song."

"Camera one," he said, "give me a closeup."

Eric turned and looked around the room. "Will somebody please find out what the hell is going on?"

Nash Cooper slowly made his way to the center of the stage and stood behind the microphone. "The first time I heard From Ashes," he began, "I knew that it was not just another song. From the first note, I got cold chills, and I knew it was extraordinary. I was at a country club, standing in the back watching Raine Waters perform it. He was sitting on a stool with just a guitar, singing the song...and it was...magic."

The crowd cheered and applauded. When they stopped, he said, "So I ran up here to Nashville to record it and well, as they say, the rest is history." The audience broke into applause again. "But what you don't know is that at first, I tried to steal it. I told everyone that I had written it, not Raine Waters."

The audience gasped and started booing. Nash held up his hands and smiled. "Yeah, you're right, and I deserved that," he said, then he paused for a beat, "Since I've been in Nashville, I've heard a lot of wild stories about him, but those crazy stories don't tell you much about the real Raine Waters. When he found out what I had done, he could've sued me for everything I had, destroyed my reputation, got me kicked off my label, and ruined my career, but he didn't do any of those things. Instead, he mailed me another song he had written with a note."

Nash reached into his pocket and pulled out a folded piece of paper and held it up. "This is it," he said, "Dear Nash, I wrote this song for you. I think it will be a good one, Raine. P.S. Don't forget to put my name down as the songwriter this time."

The audience laughed and broke into applause.

Nash waited until the room was quiet. "I'm not sure all of you know this, but Raine wrote From Ashes for his daughter, Brooklyn Taylor Arnett."

When Brooklyn walked onto the stage, the room exploded with thundering applause, whistles and cheers. When they finally stopped, she slowly walked up to the microphone and said, "My father was supposed to be here to help me sing this song. But the last thing he said to me was, 'If for some reason, I don't make it there in time, I want you to sing it for them anyway, and make sure you tell them that I wrote those words about you.'"

She looked back at Josh, who was sitting behind the piano and nodded.

Josh played the intro, and Brooklyn started singing the first verse;

"It was the only song of mine I could not rhyme

The only song of mine that was out of time

It's about the day I left three hearts behind

When I walked away from yours, and hers, and mine

Brooklyn's trembling voice broke, and she began to cry. "I'm so sorry..I...I don't think I can do this."

When she dropped to her knees on the stage crying, a hush fell over the room as the shocked audience watched in total confusion.

Amanda Jones ran out on stage and lifted Brooklyn off of the floor. With her arm wrapped around her waist, she leaned into the microphone and said, "At 7:15 tonight, Raine Waters boarded a private jet chartered to fly him to Nashville for this show." She paused and looked down into Brooklyn's sad eyes, "They were trying to fly around a storm, but...something went terribly wrong...they crashed...there were no survivors. Raine Waters...is dead."

The audience gasped then fell eerily silent. The only sounds in the theater were people crying.

"Play something'" Josh heard in his headphone.

He started playing the intro of From Ashes again on his piano.

Amanda wiped her eyes and started singing the second verse.

All that I could see or hear was me

The only thing that mattered was who I'd be

But I was deaf, dumb, and blind and couldn't see,

My wasted life on fire in front of me

But when I opened up my eyes and saw the flames

There was nothing left to see, no one to blame

Just open wounds and bleeding gashes

All that was left of me was HER,

And smoldering ashes.

When it came to the final verse, Brooklyn took the microphone and
sang,

God, I know I have no right to even pray

Because I turned my back on you and looked away

But I'm begging you before my whole life passes

Let me hold her in my arms

Resurrect me from these ashes."

When the song ended, no one clapped or made a sound.
Brooklyn lifted her hands and looked up. "Dad, he *DID* answer
your prayers. And...I will never forget how it felt that day...when you
finally got to hold me in your arms. I love you, Dad...Goodbye."

32

SOMETHING BIG

S cott Hugley had been the first to know that something was wrong when he had received a call from the jet charter company, letting him know that the Colorado Springs airport tower had lost contact with the plane only minutes after it had taken off.

The second person to know was Jake. When Scott pulled him aside backstage and told him, Jake's knees went weak, and he had to sit down. "Oh, God, no. Not this, not now."

He looked up at Scott. "Does Brooklyn know?"

Scott shook his head. "No. I don't want to tell her until we know for sure. They said they are experiencing heavy weather, and the radar may have malfunctioned. They are running a check on all their systems to make sure. I'm expecting a call back from them any minute."

Together, they walked to Raine's dressing room to wait for the call.

They both jumped when Scott's phone rang. "Hello?" he said, "Yes, this is Scott Hugley."

Jake held his breath, staring at Scott. "Oh, God," he said, softly, "What about the pilot?"

As Scott listened, he looked at Jake and shook his head.

Jake sat down on the couch, dropped his head, and broke down crying.

When Scott hung up, he sat down in a chair across from Jake. "They found the wreckage. Somehow they had gotten way off course and flew into the side of a mountain," he wiped his eyes with his hand, "Raine and the pilot died on impact."

A few feet away, mounted near the ceiling, was a television monitor. The volume was on, but it was very low. When they heard Brooklyn's voice, they looked up at the screen. Scott took the remote and turned it up. In silence, they watched her perform one of the songs that Raine had written for her album. When she finished, she smiled wide, and her eyes sparkled and twinkled in the bright lights as the audience stood and cheered.

"She looks so happy," Jake whispered, "My poor baby. This is going to devastate her, but she needs to know. I have to tell her."

Scott looked over at Jake. "What about Amanda," he said, shaking his head, "She needs to know too."

Reluctantly, Jake stood up and slowly walked to Brooklyn's dressing room. "Hi, Dad!" She said, smiling when he opened the door.

Jake had heard Brooklyn cry many times before while she was growing up. He could still remember holding her in his arms as she cried the first time some boy broke her heart. And he knew he would never forget the day he held her as she cried after hearing the news about Virginia's cancer. But the heart-wrenching sound she made when he told her about Raine was something he prayed that someday...he would forget.

Everything seemed to move in slow motion after that. Although it had only been 25 minutes, it's seemed like hours had past when it was finally time for Brooklyn to sing From Ashes and tell the world about Raine.

"Brooklyn, you don't have to do this," Jake told her, "Let Amanda or Nash do this."

"No," she said, "I have to do it, for Dad. It was the last words he said to me. I have to."

AFTER THE SHOW AIRED, the news of Raine Water's death spread like wildfire around the world. The next day, the major networks and all the cable news shows rushed to air tributes about him.

For the next few months, it was almost impossible to turn on the television or listen to the radio and not see or hear someone talking about the legend of Raine Waters.

The stores couldn't keep his records in stock, and the number of downloads of his songs was off the charts.

On the day of his public memorial, the freeways around Nashville were backed up for miles from the line of cars full of his fans inching their way to the church.

Lance McCain had received permission from the judge to bring Dave to the memorial, as long as Buster and Art accompanied him.

"Promise me you won't do anything stupid," Buster said to Dave, unlocking his handcuffs in front of the church.

"Don't worry, I wouldn't do that to Raine. I made a promise to him I was going to be good from now on."

After the service, when Buster and Art were taking Dave back to the car, Brooklyn walked up to them. "You're Dave, right?" She asked him.

He nodded. "Yes, ma'am, I am."

"I hope you know how much my dad loved you," she said, smiling up at him, "he talked about you all the time."

"Miss Brooklyn, your father, was the best friend I've ever had, and I loved him too."

She smiled. "I just wanted you to know that he believed in you. He told me that one day, you were going to do something big, something great."

Dave's eyes filled with tears. "I'm gonna try my best, to honor Raine, and do just that." Dave wiped his eyes, "Miss Brooklyn, I guess you know that you were his entire world."

She stood up on her tiptoes and kissed him on his cheek. "We both were," she said, "I promise I'll come to see you soon."

TWO WEEKS LATER, Brooklyn and Josh flew to Colorado Springs to visit Dave. They were also there to meet with Lance McCain for the reading of Raine's Will.

Lance had also asked Jake, Louise, and Coop to be there as well.

They were all seated around the conference table, waiting for Dave to be delivered by the Colorado Springs police officers.

"To be honest with you," Coop said to Lance, "I'm a little surprised that Raine had a Will."

"Me too," Louise said.

Brooklyn looked at Lance and asked, "When did Dad have you prepare it?"

The door opened, and two police officers helped Dave shuffle through the door. Without being asked, they removed his handcuffs and ankle shackles. "Let us know when you're ready to go," the officer said.

"Thanks, Dude," Dave said, "They have good coffee here. You need to try it."

He looked around the room and smiled. "Hey, everybody. It's really good to see you."

When he got settled in his chair, Lance opened his briefcase and took out some papers and a small paper sack, and sat them on the table in front of him. He held up the will and said, "Before I read this, I'd like to show you something."

He reached into the sack and pulled out a watch, a ring, and a bill-fold. "These are Raine's personal items recovered from the crash."

He handed the watch and ring to Brooklyn, "I thought you might want these."

She picked up the ring and slipped it on her finger, and held the watch up to her heart. "Thank you," she said, "I'm going to save these for Ginny."

Lance opened the billfold and pulled out a folded piece of paper. "I also found this," he said. "For almost a week, I've been trying to come up with the right words to say this, but so far, nothing I can think of makes this any easier to say."

"What is that?" Brooklyn asked, pointing at the sheet of paper.

Lance smiled, "I think it's a song or at least the beginning of one."

"One of Dad's?"

He nodded, "Yes, it's his handwriting. But before I read it, I'd like to address your questions about Raine's Will because I believe this song had something to do with it."

Lance leaned back in his chair and looked around the table. "Raine came to me the day after we settled Dave's case and asked me to help him write his will. He signed it on Monday morning, three days before he died. Of course, when I prepared it, no one knew what was about to happen, and at the time, I didn't think much about it. When I heard about his death, of course, I was stunned and sad, but I still didn't realize what was going on."

Brooklyn frowned. "I'm sorry, Mr. McCain, but I'm confused. What are you trying to tell us?"

Lance took a deep breath and let it out slowly. "Please, forgive me, this could just be a coincidence, and I don't want this to upset you, but I believe Raine knew what was coming. I think he had a premonition of his death."

Louise gasped and started to cry. "Oh, God," she said, "You think Raine knew he was about to die?"

"Yes, I do," Lance said, "And as hard as it may be to understand...I believe he was ready to die."

Tears rolled down Brooklyn's face. "How could you know that?" she asked, "Did he say something about it?"

Lance picked up the paper. "Not to me," he said, "But I think he wrote this for all of you."

He put on his readers and held up the page. "It's only two verses. He didn't finish it, but then again, maybe he did."

Lance handed the paper to Brooklyn. "I think Raine would want you to be the one to read this."

Brooklyn took the paper and read,

"Verse 1

Lord, I have looked into her eyes and kissed her lovely face
I have held her in my arms and felt her warm embrace

You have answered all my prayers; now all my pain is gone
It was all I ever wanted; now it's time to bring me home."

He looked at Brooklyn. "Are you Ok? Do you want to stop?"
"No," she whimpered, "I want to read the rest."
She looked down and continued:

"Verse 2
You lifted me off the ground and gave me strength to stand
You gave me hope, gave me courage, and showed me how to make
amends
But I'm tired of fighting demons, Lord, the urges are too strong
So while I am still standing, Lord, please, God...bring me home."

In Raine's will, he instructed Lance to set up *The Virginia Taylor Cancer Research Foundation*, funded with five million dollars from his estate, and 50% of the continuing royalties earned from the song, *From Ashes*, and he designated Jake to oversee it.

He deeded back the little house in the woods to Coop, with one condition, he couldn't turn it into some kind of Raine Waters museum. In his note, he said, "Coop, I was thinking you could use it as a play-house for the kids there at LaCita. Maybe turn it into a cool fort or something."

For Louise, he instructed Lance to pay off the mortgage of her house. In his note to her, he said, "I love your house, and I know Brooklyn, Josh, and little Ginny will too. After you and Jake get married, promise me that everyone will spend Christmas there every year. It was my best Christmas ever."

For Brooklyn, Josh and Ginny, he bequeathed 75% of his entire estate, including all current and future royalties earned from his songs. In his note, he said, "Brooklyn, there is a leather briefcase on the top shelf in the closet in the little house. Find it and do something with what's inside."

The last note he wrote was to Dave. "To David Baker, the best friend anyone could ever ask for, I bequeath 25% of my estate. Remember your promise, Dude. Take some of this money and buy that house on Cocoa Beach, I promised you. Take the rest and do something big with it."

"There is only one item that Raine did not leave specific instructions for me to handle," Lance said, "I think since you are all here today, we need to address it. What do you want to do with Raine's ashes? Do any of you have an idea?"

"I think I know," Dave said, "but could I ask a question before I tell you?"

"Of course," Lance said, "what's the question?"

"Could we wait until I get out before we do something with them?"

Lance looked around the table. "What do you think?"

"I can't think of a reason why we couldn't," Brooklyn said, smiling at Dave.

"Mr. McCain, could I ask you one more question?" Dave asked.

"Sure," he said, "What do you want to know?"

"Do I have to be out of jail before I can do something with this money?"

Lance smiled, "Well, Dave, I guess that would depend on what you wanted to do with it. What do you have in mind?"

"I would like to start a foundation. I'm not sure how much it would cost, but I think Raine would like it."

Lance opened his yellow pad to a clean page. "Ok, Mr. Baker, what would you like to call this foundation?"

Dave looked at Brooklyn and grinned, *"The Raine Waters Foundation For The Homeless."*

EPILOGUE

When Lance McCain watched the video of Sam Green's visit to Dave in the shop and heard what he had said to him, he immediately sent a copy of it to the judge and one to the governor. Although Sam Green had not given his permission to be videotaped, and knew it could not be used as evidence against him in a court of law, he realized the damage he had done to his career was irreparable. He resigned as the district attorney and appointed his deputy district attorney, Everly Moore, to take his place until the next election. In that election, Everly won easily and has served as the district attorney for Teller and El Paso counties for three years.

FROM ASHES not only won the CMT *Song Of The Year*, but it also won several more awards; the Billboard music award, the American Country Music award, the Peoples Choice award, the iHeart Radio Music award, the Glenn Gould Prize, and that following January, Brooklyn accepted Raine's two Grammy Awards.

Nash Cooper's recording of From Ashes was certified Gold, Platinum, Double Platinum, and finally Diamond when it sold over 10 million units.

Over the next three years, Brooklyn charted four number one records, won the CMA Horizon award, and brought home six Grammy's.

Three months after Raine's death, Louise and Jake were married in a small, private ceremony, standing in front of the fireplace in her beautiful mortgage-free home at LaCita.

As her music career soared, Brooklyn toured with Amanda Jones, performing as her opening act.

With Jake serving as their road manager, Amanda, Brooklyn, Josh, Jake, and Louise toured the world as a family, performing to sold-out concerts with Louise keeping a close watch on little Ginny backstage at each performance.

Coop had his grounds crew clear the half-acre that surrounded the little house and turned it into a park. A few months later, after the grass had covered the area, he installed three swings, two seesaws, a tall tube slide, and two merry-go-rounds. He also dug a shallow mote that surrounded the gleaming white "Castle" with its two towers that reached high in the air above what used to be the little house in the woods.

It took Bertha three years after Raine's death to get up enough nerve to admit to Amanda that his feelings for her were more than just a friendship.

His forehead was wet from perspiration, and he was fidgeting in his chair. "What's wrong with you today?" Amanda said, looking across the table, "You're white as a ghost, and you're sweating. Are you feeling alright?"

"Yeah, I'm Ok," he said, wiping his forehead with his napkin, "I'm just a little nervous."

"Nervous?" she said, surprised, "How could you be nervous around me?"

Bertha smiled. "I'm always nervous around you. Haven't you ever noticed that before?"

"No, I haven't. Why would I make you nervous?"

"Because you're so beautiful." he said shyly, looking away.

Amanda lifted her head and raised her eyebrows. "You think I'm beautiful? Really?"

Bertha nodded but kept his head turned. "You are the most beautiful woman I've ever seen."

Amanda didn't respond because she wasn't sure what to say. She had known Bertha for so many years as just a friend. It had never occurred to her that Bertha had those kinds of feelings for her.

"Bertha, don't turn away from me like that," She said softly, "Talk to me. We've been friends for years, and there's no reason for you to be nervous around me. Tell me the truth. What are you so nervous about?"

Bertha turned and looked her in the eyes. "I wanted to wait and give you time to get over the loss of Raine. Actually, I've wanted to tell you for a long, long time, but I was afraid it might hurt our friendship."

He lifted his water glass and took a drink. "My birthday is next week. I'm turning 60. I realize that's not that old, but it has made me rethink what I believe is important in my life. It took me a long time to admit this finally, but now I know the most important thing in my life," he put down his glass and stared into her eyes, "is you."

Her surprised eyes opened wide. "Amanda, I've been in love with you for so long. I know there's a few years difference in our ages, and you may not have any feelings for me at all, but I just had to tell you."

Amanda looked across the table at him for a long time without talking.

"Say something," Bertha said, "Don't just stare at me like that. Please say something?"

"I'm sorry, Bertha, but I'm a little mad at you right now," she finally said.

"I knew I shouldn't have told you!" Bertha shouted, "Please, don't be mad. Just forget what I said."

"You want me to forget that you're in love with me?" She said with a grin, "Bertha, I'm not mad about what you said. I'm mad that it took you so long to say it."

DAVE KEPT his promise to Raine, and for the full three years he was in the psychiatric hospital, he was the perfect patient. The years of therapy had helped him overcome his claustrophobia and confront the dark demons he had been hiding deep inside.

Through the years, when he wasn't in therapy, he worked tirelessly on his foundation. With Lance McCain's help, The Raine Waters Foundation For The Homeless had built and opened two very successful homeless shelters; one just across from the beach in Jacksonville, and one on*Diet Coke*

the beach in Daytona.

Dave had discovered that when Buster and Art were on the Colorado Springs police force, to make extra money, they had bought, remodeled, and flipped several houses together. Since he couldn't leave the hospital, he hired them to oversee the development and construction of the shelters.

Dave had always hated the name 'Homeless,' so he didn't use that name for his facilities. Above the door on both buildings was a large sign that said something that had come to him in a dream.

AFTER RECEIVING three years and two months of intensive therapy in the psychiatric hospital, the judge signed the papers, and once again, Dave was a free man.

Lance McCaine was leaning against his car, waiting for Dave when he walked out of the hospital to take him to the airport. They were flying to Orlando for the grand opening of the third shelter built by the Raine Waters Foundation For The Homeless.

The facility had been completed for several weeks, but when Lance received the call from the judge informing him of his decision to sign his release, he postponed the opening so Dave could be there and cut the ribbon.

The timing couldn't have been better because this shelter was not only the biggest they had built so far; the flagship of the Raine Waters Foundation For The Homeless, this building also contained a surprise. On the third floor, with an expansive view of the ocean, was a 2,000 square foot apartment that would become Dave's new home.

"Are you sure about this?" Lance asked Dave as he pulled into the parking lot at the Colorado Springs airport.

"Are you worried about me freaking out on the plane?"

"To be honest, yeah, a little," Lance said, smiling, "Three hours in a small plane...are you sure you're ready for this."

"It's called, Desensitization, or Self-exposure Therapy," Dave said, "Little by little each day I faced that fear, and with the doctor's help, it took me almost a year to overcome it, but eventually I did. Don't worry. I'll be fine."

When they reached altitude and leveled off, the flight attendant asked them what they wanted to drink.

"I'll have a scotch and water," Lance said."

"What about you, sir," she asked Dave.

"I'll take a Diet Coke," he said, then turned toward Lance and grinned, "That's the second promise I made to Raine; no more booze."

Dave had been quiet, not talking much since Lance had picked him up from the hospital. "So how does it feel to be a free man again?" Lance asked, sipping his drink.

"I don't know," Dave said with a shrug, "I guess the reality of it hasn't hit me yet. I'm happy, I guess, but sad at the same time that Raine isn't here. I miss him."

"Me too," Lance said, "but I know he would be proud of you for what you've done and what you're doing with the foundation."

"I sure hope so," he said, "How *ARE* we doing? How much money do we have left?"

Lance smiled. "I wanted to wait until you got out before I told you, but you don't have to worry about the funding of the foundation any longer."

Dave raised his eyebrows. "Why not?"

"Brooklyn donated 50% of all of Raine's music royalties to the foundation. That includes half of her share of the From Ashes royalties and half of the future royalties from the 88 new songs she found in a briefcase in the little house."

"So that's what was in there," Dave said, "He guarded that brief-case with his life, but he never told me what was inside."

"I talked to Bertha Brooks, who is publishing all of the new songs," Lance said, "He told me it was like discovering a treasure chest full of gold."

Dave pulled down the folding tray, set his Coke on it, and looked at Lance. "That means we can open more shelters, right?"

"A lot more." He said grinning.

Dave leaned back and thought for a moment. "The one we're going to today, this new one, is it really sitting right on Cocoa Beach?"

"Yeah, just a mile or so down from the pier. We bought two houses and converted them into one substantial structure. It's almost 10,000 square feet. I've only seen the pictures, but it looks beautiful."

"What about the trouble the residents were giving us and the city about building the shelter? How did we get around that?"

Lance laughed. "I'm not sure what he said or what he did, but somehow Buster turned everybody around. Now they seem fine with it being there, and some of the neighbors are even volunteering to work at the shelter."

"That's great," Dave said, "How many can we feed at this one?"

"That depends on how many volunteers we have to serve the food and bus the tables, but we can seat 100. Buster is hoping to turn the tables two or three times during each meal, so that would mean we could serve three to four hundred a day."

"What about medical and dental care?"

"Buster has lined up about ten doctors and seven or eight dentists so far. The plan is to have a doctor and a dentist at the facility one day a week."

"That's terrific!" Dave said, "How many churches have we partnered with?"

"Again, Buster and Art have done an amazing job lining up those partnerships. He told me he had over ten churches supplying most of the volunteers, and he received a commitment from New Life Space Coast, in Titusville, to lead the charge helping to keep the general store full of clothes, coats, socks, underwear, and shoes. Also, each person that comes to eat will get a plastic goodie bag with a blanket, toothpaste, a toothbrush, and a bar of soap."

"How many can we sleep?" Dave asked.

"There are ten full bathrooms with showers on the second floor and two large sleeping areas with 50 beds each."

"What about the homeless families with children?"

"The rooms have folding partitions we can use to separate the families from the main sleeping areas," Lance said, "and they will have a key to the private bathrooms."

He lifted his glass in a toast. "Dave here's to you and your vision. I think you've thought of everything."

Dave tapped his Coke against Lance's cup. "There's one more thing I want to do."

"Oh lord, I'm afraid to ask," Lance said, "What have you got in your head now?"

Dave grinned. "I want to start a construction company and build free houses for the homeless, and a large shelter on every beach in America with Raine's name on it."

Lance smiled. "I like that idea."

"And," Dave said, "I want to give a job to every homeless man or woman that wants one, to help us build them."

WHEN THEY LANDED IN ORLANDO, Buster and Art were waiting for them in the luggage terminal. When they saw Dave, they ran up to him and almost knocked him over with their hugs.

"Would you look at you?" Buster said, grinning, "You look great! Where did you get the new suit and fancy shoes?"

Dave smiled. "From the judge. He said he wanted me to walk out of that hospital ready to take on the world and looking sharp."

"Well, you damn sure do," Art said, "You look like you just stepped out of a GQ magazine."

"We're so proud of you," Buster said, "Now, let's go see your new shelter."

When they passed the Merritt Island Mall and came to the two long bridges that connected Merrit Island to Cocoa Beach, Dave stared out the window, thinking about the many times he had crossed over them, walking beside Raine pushing his old rusted bicycle with the leather briefcase tied to the handlebar.

When they passed over the Indian River, and Dave saw the huge Disney and Royal Caribbean cruise ships docked along the piers, he look at Lance, "Have you ever been on one of those?" he said, pointing at the ships, "I'm going to do that one of these days."

"No," Lance said, "I've never taken a cruise, but it sounds like fun."

When they turned down the small road leading to the beach, and Dave saw the beautiful structure glistening in the bright sun, framed by the blue sky behind it, his eyes filled with tears.

When they pulled into the parking lot, Dave opened his car door, stepped out, and scanned the property. He held out his arms, looked up at the sky, and whispered. "Dude, can you see this? Look what we've done."

The three-story structure was perched on top of several round two-foot diameter concrete posts.

When Dave walked up the steps and opened the large leaded glass front door, he heard, "Welcome home!"

The room was full of his friends. Louise, Jake, Coop, and his wife Mary were the first to run up to greet him.

"It's so good to see you again," Louise said, hugging him, "You look great!"

"This is a wonderful thing you're doing," Coop said, "I'm so proud of you, and I know Raine would be too."

Dave nodded his head. "I sure hope so, because I'm doing it all for him. In his honor."

"Who are you?" Dave looked down to see a beautiful little girl with long glistening black hair and sparkling blue eyes.

He squatted down. "I'm not sure," he said, "but I think I'm your Uncle Dave. Is your name George?"

She smiled and shook her head no. "Are you sure your name isn't George?"

She giggled and said, "My name is Ginny."

Dave shook his head and smiled at her. "I don't think so. I'm pretty sure your mommy told me your name was George. It's real nice to meet you, George."

She put her hands on her tiny hips. "My name is not George. It's Ginny."

"How old are you now, George?"

She frowned at him and held up four fingers. "My name is Ginny, and I'm four years old."

Dave laughed. "If I call you Ginny, could I get a hug?"

"Sure," she said, hugging his neck.

"Ok, Ginny, you can call me Uncle Dave," he said, "Did you know that I was your Grandfather Raine's best friend?"

She looked at him with wide eyes. "Mama said that he was a singer like her, but he died."

"Yes, he did, but I have a feeling that he is looking down at us from heaven right now with a great big smile on his face, because he loved you, and he loved me too...a whole lot."

Holding onto Ginny's hand, Dave walked around the facility. "You can only get a hundred in here?" He asked.

"There's actually room for more," Art said, "but according to, Arnie if we add those extra tables and chairs, it would be too tight to bus the tables efficiently. He said if we keep it like this, we should be able to clean and turn the tables faster."

"Who is Arnie?" Dave asked.

Buster grinned. "Don't you remember? I told you about him. He lives in the house next door and was the guy raising all the hell at the City Council trying to block us from building a shelter here."

"That's Arnie?" Dave said, confused, "and now he's giving us advice?"

"Yes. I did a little digging and found out that he is a retired restaurant owner. He has owned five very successful restaurants in his career."

"So, how did you turn him around?" Lance asked.

Buster and Art looked at each other and laughed. "We had just finished the demo of the original two houses, and Art and I were talking to the architect when Arnie walked over to us. I'm sure he was coming over to yell at us again, but before he could, I said, Arnie, thank God you're here. Would you take a look at these blueprints and tell this guy that the kitchen is in the wrong damn place."

"What did he do?" Lance asked.

"He scowled at me, but walked over and looked at the plans," Buster said, smiling. "When he saw what we were planning on building here, and realized the full scope of the project, he began to soften up a bit and started asking us questions, and talking to us."

"There's too many. You can't help them all," he told me.

"What'd you say?" Dave asked.

"I told him exactly what you told me," he said, "We know we can't help them all, but we can try to help a few."

After that, he was over here most of the time watching it go up. He designed the kitchen and drew the table layout."

Lance shook his head. "You're amazing, Buster. A real silver tongued devil."

After they toured the kitchen, the dining area, the general store, and the medical facilities, they walked upstairs to check out the sleeping areas. "What's on the third floor?"Dave asked.

"Your office and a surprise," Buster said, with a wide smile.

He walked to the corner of the room, slid back a section of the wall exposing an elevator. He punched in a code, and the door slid back. "This is a private elevator. It takes a secret code to use," Buster said. "It's kind of small, so if you don't want to use it, the stairs are over there."

Dave walked into the elevator and grinned. "It's not that small. Come on, get in. I want to see the surprise."

On the third floor, the elevator door opened, revealing a small hallway. Above the door on one end was a wooden carved sign that said, "The Raine Waters Foundation For The Homeless." At the other end, there was a red cloth covering the sign.

Dave pointed at the red cloth. "What's in there?"

"The surprise," Buster said, reaching up and pulling down the red cloth.

Above the door, the carved wooden sign said, "Dave's Place."

"Isn't that what Raine said he was going to call it?" Buster asked.

Dave wiped the tears from his eyes and nodded. "Yes. He said he was going to build me a beautiful house on the beach with a view of the ocean, and call it, Dave's Place."

"Go on, open the door and look around," Buster said, "I think you're gonna like it."

Dave walked around the apartment, smiling.

"Do you like it?" Louise asked, "Brooklyn and I picked out the furniture and decorated it."

Dave walked over to them and put his arms around them. "It's perfect," he said, looking through the three large windows at the sparkling ocean, "Thank you. It's better than my dreams."

THE NEXT MORNING AT SUNRISE, all the people that Raine loved gathered together on the beach near the crashing waves behind the shelter.

Brooklyn, Josh, and little Ginny; Louise and Jake; Coop and Mary; Amanda and Bertha; Lance McCain, Buster, Art, and even Mr. Beasley from the book store were there standing on the sand barefoot, holding hands in a semi-circle around Dave.

When the sun appeared, Dave slowly waded waist-deep into the ocean. He was holding a beautiful marble urn in his hands.

As the golden rays of the sun on the horizon began to glisten and sparkle off the blue water, Dave opened the urn and slowly poured out Raine's ashes into the water.

He looked up and said, "Forasmuch as it hath pleased Almighty God of his great mercy to take unto Himself the soul of our dear brother here departed, we, therefore, commit his body to the ground; earth to earth, ashes to ashes, dust to dust; in sure and certain hope of the Resurrection to eternal life, through our Lord Jesus Christ."

When he finished, he took the empty urn and threw it as far as he could into the ocean. Then he wiped his eyes with his sleeve and said, "Goodbye, my friend. I will never, ever forget you."

They all stood silently watching the waves crash on the beach, slowly retreating back to the ocean, pulling Raine's ashes along with them.

When the ashes were gone, Dave reached down, picked up little Ginny, and slowly walked back to the shelter. When he got to the entrance, he looked up and smiled, as he read the words carved into the teak plank hanging about the door.

RAINE'S PLACE

I was hungry, and you gave me food
I was thirsty, and you gave me drink
I was a stranger, and you welcomed me

WELCOME TO YOUR SHELTER...FROM RAINE

The End

A NOTE FROM BEN

When I finished writing From Ashes and sent it off to my first readers, their immediate response was, "I can't wait to hear the song. Will it be available on iTunes? Maybe even have a link to download it in the back of the book?"

To be honest with you, I was not expecting to hear those questions and didn't know what to tell them because there 'was' no song. I had written the lyrics as part of the book but never considered turning it into an actual song. Since then, everyone, and I mean everyone, who has read From Ashes has asked me about the song.

I guess I should've expected that question because after all, I have made my living most of my life as a singer/songwriter, so with the help of my good friend and great singer/songwriter/performer, Tim Boyd, we started collaborating to write the music to match the lyrics I had written in the manuscript. It's coming along and sounding pretty good, but it's not quite finished yet. When it's done and produced, it will be available on iTunes. Just search for Ben Marney/From Ashes. Who knows, maybe Tim and I will win a Grammy. Ha, ha, fat chance of that happening.

I actually finished writing this book in November 2020, but I waited to publish it in 2021. Call me superstitious if you want, but I didn't want to take any chances. Truthfully as challenging as 2020 was because of COVID 19, it turned out to be an excellent year for my writing career, my book sales soared, and I won two book awards.

My novel, *An August Harvest*, won the 2020 *Maxi Award* for Romantic Suspence, and my novel, *Another Lifetime Ago*, won the London based *PageTurner Awards* for Movie Adaptation. I am currently working on getting that novel made into a movie.

If From Ashes is the first book of mine you have read, I invite you to read my other novels that are available on Amazon.

ABOUT THE AUTHOR

Ben Marney is an emerging author of Romantic Suspense. This is Ben's seventh book.

Thanks for reading ***From Ashes*** I hope you liked it. This book is also available in print and audiobook format, on Audible.com, iTunes and Amazon.

If you enjoyed this book, I invite you to read my other novels, ***Another Lifetime Ago, August Harvest, Sing Roses For Me, Serpentine Roses and Children Of The Band***.

My first novel, ***Sing Roses For Me*** can be downloaded for **FREE** on Amazon. Just search for ***Ben Marney books***.

Sing Roses For Me is a suspense- thriller based on a true story that actually happened to me. I am very proud of this book. It's been downloaded to over 450,000 readers and has been ranked in Amazon's Kindle Free top 10 for Suspense, Thriller, Mystery and Romance categories since its release in May of 2017.

My last novels, *An August Harvest* won Best Romance novel by the prestigious 2020 Mazy Awards and *Another Lifetime Ago* won the *PageTurner Award* for Movie Adaptation.

One more thing... Writing is a lonely job, so meeting and getting to know my readers is a thrill for me and one of the best perks of being an author. I would like to invite you to join my **Private Readers' Group** and in return, I'll give you a **FREE** copy of *Lyrics Of My Life*. This is a collection of autobiographical short stories about my amazing life so far.

I really would like to meet you! Please join my readers' group here:

www.benmarneybooks.com

Made in the USA
Monee, IL
24 December 2021

87101955R00194